Listen now, to find your own bittersweet destiny in the sound of the global symphony. Everything in life immanent on Earth is fully present in heaven, and everything beyond is fully present within your own heart and power. Through the River's colors, sounds, and sentient stories you can find the correlated truth of your own beauty. If you wander momentarily into the paradisiac garden, the sweeping tides bring you bliss from whence you can see your way once again. The fragments of civilization are but raindrops falling into the unceasing Emerald River of Compassion.

Also by Rowena Pattee Kryder

Gaia Matrix Oracle

Faces of the Moon Mother

Moving with Change

Sacred Ground to Sacred Space

Tiger and Dragon I Ching

EMERALD RIVER OF COMPASSION

The Old Earth

ROWENA PATTEE KRYDER

Priscilla
with
great love and appreciation
Rowena Pattee Kryder

BEAR & COMPANY
PUBLISHING
SANTA FE, NEW MEXICO

LIBRARY OF CONGRESS CATALOGING-IN-PUBLICATION DATA

Kryder, Rowena Pattee.
    Emerald river of compassion / Rowena Pattee Kryder.
    p.   cm.
    Contents: v. 1. The old earth.
    ISBN 1-879181-13-4 (v. 1)
    1. Biology—Philosophy—Fiction. 2. Gaia hypothesis—Fiction.
3. Human ecology—Fiction. I. Title.
PS3566.A789E44   1994
813".54—dc20   94-5223
                                                                          CIP

Bear & Company, Inc.
Santa Fe, NM 87504-2860

Cover and interior illustrations: Rowena Pattee Kryder © 1994
Cover & interior design: Marilyn Hager
Author Photo: Jane English
Editing: Gail Vivino
Typography: Marilyn Hager
Printed by R.R. Donnelley

1 3 5 7 9 8 6 4 2

This book is dedicated to my two wonderful sons,
Miles Wilkinson and Charlie Leary and to all children
everywhere, young and old, who have the imagination
to see a new world and the courage to live their part in it.

CONTENTS

ACKNOWLEDGMENTS

I thank the many people who have been a part of my lives as we move through and within the great Emerald River. Most particularly I thank Judith Cope for her steady heart-felt editing through the Mount Shasta winter while I was writing this book. Thanks to Richard and Nancy Stodart for their feedback; and to Alma Rose for her encouraging comments. Thanks to Gerry and Barbara Clow for seeing "The River" and for their positive creative suggestions on its publication.

INTRODUCTION

The *Emerald River of Compassion* is a vision of Gaia's—the Earth's—reality. Hence, it is one story, but it also tells the many stories of individuals living on Planet Earth. The *Emerald River of Compassion* tells of our human realities, revealing how we coincide with or diverge from the structure of nature and what our potential participation with its inexhaustible plenitude can be.

The Old Earth, part one of the *Emerald River of Compassion* trilogy, gives us themes of our traditions, and our tribal, modern, and mundane selves. We meet characters who have learned to break down or transform cosmological, cross-cultural, and psychological forces that have dammed the River. Their trials and patterns of unfoldment are not apart from our own. Whether Japanese, Australian, Greek, European, American, or Chinese, these characters imply and express qualities that are archetypal rather than specific to one or another culture.

The archetypes within each of the Four Worlds are introduced through the cosmic story of the Creator and Creatrix. These divine beings penetrate the lives of the mortal characters as qualities and themes that can be perceived as imaginal patterns when we open to the River.

If we think of the River as a circle—a cycle returning to its source—we find that its circumference is infinite, yet there are circles within circles, like rings of waves in a pond. There are stories within stories here. We can see the obvious linear progression in the stories pertaining to a certain character, but we can also see how the continuity is possible because of metaphorical connections among all the stories. Themes of racial and religious conflict, tribalism, and technology run deep in the human constitution and operate in juxtaposition.

Each of the sixteen Old Earth archetypes contains four symbols. One way of reading this book would be to read all four stories of each archetype at a single sitting, perhaps with your husband, wife, child, or another group of people. See how each symbol is expressed in a story and how the group of four stories relates to an archetype. The interconnected stories are a stream of images wherein the tenacious source energy of the *Emerald River of Compassion* can penetrate our souls. Through story upon story, and image upon image, we can awaken to the creative stream of the universe within us, the core fountain of power that can open us up to who we really are.

Each symbol displayed at the beginning of a story pertains to the *source*, *agent*, *process*, or *effect* of its respective archetype. The *source* radiates a *golden light* that reveals either longing or enlightenment. A gift from the headwaters of the River, the golden source is our spirituality, our divinity. The *agent* is the *black invisibility* of that which is at once dissolved and restructured to become a means of transformation. This transformative *process* is delineated in the *red of change*, the color of sentience, involvement, and suffering. The alchemical *effect* of the archetypes is revealed in the *white of purification*, the separation of the wheat from the chaff. White clarifies what can be regenerated and returned as seed to the golden essence and what is best returned to the black and red compost of existence. The respective schemes of these four colors—gold, black, red, and white—are given next to the name of the symbol. The first color refers to the function of the symbol, the second to the function of the archetype, and the third to the function of the world.

This alchemical association with the symbolic functions of the archetypes is part of the tradition of discovery of our imaginal power. The tradition of *sophia perennis* reveals that the individual soul is one with the world soul that vivifies the universe and is part of the living River.

Although the linear sequence of the stories in the *River* appears historical, many stories are happening simultaneously and, in some cases, many years pass between stories. In these stories time is not considered regular like the ticking of a clock or metronome. It is, rather, like the River itself—sometimes bubbling up with the convergence of many events in one place, and at other times on a smooth glide when only a placid current flows. Time in the *Emerald River of Compassion* is continuously contracting into a dense impact of insight and meaning and then expanding into release and expression. This changing pulse of time is not divided from consciousness but is inseparable from memory, the awareness of the now, and the anticipation of continuity into an unknown future.

Everything in *The Old Earth* is tending toward either elemental decomposition or a revelation of archetypal awareness that can be seen as the seeds of the garden we are planting in the compost of what has been gathered in the past. The elements and elementals are dynamic powers that make everything useful. Memories are like ruins when they no longer match the living pulse of the River through our lives. Ashes to fire, sand to earth, mud to water, and dust to air sink to the depths of the River where they settle into an amalgam to be used according to the imaginal power of a given character to transform Old Earth qualities into New Earth qualities.

Social themes are implied within interactions of the characters. They become more complex as the *Emerald River of Compassion* progresses. The members of a group bring valor, perseverance, transcendence, patience, and purity—or selfishness and reaction—according to their inherent predispositions and abilities to *be who they are.*

All the characters, however innocent, well-meaning, or corrupt, are part of the metamorphic, interconnected passion of life. The source of passion is one, but its many tributaries *together*, with *compassion*, carry the circling seminal drop that enlivens the body of light within the body of clay. One glimpse of the power of compassion can temper the whole flood of greed presently destroying the Earth.

Future Volumes of the Emerald River of Compassion

The power of the imaginal—of the deep dream—is a power that humans, in our habitual preoccupation with production and consumption, have forgotten. Yet, the imaginal incubates and lies within us. This power runs through the second volume of the trilogy, *The Land of Zar*. In *The Land of Zar*, our characters find the inner mysteries of the imaginal. They navigate the primal language of imaginal capacities and begin from within the deeper currents of the River to re-create, in part three, *The New Earth*.

The New Earth reveals humans free to actualize on Earth the creative power that blesses the planet with inner powers harmonious with the River's own mystery. Those who have transformed deeply within themselves, become agents for the greater humanity. Humanity then realizes Gaia's plenitude through understanding its own commitment to action. Action is not only *doing*, but *being*, when our *being* coincides with the great structure of nature.

R.P.K.
January 1993
Mt. Shasta, CA

EMERALD RIVER OF COMPASSION

THE FIRST WORLD

The dark waters of heaven win back the dreams of the Creator from the certitude of light. Interpenetrating in a world of timeless depth, the Creator circles in poetic chemistry before the stars are born.

He draws the First World with a finger of intent, like a lotus stem arising from the black waters of nonbeing. Out of nothing, he lifts up the spiritual presence of his petaled hope and discovers it to be the Creatrix. Seers, seeing the invisible, and feelers, touching the untouchable, the Creator and Creatrix open to each other as one heart, one mind. Without above or below, without right or left, their love unfolds in the space of absolute reflection.

Shaking off the slumber of nothingness, they remember the beginning becoming again. The flood tide of the First World returns. The Primal Waters curve upon themselves. There is no genesis that has not dawned in the Mobius swirling patterns that eternally return. Creators of cycles without end, they once again begin a universe. Long before the original fireball, the flame of their spirits sparked pure light. Now, as then, the womb of the First World implodes with their compassion. The mystery of the River *flows from the fountain of their being and cascades into images seeking soul, substance, and life.*

Waters part in the eternal night as their incomprehensible bodies pull back the magnetism of pure contemplation. Rushing in a chorus of neutrinos, the will toward beauty presses toward time. Within their heavenly matrix, the Kingdom arises. Iridescent streams fan out from the palpitating fire and water of the spirit—running clear, long before the seasons turn.

Like the limpid currents of the underworld and the tongues of phoenix fires, eros and logos emerge from the River's burning waters. Headwaters churn with images of flashing free electrons. Beauty moves with outstretched wings while compassion fills bottomless vales of possible suffering. No sooner does the Creator dream of those who can behold and praise him than the Priest-Seer emerges. The Creatrix, foreseeing the separation of spirit and body, spills her cosmic tears. The possibility of identity invades the tenacity of primal substance, and the turbulent River spins.

THE CREATOR

Drunk on the primal essence of the River, the Creator spills forth the cosmic Word. In poetry that issues from eternity, he speaks of the One and the many—of fire, air, earth, and water. His single divine eye beholds the unity of the River flowing from the logos, the Word.

Flushed with joy, he stands at the headwaters and propels his lightning and fire into the River downstream, penetrating the waves where the Creatrix moves in delight. Thus infused with his spiritual fire, every particle dances with the potential of awakening.

Aeons pass. The River coalesces into a solar system flung out on the edge of the Milky Way. Born many times—from spirit, fire, water, and molten magma—a tributary of the River winds toward the Earth. Changing, changing, the secret of the Earth hides inside the womb of the Creatrix until it finds its purpose—to die and be reborn in the unending cycles of the First World. Propelled away from the Creator, the Earth moves toward an unknown destiny. Blindly at first, life seeds itself, its myriad forms moving from waves of light into vegetal tremors pulsing in phosphorescent seas.

Again and again, the Creatrix infuses design into the atoms dancing in the River's chaotic maelstrom. Elements rain down from the supernova of the early Sun as the Creator's crown of light becomes the auras of all things. Asteroid rains of fire fall from the invisible.

After vanquishing floods, remnants of humanity drift back to the call of the River, to some destiny faintly felt and remembered. Tribes circle the Earth in search of the Creator's source. They stand in awe of the light itself, the power that washes away the darkest of the deep violet skies.

THE GOLDEN GENESIS

Eternity
Gold of gold within gold

Being still
I reach my center
and turn, walking in eternity
one with everyone.

In the golden light there is nothing that cries. Mountains arise from the belly of the planet to be swallowed in thunderous rains, spreading dark waters into hissing hot springs. Red, spitting fire erupts from the crust of the primeval Earth. Oceanus surges in the dark womb of space. The River roars at its source within the nuclei of all things. Here in the matrix, all souls are conceived. White cliffs cool in sediments that become the bones of shellfish and mammals. Molecules transform sunlight into the energy that lifts life into the finite forms of green plants. Gods and goddesses search for the lost language of the Sun.

The eros of the Earth erupts with the kissing of fish, the spasm of newts, the sexual riding of turtles, the mating of bats hanging together in caves. Fertile oceans foam with sperm lost in quest of the mystery beyond the veil. All wombs long for the flood of creation, where each child is conceived as a messenger of eternity, rending the membranes of the firmaments.

Raphael, Maria, and Ariel

Maria's love for Raphael knows no bounds. She opens herself to him as heaven opens to the brilliant light plowing the fields of space. His penis penetrates her womb like a solar ray in winter, and she feels renewed. Through her, the Creator creates himself.

Her ecstatic cry leads Ariel's soul into the golden channel of joy. Cells unfold and migrate as his embryo recapitulates the evolutionary chain. Fish and reptile move within him, a portent of the child to be. The ape-child sleeps. Ariel curls up and unfolds a mythic ritual of creation, the fall and renewal before breath moved in heaven. The amniotic fluid of the cooling Pacific sways in rhythmic tides.

The River layers itself in gold over gold to fashion a web of sparking neurons. Organic gestures move toward a repertoire of images unfolding in premonitions of unborn landscapes. Crystalline genes orchestrate the music of Ariel's fetal form as matter oozes from etheric elements. Cells multiply into bulbous forms that stretch and yawn up the spinal tree toward a brain beholding a thousand cities in a possible future. There is before or after in this eternal womb where each self makes fields of scented flowers. Ariel, in his little world, turns through the script of the River, looking for a page of life in the twentieth century. Sensing his oneness with the blue eyes of a cat, the ruffled wings of a hawk, the lilies opening in spring, he feels the River coursing through his veins. His hindbrain becomes a compass for the primeval creatures within himself. His forebrain swells and engulfs the universe in a tiny cosmic replica.

Ariel wakes as if from a dream to Maria's breathing in the night. "Come, come!" she cries, opening her thighs to the golden River pouring through her lotus love. She echoes the chant of Raphael as he rhythmically moved above her naked body when the universe began. Beckoned by the cosmos, Ariel wails in delight, radiating heat from his hands and heart. The diaphanous veil of blood bursts into beauty. A child is born.

SEEING BEYOND THE FLOOD

Divine Eye
Black of gold within gold

Through focus
my spirit dilates
and beholds
the boundaries of form.

The watery eye of the Earth opens in the midst of blue wonder as the River awaits transformation. The gods and goddesses are quiet, listening to the falling rain of tears. Lemuria and Atlantis pass away in the floods of time, the River doubling back on itself. But the Creator feels no burden as he dreams inside the troubled Earth, his word vibrating new channels into which the River gushes forth. The water, rising from its source in renewal, rushes like the hum of bees in his ears.

The Creator walks in the etheric essence of the Creatrix, who some call Sophia. She gives birth to the shapes of mosses, fungi, and flowers. She bathes in aqua pools and breathes the power of life into darting trout and mayflies. Adorned for millions of years in her rainbow-colored robe, she weaves the fiery eye of the Sun and the silvery eye of the Moon into the watery eye of the Earth. The Sun and Moon turn, creating golden and silver tapestries from their longing. Moving in conjunction with each other, they conceive a new way of seeing. Before dawn they awake in each other's arms and whisper words of fidelity before they part, moving toward opposing realms of the sky.

Twelve tribes migrate in the night, spreading new seeds in the fertile black earth as the last Atlantean flood recedes. Bison and antelope roam in the plains and mountains. The multicolored cliffs of Santorini rise. The Sahara proliferates in lush forests where water bubbles up from caves and birds sing in the language of waves.

Like specks on a duck's egg, tribes gather around the Earth—from the Indus and Mesopotamian valleys, to the Yangtze and Nile. They migrate to Lake Titicaca and the Pacific islands emerging from the sea. Passion points to vestiges of ancient mysteries: the Chan Chan city of China, the wall in the Bay of Dubrovnik, the ancient African city of Zimbabwe, and the timbers of Mount Ararat.

The divine eye watches new civilizations take form out of the form-less waters. Ashes of ancient cities fertilize the rising plains, everywhere marked with fragments of settlements remaining from the later migra-tions: the fort of Craig Phadrig north of Inverness, the Maikop inscrip-tions of the Abkhazian peoples, and the cuneiform tablets of the library of Tell Mardick.

Mama Ocllo

After the Nazca people vanished from the plains, the people who were to become the Inca journeyed toward Inti, named for the Sun God from the sacred mountains. The rays of Inti guided them out of the abyss of fear and through the mountains and jungles in search of a holy site to settle. Among the people were four brothers who received the power of Inti streaming down from the sky. They lived the magic myths woven by enlightened ancestors who released their breath to the wind and returned all things to the Creator and Creatrix. When the ancestors passed on, their souls returned to the Sun and their blood ran back to the River.

There, where the sacred quinoa rose from the Earth, the Sun God rained down a thousand colors of prayer. The four brothers saw the pres-ent clearly. Their wives saw the future and strung words into oracles. Together, male and female, they comprised the original eight, whose hidden meanings turned in the heart of the Creator. Two of the original eight were Mama Ocllo and Manco Capac. In a later incarnation they would become mother and son, and she would guide him as Huayna Capac, the eleventh emperor of Peru.

As the divine eye surveyed the steep terrain of the Andes, the people moved slowly, carrying the golden staff of the solar ray into new dominions. With vision that was one with the Sun, Mama Ocllo led them toward their holy site where they would engage in true sacrifice, which means to make sacred: returning clay pots to the Earth with the return of the body, while the spirit sang in heaven. Mama danced in the growing grain, her serenity gleaming in the eye of the Creatrix.

One of the brothers, Ayar Cachi, hurled rocks with his golden sling and gouged ravines out of the mountains for passageways. With demonic violence, he carved the way to Mount Pisgah and then, becoming a rainbow, showered his people with hope. He led the people to the site of the holy empire, later to become Cuzco. There, the promise from the gods—that the golden staff would stand in the Earth where they were to settle—was fulfilled. And there, Mama Ocllo guided Manco Capac to build the House of the Sun, the holy edifice in Tahuantinsuyo.

The four brothers, the grain of the Earth, stand as sacred stones to those who cannot yet see the changing migrations of the soul. The divine eye is within, but how many use it?

Now Mama Ocllo lives in Peru as an astronomer who seeks to find the mirror of Earth in the heavens. She is proof of the power of the Goddess, for she traces the tracks of the stars in patterns that work magic on Earth. The sacred breath of the Creator and Creatrix move through her eye in geometries that speed the descent of the River to Earth.

"Look at my eyes," says Mama Ocllo to her people, who are huddled together around a night fire. "All that I have seen, you can see through me. From now on, I shall live on the Island of the Golden Moon."

"How will we find you, Mama?" asks little Pachacuti, whose big brown eyes grow round.

Mama turns her brown face toward Pachacuti: "If you focus your two eyes inward and marry the Sun and Moon within your heart, you shall see as I see. The blind spot of your vision is where silver and gold cross and where the golden staff stands rooted in the Earth. Accept the blackness and the serpents will rise up the tree of your spine and create rainbows."

Pachacuti grows silent as the fire flickers golden on his face.

"Will you tell us what sign we might see that promises a new empire?" asks Maucha, who holds a sword.

Mama's face grows serious: "Find the source of the River and listen. The speech of the River is as relentless as the cracks of time on temples and as gentle as the kiss of dawn on the clouds. See life as a brimming cup and the River will gather in your heart. Old empires were to anchor the River on Earth. In these times the monumental treasures of the past are to be as fluid as electricity in your body. Let the River roll through you like a shimmering rainbow. Though you are my people, no longer is the River a single color."

Maucha is persistent and zealous: "How can we live through these times of madness when fumes fill the air and surround the whole Earth? It is the white man's disease!"

"It never has been easy, nor will it be," replies Mama Ocllo, whose wrinkled face shows courage. "But as you focus on your blind spots, you shall see how to move through the black air to immeasurable glory. This glory is to behold the Sun God in people of every color. Your resistance to change is but a sign of your own enmity. If you see the rainbow, you will know the rainbow. By knowing the rainbow you can *become* the rainbow. Receive the River through your eyes and weep no more. Love makes possible a thousand deaths, each one surrendering more to perfection."

Hyperborean Mountains and Caves

Spiritual Fire
Red of gold within gold

Centering my light
into transcendent rays
I breathe
fire.

The skin of the Creator changes color with the migration of tribes across the Earth. As mountains rise out of melting rocks on the shifting continents of Asia and Europe, the cosmic Creatrix layers veils of mist over cooling lava and breathes crooked pathways over the land. Her mysterious moisture spreads life over barren rocks and penetrates into uterine caves.

Following the path of the Sun, migrations move south and west. Arctic seas shrink under a cap of crystallized ice. The brains of Atlanteans and evolving primates meet in caves where stalactites glisten. Cycles repeat over and over in the memories of tissue and cell. The crises of the Permian Ice Age send the River streaming toward fur and warm blood. Now the hoofs of horse and bison, the claws of bear and lion, speak in snow prints of the River's living water. Evolving herbivores translate the light-filled crystals of chlorophyll into blood-red meat for the carnivore. Bodies burst from wombs in caves while glaciers rip through graves.

The River water flows wherever souls who remember the Creator and Creatrix walk humbly below the maelstrom of rising spirits. In time, the River runs north of the Hyperborean shore, where it flows through the caves of Lascaux and Ahernsberg, Pech Merle and Altamira. Later, the tribes divide into the Germanic and Celtic peoples. Later still, the rounded, post-Atlantean script is replaced by the sharp edges of hatchet marks and arrowheads. Ogmios, culture-hero of ancient Britain, articulates one tributary of the River, splashing patterns of speech into signs, trying to remember the spiritual fire. The Tree of Life in the spine of the Creatrix becomes known as the language of the trees. Among the Celts, the tree unfurls in the speech of the birch, oak, willow, rowan, and pine.

Oga and Walumpu

The magical source of life is seeded in the invisible white fire of the underground. Here, in the absence of solar light, the air of Paleolithic caves hums with the ritual of remembering the primordial condition. The memory is held in the red hand that is painting the dots and hatches that portray the power of life pulsing between male and female. Chanting voices echo while incensors burn the spiritual fire. Lamps burning the fat of animals light the way to a deeper mystery where all is dark and still. The primordial condition can only be replicated in the absence of solar light.

Men and women huddle together for a ritualistic opening of the channel between the lotus crown and the lotus root. Walumpu stands and embraces Oga, who has been holding a stone goddess figure close to her body. The River vibrates within the Word of the Creator and Creatrix in the murmuring of their love to each other. The channels open and fill the lotus, the spiritual fire rising in petals of light. Atomic nuclei spin together and apart in a cascade of invisible light, a symphonic dance of fusion and fission.

The light recedes. The Creator enters Oga while the Creatrix envelopes Walumpu in her dark embrace. Their permeable bodies open and breathe the fiery infusion through their skin, their cells vibrating with the force that drives the Sun and Moon. The divine eye opens and beholds its own flame in the instant after the great conception. Neither space nor time creates illusions in this moment; only the great void lies between them. Light and darkness encompass each other. The Creator passes through Oga into Walumpu's mouth and speaks through his full lips: "I am what has not been made." The Creatrix passes through Walumpu into Oga's heart, then rises in white flame from her vibrating body. "I am the fire of becoming everything made," she cries.

Slowly, the white fire of the ecstatic fusion fades. All in the tribe, fur close to skin, seek to remember the fire returning to fire. Deep within herself, Oga wonders how she can reevoke the moment of fusion. Her body remembers, but her mind is already moving into the realm of time and heavenly history. As the centripetal powers of the Creator and Creatrix reverse and spin outward, she and Walumpu begin to etch the script of the River on the cave walls.

ARYAN MIGRATIONS

Crown of Light
White of gold within gold

Elevation
of your aura
spins in cones
of living light.

Pravin and Luqman

The greater Ice Age is an old man of 250 million years. He hibernates in the winter when the chromosomes of mutants kiss deep in the Earth's womb. His wife is the Sun who circles the galactic wheel, gathering the qualities of the zodiac from the sky. She flashes forth the imprints of the stars into the icy crystals of his bones.

Long ago, when the vernal equinox was in Sagittarius, the River of our galaxy flowed in whirlpools through the celestial north and south poles. The golden age of that time ripened in a tropical arctic.

Pravin remembers when the Sun and stars and all the elements were his gods and goddesses. An Indian tour guide, he walks along the Tungabhadra riverbank with friends who are seeking to awaken to spirit. Pravin is drunk on the wine of springtime, and passion pours from his heart, for spring is the solvent of winter. Botu is retired and has come from New York to find the fluid way, to rediscover his heart. He and Pravin walk together like two gods. Luqman follows, pensive and silent.

Maria and Heng-O walk behind, talking between themselves, the spring breeze blowing through their hair. Maria calls to Ariel. He is like her breath, moving in and out, reaching for grass and stones and now for her steady hand. Swallows dart above his curly head, and he shrieks in delight, then spontaneously breaks away and jumps into the cool water. They walk near the headwaters of the river where animals abound in the tropical forests.

Maria gasps, watching Ariel, as Pravin and Botu look back and laugh. Heng-O stretches her hand toward the jubilant child, but it is Luqman who rushes in and pulls him back to the bank. Everyone relaxes as Ariel's laughter ripples on the surface of the water. All minds gather into a single thought: It would be lovely to stop awhile and let Ariel play in the afternoon Sun.

Maria and Ariel sit down on the bank and dangle their feet in the water. Botu, a large, gentle, black man, refreshes himself with a beer. Heng-O squints into the Sun, looking up at Pravin sitting reflectively on a rock. He is remembering the singing mouths of the gods who taught him when he was a priest, guiding his people by the rhythms of the stars, away from the encroaching ice and toward a new destiny.

"You think the River is only here on Earth?" asks Pravin, whose brown face mirrors the fullness of long ago, although his heart bends like a willow over the gliding River.

"Bless us with an ancient story!" cries Heng-O. Maria holds Ariel now, cradling him like a precious basket in her arms. Luqman lies back on the grass, longing for the serenity of his friends. His gentle soul stares through wild eyes, for he has not recovered from the shock of being a soldier in the recent war in the Near East. His body shakes frequently, the blood twisting through his veins, as though striving to unburden a load of hidden feeling. He sits up and casts a fishing line into the River, watching the hook swirl in the turbulent eddies, as if caught between dimensions like his own throbbing body. When he finally speaks, his voice bears a tremor: "Yes, Pravin, tell us how you walked with the old gods of India. I feel blind. Perhaps you can help me see."

"My mouth feels hot with flame," Pravin begins. His energy is felt by everyone. "It is hard speaking of these things. The River tells all. Like you, Luqman, I have seen the evil heart, the red spit of bombs and blood. Ariel must grow like a white, bright rose into a new era. The

River will soon shake its tail. If it rattles, it is warning us to rid ourselves of blame and move out of the way."

"What we live is truth—isn't that our own way of the River?" asks Maria in a strong, sure voice. "Tell us of your journey, of what you remember of the old times."

Pravin bends down and puts his hands on his knees, preparing to tell his story: "Our Aryan root race splintered like reeds in the hot Sun. My people, the Deva-Yasnians, lost sight of the Creator, the source of the River, for we lived in hatred of the followers of Mazda. We migrated from the north through Siberia and down into what is now Iran. Our hostility was later reflected in the Turanians.

"I'll tell you of when I was a servant boy. I suffered from intense labor and the harshness directed at my people. Though born a slave, I knew the patterns of the stars and the elements. The River flowed through me. I remembered my love, Savitri, the divine Word whom I once had known in the flesh.

"My life was hellish, but my spirit wanted to dance and shout and sing. Only the Sun, stars, and elements were my friends. A priest, Vivasvat, felt my ardor and assigned me as his attendant. I washed his homespun saffron cotton and dried it in the Sun, arranged the flowers and fruits according to his dream. I could read his wishes and would well with tears of sorrow and love, all through the act of serving him. When the sacred hymns were recited, the power of my past leapt into the music and rhythms of the syllables. The holy *Nivids* dissolved the boundaries of word and presence, and I met the gods face to face. Thunderous Indra, fiery Agni, changeable Vayu—all lived within me. Through recitation of the *Nivids* I made contact with Savitri, whom I now seek to find again. She is my beloved who lives within the River."

"Is the River you speak of in heaven?" asks Maria, her golden hair flowing back like a goddess dreaming. Ariel holds a tiny flower in his hand.

Pravin looks up at the sky, as if searching for the words of the gods: "In Sumeria it was known as Eridu, the 'confluence of the Rivers'. In India the holy Ganges fell from heaven and wrought near disaster upon the Earth. The River is gaseous and tumultuous, and a scourge of truth in the darkest of times. In ancient times, to save the world, Shiva danced in rhythm with the River and caught its deluge in his hair. After the flood, tribes migrated and divided into cults, each seeking to remember the golden age. Now, Shiva's hair dangles blond on one side, black on the other, red in front, and white behind."

"The River then is in all the races?" asks Heng-O, puzzled. Botu sits listening and sipping his beer in the cool shadow of a nearby ash tree.

Pravin slides off the rock and onto the grass, facing the others. His aura brightens: "The souls of all humans flow like tears from the face of heaven. The skin mirrors the black Earth in the heat of Africa and Australia and the red Earth in the plains of the Americas. The yellow Earth of Asia rises up in powders of golden pigment. The chalky Earth of Eurasia grows in straight rows of crystals through the white face. All the races blend in the brown peoples of the oceans. The cross of the races has its source in Eridu, in the circle of the sky. Svarivara, the celestial spring, lies within each soul, whether the skin is dark or light. This spring can dissolve the madness of war."

"Is the spring the spirit that acts through the breath?" asks Luqman, his courage rising. "It seems that humanity is fragmented, with no power to act. Look at my bag of blood and bones! The suffering you bore in ancient times I now carry between my clenched teeth. My soul is thirsty for the spring you speak of. I long for my heart to cease churning, so that it may radiate like the Sun. Will my affliction hinder love forever?"

"We love you, Luqman," says Heng-O. He can see the peace in her eyes as she presses his hand. Ariel places his little hand on top and echoes Heng-O. "We love you, Luqman." Ariel looks from the white face of his mother to the black face of Botu and giggles gleefully, his own face round as the rising Moon.

"Where did the spring come from?" asks Maria.

"I feel the spring is whomever we deeply love," responds Pravin, taking Ariel in his large hands and tickling his squirming body.

On the opposite bank, the monkeys chatter and begin to scratch each other, their grooming enlivening the River. Light glides in ever-changing patterns, mirroring the colors of the trees and hills. Old Botu laughs as the Sun crests the western hill.

The chorus of monkeys is rejoined with the songs of birds offering gratitude for a day well lived. The sky turns from violet to rose, mirrored in the River that now sings its own song:

Creator's Song of the River

I am the funnel of creative power, the source of the River.
You can find me in every pivot of the changing and the unchanging.
I am the divine eye that sees all possibilities.
I am the concentrated dilation that opens on all alike.
I am the multiple views of the world.
You can find me in the light appearing as darkness to mortal eyes.
Look for me in the rose, the cradle, and the auras of queens.
I am the newborn, the child, and the ancient one.
I speak the silent language behind all languages.
Look for me in the rays that precede all waves.
You can find me in the seed, the sun, and simple things.
I am my own mother and father and dwell in the houses of everyone.
I live in the call of the wild, the primal sound.
I am the blessing of every wish and source of all hope.
Look for me in your own crown and the rays of the Sun and stars.
I dwell in every body.

Are you the talk of the ages?
I am unspeakable.

THE PRIMAL WATERS

While the Creator watches from his transcendent eternal home, the Creatrix dances on the firmaments. She never tires. Offering up her days to all who receive her myriad ways of becoming, she touches the depths of the sea and the heights of the sky. Entering the facets of crystals and gems, she weaves the reflecting and refracting rays of the Sun to engender a million designs. The source of eros, she dances not the form of things, but the pulse of power behind the patterns yet to be.

She orchestrates the River into symphonic patterns of possibility and seals the dark secret of its depths within each string of cadences. Turning endlessly upon itself, the River vibrates with waves of eros and logos until, out of infinite chaos and seething mystery, the cosmic egg appears. All forms of matter and sound, life and language, swirl in the movement of its continuous curves. Positive and negative powers undulate within its translucent shell, generating the cosmic language that is the script of the River.

Now the Creatrix stirs the Primal Waters, spattering the script into the ethers. The ancient tongues of Sanskrit, Hebrew, Arabic, and Aramaic catch the rhythm of the water in midair. Upon wandering tribes the script rains down, like the sinuous curves of snakes who know the language of the heart. But they cannot fathom its mystery. All are innocent in the Primal Waters, for neither judgment nor death yet shadow the human race.

The Creatrix moves between darkness and light, chaos and pattern, then vanishes into the depths. Few can behold her nebulous becoming. But those who follow the curving path that returns to itself can see their own reflection in the water. Returning from too much wandering, they can enter infinity. Poetry bursts from the tongues of innocents who can be still and see the script of the River.

THE CHAOS OF THE SOURCE

Source
Gold of black within gold

The spring
of primal substance
spirals
within my being.

Karl

When the world was formless and void, darker than shadows in the abyss, Karl's soul rose like a fountain on a stream of universal being. Riding the waves of the Primal Waters, he heard the chorus of primates and birds chanting the Creator's song of the River.

His soul remembered when the Creatrix went out from the Creator and her diaphanous body turned into the firmaments that hid the gods from the eyes of mortals. She entered time, rising from the primal fountain. Her heart was warm and her womb was moist. Her hairs were silken strands of possible worlds, waving in the waters. The Creatrix became the River of change, the branching rivulets that veil the source. Without knowing it, Karl searched for the source in her mystery of transformation.

Son of a Lutheran mother and a Jewish father who was gassed by the Nazis, Karl hid in the Black Forest and survived on canary grass, ground ivy, snakes, and rabbits. He learned the patterns of edible leaves and roots as he wandered through thick terrain. Sometimes a German uncle gave him shelter in an old shed, but mainly his house was hidden in his body, which moved like the River when it was pristine and pure. He lived with trembling hands and sensitive ears, listening for the question that arose from raw instinct: *What is chaos?* For the raging bull of war had overturned the semblance of civilization.

As he grew older, Karl would remember the stories his mother told of Voluspa, the blind seeress. She would say: "In the beginning, there was nothing but the Yawning Gap with the Chill Stream, flowing from the Place of Fog and Mist."

"What is the Yawning Gap?" he would ask, opening his hands and looking into his empty cupped palms. "How do people come from nothing, Mama?"

"The giants come from nothing. They are not people. They are forces like water, fire, and mist."

"Where do the forces come from?"

"The void, the abyss."

"How did the world come from the abyss?"

"The World Tree stands in the midst of the abyss. All nine worlds grow from its branches."

Now a scientist in the theoretical division of Los Alamos National Laboratory, Karl still stirs with the old myths and the question of becoming, the origins of creation and destruction. The intensity in his body summons the primal things that trembled before the stars were born. As he walks alone in the New Mexico mountains, he watches the raindrops of a summer storm form out of the whorls of changing clouds. Moving like a serpent into the turbulence, his soul approaches timelessness, perceiving the world in slow motion and beholding the perpetual perturbations in awe. Water droplets merge and scintillate in endless recursive patterns, dancing and dividing in tiny vibrating globules. *What is universal?* he wonders. *What is the source of the self-similar fields of whorls and drops?* His perception accelerates to catch the momentary transition between nothingness and mist, chaos and form.

The nonlinear flows and oscillations found in the perturbation techniques of modern chaos theory do not take Karl far enough. He seeks the source of endless feedback loops. The random output from one calculation becomes the input of another—this is the cosmic egg that is ever giving birth to itself! Cycle without end, the Creatrix dances in the darkness as computers click in the labs on the hill above.

Karl seeks to utter the name of the source, to call himself magically into the arms of the unknown. He wants to understand sound and silence as the source of music. He wants to find the luminous darkness where destinies are born. He wants to discover the origin of chaos, the recursive branching of being, born from nonbeing. He knows that the computations of period-doublings—the flight patterns of bees, the variabilities of weather, the migrations of people—all result in a geometric constant. Like a boat carrying a million people over turbulent seas, this constant carries the digits to the other side of zero and sets them down on a finite shore.

Karl listens and watches the dark sky overhead. A lightning bolt leaps between heaven and Earth as the Creatrix flashes through the veil of clouds. Poised between will and fate, Karl sees in his mind's eye a toroid pattern turning endlessly inside out. The geometric constant born of infinite randomness gyrates out of zero into finite forms, then turns back into itself, as if to gather the blossoms vibrating on the Tree of Life. The rain streams down without wind.

He races, stumbling, up the hill to the lab, his long hair flying and his heart pounding. Toroid turbulence has led him to the center of chaos. He goes to the computer to calculate the geometry of the torus as rings of subatomic particles fuse and split inside the matter and antimatter bubbling up from the Primal Waters.

THE MESSAGE IN THE WAVES

Cosmic Egg
Black of black within gold

Cosmic seed
of divine potency
implodes and explodes
in universes.

Pahulu

Pahulu is trying not to lose her mind. After running on the beach
and wading among the waves, she plops down on the foamy sand, her
round belly resting on her thighs like a ripe fallen fruit.

As brown as the Earth, Pahulu embraces the day like a hibiscus
opening to the light. She is the perennial spirit that drones with the call
of the whales and surrenders to the fins of dolphins. The spirit of Ha-
Wai, the joyous Sun Goddess from ancient Mu, the motherland of
Lemuria, lives in her cells. Her lineage is as vast as the waves of the sea:
Born of Mau and Maumau, born of Nana and Mana, born of Kake and
Make, Napa and Nala, Pala and Kala, Paka and Papa, Kalakala and
Huluhulu, Halahala and Palapala, Pea and Lupe. . . . Pahulu is the darkness within the Sun, where the light touches the sea. The laumilo eels,
sea-urchins, and kuopoupou fish all vibrate to her presence, except
when she is angry.

She is angry now. The modern male drives her insane. Sexual madness is all she sees, rather than truly erotic love, which seems as rare as

ice in the tropics. Having become impregnated in a moment when she lost her center of truth, she later wept—not because she loved a white man, but because she succumbed to his attitude. She let herself be manipulated instead of being an active source of love.

Sensual as a squid, Pahulu moves in great empathy with all who touch her. Supported by the rippling waves of nature spirits and the abundance of the island, the bounty of fish and fruit, she gives and gives with no thought of lack. But the white man, Gus, lived inside a contracted aura. She felt sympathy for him at first, seeing him as a child who needed a mother. And she was willing to be mother to him. She knew from the old legends that males are born in the night of creation, whereas females are born at the approach of dawn. Like the Sun Goddess, she shares her light with all, because she knows the darkness of the Earth and the sea.

Pahulu watches children turning somersaults on the sand, jumping in the air and tumbling over each other. For a moment, she forgets her anger, remembering that the night of creation gave birth to turtles and lobsters, too. Gus knew nothing of birth, she muses, only the pain of abandonment, of lack, of the struggle to get, to take.

Suddenly anger seizes her again and her body surges with heat. She remembers the moment of being taken as an object, instead of as a person or spirit or wave of abundance. Gus came and went quickly, like a sharp sword lopping off a fruit. She holds her belly and listens to the call of the gulls and terns wheeling above her head. "Where does anger begin?" she wonders to herself. "The rottenness of others must be inside me or this acid would not rise to the surface."

She rises from the sand and strides out toward the sea. The Creatrix dwells within her, and with her power Pahulu walks toward truth. She tests herself in the waves whenever she senses trouble. Wading out to the breakers, she dives into their rolling motion and plunges beyond into the depths. The outgoing tide turns her inward, and she descends between currents of positive and negative pressure.

Pulled in two directions, down and up, she undulates like a panduras vine sprouting leaves. She becomes a serpent, a kauwila eel, an ulei tree, wiggling in the ocean. She swims inside the turning tide, the cosmic egg that spills its protoplasm to the cadences of ancestral plans. She becomes an unhatched egg in the great Pacific, a cosmic embryo carrying a human embryo. In her body she feels a cleavage cutting through her animal-vegetal spine. The spheres of her being stretch her from crown to root, crossing her left and right, female and male, uterus and testes. Eros rises within her. As she spirals into the dark space of the sea, her soul calls to the Sun Goddess to be washed clean of anger.

The child inside her lies waiting for birth. Like a cyclops, the single luminosity in its brain grows between unseeing eyes. It struggles for life within the womb as the mother surrenders to the changing sea.

Pahulu lets the Primal Waters determine whether she is to live or to die. She becomes one with the living magnetic field and moves into a four-dimensional matrix where time and space turn inside out. Gravity pulls her down toward the center of the Earth. Knowing the purity of her will, the Creatrix calls to the sonorous cells of dolphins to lift their listening to Pahulu's body. In a symphony of movement, the dolphins ride the turbulence down to the depths where the lifeless body rolls in the crossing currents. All sense of separation momentarily vanishes between Pahulu and the dolphins. Powerful dolphins embrace the fragile human species in Pahulu, turn the inner centripetal motion upward and outward, and carry her body to shore.

Lying naked on the beach, she heaves the fluid from her lungs near the pulsing umbrella of a jellyfish. At once she begins to breath heavily, and she sighs as the Sun touches the horizon.

THE CITY BLACKOUT
AND ANCIENT MEMORIES

Movement
Red of black within gold

Interference patterns
of divine thought
ripple and spread
through the darkness.

Zoa, Mujaji, and Nummo

After ten hours behind the wheel of a cab, Zoa often goes to the bar to relieve his pent-up energy. Every day he drives the streets of Manhattan from Harlem to Little Italy, unconsciously seeking something of the old times, something floating within his cellular memory. The driving itself occasionally brings release, but today an irritable woman of obvious wealth railed and shouted at him as though he were a dog.

Inside the tavern, men snicker at a woman swanking around the room. Soured old throats gulp whiskey and beer to appease unfulfilled dreams while the dead, fermented grain struggles to come alive in spirits rising through the men's consciousness.

A young man with liver-red lips approaches Zoa at the bar and announces, "I'm free!" His fuzzy hair and dark skin reveal a distant ancestry similar to Zoa's.

"Free of what?" responds Zoa, looking at the mouth full of rotten teeth.

"I've inherited two thousand dollars from my uncle!"

The old men's eyebrows rise. "Shut up," Zoa reproaches. "Don't speak of what can be taken from you." He gulps down his whiskey and withdraws alone to a corner booth.

Slowly becoming intoxicated, Zoa sinks deeper into himself. His gold bracelet and neck chain speak not only of pride but of remembrance of golden days that purge the deadening grind of the city. Depressed from the endless routine of driving without purpose, he sinks into blackness and falls unconscious. The Creatrix moves in the alcohol to release the light of memory. One by one, his brain cells burst into flame, and he dreams of other times.

He roams places unnamed, riding the River as it flows before the titans fall into bodies and the manna of heaven spins into matter. He dreams of walking on water, of dancing on the holy matrix when the Moon dwells in the Pacific. He is pre-Polynesian, able to expand or contract at will. Master of ectoplasm, he enters the spirit of the waters and fearlessly walks through the starless night. He dreams of being a rongorongo man, chanting alive the script of the River as the sea.

He sees the hand of Tangaroa, the Creator, and cries out, "Show me the way to liberate my people!" The hand points to an eel swimming in the black sea.

"I am a black man! How can I be free?" appeals Zoa, trying to make himself understood.

Tangaroa speaks in riddles: "You are a giant! In primeval times you pushed up the sky with the spirit of Maui and let the gods and goddesses move between Papa and Rangi, the Earth and sky. I embrace you always. Move as eels swim!"

Zoa kneels in the stern of his canoe, feeling its every movement in his body. Waves reflected from the island shore cross those from the greater sea, creating patterns of an animated alphabet in the water. With his *mattang*, a navigating tool made of twigs curving outward into arches and tied to a crossed square frame, he precisely gauges the patterns of the waves. A man of the whole Pacific, he feels his freedom, centered in the pure process of the Primal Waters. Tangaroa has enabled him to summon rain and Sun from the power of his own hand and heart.

The peace of the waters abruptly gives way to human voices that jolt Zoa out of his reverie, and he awakes to find the tavern completely dark. He struggles to determine what world he is in, startled by the incongruity between his dream and a metropolitan blackout in the depth of winter. He could linger there a long while, soothed by the darkness, but for the thought of his family. He stands up and stumbles out the door only to confront traffic moving chaotically to the incessant blare of horns. Too drunk to drive, but not to feel angry, he knows that in the city he will never be free.

He breaks into a run, gathering his dreams as a sailor hoards his treasures, his powerful frame bursting into a cleansing sweat. Love for his family wells up in his chest. He wants to renew himself in the flow of his children as he did in the ancient seas. His ancient *aka body* calls through the darkness, erupting like a volcano from one of the old continents— Bara Bara, Tongo, Samoa—and transforming his red anger into white hope in the blackest of nights. He feels the marrow bones of lived myth rise from Rano Raraku.

Exhausted but exhilarated, he finally arrives at the tenement to find Mujaji with the children hovering anxiously beside her. His son, Nummo, hugs his waist and legs as he throws his arms around them all, and the pulse of four hearts move as one.

On the following evening, Mujaji sits waiting for Zoa to arrive home. She does not want him to notice that she has been crying, for that would upset him, and driving a cab is hard enough. Usually, she is a sorceress of joy, burning up transgression in her heart.

When Zoa comes in, he sinks his large body into a chair next to the radiator: "The ice is bad out there. I slid on Eighth Avenue and almost hit someone!"

He smells the stew simmering in the kitchen, then looks softly at Mujaji in her bright African robe. "Mmm, smells good, honey," he says with a big sigh. "I'm a lucky man. You and the kids are all I've got."

"What about your dad, old Botu?"

"He's doing his own thing—on the go all the time. I got a card from Burma—says the people he's traveling with have a lot of spiritual awareness. He loves the guide—I think his name was Pravin."

Mujaji murmurs to herself, thinking how lucky Botu is to be out of the city. She hesitates before she speaks. "Honey, I've been thinking we should move from here before it gets any worse."

"Move? How? Where?" asks Zoa, hardly believing she is serious.

Mujaji gestures with her arms: "The world is large. You hurry home to my arms, but you grow more tense every week that passes. Nummo goes to a school that is like prison. Fa has started university by getting a scholarship, but she is unhappy."

"But where could we go?"

"Marinda tells me the West Coast is more spacious and has more opportunity. We could even go to a remote place where we could return to native ways. It's not impossible. You always tell me your dreams and your memories of former lives. You're a sailor, not a taxi driver! I want to see you alive again."

Zoa falls into silence. Images from his dream-encounter with Tangaroa pour into his head.

"Mujaji, I know you speak out of love, but we can't afford to move clear across the country."

"Think of the journeys you've made! Have heart!" persists Mujaji. "I can't hide my worries anymore. Crime is getting worse. Fa almost got mugged in the park today."

"What! Is she all right?" says Zoa, his face hardening. "I'll rip apart anyone who touches her."

Mujaji holds her head between her hands: "Yes, she's resting now. She said she saw a great white snake rise up and carry her away. Next thing she knew she was dreaming."

"What do you mean—a great white snake?"

"It wasn't what you think! She said the snake was a protector of some kind—that it blazed with gold and red in the darkness."

Zoa leans back and buries his face in his hands. Two tawny cats curled by the radiator blink sleepily at him. "We can't move, Mujaji. We're barely making it here. Nummo can learn what he needs in the city. He'll survive in school."

"Survival is not enough. He is losing his spirit. He's a good boy, but this culture may drain that out of him. His anxiety has smothered his dreams. We've always made our home the place for dream-telling. Now he's silent. He doesn't dream anymore. I'm to the point where I'll do anything to give our children a better life. And I want to sing and dance again."

"Can't you dance in New York? There's the Afro group and the ballet school. We have enough extra for that."

Mujaji turns away and looks out at the flurrying snow. Zoa stands up and calls to Nummo, who comes in from the bedroom. Small for his seven years, he lowers his eyes as he sees his father.

"Come here, son."

Nummo bursts into tears as his father reaches out to him.

"What's the matter?"

"Nothing."

"Let's sit here and dream a while," suggests Mujaji.

"I can't."

"Let's play a game then."

"What game?"

"Three frogs dancing and singing!"

"Will daddy play?" asks Nummo, his face brightening.

"Whraaaock," mimics Zoa as he squats down on the floor.

While playing with Nummo, Zoa can see how repressed his son has become, how out of sorts he seems. It puts him in touch with his own sadness about not being able to live more freely. He has become inured to the status quo, to thinking that getting by is all that is possible.

Later that evening, Zoa turns to Mujaji in bed: "Honey, I've been thinking. You're right. I endure too much. We all do. We're selling our souls here, and we don't even realize it because of the pressure. The children suffer without even knowing they suffer. I'll find a way to move."

THE STONE BUDDHA

Infinity
White of black within gold

Multitudes
of clouds
pass through
the infinite sky.

Yu and Kau Chiang

Yu paces at the feet of the Leshan Buddha that overlooks the confluence of the Kialing Kiang, Min Kian, and Wei Ho rivers. A youth of seventeen, he is as restless as the waters bubbling together toward the Yangtze. His father, Kau Chiang sits serenely on the toe of the colossal Buddha, carved out of the cliff long ago. Ho Liu, his younger sister, hops on the steps winding up the cliff to the Buddha's monumental body.

Yu longs to study in America, yet his heart dwells in old China. Thoughts of the recent quakes in India and California storm together in his mind with musings of the wise men of old. He looks up at the Sun through the trees above the cliff and thinks to himself: *Solar flares are peaking now.* He wants to learn more about the correlation of Sunspots with magnetic conditions on Earth and the resulting effect on human stress. Although he has not mentioned it before, he decides that now is the time to approach his father.

"I want to go to America to study," Yu says directly, without preparing his father in any way. "There is much I can learn there."

Mirthful lines slant across Kau Chiang's calm forehead as he gazes upon Yu, thinking that the corona of the Sun seems to surround him. "It is good to learn the Western way," he replies, "but you must not forget the old Chinese way."

"There are so many ways!" exclaims Yu in exasperation. "Mathematics, science, psychology, art, literature! In the modern world I must choose among them. You are not of the modern world, father. Your ways will not extend to the building of new bridges. Old Buddhas stare out of stone here."

Kau Chiang glances at Buddha's stone fingers resting on his immense knee. After a long pause, he responds in riddles: "Jewels are the stuff of universe, and each one reflects all others to infinity. You cannot separate what is inseparable. The Tao is in the Buddha and the Buddha is in your travel to America. You may go, but if you divide birth and death, art and science, East and West, you will lose the Tao." He adds quietly, "Yet the Tao will never lose you."

"There is so much wrong in the world! I hate it!" cries Yu, now pacing anxiously. "I want to get to the root of it." The roar of the rivers rushing together drowns the sound of their voices.

Kau Chiang stands and speaks loudly: "The flowing, swirling, and teeming of the River are its language. There is no need to drag in right and wrong! Choose a way and go deep, and it will become a road to your starting place. Now, let's climb to the top and start home. Your mother returns from India tomorrow."

Ho Liu is already jumping up the steps carved in the cliff. Kau Chiang gently puts his hand on Yu's shoulder. "How is your English coming?"

"I am having trouble with the conjugation of verbs! I want to write poetry, but there is a strange thing about English."

"What is it?"

"You need a knower to know something, a doer to do something. The verb in English must be set into motion or acted upon by a noun or thing. In Chinese, the mountain needs no mountaineer. What is it that divides subject and verb in the West? Our ideographs are very precise, with symbols that are noun and verb at once. Very few English words resemble their meaning. They are not pictures of what they describe."

Yu longs to become a craftsman of words, to speak of the mysteries in the Sun and Earth and all of life. Seeking to know source, he finds himself in the midst of a thousand things, caught in a continuously unfolding chain of events. Seeking to choose among professions, he finds himself always between them. The way of the Tao flows in his blood. To fit into a modern niche, he longs to cut through the Buddhafield. Yet no sooner does he sever it, than it weaves itself into a new pattern.

As they reach the fifth landing of stairs, Yu asks his father, "Did you know that the planet Mars is a trigger for ninety percent of all solar magnetic storms? They begin after Mars moves into a hard angle with another planet."

Kau Chiang laughs. "We all live inside the Sun, for the Sun is the heart of the solar system. When your facts spin into the Sun and roll out as poetry, you will know the true trigger."

They reach the top of the stairs, where they stand looking at high cirrus clouds stretching out like the wings of birds. Kau Chiang hears a song emerging from Buddha's heart, although his lips bear the silence of stone:

Primal Water's Song of the River

I am the high source of the River,
running through the invisible firmaments.
I am the oceanic continuity of all change.
You can find me in mist and water waves.
I am the vibrations that undulate everywhere.
You can find me in the iridescence of opals and the sheen of pearls.
I am the implosion of the cosmic egg.
Look for me in every nuclei tending to expand,
in the song of the dolphin and waltz of the whale.
I am the spiral of growth in every seed.
I am the mysterious deep where simplicity reigns.
Look for me in chaos and turbulence,
in the swirling dance of breakdown and renewal.
I am the paradigm shifting.
You can find me in the fountain and reverberating ripples.
Infinity is my home and end.

Are you the mystery of change?
I am the great wave that precedes the world.

THE KINGDOM

Through his single divine eye the Creator beholds the mysterious Primal Waters and proclaims, "It is good. This dream captures the fragrance of my soul, but it is formless and unconscious. I need a body. Let us conceive of a divine Kingdom!"

The Creatrix parts the sea foam with her finger and draws forth a budding stem. She curls herself around it, feeling content and renewed as she floats naked upon the waters. "The Kingdom is in all parts of me, as I am in you," she says softly. "This bud will bloom when you are remembered in the prayers from Earth. Your body will grow from this stem, the axis of the world."

Thus the Tree of Life rises from the Primal Waters and climbs through the spine of the Creatrix, emerging as a staff of power within the vertebrates to be. Through the guidance of this direct vertical axis, the Kingdom touches the Creator.

However, Courage is needed to draw the spiritual alignment down into a more humble world. "Courage cannot be formless," says the Creatrix. "It must face adversity from an open field of optimism and spread gifts to the four directions."

"Optimism?" questions the Creator, who yet has no doubts.

"Abundance. Connection to the source of the River and the infinite possibilities of creation."

"Adversity?" he asks again, knowing only the unity of flux in the River.

"The electric charge of your light waves is broken into the duality of positive and negative, clashing against itself and struggling against the creation of birth and death."

At that, the Creatrix vanishes once again, and the Creator is left to contemplate how his Kingdom might endure the turmoil of the everchanging Primal Waters. He lives in the memory of the interlocking curves of their divine embrace.

Now the rhythm of the River and its permutating ambiguity seek a clear geometry. After millions of years, the Creatrix returns, her arms filled with patterns of simple isometric forms. The Creator is pleased with the triangles, squares, and pentagons that pivot through themselves, creating symmetrical, mirror images of order. He places the forms in the four directions and, observing what lies above and below, ahead and behind, beholds the hierarchy of the Kingdom.

"From these forms shall come all order!" Rotating a drop of the Primal Waters, he charges it with his power and imprints chains of periodic order upon the nuclei of all atoms to be. Sometimes centripetal, sometimes centrifugal, the energies dance in gyrostatic equilibrium, flowing in the undercurrents of the River, and then rising up through hierarchies of form to meet the pyramidal hierarchy from above.

However, the permutations of the pentagon concern the Creatrix, who foresees in it the efforts of future life and culture. "What about this form?" she asks.

"It is the medium of our vision," responds the Creator. "The geometry of the pentagon is the mystery that reveals the harmonic proportions of our love and compassion. We need it to draw creativity out of beings who long to return to us. Otherwise creation would go astray. It is here, in my body of the Kingdom, that I establish the culture of the perennial wisdom through which souls will find their way back to me."

VISION QUEST

Guidance
Gold of red within gold

Orientation
to the four quarters
guides
the hungry heart.

Nesaru

Nesaru remembers when, as a child, she listened for hours to the stories of her great-grandmother. She told Nesaru of the time when the Christian padres persuaded seventy-three Hopi in the Awatovi village to be baptized. Although the Hopi hated the missionaries who took away their ceremonies, leaving their spirit scarred and burned, baptism continued to spread over the land and cause rifts among the tribes. Other Hopi even attacked Awatovi, stealing up in the night before the Wuwuchim ceremony. They shot arrows and flung bundles of burning greasewood into the kiva, where tribal brothers and sisters were lighting fires at dawn. Like the vomit spewed by a sow on her own young, the fratricide has plagued the Hopi ever since.

Great-grandmother was spared only because she had not been baptized. She was versed in the clan songs and Hopi rituals, and she held the sacred *tiponis*, the clan fetishes.

Now Nesaru feels impaled on a serpent's tooth. Although she has received Hopi traditions through her ancestors, she seeks to find the body of the Creator in new ways. Separated from her husband, Wickvaya, since his imprisonment, she decides to fast and seek a vision—for herself, for her Native American people, and for humanity.

She walks by starlight to the sacred circle that she prepared the day before, daring to do what her people have not done: to quest by herself and find a new way—to break the rigidity of the old, yet breathe in the traditional spirit. Her body casts no shadow in the night as she climbs the round red rocks outside of Sedona. The indigo robe of the Creatrix spreads over her, and she feels the tension of the Sun and Moon in her heart.

Nesaru enters the sacred circle from the north and bends down in the center, where she touches her head to the ground. She plants a pole with seven feathers, then sits facing the west and prays to see her fears.

As she stares out into the hills, the fears come. Faces appear in the rocks. The trees dance in the wind like contorted bodies writhing with madness, their branches gesticulating like arms crying for help. Inside a rolling bush she sees humanity, bound and chained to itself.

Nesaru lies down, afraid of her own madness and of never escaping the chain of domination. She sees the branches of a nearby juniper tree change into the veins of her own womb and turn to black worms. She sees her own children, born from the wounds of ancestors, and reflects upon the senselessness of passing on hurt from generation to generation.

She sits up and offers a prayer: "Help me, Great Spirit, to see things as they are. Help me to forgive myself and others." The sky begins to brighten.

Nesaru looks down at the shriveled skin of her hand. She is only thirty years old. She sees her leg decaying and her body melting, becoming a river of change, the flow of time running through it. "The fear of death is the sting in every pleasure," she thinks.

The sky grows brighter still, with a piercing ray that opens her heart of hearts. She asks forgiveness for her apathy, her resistance to change, and her fear of madness and death.

A rattlesnake approaches from the west and slithers behind her. Nesaru feels the sting and burn of the poison of the ages run up her spine. The snake becomes still, and its spirit speaks: "I am formed of the waters of life, driven into poison by fear."

"I receive your medicine and become one with you!" responds Nesaru, feeling the rattlesnake crawl up her spine, and the blue light bursts through her heart. She gives thanks.

On the second day Nesaru spreads a quilt and faces north. When she begins to drum, she senses that something behind her is drumming through her, asking, *Where are my people?*

"Forgive me my pain," she prays. "Forgive the scattering of my people and the forgetting of who we are."

The drumming and praying enliven the pole in the center, turning it to a column of gold. Her arms become wings. She hears the piercing cry of the eagle, the cry of her own voice, of her people. The flapping wings of the eagle beat the drum. She receives the eagle through her shoulders and exclaims, "I receive your medicine. I become one with you!"

On the third day Nesaru sits facing the east. She shakes her rattle, which becomes the Earth. She feels the sentience of all insects and creatures in her body. Though physically weak from her fast, she is strong in spirit, and she shakes the rattle for all of life.

The rattle shakes itself.

"I am an old crone," she cries. "I am the new born. I am a child. I give birth to myself!"

The rattle shakes right through her heart. The sick Earth weeps. The rattle becomes a turtle. She cannot see it, but she can hear it. The turtle becomes the Earth.

The rattle stops.

Nesaru bows down irresistibly to the Earth. She remembers her childhood when, in respect of life, she did not walk on grass and did not eat meat. But then the white man's ways came into her, and she killed bugs and poisoned mice for no purpose. She asks the Great Spirit to forgive herself and all white people.

The leaves on the bushes glisten. The rattle turns green. The Earth is greening.

On the fourth day, Nesaru faces south, where the flame of the spirit flares. At noon she strikes a golden bowl, the ring piercing the air. The Sun blazes down on her skin, which is once again young. She is drawn upward, her arms spreading. A high, tremulous tone quavers from her throat. Then a steady, penetrating tone comes forth, followed by a higher tone—three times the sound of energy—that permeates heaven and Earth as the pure light brightens. The trees that had gesticulated with humanity's madness now sway in gentleness.

Nesaru takes stones and gems from her medicine bundle and constructs a mandala, then begins a series of prayers to the Great Spirit.

Placing purple stones in the west, she prays for the black people to grow in the greatness of their love.

Placing lapis lazuli stones in the north, she prays for the white people to be just and understanding.

Placing turquoise stones in the east, she prays for her Native American people to receive the light of the Great Spirit.

Placing golden coins in the south, she prays for the yellow people to know the old wisdom.

Having faced the four directions and prayed for all peoples, Nesaru knows that the period of questing is finished. Before returning to her tribe she offers one final prayer: "Help me to find my family and my people," she calls out. "Help all humanity to awake, that we may find our destiny. Thank you, Great Spirit, thank you!"

Journey Home

Courage
Black of red within gold

Guided intent
of heartfelt words
brings forth
courageous action.

Luqman

Luqman feels like a donkey stumbling down a mountain with the burden of war on its back, flung half into the other world from the whip of suffering against its backside. Having left Bangalore, he carries Pravin's remembrance of the gods and goddesses with him on his journey to his native Iran. Usually walking, sometimes hitchhiking, he moves from Bombay through Ahmadabad to Hyderabad in Pakistan. Before he crosses over the mountains, he finds a rocky, secluded place near the Indus River to rest. Longing for a place of protection, a house of God, he remembers the words of the Prophet, revealed at Mecca:

XXXIX, 2, 3: "Lo! We have revealed the scripture unto thee with truth; so worship Allah, making religion pure for him. Surely pure religion is for Allah only. And those who choose protecting friends beside him say, we worship them only that they may bring us near unto Allah. Lo! Allah will judge between them concerning that wherein they differ. Lo! Allah guideth not him who is a liar, an ungrateful one."

Continuing on to Mecca the next day, Luqman meets a man fervent

41

in his dedication to the One God, Allah. The pilgrim sees Luqman's tattered clothes, matted hair, and unkempt beard, and wonders.

"Who are you?" he asks Luqman. "What are you seeking?"

"I am a spirit walking in the darkness seeking light."

"I can help you! Come. We shall receive the light in Mecca. The Messenger walks with us!"

Luqman decides to travel with the pilgrim, but eventually he feels the discrepancy between his own humble faith and the fervent, almost fanatical faith of his companion. After crossing over the mountains, they part ways. For the next three days, Luqman proceeds wearily toward Isfahan until he is finally offered a ride by three travelers who take pity on his exhausted state.

He settles with his bundle into the back seat of the car and looks shyly at two healthy Arab men and a young woman.

"Come with us to Anar," offers one of the men. "We have friends there with whom we shall eat and drink. It will do you good!"

Luqman feels uncomfortable and shakes his head. "I would rather be miserable seeking the blessings of Allah than be in paradise without him."

That night they drop him off in the streets of Anar. Luqman wanders about, confused in his soul, not knowing whether to laugh or cry. When he comes upon a mosque, he decides to seek comfort inside. As he enters, he is so absorbed by the candles lighting the niches and the bright prayer rugs on the floor that he doesn't see the sheikh in the corner.

Feeling divinely wretched, almost possessed, Luqman prostrates himself and involuntarily drools on the carpet. As he struggles to his feet, he perceives the evil of war to be wrapped around him like mummy rags. He tears off the imaginary rags and spits upon them, then throws them into the fire as new blood surges in his marrow. Beginning to dance, he spins around and around, the images of torn flesh, phallic missiles, and blood-covered Earth passing before him. He pours some oil over his head and offers a silent prayer: "Allah! Grant me a new life! Let these memories pass from me!" Then he implores aloud: "Let me not die without a lover! I am on fire with a dark Sun. Saints frighten me as much as worldly people. What am I to do?"

The flame burns high as he spits dark memories into the fire. He dances on, spinning into a spiral, until he is suddenly lifted by a point within his soul. The evil falls away, devoured by imaginary vultures. Almost collapsing as his heart continues to swell, he is caught in the wings of an angel. The River sparkles with golden streams spun from his dance. The Creator's body bursts into full bloom on the stem of the Kingdom, filling the mosque with a mysterious sweet fragrance.

Suddenly, a voice blurts out, "You shall put no one before Allah!" The sheikh, having heard only Luqman's appeal for a lover, steps out from the corner.

Luqman is astonished to see the sheikh, but he stands liberated from his wretched possession. He sees the supreme name of Allah emblazoned in the air. The fiery letters transform into the bodies of women, children, young men and old.

"I am drowning in Allah!" he shouts. "She is rage turned to remembrance! She is the companion of fear, the mistress of tears for the wounded and sick! She is the blood of war's slaughter turned to love! Oh, lady of love!" With tears running down his face, he turns to the sheikh and kisses him.

Astonished, the sheikh jumps back. "You scoundrel! Go away! This is a sanctuary!"

Luqman becomes still and stares at the sheikh. "Allah is in all beings! I stand naked before you, willing to be examined by Allah. I will lie down as a carpet for everyone's prayer. Do you feed the hungry and give water to the thirsty? Yes, I am a beggar. I have no pretense. I have participated in the great evil of war. Pray for me!"

"Get out of here! Guards!"

Luqman's flame draws only the smoke of hatred from the sheikh. Seeing the sheikh's hypocrisy, he stands in wonder, still filled with spirit. He is thinking to himself, *a devil in sheikh's clothing*, when four men close in on him. They beat him up and fling his limp, bruised body into the alley, where a donkey stands tethered to a post.

LESSONS AT THE ZOO

Order

Red of red within gold
The hidden hierarchy
of orders and species
are released
into time.

Maria, Pravin, and Wilson

As Maria strolls with Ariel beneath the eucalyptus trees that grace the walkways of the San Diego zoo, she cannot help but reflect on her years in Asia. The animals dwelled in the natural freedom of the wild there, in stark contrast to the confinement she sees before her. She watches Ariel, now six, running from cage to cage, wanting to get in with the creatures. In India he had come to know the birds of the air, the fish of the river, even the monkeys, like his own body. The axis deer, otter, and oxen were as familiar as his own mother. Now his friends are unreachable.

"Can I go in and hug the monkeys, Mama?"

"Not here, dear. We can just look."

"Why are they inside when we are outside, Mama?"

Maria stares dumbly at the tigers in the cage, feeling their lethargy, and thinks, *Maybe we are the ones who are locked in. All I've seen in the wild is captured here.*

"Can we go and see the bears?" asks Ariel, eager to interact.

"Maybe later. We are to meet Pravin and Krishna here by the tiger's den."

Not far from where Maria and Ariel are waiting, some junior high school students have gathered with their teacher, a man with a scholarly air despite his stocky build. Gesturing in all directions, he begins to speak: "As we have discussed, life has distributed itself in all environments—in the sea, the mountains, the forests and deserts, even the icy arctic. How do you think the different species we have seen in this zoo have adapted to their environment?"

A tall, red-haired girl answers like a tape recorder, parroting what she has heard: "The fittest of species survive. The order of nature's niches comes about from natural selection, by adaptation."

The teacher nods and smiles while several of the other students take notes. However two Native American children, recently admitted to the school through a trial program, seem very puzzled. Unfamiliar with modern science, Lomo looks to his older sister Kuksu for reassurance. "Those tigers look unhappy," states Kuksu boldly. "Does that mean they are not adapting to being captured? Does that mean they will not survive?"

The teacher tries to be patient. "Adaptation to a zoo is different from adaptation in the wild. The struggle for survival in nature is real. The animals will survive in the zoo because they are fed and cared for. Now, who knows what mechanism controls variety and adaptation?"

Pravin, with little Krishna by the hand, emerges from the crowd on the walkway and embraces Maria warmly. Krishna stares at Ariel for a moment, then digs into his pocket and pulls out a lizard. "Oh! Let me hold it!" cries Ariel, putting out cupped hands. The boys stoop down together in delight.

"Listen to this school lesson," says Maria, looking at Pravin with dismay. "It is no wonder everything has become so denatured and mechanical in the West. I don't even understand what a control mechanism for adaptation is."

Pravin, having heard the some of the discussion as he passed by, turns to look at the students. One boy addresses the teacher hesitantly:

"You told us that genes determine growth, traits, and species. Is genetic control the mechanism you are asking about?"

"That's right. Genes control both the forms of species and the rate of growth through a coding of proteins and enzymes."

"But what causes mutations?" asks a bushy-haired girl, wrinkling her forehead. "We learned that two different species must originally have had a common ancestor. Once a mutation occurs, the species continues to express the new pattern as if it were there from the beginning. Where does the mutation come from?"

"A very good question!" replies the teacher. "Purely random genetic alteration. All patterns of life have come from such randomness."

"Excuse me, sir," interjects Pravin, his dark eyes shining. "Do you mind if I ask a question? I am a visitor here and have much to learn."

"Not at all. Please go ahead. I am Steve Wilson, and these are my science students. They will benefit from a different point of view."

"Would you say that nature acts as a whole? And if so, what is it that orders the niches of nature?" asks Pravin.

"Evolution is simply an orderly progression that develops from chance strains of genes," states Wilson categorically. "The niches occur as a result of the survival of the fittest."

"Do you teach your students that our destiny is wholly determined by natural selection? Does that mean that either we must overpower others or they will overpower us?"

"Destiny is ruled by our anatomy, which comes from a determinative framework of genetic strains that emerge randomly. In some sense, all creatures are at war."

Maria feels exasperated but tries not to show it. "Do you explain the evolution of humans in the same way as kangaroos, wasps, and whales?" she asks.

"Genes that spread during the Pleistocene epoch brought a humanizing influence," replies Wilson, stiffening. "Those genes reduced our apelike muzzle and increased the size of our cranium, enabling us to face one another eye to eye as we do now. Through genetic control and adaptation, we have shed our claws and heavy hair."

"Now we face a new challenge, do we not?" Maria asks straightforwardly.

"What do you mean?"

"In a strictly statistical sense, we are headed for starvation. My child here is not likely to survive. Can we adapt to an environment polluted with noxious gases and radiation? The mechanistic view, which holds that domination of others is the key to survival, has brought us to this point. We have pirated the Earth. Entire strains of races and cultures have already died out. Now the entire human race is in question."

"We all struggle to survive," responds Wilson with a shrug. "At one time, the Earth abounded with small creatures who could not breathe oxygen. Then organisms evolved that could change light into chlorophyll and release oxygen into the air. The war of adaptation is great. Creatures have become extinct in all eras."

"Does that mean we may become extinct?" asks Kuksu.

"Nature rejects those creatures that don't become part of the entire life-web. Like animals, we may become extinct if we can't adapt to nature's laws."

"Might nature's laws have come from a source other than chance?" asks Pravin, his eyes flashing.

"Since you come from another culture, sir, and seem educated in these matters, I'd like to ask *you* to explain the amazing order of nature. Look at these carnivores. The vegetarian antelope and deer are their prey. How did nature's web evolve in your view?"

The students wait expectantly while a flock of sparrows flit around them. Pravin welcomes the chance to elaborate: "In India, I learned to see nature as a fabric of cycles that act as a whole. The legend is that a divine being, Purusha, manifested himself in an ocean of love that became matter. Everything in nature is hierarchical. What you call chance or randomness is but an imperceptible act of one or more of the five elements called *tattwas*—modifications of Purusha's great breath— that created the hierarchies of order. His breath spreads in four directions. Perhaps the four elements of fire, air, water, and earth, which come from the fifth element, *akasha,* are similar to your terms for various states of matter—plasma, gas, liquid, and solid. All the elements are permeated by *akasha,* sound. From these five elements, all order in creation is derived."

Lomo and Kuksu look at one another and smile. Pravin, noticing their response, asks, "What do you think of that story?"

"Your story reminds me of a prophecy our people have," responds Lomo. "It is different from our teacher's explanation and also from your story, but your story feels more like it."

"Can you tell us of your people's story?" Wilson invites.

"I can try. In the beginning, there was only the Creator, Taiowa, who made four worlds. But the worlds were destroyed, one by one, and in each subsequent period there was less purity and more density. My father told me that, long ago, we had a door on the top of our heads that was open, but now it is shut. This is why we can't remember how order came about. Our story sounds just the opposite from what our teacher says. I don't know what is true."

"Will reality please stand up and explain itself?" quips Wilson with a broad smile. Everyone laughs, including Pravin and Maria, as he continues, "We don't know whether life resulted from a rare chance event or from an orderly pattern, but we need not invent stories to explain natural law."

THE EGYPTIAN RITE
ON THE ISLAND OF MALTA

Culture
White of red within gold

Luminous ark
of sacred culture
transmits
perennial wisdom.

From a star in the Creator's crown a ray shoots down to Earth, where a luminous being covered with fishlike scales rises out of the Primal Waters. As the Tree of Life bursts into bloom and the fragrance of heaven permeates the planet, the being talks in riddles: "The body of the Creator longs to find its likeness. Beware of endless procreation and conflict among yourselves. I am the seed of the perennial culture. Where I stand is a throne. Where I dream is an altar. The divine ruler is lord of the universe. His queen is his power. He shall guide you to light and deliver you from the uncertainty of the waters."

Amid the swirling eddies of the River, where the banks of history harness the metamorphosis of nature, the Creatrix divides herself into multitudes of powers. She moves like a turquoise snake, flowing and dancing around the tribes scattered across the Earth. She fills the Creator's body with the instinct of animals, watching it widen as he strides forth in four directions through the races who seek a Kingdom. Although his footsteps reveal a path to the hidden flame of his crown, each tribe of each race must find its own way to the axis of heaven.

Channon and Fariba

Channon sits in the study of his home on Malta, reflecting on the ancient culture-heros. He remembers from past lives how he sang the songs of Ra, the great Sun, rising at dawn between the hills of yesterday and tomorrow. Even as a child in this life, he loved the familiar forms of the hieroglyphs, the pyramids, and the Egyptian goddesses, whose bodies were filled with stars.

Now he dedicates his life to remembering, to putting back together the scattered members of the body of Osiris. He studies the ancient texts, hoping to find traces of the great body of light that shines above the fallen body of nature. The aging and decay of his own body trouble him, as time steals the precious fluids of his vital energy and pushes him toward forgetfulness and sleep. But he is stubborn. He studies long into the night as though to counter the forces of nature, to run back up the River toward its source, to pass through the narrow opening of the eye of Ra and enter the mouth of Temu before the living Word is ever spoken. His mind reaches into the black void where the bright Word circles beyond the sky. Working through a matrix of stones, stars, and the art of mathematics, he finds a pathway to the body of light, which transports him in ecstasy.

Here on the island of Malta, an ancient jewel set in the turquoise waters of the Mediterranean, Channon lives with Fariba, his wife of Persian ancestry. Though he loves the deep silence of his seclusion, he knows his fate is tied to those who desire to learn the hidden wonders of Egypt's timeless realms. They too seek the body of light, and they come to attend his weekly classes on the divine Word and the knot of eternity, the flowing perennial wisdom that was once crystallized into form in ancient theocracies. Thirty-three have gathered this summer to receive the nectar from Channon's lips as he breathes out the story of *being* the divine body. Blown by the wind of their own purpose, and wanting to do more than just contemplate the old wisdom, they have planned a sacred rite in the stone ruins of Channon's garden.

The play begins on the night of the October Full Moon. Adorned in a golden robe, Channon lives the part of Osiris. "I come out of Temu, the River that ran eternally before anything existed," he declares. Temu is his father and mother, the he-she that regenerates all things, reaching into the unknown and drawing forth his crown of light. Ra, the ever-shining, lives in his crown and runs through his erect body, filling heaven and Earth with seeds of culture. "I am the sacred River," he continues. "I spread my glory through the gates of birth and death. I am the circle of life that never ends!"

Fariba, clothed in silver as Isis, embraces him. "I stand amazed in the presence of thy radiant crown and thy dark body!" she says adoringly, gazing directly at him. "My passion moves in your power. Our love is the beginning and end." She seems to dance in the vortex of heaven's velvet sky as the midnight stars move on.

As they embrace, Channon feels himself drawn through the genesis of the world. "I rise as a golden sea of infinite being from the netherworld of the gods!" he exclaims. "You are my lady of mystery! Through you I lift the silken silver veil. Together, we rule heaven and Earth, encircled by mountains of memory."

Crowned with the Moon, Fariba's black hair ripples back over her shoulders. "You are the face of justice," she responds. "My balance comes through Maat, who holds the feather of righteousness. Together, our crowns bless all worlds to be."

From his robe, Channon draws forth small cakes wrapped in green foil and offers them to Fariba. A girl dressed as a genie enters carrying glasses of wine on a star-studded blue platter. "The ways of becoming are through my body and blood," declares Channon through the lips of Osiris.

"I live to serve you to humanity," responds Isis, offering the cakes and wine to those assembled.

The essential fragrance of the Creatrix embalms those who receive the body and blood of Osiris. They are lifted by music that reaches up to heaven and returns with the rhythms of the gods. Cypresses stand in the background inside the circle of stones that separates the sacred and profane.

By the light shimmering to the sound of cymbals and harp, Osiris stands naked with his penis erect. Isis entwines herself in his arms, veiling him with her silver robe as he becomes lost in her streaming hair.

The chorus rejoices at the union of the king and queen. Osiris and Isis then circle the gathering before departing to the joyful sounds of Egyptian sistra, castanets, drums, and bells—all resonating to the chorus of heaven.

The seekers, feeling they have stepped into the knot of eternity, form a great circle under the moonlight as the first rains of the season begin to fall. Having returned to the source and been touched by Temu, most hear the "Kingdom's Song of the River":

Kingdom's Song of the River

I am the vista from the cosmic mountain where the River gathers rain.
I am the inward view of heaven.
Look for me in utopian longings and the beginnings of every plan.
I am the city of God in every neighborhood.
Look for me in the symbols of the world.
I can be found in the columns and cornices of every temple.
I am the leader in every person.
I am the edifice that mirrors heaven.
You can find me in flowers turning toward the Sun.
I am the miracle of the fugue.
I am the orientation of all mandalas.
I am the birdsong breaking through every cage.
I am the height and breadth and depth of the landscape.
Look for me in the body of God.

Are you the hierarchy of government?
I am the heavenly city that precedes Earthly rulers.

THE PRIEST-SEER

The Creator throws open the doors of his mind and beholds the Kingdom as a gigantic crystal. He draws forth the Priest-Seer, the embodiment of divinity in the later priests and priestesses. To them he proclaims: "You are the antennae of humanity. Through you the people of the world shall know me. You shall guide the king and the populace. This crystal is my house, and its facets are my temples. Here we shall have communion and balance all opposites."

The Primal Waters lap against the shore where the giant crystal stands. Facing the Creator, the Priest-Seer plucks a golden rose and a white lily from the foam. He divides into a priest and priestess who place the rose and lily upon the altar. "Here we shall commune with you by day and by night," they announce. "Here, we shall initiate the divine plan, the reciprocity of eros and logos. What is our quest?"

The Creator's crown grows radiant. "Your quest is to find the language hidden within the mystery of the Primal Waters and the Kingdom. They are my soul and body. You are my mind, and your realm is sacred thought. Through the hidden language, you shall execute the divine plan and make sacrifice. To do this, you will keep my sacred fire burning and never forget me."

Fire leaps from the Creator's brow and ignites the subtle essences inside the crystal. Instantly, its sacred flame lights the censers of every temple. "Within this fire is my divine Word, the light of the logos," he pronounces.

The Creatrix envelopes the crystal and blesses the priests and priestesses. For thousands of years they make the elixir from the sacred fire. They mediate heaven and Earth, chanting hymns that glorify the cosmos and fusing eros and logos through joyful inspiration.

Through the wholeness of the Priest-Seer, the cosmos lives within the chaos of the River. The cosmos circulates the vital energies of the water among the stars, brings elements to life, and gives birth to consciousness. Through sacrifice—the making of the sacred—the River renews itself. All in the cosmos is sacred, for all comes from the sacred fire.

The logos of the Creator is the source of order within the cosmos. The eros of the Primal Waters is the vital source of chaos. The divine Word is forever changing chaos to cosmos. Eros is forever changing cosmos to chaos. Chaos churns as a mystery of the River's burning water and brings humility to mortals, but some begin to perceive chaos as evil. This is how it happens:

The invisible powers of the wind break the surface of the dark waters and hurl them into wild, turbulent spray. The priestesses, knowing the wind is an elixir carried on the breath of the Creatrix, inhale the streams of air, which awaken their minds to the hidden language. They behold the Creator's very soul and body—the Primal Waters and the Kingdom—in splendid geometries of light and color.

The turbulence makes some of the priests afraid. After conferring among themselves, they decide to conquer the wind by walking forward into the face of it, against the force of the Creatrix. But their resistance only intensifies its power, and the wind grows into a hurricane that almost extinguishes the sacred fire. The tension of their struggle even cracks the giant crystal, and the Primal Waters flood through its fissures, revealing the fluid, erotic language arising from the ecstasy of chaos.

Now, the priests are terrified. Though they feel the River's power, the geometry of its script eludes them, and they stand outside of the mystery, their vision blinded by the fire itself.

When the crystal breaks, it shatters the Creator's divine eye into many ways of seeing. And so the Priest-Seer divides into many sects, each becoming a cult claiming to know the hidden language. The priests say the language comes from the sacred fire, whereas the priestesses see its source in the foam of the Primal Waters.

Each faction seeks to control the mystery by erecting temples and writing scriptures to make meaning absolute. Sepulchral lamps light the way to Egyptian, Babylonian, Chinese, and Hindu religions. Beholding the bright Word of the Creator through the dark fabric of their minds, the priests translate their vision of the sacred script into cuneiform, hieroglyphs, and ideographs. In time, the mystery is forgotten, and only words and rites remain.

Wishing to emulate the crystal that mirrors every facet of eternity, the priests seek to reflect the Creator's divine essence in precisely chiseled stones. *The energy of the River becomes trapped in cyclopean monuments that honor the cosmos as the order of gods in heaven, not the order inherent in nature. Some priests create* temenos, *sacred enclosures over the graves of the gods who once descended from heaven with flashing wheels and wings of light. Around the shrines arise the cities of Ur, Uruk, Eridu, Lagash, Nippur, Jericho, Palenque, Teotihuacan, Mycenae, and Çatäl Huyuk. Ziggurats, pyramids, and temples, once commemorating the cycling of chaos and cosmos, now reveal the intent to stand against time.*

Thus the circle of the eternal return is broken. Weaving the tapestry of remembrance of the body of light, the Creatrix tries to balance the nebulous enigma of the Primal Waters with the sharply formed pyramids of the Kingdom. Her fingers move quickly, for the priests still dream of ways to calculate the incalculable and to overcome the rampage of eros with knowledge. They tend the fire diligently. Wishing to dispel their fears, she blesses their souls and dissolves into mist to create a new brew of inspiration.

VISITORS TO THE FESTIVAL OF SUKKOTH

Balance
Gold of white within gold

Equanimity
amid turbulence
centers
the cosmic current.

Fariba, Akrisios, Henshaw, and Aaron

Every year Fariba travels with two friends to explore the many ways of the spirit. One is Akrisios, a large, highly spirited woman from the Greek island of Lesbos. The other is John Henshaw, a retired American professor who has known Fariba over the eleven years during which he has periodically attended Channon's summer classes on Malta. They have all come to Jerusalem to attend the Jewish festival of Sukkoth.

Inside the synagogue, a radiant rabbi presides over the sacred harvest festival held in thanksgiving for the abundance of life. Although praise and gratitude come less easily in this third year of a worldwide recession, there is great conviviality among the participants. Holding citron, palm branch, myrtle, and willow, they recite psalms and sing hymns, their procession spreading in four directions. The entire congregation is flooded with the sweetness that comes from the pain and struggle of bending one's will to Yahweh.

When the processional ends, the worshipers cluster together in branch-covered booths to receive bread, water, and fruit from this year's harvest. The booths symbolize the Sukkoth "divine booth" that in times to come will receive all of humanity under one Heavenly Father. Fariba and her companions learn that the ideal of the Sukkoth festival inspired Zechariah's vision of all nations assembled under the wings of holy Jerusalem.

After the nourishment, everyone breaks into groups to study the Torah. The three friends join a group facilitated by Aaron, a bright young man who reads from the Torah and recounts the history that gave it birth. Akrisios, especially, feels great empathy when she hears once again how the Jews were assaulted by storms and enemies alike during their migration in the wilderness. In the processional, her voice had blended in genuine feeling with all the others, but now the laws of the Torah weigh like a heavy patriarchal hand on her head. Aaron reads phrases that draw out her anger: *Fear God and justice shall be yours....* *Separate yourself from all that is opposed to the will of God. Worship no idols, practice no divination or magic of the pagan ways.*

She summons the courage to speak. "Does living a holy, good life have to mean separation from all that is physical, wild, and natural?" she asks Aaron, trembling with an indefinable feeling. "I am here to learn, but I am troubled by a divine righteousness that denies pagan rituals and the eroticism of the body. I feel everything through my body, and I know the joys of love are greater than the wrath of Jahweh. Didn't King Solomon become enamored of the Queen of Sheba and summon her to Jerusalem from Yemen? Now you hold festivals in simple synagogues, but Solomon's temple and the royal city of Jerusalem both once expressed lavish wealth. What about the simple shrines of nature? Do you regard tribal animal powers as idols?"

Aaron blushes and struggles to maintain his composure. "The senses bear false witness of Jahweh," he responds. "Solomon and his house of worship were destroyed because of his dissolute living and abuse of power. He built his gold-lined temple for Jahweh's glory, but he later allowed the worship of idols and brought down shame upon himself. The Torah forbids the worship of idols and the practice of pagan rites, for without single focus upon the One God, people fall into evil ways.

But we honor nature's laws through festivals such as this one, based on the lunar cycle. In this way we maintain rhythm with nature without idolizing any of her creations."

Henshaw decides to interject, "According to historical records, at the time of Solomon, Arabs and Jews shared a peace and prosperity that they haven't experienced since. Solomon built alliances with his neighbors and consolidated warring tribes in unity. From that time on, Jews have been wandering the world in exile. Is that not so?"

"What you say is true," replies Aaron, nodding his dignified head. "We have been wandering since the Romans destroyed Solomon's temple. It did not cease until our nation was reestablished after World War II. But we were not robbed of the *Torah*. The gift of immortality of our souls remains, though our bodies have been tortured, gassed, and mutilated. We suffer for Yahweh and shall endure through time. The guidance and power of the *Torah* enabled us to rise from the ashes of the burned temple."

All three friends feel a mixture of excitement and irritation when the session closes. They walk over crumbling stone streets toward their inn, watching the synagogue vanish into the night and thin clouds dancing against the Moon. Akrisios shares her reflections first: "To worship together is a beginning. The music and dancing were wonderful, but to hear of Yahweh's Word as the final and absolute authority makes me want to weep. I feel like a jackal that would eat the dead Word and transform it inside my body, turning it into acacia trees and canaries and the flesh of wild animals."

Fariba, too, feels flushed with sorrow: "Love grows in me like a fragrant magic filling the air. I know the mysteries that live in your body and blood, Akrisios. The Egyptian mysteries reveal a circling River, the eternal return that issued from the Word of Temu. But this Word was not an absolute genesis, nor did it give birth to a unique, chosen people. In Persia, the great polarity of the god of light and the god of darkness created a cosmic tension, like a bowstring pulled back by the emerging voice of revelation. But a curtain was drawn over the sacred groves and the subterranean places where women wailed for the Moon, because they wanted to shatter the veil between eros and spirit."

As they pass through the dark streets, Henshaw remains silent, like a mirror reflecting the fire of the two women.

Akrisios now burns with a passion that melts the restraint that covered her soul in the synagogue: "Religion without spirit hollows out my bones and empties my veins. I feel the pain of the ages. Social law, in the name of religion, demands blood and drives men to war. My power is within me! I remember the animal love of cave art shining through the darkness of the patriarchal ages. I remember the rites and theater of the dancing Greek maenads. That is how I find the ecstasy of the spirit."

Nothing is too far removed for the erudite Henshaw. "As I see it," he begins, "it was inevitable for the *Torah* to become law when Greek mask and theater succumbed to written scripture, which was seen as an antipagan, antimythical, prophetic revelation. It kept eros and sensuality in check, as did the Old Testament biblical revelation and the disguise of its source. It depends on whether you believe that scripture was actually the revealed Word of God or that it was the design of priests who had their own motives. After the Jewish prophets, both Christianity and Islam canonized scripture, probably for the same reasons. The written word prevailed over the oral tradition in order to control people's passions. Your outcry, Akrisios, is precisely what the prophets feared."

"We must keep ourselves centered and curb our own passions through *inner* work," says Fariba. "We cannot change anyone. The entire Earth is perilously balanced between destruction and renewal. We must watch ourselves each moment and fight the fear that is within and the fear that is institutionalized in any form. Fear and anger are like gnashing teeth that grind up our truth. Blame is born of failing to live our inner truth, and war is born of blame. We must *become* the Word before it was uttered and live from our own power."

"When I was an alcoholic," responds Akrisios, "I was lost to my true being and gave my power to masculine authority. I have battled inside my own body, but I have managed to reclaim my heart from darkness. It is nature, the wild, that keeps me in balance. It seems to me that Israel abhors the mystery of the dark—the unknown pagan gods and goddesses—because they are alive and full of change, fecund like ripe fruit. Jahweh, unlike the dying and resurrected Attis, Adonis, or

Dionysus, never became the consort of the Great Goddess. Why not? The ecstatic silver fluid of sex is true eros, the essence of life!"

Akrisios feels the current of the River moving within her. "Bless the Jews and the Christians," she concludes. "Let us weep for all, but then rest in the fields of the Earth. My ancestors are the lilies, wheat, and corn—the calves whose blood was spilled by knives of priests. I do not yet rise, but sink deeper into the mystery."

Carried by the winds of their words, the three suddenly find themselves at the garden beside their inn, where they pause to bask in the nourishment of the starlit sky and each other before retiring.

THE CELLULAR MEMORY IN THE BLACK FOREST

Plan
Black of white within gold

God's design
in the Tree of Life
grows
from the cosmic axis.

The Creatrix mingles air, fire, and water into the brew of inspiration—three drops, three paths, three tongues that seek to awaken the Earth. She sprinkles the brew into the River and weaves pathways by its banks, where ancient tribes behold her mystery in the patterns of waves. The River's script flows through the sweet laughter of children, the ecstatic breath of lovers, the shining eyes of the dying. As the Creatrix drinks and fills herself with the essence of the perennial waters, the Tree of Life awakens in her spine, rising through the rivulets of her whirling sacred centers to proclaim to all realms the great trust, the abundant endowment, inherent in the River itself.

The Creator focuses the laser beam of his mind and sends the scroll of the divine plan directly into the Tree of Life. Standing on red, black, and golden pebbles that line the River's floor, the Creatrix receives the plan through her feet as burning water rises through her diaphanous body.

Now the gold of heaven penetrates the darkness of Earth, where colored flames ascend the spines of those who have settled in ancient cities. The seeds of human souls, cast deep into the soil by fearful priests, quicken with the Creator's thought. And, within the Creatrix, the Tree of Life opens into a giant hologram, pulsating thunderously throughout her body with the language of color, sound, movement, and form.

Christa and Horst

Christa's soul lived then, too, creating life as a goddess of the burning water. Her body remembers the brew of inspiration and the miracle of riding upon the spirits of fire, water, and air. Her spirit is strong still, her cells alive with the memory of eons, for she is a child of the tree language, carrying the branches of the Creator and Creatrix in her veins. Over many incarnations she has experienced the various facets of the Earth and its children.

Now Christa lives in an elegant summer home near the Black Forest of Germany, where the perpetuity of the River still moves through her womb and brain. The two passages of the Earth intersect in her mortality as she spreads herself between inner and outer, between root and flower. She had married Horst with her flower in her root, naive about his controlling and possessive impulses. But there remains a wildness in her that cannot be tamed.

During the day, she tries to fulfill Horst's expectations by directing the maids, overseeing the garden, and serving the innumerable guests according to his precise, aristocratic etiquette. Horst seeks to absorb all her energies in his own affairs, for a deep frustration lies within him: he desires to control the uncontrollable, to strangle the beautiful madness of her creation that also attracts him to her. He does not understand why his breath is shallow, his joints tight, and his thoughts erratic. Drawn to Horst by the power of opposites and the unknown past, Christa now wonders why she married him.

She longs for the free rhythms of nature. Over many lifetimes, she has tried to regain the magic of ecstasy, to bring herself back to the moment of spiritual conception when root and flower meet in love. Her soul longs to recapture the inspiration of the wandering minstrels, whose songs invoked the nature spirits and lovers in other ways. At night, while Horst sleeps, she draws and paints the multitudes of patterns that twist and turn in her mind, swirling from abstract spirals, crosses, and circles into whorls of clouds, wings of geese, orbs of the Sun and Moon, and branches of ash and alder.

Alone in the night, she can come into herself and feel the River's current move through her art. She breathes deeply and dances freely. She momentarily sees the architecture of nature as a luminous flow of shapes rising into ecstatic song. Such making and melding with color and form eventually lull her seething mind to sleep. Seeking to awaken her soul from the recoil of ancient wounds, her mind returns to the past and its obstacles to deliverance. Traveling through the night on the swift wings of the ethers, she dreams.

She is Amsu, the son of the high priest Manesis, who desires that Amsu succeed him in his priestly role. Detecting the smell of death inside the temple, Amsu goes outside and watches his father dam up a river and create tributaries. Then he rearranges gems on a gameboard. A tree stands to Amsu's left. Each time Manesis changes the position of a gem, the tree multiplies in mirror images. Once he has changed all the gems, Manesis goes to the trees and plucks their flowers and fruits. The mirror images then vanish and the original tree splits into two and bursts into flames. A wailing voice, rising from the trees, jolts Christa out of her dream.

In a semi-awake yet lucid state, she probes the meaning of the dream. Amsu discovered his father's plan to change the River's course in order to hoard the sweet-smelling essences that spring from the invisible light of the Tree of Life. Amsu recognized the symbols. Manesis' plan was to separate the ecstatic flame from the vegetal human root and to use the energy of the River to control both nature and humanity.

Christa awakens further, feeling very strange, knowing she has dreamed that dream before. She sees the eyes of her husband in the eyes of Manesis and falls asleep again. Dreaming again of Manesis, she is now his daughter, a priestess. Beholding her father's covetous look and his desire to control, she cries out in rage: "You cannot change the course of the River without killing the trees. The Creator and Creatrix are embraced in their branches! I will have no part in this!"

"You *will* help me!" Manesis shouts back, his face like a star fallen to stone. "We shall make dams and create trees with mirrors in other places. We can now be masters of all. Our access is through the ancient channel of the male and female root and crown that oscillates through the Tree of Life. Priestesses such as yourself must be virgins. You are my double from long ago. Nothing will ever part us."

In her dream, Christa speaks words that cannot be translated: "Your face holds a passion for a dead eternity, and your words twist like poison in my gut! I will never help you in this sacrilege! I can see down the long road inside the belly of the serpent, where children cry from lack of food and men trample forests and kill one another for power. I see the River carrying fertile soil to the sea, where it mixes with the blood of innocents. Only dust blows in the hot wind."

THE FLIGHT OF THE OWL INTO THE BLACK FOREST

Quest
Red of white within gold

> The shield
> of changing winds
> strives
> toward infinite complexity.

Christa and Horst

On the morning after her dreams, Christa is a soul on fire. "I must leave," she tells Horst. "I cannot live with you anymore. Let me go." Her hair springs out like loose steel wool and frames her small face.

"You will not leave me! Your place is here!"

Horst's flesh seems to burn from her glance as he erupts in uncontrollable anger. Their argument races like a roller coaster through the hot summer air as it has done many times before. He is obstinate: "Here you have leisure and social admiration. What more can you want?"

Christa's flame burns steadily after being nearly snuffed out altogether: "I want freedom! You don't even see me. You are possessive and think you can own me. I'm leaving for good!" Her arms flail as she flings her wedding ring at his feet.

Horst backs away momentarily, stunned and in obvious pain. "By God, you will stay!" he rages. "Though you cost me a fortune, you *are* my wife!"

His face contorts in a way that Christa has not seen before. She begins to feel sympathy for him, realizing how she is always caught by the pain she inflicts.

Turning, tortured, she moves toward the door: "I alone, I alone know who I am. I belong to no one."

Horst watches helplessly as Christa flees across the manicured lawns into the wilds of the forest. She draws air like a pump, her pulse and breath quickening while her skin warms to a reddish violet. She thinks to herself: *Nothing will separate me from the real Tree of Life.* Branches break under her pounding feet as she tries to outrun the chaos of her feelings, but her mind races ahead like a stampeding horse.

The leaves appear like fiery eyes that open and close to the howl of the wind. Furling clouds send shadows fluttering eerily across the forest floor. Her motion stirs a resting owl that rises with a fierce rush of its great wings and drifts toward a hidden place in the north. Like a butterfly burst from its cocoon, Christa follows in quest, seeing the bird as a sign of hope. *Give me the ears of an owl! I want to hear the sounds of freedom and the language of the trees.*

She looks toward the west as the Sun descends. *May I walk into the Sun and burn until I find the imperishable! Where is my home?* Her beating heart becomes one with the vermilion ball on the horizon as the world darkens and settles.

The owl observes her silently from the tree. She stops and becomes still, then sees an owl feather at her feet and kneels to pick it up. Silver threads of starlight stream down into her eyes and entwine themselves around her soul. They calm her and seem to speak: *You are a daughter of the night. Your fire will smolder unseen as long as you look to the fearful for sustenance and acceptance.*

The stars fade and the threads loosen as Horst returns to her mind. The wind has died and the forest stands silent. She sighs in confusion and nods like a hyacinth closing at dusk. Enfolded in darkness, her whole body sinks into the Earth.

In the dark, silent wild, her soul grows happy, fluttering with the softness of winter snow. Sleep comes and gathers her dreams of long ago. An old man and an old woman appear before her. "Write my book," commands the man. "I am old, and the people no longer behold me in the language of the trees. I have traveled the Earth and found few who will follow my plan except those who are invisible to their fellow people. Changing the course of the River has brought untold suffering. The Tree of Life is dying and the Earth is becoming a wasteland. Mines rip open the bowels of the mountains. Forests writhe in the pain of slaughter. Poisons fill the blood of the rivers and the breath of the air. Few even want to remember us. We know you can see us as one! We are weary of moving in the circles of the Sun and Earth while men and women move in confusion and addiction. I long to return to the center."

As the old man retreats and vanishes, the old woman speaks directly to Christa: "I will accompany you on your quest, wherever it takes you. It will be long. You can see, though you are unseen. Take the owl feather and write what you see. A time may come when others will understand your words. Write with the red of your blood, and the white fire will be there, too."

THE EXCHANGE OF CHAOS AND COSMOS

Sacrifice
White of white within gold

The temple
of the Earth
quakes
to find renewal.

The constancy of the logos is revealed in the changing order of the River. Circling through the gates of birth and death in sacred groves and lakes, the Creatrix spreads the elixir in the drops of rain, the sap of trees, and the blood of animals. She dwells as the brew of inspiration in the human heart, resurrecting the white flame of spirit and the red blood of eros through the living body. But the body decays, whereas stone monuments stare into space from the face of the Earth through thousands of years.

The Creatrix guides the alchemy of heart, lung, brain, and swirling centers that link the mortals to heaven. She walks on celestial dew condensed from the spirit of the sky and spread out within Earthen forms. But the tumult and clamor of the world—the wars, psychic noise, and pollution—hinder renewal in the celestial dew. Knowing that the Tree of Life can only be touched by those who have not severed eros and logos, she seeks to help mortals find the universal solvent in the temples of the body and the Earth.

As the forms of the cosmos change through cycles of time, the script of the River becomes garbled in many towers of Babel. The ancient myths of sacrifice tell of the loss of the paradisaic garden of the First World, the spiritual world, the world of sources. Though mortal ears hear the truth in golden sleep, the mortal mind turns the mirror to reflect the gods and goddesses as it wishes. The mirror is backed with shadows that clothe the truth in many stories.

Having heard the stories the mortals tell in their Earthly temples, the Creatrix returns on silver wings to the Creator and speaks plainly: "The air sizzles with confusion. Your Word lies broken like a fallen crystal, fractured on the bones of mortals who spit back the River in half-truths."

"Tell me," responds the Creator. "Let me hear how the threads of eternity have been cut and woven into stories."

Waving her arms in patterns of the River, the Creatrix begins to tremble as she sings: "Some say that I fell from the highest heaven as Sophia. They speak of the twelve rulers who became jealous of my pure spiritual essence. They say a self-willed one, emanating a lion-faced power, showed himself in such glory that I mistook him for you, my true treasury of light. On my descent to meet him, the twelve rulers surrounded me, and the lion-faced power devoured me and flung my body into chaos. They say I weakened and prayed to the light that all who receive the mysteries of Sophia be lifted up. The twelve rulers I know are within me."

The Creator's heart fills with fire, and beads of crystal dew spring from his brow: "May they remember your sacrifice. What other stories do they tell?"

"They speak of the light beings you created in the beginning, the ones that fell as stars. The stars strode out in the bodies of angels and entered the wombs of mortal women. Some say the angels flew in spacecraft through the azure sky, materializing their bodies out of celestial vapors in order to taste eros. They speak of women's blood mixed with the flame of angels, red within red, as the origin of evil on Earth. Others say the root of this evil lay in your heaven, from which the angels descended. In these ways they explain themselves as unEarthly creatures, part beast and part angel."

"The ways are arranged," replies the Creator softly. "But do none speak of the memory of my golden field where the white flowers bloom?"

The Creatrix washes her diaphanous body in the burning water and looks at the Creator in wonder. "Yes, many speak of a garden of paradise where you revealed yourself in the vibrating field that gives rise to all things. The Tapirape Indians of the Amazon tell of a time when their people dwelled on the bottom of a lake penetrated by your golden solar ray. They say a mortal man fell ill because he embraced power instead of love. Two young men from your golden lake then ascended the solar ray. Obelisks were later made to reveal this ray. The Earth above bewildered them, but they were guided by a deer to the liquid fire, the healing burning waters. They were able to go back into the lake and heal the sick man. But the two men told everyone of what they had seen above on Earth. Although the high priest tried to stop them, they returned to Earth and wandered there, never finding their way back to your golden lake."

The Creator sighs: "It seems that mortals seek comfort, but only suffering awakens them. Why do they not know that the only comfort is in opening the doors from root to crown—from Earth to heaven and back again in cycles of renewal?"

The Creatrix, resting on the white carpet that absorbs all suffering, goes on: "There is another story that is most popular among the people."

"What is that?"

"That you walked the Earth as an incarnate god who was slain, castrated, and crucified, your body cut up and your members scattered about the land. This story draws the celestial energies into the agricultural preparation of the Earth through the human souls seeking to unite us in themselves. This god is lord of eros, fertility, and cultivation, as well as the resurrected all-embracing healer."

"Who do they say I am?"

"Many are your names in different cultural disguises: the Cretan Adonis, Egyptian Osiris, Greek Dionysus, Babylonian Tammuz, Hittite Attis, and ancient Mexican Quetzalcoatl. These are but some of the names for this god, who is seen as my husband rather than as my father. Those who follow the ways of this story tend to be of the ancient red race—the survivors of Atlantis, the Cretans, the Pelasgians, the Lycians, the Israelite Kaphtorium, the Egyptian Kefti, and some of the tribes of the Americas."

"How can this view of me deliver them from their pain?"

"This god voluntarily sacrifices himself, for he is the consort of my essence as the Great Mother Goddess. The god's fiery phallus represents my baptismal candle. Sometimes the males castrate themselves and dedicate themselves to the Mother. Phallic columns stand on the graves of their dead. Through the fusion of fire and water, the blood of the son enlivens the Tree of Life, permeating the air with the fragrance of eternal spring. Many of their leaders are cast adrift as babes in baskets upon the waters. They speak wise poetry and are baptized in the River. This is their sacrifice. Through this cult their dreams are sparked, and some are lifted into ecstasy, like the one called Dionysus."

Akrisios and Fariba

Akrisios, Fariba, and ten other women have come to the island of Lesbos to enact a sacred ritual of renewal for themselves and for the Earth. Dressed in crowns of ivy and long flowing robes, the twelve women dance over the hills of Lesbos in the light of May's Full Moon. They clash cymbals and fill the valleys with exultant songs, their hair flying free in the wind. Some carry torches, others a *thyrsus*, a lance crowned with a pine cone. Akrisios and two others hold snakes that coil and writhe in their hands. They sing and dance to invoke Dionysus, who embodies the eros of the Earth.

Like the ancient maenads, the mad ones, they draw the magic of the Earth through their bodies. Call it madness, call it chaos, call it the sanity of the wild, call it the vibration of the Word, they swirl, flushed with ecstasy, in the liquid light of the Moon. Their bodies spring with the fervor of love and the power of animals. But their hearts, so open to feeling, are grieving for the dying god within the Tree of Life. Moving slowly now, they weave a path toward the great oak tree on the crest of the hill.

Weeping for the dying species, the depleted rain forests, the toxic waters, the waste-filled Earth, their empathetic bodies expand to embrace the evil and greed of the world, to transmute it through the fire of love in their cells. Both enlivened and entranced by this energy, the snakes grow still and gaze into the eyes of the ones who hold them. The group reaches the giant oak with new power to battle the source of old wounds. The filth of the world rushes into them, impelling them to draw forth the red flame from the Earth's depths into the red blood of their hearts. Passion pours through their bodies. Flushed with the united power of eros and logos, their hearts transmute the evil caught in sentient forms. The density of ancient chaos, imprisoned by a judgment of evil, explodes into a rich fragrance of spring flowers in the cool night air.

The women gather around the great oak and embrace the ancient bleeding god within it—Dionysus, Attis, Adonis, Osiris—the god of many names. Perspiration drips from their bodies. Leaf buds unfurl on the tree's outstretched limbs.

Akrisios pounds her chest to the rhythm of her heart, the rhythm of the wind winding through the grass, the rhythm of the clouds passing over the Moon. Soon all are pounding lightly in one rhythm, one heart beat, as the burning water of the River washes over them. The heart of the sacrificed Dionysus pulses within the oak as the tree deva rises from its crown. The women lie down on the Earth and face the sky, their feet touching the tree. Each one feels the deva's presence. Some hear its meaning.

When the great purge and transformation have ended, Akrisios feels compelled to speak, even though she is still trembling: "I felt a flame rush through me, and with it came the words, 'I live in celestial fire until the hearts of all mortals beat in one rhythm.'"

Fariba gestures from her heart to the trunk of the great tree and seems to draw a heart out of it. She holds the bleeding heart up to the Moon shining through the contorted branches. "Through me the bleeding core of the red Earth turns to gold," she declares. "I lift Dionysus' heart to the face of the Sun-blessed Moon, that he be reborn within me."

Carrying the emerald leaves of the Tree of Life, the winds hum a requiem for the death of the god. "Weep not for me," the god calls out. "Weep for yourselves. Weep for the children. Look to the future. How shall you consecrate yourselves? Let your sorrow fall and your bitter tears drop. I am immortal and cannot die. Come into yourselves."

From the heart of the tree, the women hear a song:

Priest-Seer's Song of the River

I am the wand that dispels the doubt of the atheist.
I am the thirst for renewal in the seed.
You can find me in the balance of the stalking heron.
I am in every sincere prayer.
Look for me in the anonymous lover and the monk's passion for truth.
You can find me in sacred ceremonies for the Earth.
I am the light in the mountain where the River runs underground.
You can find me in jewels and crystallized water.
I am the snow on the mountaintop and the vista below.
I live in the continuous invocation of the beloved.
I am the baptism of the spirit into life.
I live in the waters of life and the winds of the spirit.
You can find my quest in everything sacred.
I know the divine plan and live in the web of life.

Are you the spiritual authority?
I am the beginning and ending of knowing.

THE SECOND WORLD

The babel of priestly tongues stirs the Creator from his cosmogonic reveries. "Why have they lost the mystery?" he asks the Creatrix. "The hidden language remains invisible to them. Though the sacred fire still burns, the stories of our reality are confused."

"They fear that which they cannot comprehend or control," she responds, trying still to balance the chaos and eros of the Primal Waters with the cosmos and logos of the Kingdom. "The ecstasy that once inspired them to sing your praise is lost. They have cast the mystery of the River into stone."

"Is that why they no longer praise me? Their hallelujahs and chants are spiritless. Where are the priestesses? Don't they know the script of the River?"

"They are no longer permitted in the temple of the Priest-Seer, nor am I now honored there. They have gone into caves, hidden like language itself. Already, knowledge of the elixir is threatened. But the priests and priestesses need the essence of one another. The River still flows through their spines, but only in broken tongues. We must heal their fear and dispel the amnesia of our presence within them."

The Creator responds with light beaming from his crown. "Let us create beings who embody our power and love and who will not try to turn the River's mystery into rigid law. Let us create another world."

The Creator and Creatrix fly wing-to-wing, the new creation shimmering between them in streams of color and sound. Darkness through light, and light through darkness, prismatic colors refract in the sacred flame. Silence through sound, and sound through silence, the symphony of the Second World resounds.

The Creator draws the Immortals of the human spirit out of eternity so that the spirit might realize its deathless nature and stand outside the confusion of time. As the logos rushes forth from the Creator's mouth, the Creatrix blesses the new all-knowing spirit. Through the Immortals the Creator's Word rushes forth in deep gutteral sounds of "hu, hush, green gifts of home."

Now the Creator's divine eye beholds the possibility of the human soul. He draws the human forth as love from the logos of his Word, but his fractioned eye resists a unified vision. Children spring out of the song of the human soul, each with a different feeling and view, the prefigurations of the Antagonists.

The symphony of the Second World rings out to heal the separation of priest and priestess. The Creatrix returns the sounds of the logos through the movement of the hidden language, the palatal tones of the River rolling and rippling with the birth of human souls. Naked and rapturous the souls romp, running and leaping into the lush liquid of life, their sweetness softening the contentious sting of the Antagonists.

The human body is formed from the Creator's spiritual fire, from the glowing particles that meld with the River's burning waters. Moving to the trumpeting sounds of tempests and deep dental tones, the Creatrix draws the Primal Pair out of the deep dreams of the soul and infuses the body of the Pair with the erotic intensity of life.

The Creator concludes the symphony through the labial tones of the logos. The rays of his crown vibrate with the thoughts of his mind until the River billows with concept. Scattering the views of the mind into matter, the rays are immersed in profundity and rise as the thoughts and illusions of the Trickster.

THE IMMORTALS

Fire returns to light as the River carries the human spirit to the shore of the Immortals. The Creator gazes into the calm, clear waters and, seeing his own reflection, looks deeper, beholding the human spirit in the children of eternity. "They are of my essence. They are reflections of my eyes. I am Hu, and I shall live in them forever. Let them become Hu-man. From my own image shall I draw them forth in rainbow colors."

Like the infinite eyes of stars in the sky, the spirits, yet to have soul, body, or mind, momentarily realize their oneness with the Creator. The intention of each one is uttered in the River as a spiritual name, empowering it to meet its true destiny. The burning waters cleanse the toxic wounds of the priests and priestesses so that they can remember their original vow. As the Creatrix releases the spirits to the River, their rainbow colors resonate to the red, yellow, green, and blue starlight filtered through her iridescent wings. She weeps at the purity of these immortal ones, washing away the pain of the First World with her tears. Her breath showers the glassy waters with the elixir of inspiration and her movement illuminates the shadows with flashes of intuition. Her glance becomes a dispeller of darkness. The gift of her vision enables the spirits to glow and to begin to recognize one another. Through the black field, the River becomes a mirror, reflecting everything that shines above. The Creator beholds it all from the golden fields of his home, and he is pleased.

THE GOLDEN INTENTION IN THE BLACK GROUND

Intention
Gold of gold within black

Genesis
of the human spirit
embraces
the uroboric paradox.

Kau Chiang

Following the flooding of the southeast China river valleys, Kau Chiang decides to visit a refugee camp, where he erects temporary shelters for those whose homes were swept away. Although healthy for his fifty years, Kau Chiang grows tired from the intensity of the work. Exhausted, he lies down in the camp infirmary, letting his mind wander and reflecting on the good fortune of his son, Yu, who has gone to America to study. Soothed by these thoughts, his mind wanders further until he falls into sleep and the memory of ancient times.

He dreams of his lifetime in old Alexandria, which, in A.D. 400 stood in the desert as a cultural oasis of diverse beliefs. He was the brilliant mathematician-philosopher Hypatia, who raised light against the darkness of the times. Truth burst like butterflies from her lips, nourishing the poor and downtrodden. Weaving the eternal thread of wisdom that linked East and West, she taught Greeks, Jews, Egyptians, and Christians alike.

Kau Chiang's delirious awareness sinks into the pain in his back where Hypatia was stabbed centuries ago. Memories edge toward faces that flow and spin in the River's current, the dark tension in the golden source. He lives the stillness of *being* the matrix, as pain becomes pure energy. Angelic choruses fade into mad voices that vanish into the piercing pitches of white sound, void of holy balm. He sees heavenly armies of fallen angels descend to earth amid Atlantean swirls of divine pride—pride that is consumed in smoke as the great Alexandrian library burns.

As Hypatia is dragged from her chariot, her soul sails to the edge of heaven and gazes down upon the impalement of her spine, the dismemberment of her body, the scraping of flesh from bones with oyster shells. She watches from above as the sectarian Christians rampage against the Jews and pagan Greeks.

This brutal smothering of Kau Chiang's truth shatters his spirit like a mirror pierced by a bullet. No longer a single voice for East and West, his soul splits into two, one part going to the West, the other falling from the sublime gold of the spaceless matrix into the vast hills of China, where Kau Chiang follows the dark veins of the dragons.

Concurrent with Alexandria's fall is China's revolutionary tumult, brought about by the chaos of six rapidly changing dynasties. The Confucian order disintegrates and crumbles into dust, casting a millennia of temples, libraries, and schools into a pit of ignorance. Only Kau Chiang's intention sustains the values of the past against the confusion of the mobs.

Kau Chiang turns in his bed, soothed by the memory of Chinese landscapes. Snow-covered mountains, rising through the mist, appear from black ink that spreads in quick splashes across silk. His hand is quick and precise. The winding pathways amidst emerald pines lead to the singular breath that reaches a feeling of iridescence. In landscape painting, his intention is present.

Three times Kau Chiang incarnated during China's six dynasties, each time seeking to join the Eastern and Western roads in his heart. The dragons know the way, the Tao, the River that fears nothing. In the fifth century, Kau Chiang stands with a golden brush in one hand, a knife in the other. His body reveals a warrior, his spirit a poet. He follows the glistening path of the dragons that link the golden dust of dawn in the East with the high mountains of the West. He drinks in the dew of heaven while swimming in the Taoist cascades and climbs the hills where birds built their nests from the grasses of eternity.

With his knife, he cuts the edge of public life and traditional values. With his brush, he writes what the dragon teaches him: "Without attachment, *feel* the living web, and compress your intention in a single focus. Find the headwaters of the River in the blackness of flowing ink! The River is wherever the light is undivided from your eyes. Live where the sound of white water is one with your ears. Attune to the mist and the backbones of trees. The Sun circles the Earth, and the Earth circles your hand. Be one with the River that never changes, and you will meet the Hsuan-P'in, the Dark Spirit of the Universe."

"I am not afraid," cries Kau Chiang as he looks into the obsidian eyes of the dragon. "I walk through my own blood and scrape my own flesh from my bones. I forgive all pain and offer myself to the divine darkness!"

The dragon spirals several times. "Accept being mortal, so that Immortals may live within your spirit."

The dragon arches its back and floats between two clouds as Kau Chiang's doors of memory open to an Indian incarnation when he is dipped in the sweet dew of Buddhism for further healing. Inspired by something so fine and invisible, he journeys across the Indian deserts to paint Jataka scenes in the Chinese caves of Tunhuang. Seeing this intention in the patterns of diamondlike hills and the brushstrokes of trees through the golden body of Buddha, he follows the gnarled road to the River. "I am a man dedicated to the Tao. Lead me through the twisting caves of the world to the liquid light of the Buddhist void. I accept the darkness, though I love the gold. The Immortals live in me!"

Thus, Kau Chiang cuts loose his body and frees his soul in the darkness. He moves in the bodies of the dragons and passes like incense through the nostrils of the gods. He eases the pain and sorrow that arise from the destruction of times of glory, wealth, and knowledge. He breaks the seal on the book of his own spirit and humbles himself. His obscurity, anonymity, and invisibility are strong medicine in the dark circling currents where the human spirit is born. The human microcosm begins here in the nothingness where everything changes, for nothing is still.

And so, as the arrow of time parts East and West, Kau Chiang's identity divides into two reflections, clouds of opal and black obsidian. In the East, as Kau Chiang, he plumb the depths to live in the obscurity of the Tao. In the West, he becomes Zapana, who builds empires and erects monuments to the Sun.

The Black and Golden Ruins of Incahuasi

Inspiration
Black of gold within black

Father-mother spirit
in sinking spirals
descends
on angels' wings.

Zapana

In his dream, Zapana walks with the Western stream, where he encounters the Immortals, surrounded with golden radiance. They say, "We have divided the Earth into East and West."

Zapana awakes, surrounded by rubble and rotting food. Hearing the ancient songs of Incan priests rising from the Incahuasi ruins, he weeps.

Before her death, Mama Ocllo, Zapana's mother in a previous life, laid down the treasure of her existence: "I give this life for you, my son. Take it and wrap it in cloth. Roll it up with respect and bury it. I am with you everywhere. Rule in peace. I shall be watching from the world beyond the veil."

Mama Ocllo passes through him like water through a sieve. Through her, he sees the turning of the tides and ancient Incan boats, floating amidst the reeds. But he is angry and confused, for he also sees every store in Cuzco filled with technological trinkets. In his mind, he beholds the hypnotized public, the dead hearts of consumers, the widespread pollution, the broken hoofs of donkeys, all in a confused jumble against the once-golden splendor of the Incan empire.

Now, wandering amidst ruins, he wonders, *Who am I? What has happened to my people?* He leaps from thought to feeling, and from feeling to life after life. *Once I ruled here in a golden age, but after me came only shadows, scarlet blood, and white candles. The ancient Western flame is dying. I can see out the open windows, but I can't fly through! Oh! Ancient gods of the golden Sun, help me!*

The memories roll on like the River from the mouth of Mama Ocllo, who speaks within his mind: "Do you remember when you celebrated rituals with great pomp? Your heart was pure, but your naiveté was great. Now you must learn discretion. The mutiny of your outlying people weakened your power. They took possession of the *huaca* (holy power) of war kept in the sacred enclosure. With this prize, they marched back to Cuzco with victorious elation. You summoned your priestly hierarchy, but this only led to war, for the priesthood was already too weak."

"Yes, Mama, but what could I have done? Wasn't it inevitable that our great empire crumbled to ruins? Isn't the priestly hierarchy outworn and useless in these times? We live in another time now. What can I do?"

"Your mother awaits you, but you cannot return to her until you clear your confusion. Stand before yourself and drive the scorpions from your mind. Embrace the white man, although he drives you from your empire. The wind carves rock. Cradle the Western chaos with gentleness, or you will sink like lead in the seas of time."

Zapana wipes tears from his eyes: "Yes, I have seen the bearded whites who brought spiritual corruption and disease. Their hierarchy is of another kind. They do not worship the Sun. Their god is a conquering god, whom I cannot embrace. Yet we are both of the West. I am confused."

"You, Huayna Capac, must restore the empire within your heart. Do you remember the night the apparition brought you a gift?"

"I remember the overwhelming darkness. Within that darkness, the apparition materialized and said, 'I bring nightmares to the proud ones.' He handed me a box and vanished. When I opened the box, swarms of wispy creatures flew out. In a week, two hundred thousand men, women, and children lay dead from the plague. It was not hard to prophesy my own death. Those were horrible times."

"Your mummy was restored to Cuzco in imperial triumph. But your will was vague, and thereafter the golden age of the Incan empire degenerated. Now you herald the darkening of the gold."

Zapana turns in confusion and protests: "All these ruins are stained with death. What is permanent? What hope is there for the world when the greatest empires crumble to dust? The white man still brings plagues of armaments, addictions, and mental disease. I cannot see how to change time."

"Remain the witness so that you will be awake when you sleep. Dust your feet with the rubble and embrace the white man. I am one with the Sun, the eye of the one. Be aware through my golden eye, and inspiration will come to you."

REBIRTH INTO THE RAINBOW SNAKE SPIRIT

Intuition
Red of gold within black

Timeless windows
of initiation
flash over thresholds
into dreamtime.

Jingo

In Arnhem Land in northern Australia, twelve summers after his birth, Jingo is told by his father, "The Rainbow Snake is veiled from your sight. It is time that you receive the mark of your ancestor and reach the womb of the sky. No longer can you grub roots with the women. Now you are to hunt kangaroo with the men."

Jingo knows of the rites of circumcision and subincision that initiate youths into the mysteries of his tribe, but the child within him recoils at his father's words.

At dawn, Jingo and the other boys his age are led to a great circle. The entire Gunwinggu tribe is present. The men grab the boys and toss them into the air while the women dance and shriek, releasing the energy of the Rainbow Snake with their cries. Jingo feels disoriented as he is tossed by the men.

Jingo falls to the ground and looks up to see a woman leaning over him with colored mud and bird down in her hands. She is from a group of women that includes the one he is to marry. Panting deeply, Jingo remains still as she paints the pattern of his Dreamtime ancestors on his chest and back. He feels the undoing of his past and a powerful connection with some web of life beyond his understanding. Through pure intuition, he enters *Altjurunga*, Dreamtime. His breath seems to rush through the patterns painted on his body as his flesh changes and moves into a new vibration.

One evening, several weeks later, Jingo is out in the bush wondering how it would feel to be on a hunt by himself. He is suddenly seized by three men who carry his struggling body once again to the ceremonial ground. As the Sun sinks below the horizon, Jingo realizes that the entire tribe is there, singing and dancing. All are decorated with red and yellow ochre, and white and black clays, mixed with blood and bird down. They have entered into the heated power of the ancient River of Dreamtime, where all things glisten in rainbow colors. Jingo feels the spirit enter him as he watches the singular movement and listens in awe to the sound of their transformation into Dreamtime beings. He does not resist as three men twist fur around his head and place hair around his waist, then guide him through the dancing bodies to a remote bush. In a low, stern whisper he is told, "Never speak to any woman of what you learn here, or you will lose your power."

In the women's camp, his mother, Wibalu, keeps a fire burning, her heart beating in unison with Jingo's. Double flames lick in the fire as her tongue chants, "My son, my child, may you endure everything like a woman in order to become a man." Orange flames leap out of her mouth from the fire of her heart and womb. As dawn approaches, she ignites two sticks in the dying embers of the fire, accompanied by Jingo's aunts and Bambara, the mother of the woman he is to marry. She carries the torches to the men's camp.

More men are immersed in the ritual dances, beholding rainbows around the fire, as the Rainbow Snake touches Jingo with her tail. Standing in front of Jingo, his mother, Wibalu, passes one fire brand to Bambara, who hands it to the boy. Bambara then ties fur strings around his neck and admonishes, "Hold fast to your own fire. Spit no flames into the womb of any woman other than Brogla, your promised one."

Jingo is once again taken by three men, this time to a eucalyptus grove to fast alone for three days. The torrid air of the desert sweeps up into the forest by day and lingers in the fragrance of the eucalyptus trees at night. Jingo struggles to conquer the fears within himself: the fears of hunger, of darkness, of being alone. Drowning in imaginary whistles, roars, and groans, Jingo sees the trees turn into wild animals. He feels the Dreamtime wind will tear him apart.

At midnight on the third night, the men come. They blindfold Jingo and lead him out of the grove, through the bush, to the edge of the men's danceground. There, lying face down, Jingo breathes the Earth and smells the blood of his ancestors within it. When his blindfold is removed, he sees before him a man in the semblance of a wild dog. In the distance, he can see another imitating a kangaroo. As if before a mirror, he sees himself in the men mimicking the dog and kangaroo. Jingo shivers as the kangaroo man calls the cry of the kangaroo. The dogman growls and begins to tear at the kangaroo's flesh, then turns toward Jingo. The dogman approaches, pausing to paw and sniff him before leaping upon him. Then the kangaroo leaps upon both Jingo and the dog. Jingo is terrified, but by staying attentive through this act, he has overcome fear of madness and death. For six days and nights, Jingo and the other boys pass through trials such as this, reenacting the men's secret stories of the Dreamtime ancestors.

Then the fateful moment of circumcision arrives. Jingo is encircled by wrathful men with their beards in their mouths. Amid deafening yells, one approaches and cuts off Jingo's foreskin with a flint knife. The women, hearing the shout from the men's camp, begin responding with bull-roarers, the source of the voice of the initiating spirit, Twanyirika.

Jingo's blood flows onto a shield as his soul flies to Dreamtime. He sees the open mouth of the Rainbow Snake. Transported beyond time and space between the jaws of the snake, his thought is pulverized like crystals into sand. The white dust rises within his spirit to pure intuition. Reborn, Jingo's spirit shines through his black eyes.

His wound heals over the next few weeks. Jingo has changed, but his soul has yet to embrace the female in himself. He begins to see the Dreamtime beings, and he walks with greater assurance. Still, the next month of Dreamtime enactments terrify him. The woman in him lives within the Rainbow Snake, just as the man in a woman does. Sometimes, Jingo's female appears as the hideous face of a witch, or an open mouth attempting to devour him. Sometimes it appears pure, soft, and full of the fragrance of spring desert flowers. Aeons of male and female lifetimes stir passion in his body, casting long shadows over the

Earth from the changing shapes of the Dreamtime ancestors moving within him.

Now, in the men's camp, Jingo watches as the men plant the tall, feathered, sacred pole in the ground. He is led by the men to embrace the pole. Nearby, a Gunwinggu man lies face down in the dust, and another lies on his back, the two of them open to dust and sky. Jingo is lifted and placed face upward on top of the living human altar as his initiator approaches him with a flint knife.

With a loud shout from the men, the energy is released to unite the masculine and feminine in Jingo's soul. His penis is slit from below. The cry of the men signals all the women to be slashed across the belly by Wibalu, drawing blood. Their blood is mixed and made into a paint to invoke the Rainbow Snake.

Jingo is snatched from his past and bathed in the blood of another birth. He earns the secrets of the men's lodge and the mystery of the female womb. The rites culminate in the wedding ceremony of the boys, reborn as men, to their assigned wives.

During the ceremony, the sound of the bullroarers sends Jingo into the belly of the Rainbow Snake. He rides up the backbone, thrashing, until suddenly his fear fades away. Silent and still inside, he hears the sound of his secret name. He can neither speak nor move. Suspended in the awesome awareness of the dual sexuality of the Rainbow Snake, Jingo's senses fade completely. He rides on the wings of intuition to the home of tribal secrets. Seeking to remember the ancient mysteries of his soul, he is reborn into a new understanding of life. Jingo the boy is no more.

That evening, Jingo takes Brogla into his mud hut for the first time. Slowly and fluidly, their bodies flood with colors from the Rainbow Snake.

THE GOLDEN BOND IN THE CAVE OF DARKNESS

Crown of Vision
White of gold within black

The spectrum
of the inner eye
reveals
a virtual source.

Raphael and Zapana

In a journey to the ruins of Peru, Raphael encounters a youthful native Indian with deep sadness in his eyes. Intuiting the Indian's misfortune, Raphael speaks out boldly: "The gods who shape us are golden columns who still stand though their houses have fallen. We live for a while, send out a call, and pass away." Raphael himself stands very proud, a youth of splendid golden aura from lifetimes of service to the Immortals.

Zapana resounds with a poisonous look at the bearded white American.

In spite of Zapana's harsh glance, Raphael thinks to himself, *I discern light from fire, and fruit from poison. Help me to dispel your hatred, my brother! You confound me with old memories!* But he says, "I offer good fortune."

Zapana's eyes grow wide as he glimpses Raphael's aura through the divine eye of Mama Ocllo. "I sit like a man with two heads, one in confidence, the other in fear. What good fortune could you bring?" he remarks.

Raphael invites confidence with the brightness of his brow. "Tell me if you can. I have come here to dream of the future in the past. Our meeting has a purpose. By telling our stories, we perhaps then shall know the truth. I have a vision I'd like to share. I'd like to hear your story."

Zapana remembers, "Here at Incahuasi I once ruled. Where are my people now? No one knows who I am, not even myself. Now I live in poverty, without identity. Are the gods just? My path is narrow. I want to move toward my destiny, but I no longer know what I stand for."

Raphael's response is hopeful: "It is my belief that I crossed the Urubamba River to meet you. Your past may seem irreconcilable with your future, yet you seek who you are in the present. This ruin is the manure for some unseen seed. My quest is to go beyond the paradox and unite the opposites within me. I am looking for my own shadow, but my light is too bright to behold it. Perhaps you can help me."

"I, help you? I am helpless myself!"

"Look, you and I are opposites, yet therein lies our hope. My thoughts brighten too quickly for the world. The Earth spins and turns red at the end of each day. Since I am neither steady nor constant, I am always expressing myself in new visions. I came to these ruins to find the past, the darkness that is asleep in the fields of my unconscious. You, too, dream, I believe. Can you dream of another empire, one that does not depend on perishable buildings?"

"I don't know. It sounds empty like the sky—as hard to grasp as dancing in the wind."

"The sky is the River of unseen possibilities. If you know your dream, you can carry it through this Kali Yuga toward a new destiny."

"Kali Yuga?"

"The Dark Age. We live in an age of darkness, but in the ruins, in the desperation, is the golden light. I am filled with light. The white and gold blend in the darkness through me. If you bring me the gold of the Sun, I will fuse the white flame that can awaken our visions. May the Immortal Sun God pierce our hearts and make us brothers. Come with me to North America. We can rebuild your empire from the River of the sky."

Zapana looks up in astonishment at Raphael, whose bright face stands out against the blue sky: "I am breathless, but I see you. You speak of the Sun God as though you were like one of us. Mama Ocllo sees you through me. Sometimes I see too much, for she watches even when I sleep. I have seen the passing of many centuries just sitting here."

"I believe you. What will you do now?"

"My mother and sisters in my village depend on me. My blood mother is not the mother who watches over me, for she is more helpless than I am. I must return, though I have nothing to bring them. I came here to find myself, to return with the gift of myself. You have brought me vision in spite of myself."

"The vision is yours. Alone, I am blinded by my own light. You can see clearly, but cannot manifest what you see. Let us enter together into the undergrounds of this ruin and ask the Sun God for guidance."

"But the Sun God dwells above the Earth."

"At night, he descends into the underworld to offer a new vision to those who would receive it."

Raphael, who has visited the ruins of Incahuasi many times, leads Zapana to a giant stone that hinges invisibly inward when pushed at a distinct angle. They enter amid shafts of daylight that illumine the dust circling in the passageway. As they continue into darkness, Zapana sees Raphael's aura radiate like the Sun. They pass through a corridor and descend a stairway, somehow surrendering more deeply to the darkness and to the Sun God.

Memories of ancient times stream through Raphael, who fears the darkness. After a long silence, Raphael begins to speak: "I came here once before to face what I fear, but it is still withheld from me. May you help me find the unseen, and may God grant the ability to help you manifest your dream."

They sit down in a dark chamber, where Zapana begins to chant. Raphael feels his spine growing increasingly erect as the light rises through it. Zapana beholds spirals upon spirals of golden light rising from the crown of Raphael's head. His chant continues like the humming of bees circling around a hive.

Raphael then speaks: "Look back no more, Zapana. We are brothers in spirit. You are distracted by memories of a golden past. The ruin of your past lives on as a light in your body. Help me to serve you. I grow too tall and arrogant without you."

Zapana listens quietly, then speaks deliberately: "Will you come back to my village with me? My chant has shown me many families screaming in need. Humanity is lost in darkness. You have helped me to realize that darkness is the place of germination, that ruins are the site of new construction. I feared the white man until this moment."

"I feel like a baby in the womb of the Great Mother. I am a white man, but my soul is of the ancient red race. I am your brother."

"Your aura shines like the stars in the night. Come back home with me."

"You are an ancient one dreaming, like old clay longing to make a new form. We can make what we imagine. I will go home with you and labor for you. Perhaps then you will come home with me."

With their hearts wide open, Zapana and Raphael are able to hear a high, almost angelic sound:

Immortal's Song of the River

I am the rain that washes everything clean, falling on all alike.
I spread everywhere, yet I live in each drop.
I am the vaporized energy of the spirit.
I am centered in each atom, yet expand outward in great fields.
I am the 'magnetic moment' in all purpose.
You can find me in the focus of human intention.
I am the spinning electron that returns to itself.
I live beyond time and space, yet rest in every place.
I flow through all fields, yet thrive in a vacuum.
I give birth to all vision like a star rising after the evening rain.
I am the inhaling and exhaling of the endless sky.
I am effortless knowing without a trace of mind.

How can you be effortless?
By knowing nothing and being all.

THE ANTAGONISTS

The Creatrix crosses the River at a black bend. There, an island of dark pebbles divides the current into two streams, mirrored in the galaxy by stars that spread into two spiraling arms. And there, at the separation of the burning waters, she beholds the human spirits vibrating between the pebbles.

Gently lifting the ones so uncertain of their destiny, she kisses and cradles them, her hands and fingers serving as a basket woven of hope. She draws from her heart a nest of possibility, where, like a baby eagle, the human soul is conceived. Each soul shimmers in the golden light of the spirit. Holding them, her body burns.

Sensing the tension between the two streams rushing to her right and left, the Creatrix gathers the spirits for the great adventure of the soul. The magnetism of her attraction to the Creator flows into her hands as she aligns her will with his. Divine energy rises up her spine and spills down onto the human souls. She holds her magnetized hands apart, showering the souls with the dewy essence of love between herself and the Creator. The sphere of the human spirit expands while the parabola of the human soul stretches toward opposing poles, finally stretching to a hyperbola of males and females who face one another in awe and astonishment. Masculine and feminine, light and dark, positive and negative churn in the waves, oscillating between duality and the oneness of the single eye.

The souls respond to the creative noise of the Primal Waters flowing through the hands of the Creatrix. They reverberate first with love, then desire. Both wondrous and terrible is their fate, thinks the Creatrix, who foresees the pain arising from projection that cannot match the reality of love.

Sighing, she places the fused spirit and soul at the division of the two streams. There opens an abyss, a black chasm filled with the shadows of anger and hatred. In the darkness she creates a lotus seed and fills it with compassion to redeem all possible misery. As she releases the human souls to their destinies, she murmurs a formula of tones and hues through which each one can recognize its true spiritual name and original vow. "You shall break and be reborn," she tells one. "You can remain here, but then you shall never know one another," she tells the next. "You may be crushed, but can rise again by growing deep roots," she tells another. Moving among them, she whispers, "You may devour each other if each of you does not learn your own song. You can count the stars and never know your own soul." To a pair floating in a pool, she admonishes, "If you hold the River in your veins, the waters will turn to poison." To those already clinging to one another, she advises, "If you let each other go, you will meet." And to those who have already invented dramatic scenarios, she declares, "Your purpose is to be simple."

Again and again, into millions of souls, she breathes the numinous power of love that can draw them out of the abyss and shape their destiny. However, it is the seed of desire that drives them on.

THE GREAT DIVIDE OF CONSCIOUSNESS

Love
Gold of black within black

The eternal flame
of unconditional acceptance
touches
the untouchable.

Channon and Fariba

Fariba has returned to Malta from her travels to Jerusalem and Greece with a renewed sense of vitality and clarity. Through the years of their common search for truth, her love for Channon has matured like a good wine. She is eager to be in his presence, to be with the refinement, the sensitivity, and the creative energy she feels in him. These qualities are gradually emerging and stabilizing in her own soul as she moves among different kinds of people in the world.

Channon is not possessive of her. He is pleased that she travels, even though he misses her presence and her assistance as hostess and secretary. She spoils him at home, and he is happy that she is back with him. She has returned from Greece with the gift of a genuine artifact from the Dionysian rites, which he receives with a twinkle in his eye.

The ecstasy of their love is silent and deep, an experience attainable only by those who unveil their own souls. Each being a Sun in the other's heart, the two streams of the River move closer together through them. Fariba sings as she moves through the house, filling vases with sweet-scented roses from their garden, her heart full of the happiness of being once again in Channon's presence. Her soul emanates music that Channon hears inwardly, prompting him to rise from the contemplation of a mathematical puzzle. Embracing her lightly, he whispers softly, "You are the answer to my every question."

A breeze wafts through the open door, carrying them to love, as Channon draws Fariba's lips to his. The very intention of the Creator vibrates through his tongue as the luminous colors of the Creatrix disperse through their blending auras. Their love emanates into soft, swirling clouds that drop sweet rain upon the land, even where drought has squeezed the River from the Earth. They grow young, as the eternal spring of their souls renews every cell in the balm of colored music. The synesthesia in their brains is created in their hearts.

After the expression of their love, Channon and Fariba stroll out into the garden to the music of the growing grass and the song of the vibrant Sun, the music's orchestral strings reverberating in the colors of a thousand angels dancing on the rays between heaven and Earth.

The distance between moments is every eternal now that Channon and Fariba feel through the space of their existence together. Looking out over the swelling turquoise waves of the Mediterranean, they linger to pluck a ripe fig from a great tree that offers its fruits gladly to them, as though happy to be a part of their love.

They descend the winding path to a swimming hole, an open cove where giant boulders protect a calm pool from the thrashing sea. Fariba strips and dives into the clear blue water. As Channon watches the lithe figure of his wife plunge and disappear, he feels a strange sadness rising in his chest. He is older than she, slower, and, though brilliant in mind, more uncertain of existence.

Channon sees Fariba's shining face emerge, then moves to the edge of the rocks and removes his clothes. He is tired from the strain of intense study, travel, research, invention, and the teaching of esoteric truths. Feeling the blessing of ancient dreams, he leaps and plunges down, down, unendingly down, until, with a kick, his body lunges upward.

Without warning, Channon's brain is pierced by the lights of the Egyptian gods. He struggles against the pain, and even more against the uncertainty of life, as blood rushes from where he has struck his head on a submerged boulder. The doubt that lay deep in his soul flies like a black moth toward the light of his genius, trying now to emerge as a deliverance from drowning. Feeling as though he is about to burst from a womb, he is only partially aware of Fariba's arms around his large chest.

She kicks furiously, conscious only of the effort to keep her tiring legs moving, until her head finally shatters the bloody froth of the surface. The grace of the gods has placed a smooth outcropping within arm's reach, and she manages to support Channon against it, then climb onto it and drag up his body. Barely conscious, Channon feels the sharp edge of the abyss that stretches between the immortal spirit and the mutable soul. Fariba breathes into his mouth, drawing up the moist turbulence from his lungs, while stroking his bleeding head. Amid a maelstrom of spirits swirling beneath the sea and above their pulsing naked bodies, she resuscitates him.

Channon's physical recovery is swift, but the accident has imprinted his mind and soul. As the days pass, instead of moving closer to Fariba, he succumbs even more to the fear that severs the eternal reality of love from the uncertainty of time and existence. Sparks fly from his brain as he looks for a way to reverse the downward plunge of time into old age and death. The old wisdom of ancient manuscripts is forgotten as he struggles to grasp the secrets of immortality. His absorption into inventing nets to capture the ungraspable simplicity of love alienates Fariba. No longer does he speak softly to her or walk in the garden, where the music of their souls once blended. All his waking hours are spent designing circuit boards and programs that reverse time and erase mortality.

One night, Fariba decides she can bear it no longer. For many weeks she has been unable to sleep, disturbed by the convolutions of Channon's energy that actually hastens the death he is seeking to overcome. Walking under the stars, she converses with Nut, the Goddess whose body fills the night sky. *How will he return to me? How can I restore the love that turns all poison to the elixir of eternity?* In the ensuing silence, Fariba hears distinctly that she must leave for a while to make peace with her own soul.

She returns to the house and dares to interrupt Channon's cogitations: "I feel a need to journey to London. Akrisios has written and said that she plans to be there next week. I want to be with you, but you are no longer with me."

Channon looks at Fariba over his thick glasses, then stares down at the books and charts that exemplify his own longing. "Oh, please don't go. I need you here."

"But you never see me any more. I serve you meals and type your proposals without a sign from you that I even live. I need to go to find my own peace."

Suddenly, Channon surges with defensive anger, "Go then and never come back! I am finding a solution to the greatest problem of the human race, and you decide to have no part in it."

"Please don't react so. I long to strengthen you with love, but you don't seem to care. You only use me. The accident has changed you. You've grown afraid. Aren't the coiling wires of your inventions just the unraveling of your uncertainty? I want to share my life with you, but you no longer radiate the light of Temu."

Channon's anger persists as he chases his fragmented thoughts: "How dare you? I am close to discovering the ancient secrets of resurrection and immortality, and here you are, ranting at me! Either apologize or leave this house."

Fariba has no words. She turns away from him, unseen as air on a clear day or shadows in the dark night. She lies down to rest on a couch until dawn. In the morning, as Channon finally sleeps, she leaves for the airport.

The Preservation Chamber of the Soul

Desire
Black of black within black

The polarity
of subject and object
rotates
the wheel of life.

Desire arises in the darkness of the boundless sky. The Creatrix stands before the fire where the souls ever long to fulfill themselves in the opposite sex. She casts some cedar incense into the fire, knowing that a million years will pass before its ribbons of fragrance reach the Creator. When the time has passed, he breathes in its sweet prayer and exhales a turbulence that fans the fire of desire into every soul that trembles through the passion of the River.

Whenever the souls remember the formula of the Creatrix that protects them from oblivion, their spirits glow in great spheres. But the golden scrolls of the First World unfold through the ages into the dark invisible mystery of the human world. The souls spin in all directions, seeking to preserve what they desire from the ravages of time. However, desire only impels the one-way torrent of time into ever more branches of the River.

The Creatrix rises from the fertile River bed where the two streams branch. She throws back her head and calls out to the Creator in the First World, "Imbue them with free will, that they may not only err, but learn through the language of the heart how to move in the River and return to us. May they no longer be innocent, but knowing of their own souls."

The Creator's Word vibrates in the River's mingling waves. It whispers to the questioning souls: "The way downstream is perilous. Antagonism is the price of creating your own destiny. Your acts are mirrored in each other and in us. You long for unity, but if you engage in fear and deceit, you will never recognize each other. There, in the notes of your own music and the colors of your own aura, you can find the courage to be who you are."

A millennia passes before clouds gather to press the pain of the ages into a furtive sky that eludes the fearful souls. Having forgotten their rainbow journey together through the teeming rapids of the River, the tribes of the world contend for the land of the Creatrix as if it were their own. Greed blooms into territorial expansion. The dark sediments of desire and possession muddy the River waters and blind the soul to the beauty of its double. Anima and animus divide, desire driving one toward the other. The male seeks to rule over the head, bosom, and thighs of the female. But when she withdraws in fear and confusion, he moves on in frustration to conquer the body of Mother Earth.

The clashing of male and female souls forces the occidental and oriental streams to branch into ever smaller tributaries. Aryan tribes descend from the arctic to the plains between the Dnieper and the Danube rivers, then disperse into Greek, Italic, Celtic, and Germanic tributaries. The thundering hooves of the patriarchal Aryans and Semites trample the Mother Goddess, who takes refuge in caves with snakes wrapped around her spine.

Warrior nations move into the Caucasuses near the Aral Sea. They divide into Prussians, Latvians, Lithuanians, Czechs, Poles, Russians, and Persians. Amidst whirling wind and dust, the wild ravaging male tries to subdue the dragon of the female, whose soul still embraces the mystery of the Primal Waters. He has forgotten the nourishment of the reservoir and fears the waters will swallow him. Afraid of his own unlimited depths, he projects heros and gods to control hers. Yahweh overcomes the Leviathan, Marduk slays Tiamat, Apollo kills Python, Perseus beheads Medusa, Hercules destroys Hydra, Zeus attacks Typhon, and on and on. The names change, the war is the same. The patriarchal warlords plunder the Earthly garden of the earlier matriarchy. Semitic tribes

—the Akkadians, Babylonians, Phoenicians, Hebrews, Arabs, Iranians, Armenians, Phrygians, and Slavs—erect new nations on the ruins of the Goddess's body, each waving the flag of its own religion. Angry men build nations in the sands of time as they seek to control the uncontrollable metamorphosis of the living River.

The circle of eternal return breaks, and the divine gift of free will emerges corrupted as the quest for victory. The women weep for dead sons and lovers, and they wonder how the River can bear it.

Channon and Horst

Though Channon longs for Fariba like a flower for light, he buries his desire within his heart, where it stews and mixes with fear. His blood becomes impure and his shadow grows long as his spirit darkens with the sunset of love. Her refusal to apologize and remain with him festers inside him as a nagging abdominal pain. He sinks into isolation and closes his door to the questers for truth, seeking to preserve only his own mind and soul from the travesty of time.

Already, his own memory of the resurrection of Osiris rubs against the uncertainty of age crackling in his bones. All his longing for Fariba is driven deep into his marrow as a single desire to outwit time. He tries to command his body to enter the fire of immortality. Undesirous of a future mired in the noise and evil of the modern world, Channon relies upon his own memory to mold the future out of the shapes and shadows of the past. His persistence through long nights and days culminates in the invention of a cybernetic after-death chamber.

The longing of Channon's soul has converted the memory of his spirit into this cybernetic machine to preserve the images of his desires. His deeper question, *How did I kill what I loved?* is forgotten as his memories of the Egyptian mysteries deteriorate into a more narcissistic question, *How can my soul live forever?* Under the spell of his own self-image, Channon now realizes that this invention could fund his other esoteric projects, and, like a thirsty camel, he moves toward the mirages produced by the shimmering heat of his ambition. After performing an elaborate rite, he announces his unique investment opportunity to venture capitalists throughout Europe.

Death perches on his shoulder like a crow as the River runs downstream in double black currents, hidden from his desire-driven soul.

Horst, who, like Channon, suffers from the loss of his wife, seeks to overcome his despair by amassing even more wealth. His passion now is to enlarge his estate and pass on an immense inheritance to Erhardt, his twenty-seven-year-old son. Horst's desire to give to Erhardt is exceeded only by his desire to control him. But Erhardt is soundly independent and refuses to submit to his father's authority. Feeling powerless to control his son, Horst responds with even greater possessiveness.

He stands before a mirror, momentarily contemplating Christa's departure and Erhardt's unsubmissiveness. Unable to comprehend, he decides to vent his frustration by pursuing high-risk opportunities in the stock market. Having been informed by his broker of Channon's astounding invention, Horst decides to consider it as an investment and calls Malta to arrange a meeting.

Face to face in a conference room of a Frankfurt bank, the two men echo each other's desire. Channon's portfolio is full. He has translated the Egyptian gods into a hybrid of artificial intelligence and human gene pools. He has captured the entire zoology of animal-headed gods and goddesses in a network of silicon chips, circuit boards, and the living brain. He has even designed a virtual reality suit, whereby desires can instantly manifest into the sounds and images that mirror them.

Channon has not lost faith in Temu and Egyptian metaphysics, but he is cynical about human nature. Horst, whose concern for marketing is foremost, asks, "What is happening in society that makes the immortality chamber timely? Why would anyone want to buy these products?"

Channon's eyes gleam. "The management of the dying has always been big business. Priests, rabbis, mullahs, hospitals, nursing homes, insurance companies, undertakers—all take advantage of the fear-driven, dying soul. I want to free the dying person from these vulturous 'services' and also establish a sound business that will fund other humanitarian projects I have in mind."

Horst, with mixed motives, frowns and then smiles, like smoldering rot that cannot burst into flame. "In America, where the consumer is addicted to mechanical solutions, it might sell."

Channon continues: "People in any culture who are conditioned to linear time will be interested, for the simple reason that the fall from paradise into incarnation and mortality calls forth a resurrection after death. With this device, death is bypassed, not for the body, which will perish like fruit, but for the soul. The preservation of the continuity of the soul over millennia requires only two things: the desire to be immortal, and a unique past-life soul code to retain the pattern of dendritic growth in the nervous system."

"Does such a machine induce something like an out-of-body experience or a hypnotic preincarnational memory?"

"Yes and no. It can enable the soul to overcome the greatest human fear—death."

"But, as you say, it does not preserve the body. Is it not the death of the body that people fear?"

"Perhaps. But even more, they are afraid of total annihilation, even of the soul. Buddhism is one of the greatest proponents of this insidious belief that the soul is impermanent or even nonexistent. I must admit that the chamber is not likely to sell in Buddhist countries."

Horst responds: "I'm willing to invest in a device that will not be difficult to use and that will insure people against their own fears, whether it immortalizes the soul or not."

"Even a simple anesthetic could meet those two requirements, but this device enables people to have conscious, voluntary control of their soul experiences."

Channon sits back, smiling at the recognition of Horst's own soul. He realizes that he and Horst have concerned themselves with similar themes in previous incarnations.

Horst still questions: "How can it do that? Can ordinary people use it? Doesn't it require great training?"

"Does the world die when you sleep? It is one's interpretations of the world that live on in the mind. This device does all the work as long as the user desires immortality. That is freedom from illusion. It is desire that creates the world, and desire that destroys it. Desire splits the self from the world, the inner from the outer. This device disengages desire from the world illusion and directs it back into the source of the soul. Would you like to experience it?"

Horst fears going too deeply into memory and shattering the illusions he has created as a defense against the pain of reality: "I'm fascinated, but I don't see how reversing time is possible without the attendance of great fear."

"Time appears as a one-way movement of the soul toward objects of desire. It is this propulsion that wears out the soul. Fatigue, old age, and death result from the unwinding of time and the dissipation of desire.

Time is deeply rooted in desire, don't you see? When desire is pointed back into the soul, time stands still and immortality of the soul is attained."

Horst is silent for a while, then drops his jaw and sighs: "I would like to try it. If I can recall past lives, and experience what I presently don't remember, it will be enough to convince me of its viability as a product. It sounds at least as good as hypnosis, and cheaper."

"Will you invest if it meets those requirements?"

"Yes."

Horst and Channon set up the immortality chamber in Channon's hotel room. As Horst lies within the chamber, Channon speaks in a calm, soothing voice that turns into a hypnotic mantra: "You can stop the process at any time by pressing this button. You have complete control. Breathe deeply and relax. Above all, you long for immortality. Let yourself dream. Whatever you see, you will remember. Go back—back to the source of your soul."

The device directs the vibration of Horst's soul ever backward, until he reaches the edge of the abyss. As Christa appears before him, his breath becomes quick and shallow. She cries, "I will never come back. You are a tyrant." He restrains himself from stopping the experiment, although his pain is intense.

Then he moves further back into a time in Egypt. He is the high priest Manesis, conferring with another high priest. Together they are studying papyrus charts that depict the changing angles of the stars with respect to the Earth's rotation. The powers of the animal-faced gods emerge through the stars and are mirrored on Earth. Paintings and hieroglyphs on the walls affirm the correlation. The other high priest says, "When the pharaoh's time is come, we will mummify him and enter his magical name as a code to the door of heaven." Manesis looks up at the face of the priest. It is Channon.

Involuntarily, Horst presses the escape button. The time travel ceases, and Channon slowly assists him out of the chamber.

As Horst comes to himself, he declares, "It was you!"

"What do you mean?"

"In Egypt, we sought to immortalize the pharaoh. There was something about a computer in the sky . . ."

Channon realizes that Horst has seen their ancient connection.

"Yes, we worked together on separating the cosmic computer of stars in the sky from the vegetal erotic root of the body. Listen—we were once dark seeds longing for light. Now we have light. It is time to fulfill what we set in motion then."

"What do you mean? How is the ancient separation similar to this immortality chamber?"

Channon smiles as the air virtually crackles with returned ancient thoughts of conspiracy: "The cosmic computer of stars is a time machine, a cybernetic matrix of information that releases, in precise order, codes from its zodiac of qualities. We are now at a time when the separation of astral information and bioplasma is possible. We tried then, but the stage of history was set on another course. The world has had to wander through this incredible technological jungle in order to externalize what we long ago knew in our souls. Now computer technology enables us to spread the secrets of the ancient pharaohs and priests to the people. The soul is a mirror of the stars just as the body is a mirror of the Earth. By separating them through time reversal, the soul is freed to be a source, rather than an agent that is ever questing for meaning. As a source, it returns to the stars from whence it came, and it operates as extraterrestrial intelligence."

Horst's past and future suddenly converge in his terror of the present. His painful encounter with Christa in the chamber returns to him, casting him into deep ambivalence: "Let me see how the chamber works with several other types of people. Then I will decide on whether to invest in it."

THE SHATTERING OF A SOUL

Projection
Red of black within black

Identification
with the mirror
creates
illusion.

The male soul looks in the mirror of the River, backed by the darkness of the Primal Waters. He sees his beloved, sweet and innocent. But
she metamorphoses into a temptress with flashing eyes, a vengeful
witch. His anima is alive with the fear of her mystery. Once erotic and
full of passion, she now looms before him as devouring and terrifying.

The female soul looks into the mirror of the River, backed by the
darkness of the Primal Waters. She beholds her beloved as the bright
warrior, protector, husband and father. But he is transformed into a
rapist, tyrant, and terrorizer. Her animus is alive with the fire of his
power. Once protective and full of passion, he now rages with authority
and judgment.

The storm of the River turns pitch black, falling down and back
through time like torrential rain. The River teems with projection as the
Goddess births minotaurs and monsters out of a mad fear of the male.
She weaves a labyrinth around the wandering souls of men, who twist
and turn in futile search of escape.

Souls, crying out for the return of love, create masks to conceal their
own loving essence. The persona changes with every turn of the head,
with every profile projected from inner confusion as inner and outer, self

and other, separate into enemies. Desire breeds frustration and festers as anger and hatred.

The female invites birth, death, and rebirth to pound the rigid, imposed cosmic order back into fertile compost that can be churned with the organic flow of the River. She sees imposed order as profane, the mutability of life as sacred.

The emerging warrior sees the female as the dark dance of Kali, the mad Lilith, Hecate, Gorgon. He sings immortal songs of passion, asking his God to spare him from the mortal travesty of birth and death. With the persona of the hero, he creates a fixed, orderly cosmos and projects gods to repel the power of the Goddess pouring forth from the chaotic Primal Waters. He sees change as profane, the cosmic order as sacred.

Petruska

Sasha and Petruska, sisters from Moscow, are visiting Frankfort on a long-awaited holiday. Sasha, the older of the two, is plump, practical, and steady. She enjoys the simple things of life and does not question much. However, the demands of Alyosha, her ebullient, carefree husband, and Fdyor and Tania, her two young children, have begun to weigh upon her. Always dancing to a new tune, Alyosha demands that life be a high-pitched drama. He has bounced in and out of music, theater, dance, and even acrobatics. Tired of the burden of household management, Sasha has come to Frankfort for a respite from her duties as wife and mother.

Petruska's reasons for the journey run much deeper. An astronomer at the Academy in Moscow, Petruska is seeking some sort of therapy, some modality, to help her regather the fragments of her soul from the pain of times she cannot even remember. She feels desperate, for just being in a body has itself been difficult. Over the years, she has sought healing through various medications and therapies, including hypnosis. Yet still she lives without foundation, as though falling from a great height to a limitless abyss. Even as a child, her relationships were tumultuous. She was constantly battling an older sister, then picking on her younger brother in revenge. Always she felt attacked, unloved, undernourished. So she began to find ways to sap the energy of others. As a young woman, she would seduce men, and then become hurt and angry when she realized they did not love her. Like so many women, she sought to please, only to feel victimized at giving away her power. She once desperately resorted to some psychedelics acquired through the black market, but they only intensified her madness.

For the past eight years, Petruska has taken to wearing drab army surplus clothes and strutting around the observatory with a chip on her shoulder. One of only a few women among the astronomers there, she refuses to perform the menial tasks expected by her male counterparts, and, being quick with aggressive retorts, she is frequently baited into arguments. Although she has an excellent mind for science, to the extent that some of her male colleagues feel threatened by her diligent observations, her brilliance in the laboratory is overshadowed by emotional outbursts that have led to her being called "the mad Petruska" behind her back.

Now, Petruska's condition has deteriorated to the point that she has become obsessed with ideas of suicide. Frequently dreaming of falling, drowning, or being shattered into a thousand pieces, she awakes in the night, crying uncontrollably, her mind an embittered prison of denial and self-hatred that she seeks to evade by taking revenge on someone, anyone. Desolate and depressed, she feels that she is dying, but that she hasn't yet lived. Having grown so irritable and lonely, Petruska was at first relieved that dependable Sasha would accompany her to Germany. But, now, in Frankfort, as Sasha assists her in her search for therapy and looks out for her general needs, Petruska grows resentful.

Late one morning, as Sasha is being especially solicitous during a walk in a park, Petruska blurts out, "Don't mother me! You are so self-satisfied, but what have you done with your life? You can't help me, anyway. No one can."

Sasha looks compassionately into Petruska's bloodshot eyes and says simply, "You will be all right." After a while she suggests, "Let's have lunch. Then, if you wish, we can go our separate ways." Defensively, Petruska nods in agreement.

The restaurant is crowded due to the lunchtime rush, and Sasha decides to peruse a newspaper while they wait for a table. As though deaf to her sister's complaints about meddling, she exclaims, "Look Petruska! This might be an opportunity for you."

"What is it now?"

"An ad. It says, 'Find your own soul. Experience your previous lives through a unique immortality chamber. Call for appointment.'"

Petruska is surprised at the hope she feels upon hearing of the chamber. "If only I could find my own soul. But immortality? To live forever? No. Not like this." Her red hair shoots out wildly, framing the tight features of her face. She suddenly stands up and tells Sasha that she is going to go and call the number in the ad. When she returns a short while later, she announces, "I have an appointment in thirty minutes."

"Do you want me to go with you to see what it involves?"

Petruska's lower lip quivers: "No, I'll go alone."

"Should I wait there for you?"

"No, I must do this alone."

Petruska enters Channon's rented office with both hope and trepidation, her fiery red bundle of hair belying her quivering lips and the thick wall over her heart. She does not know that Horst is sitting in the next room, where he can observe how the machine amazingly transforms electrical impulses of the subject's brain into past-life images that are projected onto a screen.

Channon sees the curtain drawn over her soul, but his soothing manner invites her confidence and trust. He speaks briefly of his own background, then comes directly to the point. "What is it that you want most?"

"I want to find my soul. That's what the ad said I could do. But I'm afraid."

"Don't be afraid. Nothing can harm you. This experience enables you to go back into time and dissolve your fears."

"Back into time?"

"Yes. All you need to do is breathe, relax, and focus on the light inside your head. All the rest will be done for you."

"I'm afraid of something. I don't know what."

"Is your greatest desire really to find your soul?"

"Yes." Petruska nods affirmatively.

"Good. You have a great opportunity to do so. But before you do, we ask that you sign a release form in which you agree to take complete responsibility for whatever results occur."

"Is there danger?"

"It is highly unlikely."

Before she enters the chamber, Petruska prays for protection from harm and for rebirth into a new life.

As Petruska lies within the chamber, the initial emergence of her unconscious floods her with terror until Channon is finally able to attune more deeply to her soul and find the code of her ancient name. The numerical sequence of this ancient name resonates with a vibration of her original purpose as a monadic spirit.

Suddenly, Petruska finds herself standing before a mirror in which countless lives pass before her soul's reflective eye. As though dreaming, she beholds hundreds of incarnations, their failures and triumphs, and the nourishing grace of communing with the stars. Always, the stars save her from oblivion. Wandering through dreams and nightmares, she feels submerged in endless waters of time and space.

The slightest thought takes her anywhere. She drifts into a life as an Indian child who wanders from tipi to tipi, comforted by the loving acceptance of everyone she encounters. She offers a piece of turquoise to an old woman, and, as the shriveled brown hand closes over the stone, asks her to be her mother.

However, an angel appears and says, "Be awake and aware. The flame of your tongue is tied up in your heart."

Now Petruska is aflame, recoiling in agony as she inhales the stench of her own seared flesh. She is being burned at the stake as a witch, and her soul reflects the fear that shapes her destiny.

In her hand is a dead man's liver, which she has sprinkled with herbs to weave black magic against a woman who has stolen her lover. Her heart remains hard and sealed against the love it longs for. The sand at her feet soaks up the blood of her victims and turns into a coat of bitter charms.

Again the angel appears: "You cannot yet hear your soul. Look deeper. Stare into the eyes of your demons."

Petruska almost lapses into total unconsciousness, but the chamber keeps her attuned to the track of her past, coiled within the labyrinths of her closed heart. Finding herself face to face with a priestess whom she envies, she demands, "You must give me the keys to the temple so that I may know the secrets. If you are my friend, you will do this. I will have this knowledge or I shall kill myself." She immediately transforms into a wild animal, gnashing its blood-red teeth and clawing its victim.

Although still immersed in her own self-hatred, Petruska is lifted upon the wings of the angel. But the strings of confusion only grow tighter around her heart.

The angel disappears without warning, just as it appeared. Petruska withdraws into a embryo that whirls into nothingness. Back, ever back, her soul falls—now to an incarnation in Egypt during the reign of Amenhotep III. Again she falls into envy and competition, this time for her older sister who has already been initiated as a priestess. Petruska is obsessed with obtaining the same status.

She has studied hard and memorized much—the glyphs of the stars, the secret names of the gods, the meaning of the sacred symbols. But when the high priest finally questions her, he grows impatient in spite of her quick responses: "Your words are right. But you only know the language, not the meaning. Though the gods are speaking to you, you do not listen. Your place is not here, for you are not open to the movement of the gods through your heart."

Petruska's soul is desperate. She cries aloud, "There is no other place to go. I will try harder."

The high priest pauses, then continues: "To enter the chamber is to risk your life. If you cannot hear the gods, you will be mortified. Knowing the language is not enough. I cannot permit you to enter the chamber."

"But I am determined."

"Have you ever felt awe in the face of anything?"

She feels the fear in her soul. She gazes up at the expansive stone ceiling, where five-pointed stars have been painted to form the body of Nut: "The stars. I am in awe of the stars. I want to be their priestess."

The high priest seems moved and finally relents: "You may enter the chamber if you are willing to assume complete responsibility for your life. You know that I, realizing the state of your soul, cannot recommend it." Petruska twists and turns, feeling abandoned yet again. She feels she is falling, but her fear of the abyss shakes her into acquiescence, and she agrees.

As she enters the cold stone chamber, a thick darkness closes in upon her. Time expands into eternity, and her soul again spins back, back. She tries to remember the spell that will call forth the gods, but she is frozen with terror as she confronts once more her demons and shadows, her desires and projections. She transforms into each one, painfully metamorphosing into what she most hates. Only the stars offer her hope. The very cells of her etheric body stretch toward their light. Reaching for the light, longing for the source while being weighed down by the horror of her past emotional reactivity, her soul shatters into pieces and disperses into the darkness.

Having always feared death, Petruska now longs for it. She blames the priest. She blames her sister. And, tragically, she blames the stars as she plummets toward the abyss in abandonment of her own soul.

Seeing Petruska's plunge into nothingness, Channon punches in the numerical rescue code. Beads of crystal dew form inside her cells as she is flooded with light. Her mind is consumed in fire and her soul infused with blood. For a fleeting second, she beholds her face in the mirror of her soul, then returns to an awareness of the senses, her body tingling. She is still dizzy as Channon assists her from the chamber into a chair.

Petruska sits down just as Horst, who has witnessed the entire journey on the screen in the next room, enters. She immediately sees in his face the face of Manesis, who permitted her entrance into the Egyptian chamber. Before Channon can introduce them, she screams, "Give me my name! You took my soul, and I have wandered lost for thousands of years because of you!" She tries to stand up and strike Horst but stumbles in total exhaustion.

Horst feels no sympathy, only rage and hatred, for like attracts like. Because Petruska died in the chamber thousands of years ago, when the gods could not enter her impenetrable heart, he was subsequently expelled from the priesthood. Horst's soul, too, has been wandering lost ever since.

THE SEPARATION
OF DEBRIS AND VALUES

Shadows
White of black within black

The denial
of pain and guilt
smolders
beneath the dark surface.

The Creatrix beholds the many faces of the souls that turn and return with distorted disguises, like ghoulish larvae devouring everything in their path. Eaters of time, they are fueled by desire until they are lost in the smoke of a dying fire, suffocating from the stench of their own decay. The red fire smolders in darkness and rises as pain, veiling the souls from the vibrating sphere of their spirit.

The Creatrix holds the golden thread of love taut within her spine so that souls will feel the strength of their own inner beauty. Her backbone runs through each one as a ribbon of celestial essence, standing to be strung with beads of glory. However, few can feel this alignment within themselves. Even she begins to wonder if the Creator has bestowed free will in vain.

Allen and Martha

The incessant smoke coils upward from the burning city dump, choking even the coyotes trapped in the back yards of the suburbs of Vicksburg. Amid the pervasive stench of garbage and debris, Allen

113

directs Bill to a mound of unwanted scrap. "You can unload the metal here and the other stuff over there," he says as he points to another mound of drywall scraps, insulation, newspapers, and Christmas wrapping.

Bill, an archaeology student working at the national park, stares in amazement at the bulldozer plowing through the wreckage. His thoughts bear the scars of a quester of the past, for he cannot help but think of the buried cultures of Zimbabwe, Angkor, Tiahuanaco, and others. He wonders if future archaeologists will know the difference between the dumps and the cities of current times. What will they make of the twisted metal and steel, the broken glass, the piles of electronic gadgetry? *Few treasures, little artistry, in these graves!* he thinks, posing his own judgment upon a civilization of mislaid values.

Bill flings his bent aluminum saucepans and broken radio onto the heap of metal, then coughs from the fire vapors suddenly blowing into his face. As he moves to unload his garbage, he passes Allen once again: "Quite a job you have! Grand Central Station, eh?"

Allen squints and responds, "Eventually every form of matter comes through here. This is the ultimate exchange station. But more and more of this stuff doesn't decay, and it's piling up. That's our problem, these plastics."

Bill verbalizes some of his recent thoughts: "Have you ever wondered what people in the future will think of us?"

"Nope. But I see what you mean. Our junk tells the truth. Sort of like why a doctor inspects a stool. Our ways have their diseases, I guess."

"Do you think plastic is a disease?"

"Well, it grows like a tumor, but it doesn't break down. I understand they are starting to reclaim it and use it again, but there aren't very many recycling plants. Too expensive."

Bill nods and gets into his car. As he drives away, he takes a last look at the gulls swirling over the debris. Even back in city traffic, he continues to silently reflect. *Trees, flesh, even bones will rot, but synthetics proliferate like a cancer. Do we embrace synthetics out of our fear of death? Future archaeologists may wonder, 'What ignorant terrors led the people of the late twentieth century to live in cubicles? The remnants of their computer programs show them to be imprisoned by linear logic. Their microscopes and telescopes merely extended their senses, which were trapped in the illusion of an objective world.'*

Day after day, month after month, Allen's body grows more toxic from the constant ingestion of fumes. "Everything dies," he muses, "except the dead." Gazing into an old cracked mirror that shows his weary, red-faced reflection, he feels the chaos in his soul and wonders, "Am I going to die here?" He lives only for his day off, when he can hunt in the wilds.

Leaving the dump later that afternoon, Allen watches a snake slither out of a bottle at his feet. He realizes that he feels like the snake, coiled in a glass world seeking escape, writhing and slithering in smoke and dust until he grows old.

Allen is barely in the door of his suburban home before he flops into a shabby overstuffed chair and shouts to Martha, "Get me a beer! You ain't been doing nothing all day." Little Melissa shrinks back from her father and runs to her room, but fifteen-year-old Pete stands and stares. Summoning the courage from his gut, Pete cries, "Don't yell at Mom! She's been working here at home all day!"

Like the snake he has just seen, Allen uncoils and whacks Pete across the face. Martha tries to tend to her son's bleeding cheek, but he says, "I'm okay, Mom." He backs away proudly.

The pain in Martha's face follows the lines already worn there from years of anxiety. She bolts from the house and runs, sobbing heavily, toward the nearby Mississippi River. Her mind whirls with images of her children, who live with an abusive father and a fearful mother, and of Allen, who at once attracts her and repulses her.

Martha reaches the river just as darkness begins to hover in the reddening sky. Her eyes redden, too, with the deep dark of helplessness, as her tears merge with the waves at the river's edge. She takes off her shoes to wade in the mud. She breathes and breathes, yielding to dread, gulping for hope, unconsciously seeking to transform the fire of hurt and anger into the fire of light.

Lifetimes of repression flow out with her tears. Denial spills out on the ground of her heart; the blood of her children seeps through her skin. The blood of Allen runs with her own, weaving a braid, stirring a languid strength deep within her as she trudges on.

She tries to blot out the excruciating pain as hatred rises within her. Like a wailing Isis looking for the scattered members of her beloved Osiris, Martha recoils from the hot wind as the Sun descends toward the horizon. She throws a stone at a hungry black cat, meowing in need. Crows fly overhead, mocking her with their caws. The wind wails through hovering storm clouds. The gnarled shapes of dead trees cast elongated, reptilian shadows that seem to emerge as a voice within her. *I am the black Earth, the blood of suffering that will lead you to your soul. Do not deny me, or your family's own flesh will burn within you.*

The terror of the heat of transformation drives the darkness deeper within her. She responds by turning away from the dying Sun, the river, and the shadows as the clouds finally burst open with the large raindrops of a summer storm. Hurrying now to find her shoes, she falls face down in the mud. She cries without hope, assaulted suddenly by the child-hood memory of being harshly punished by her father for playing in the mud. Ever since, she has framed her life with the guilt and fear instilled by her ancestors. Feeling her very soul to be dying, Martha gives in to the dark whirling dread.

Only the rotten odor of the marsh brings her back to full conscious-ness. It passes over her and cleanses her, permitting the denied shadows of her soul to loom clearly. And with that clarity comes the rising power of her own anger—anger at Allen, anger at her father, anger that explodes into rage at generations of tyranny and repression.

The pressure of her repressed emotions seethes like billowing gases inside a bottle and builds to an intense scream, like a blown cork. She screams from the depths of her soul.

When the inner pressure is released, she begins to see, in the shad-ows of her own soul, the root of her denial. *I have allowed it. My hurt, anger, and rage are no one's fault but my own. My parents passed it on to me and I do not want to pass it on to Melissa and Pete. How can I change this vicious cycle?*

Filled with new awareness and determination, Martha knows she is ready to stand up to Allen, to insist upon a different relationship with the children and herself. The storm is over. The brilliant orb of the western Sun gradually expands, dispelling all fear with the dark clouds. Her solar plexus vibrates with waves of white fire, reflected in the final glow of the Sun as it sinks beyond the river's far shore. Walking in silence along its banks, she hears a song arising within her:

Antagonist's Song of the River

I am the center of love and love-absorbing desire.
Look for me in the billowing clouds that cover the Sun.
I am the storm of rampant desires seeking fulfillment.
I am the estranged lover who longs for reunion.
Look for me in frustration, blame, and anger.
I am the lifetimes of longing for the twin of your soul.
I am the angelic and daemonic powers in conflict.
I am the soul projection to the outer world.
Look for me in the shadows of all things.
I am the splitting of the male and female powers.
Look for me in sexual and emotional tension.
You can find me in every expectation and demand.
I am the darkness of the river where storm clouds swarm.
I sink as mud to the bottom and rise as mist.
You can find me in the rain, sleet, hail, and wind of storms.
I am the primal emotional body.

Are you repressed creativity?
I am the stimulus to discovering it.

THE PRIMAL PAIR

The astral shadows of potential life float in the River as chemical froth, stewing eros into a translucent jelly. Beholding forms of things to come, the Creatrix bestows the sheaths of the protoplasmic flux with her ancestral language of wisdom. Knowing the soul cannot incarnate itself, she channels its desires through the Primal Waters to create the diaphanous human body.

The human image still sleeps in hermaphroditic form, a blueprint drawn from the First World, where the Creator and Creatrix entwined in tender love. Using symbols that mirror the Tree of Life in her spine, the Creatrix shapes the human body through the concatenation of the genetic code. The ancient cellular language recapitulates the spiritual inception of the cosmos and later speaks on Earth through the Archeozoic anaerobic forms, the Proterozoic algae, the Paleozoic fish and plants, and the Mesozoic mammals. Each of these evolutionary phases is stored in the brain of the emerging human.

The Tree of Life pulses with the potential of existence rising to meet the descending essences of the River. Cascading etheric liquids merge with upward-swimming stardust, magma, bacteria, and plants to form a single confluence of the Tree's vital sap. Each being is a silent effigy until her breath infuses it with the power of life and consciousness.

With form-giving vibrations warbling through her lips, the Creatrix shapes the organs of body systems, her song reverberating through astral Dreamtime. She pronounces the stars, the sounds, and time itself through the human image before waking it from its dream in the paradisiacal waters. The cosmic tones lie sealed in the human brain, to be unsealed only by human speech.

As the desire of the soul is driven deeper into form, the Creatrix divides the hermaphrodites with her song. She bestows the gifts of sexual passion upon every man and woman, that they might satisfy their longing for one another through the intensity of the life force. Labyrinthine patterns of love, desire, projection, and shadows now permeate their unconscious memory. She completes her chant with a secret name for every part of the human form, imbuing its consciousness with dimensions forbidden to the emerging plant and animal.

THE LABOR CAMP

Human Image
Gold of red within black

The passion
of the hermaphrodite
is divided
into male and female.

Wickvaya

Wickvaya longs to return to Nesaru and his family. A Hopi shaman, he is incarcerated as a political prisoner in a federal labor camp for refusing to join the military during the Korean war. When presented with a draft notice by an Indian agent, Wickvaya had said only, "I have renounced weapons under the guidance of the Great Spirit. I refuse to join the army."

Federal agents consequently took Wickvaya to Oraibi, where he was given a few crackers and a Coke for his dinner. Initially, he felt confused as to who he was and where his power lay. He thought people were put in prison for murder, not for refusing to murder. On the following day, he was taken to a nearby town where he was presented with conscription papers and told, "If you sign here you won't have go to prison. You can go to war instead."

Wickvaya remained calm, the flowing Sun in his heart rising to meet this cruel barb. Directing his clear black eyes at the agent, he said, "It is for my people that I will not sign. I will fight no human being."

He refused to enter the white man's mirage of targeted enemies. In a powerful visualization that lasted only a moment, he saw the corpses of a thousand battles splattered across the pages of history. With that single glimpse of reality, Wickvaya's convictions solidified to expose the pathological tide of war. His objection brought the shadows of Napoleons and Hitlers out of their graves.

Wickvaya suffered deeply as he was taken from his land and family, but he chose to stand firm in his decision not to fight. He had already accepted the unacceptable and was used to the deceit and hostility of the white man's government, which made promises with no intention of keeping them. He knew that the white invaders, with their technology and illusion of progress, did not comprehend the mysteries of the Hopi's nine rites of life.

When Wickvaya was finally tried before a judge, he stated only, "I have committed no crime. I refuse to kill, for my beliefs do not allow it." He was found guilty and sentenced to four years of hard labor. As with so many other conscientious objectors, his spiritual ways were not recognized as a viable religion.

During his time in the labor camp, Wickvaya continues to reflect deeply on his purpose. He finds support in the friendship of four other Hopi men, among them Hano and Seno. One evening, after they have been in the camp for about two years, he gathers his four friends together. He begins by saying, "We must remember the Road of Life, even though we are herded like cattle and trapped between this terrible existence and the guns of the white man's enemies. Even though there is no name in the present world for the great wheel of life by which we used to live, the spirits of the corn, the talking stones, and the deer horn are very much alive. The stars know our sacred language—Wuwuchim, Owaqlt, Soyal, Lakon, Powamu. We must labor in the spirit of digging a kiva, a kiva large enough to include the white man. We still have our tools of power—our sticks and pollen and eagle feathers."

"You are mad, Wickvaya. White men will never understand our way. Their faces are double," responds Hano, who feels angry and helpless.

But Wickvaya is determined: "I do not want to make enemies within me. I suffered from hatred as a youth. I fought at every provocation. The bitterness consumed me until I prayed to Masaw, the guardian of the spirit land. He helped me to realize the deeper meaning of the male-female *paho*, or prayer feather. Nesaru also helped me to understand. I sion was a weakness, a perversion of our natural instincts as creatures. The whites have never learned how to make the male-female *paho*."

Seno reflects, "It is true that they do not realize that their enemies will be reborn among their own people until they are healed. But how can the *paho* cure them, Wickvaya? How can you expect the white man to perform our rituals? Our sticks and feathers are useless trinkets to them. That is why they permit us to have them."

Wickvaya is silent for a long time. "They will not perform our rituals. But perhaps there is another way they can realize the meaning in them. My grandfather told me that the male-female *paho* lives in every person's cells. If either the male or female part loses its identity, it seeks to find it through domination. War is the result of the frustrated primal hunger of man and woman for each other. When men shoot wolves from helicopters and leave their pulsing bodies rotting in the snow, or when they kill buffalo only for their tongues and hides, they are ceremoniously acting out of fear of the female within."

The men listen intently. Finally, Seno speaks: "I see that the male and female *paho* sticks, when separated, cannot receive the nourishment of life. But how will the white man come to accept the woman within him?"

Wickvaya shakes his head. "I do not yet know. You see these prayer feathers, these *pahos* I tie together? The string that binds them is the umbilical cord of life. It is tied to this eagle down to remind us that the breath of life flows through us all. The turquoise blue is our female waters. The corn pollen brings the fertile essences that, even here in prison, connect us to our wives. As you know, the two feathers tied together represent the Creator as both male and female. Fertilization is the gift of life. When we are torn apart, our pain makes us want to fight. Maybe for now it is enough that we try to understand the white man."

Hano, though exhausted, gestures violently: "In this camp we are all men, men of many colors. We are taken from our wives. I am still angry, and I still feel like fighting!"

Wickvaya answers, "Hano, I long for Nesaru as much as you long for Yuki, but here we must remember that our woman is also inside of us. It is only when I feel Nesaru within me that I can overcome my hatred. We must dig in the mines as though digging a kiva in which the white man can awaken to his woman within."

THE ANCESTRAL CHAIN

Genetic Code
Black of red within black

Crystalline formulas
of sentient ancestors
create bodies
through generations.

Galaxies turn in the River, where the yin and yang of female and male polarities meet in a whirlpool of the soul's desire. Every star, contracted into a spiritual soul longing to incarnate, trembles within the swirling water.

Through the rhythmic pulses of her song, the Creatrix translates the longing of desire into the spiral staircase of the genetic code. She selects elements from the periodic pool of possibilities and strings them into myriad forms. The descending stream of the spirit blends with the ascending stream of molecules to spin ribbons bound together with nitrogen.

The Creatrix arranges the simple four-letter alphabet in patterns that spiral up and down her spine. The whirlpool continuously passes through itself, combining sugars and phosphates to form the genetic backbone supported by the sap in the Creatrix's Tree of Life.

Millions of miles of genetic helixes stream forth from the whirlpool. Bound in their intrinsic chemistry is the simple message of the Creator and Creatrix: "Embrace your differences. Love one another." Their tantric union brings spiritual nourishment to the raw organic sequences of matter that are designed to ease the longing of the human soul.

As the double stream of amino acids spins within the cells of the Creatrix, the straight line of proteins, extruded in the outer cosmos, twists and loops back on itself, improvising qualities of potential blood, bone, nerve, and flesh. The Creatrix dances in the moment, orchestrating the metamorphic assembly of the human body as both an anticipation and a recapitulation of innumerable forms of life. The blueprint of the human body evolves in embryonic form long before the world of organisms begins.

Fariba and Akrisios

Fariba moves slowly through the jetway at Heathrow airport in London. She is still deeply disturbed, for the pain of her misunderstanding with Channon pulses in her blood. Worn down from sleepless nights, her body is both a vortex of frustrated desire and a stream of radiant love. Yet she is strong enough to face the changing reality of their relationship.

Fariba's heart expands when she sees Akrisios at the airline gate. Though usually restrained and conservative, she responds warmly to her friend's embrace. Akrisios immediately sees Fariba's emotional exhaustion. "Come," she offers, "let us get your bags and then drive to Hyde Park. I have a spacious hotel room nearby that we can share."

The ride into London passes quickly, for the motorway is lined with jubilant spring flowers. Upon entering the hotel room, Fariba's eyes immediately fall upon a photograph graced by a shaft of sunlight.

"Who is that, might I ask?"

"Maurya, the true love I once savored."

"Is he here in London?"

"No. He was a lover of long ago, but his face still nurtures me when I feel lonely. It has been twelve years since I last saw him, and I no longer know where he is. He has our daughter, Athene, who would be thirteen years old now. I lost contact with them when I was hospitalized. But come, you are tired. Put down your luggage, have a shower, and make yourself at home. I'll put on some water for tea."

"I'm more than tired."

After refreshing herself with a shower, Fariba sits down to tell her story. Akrisios listens with silent compassion and says only, "Your love will see you through, no matter what happens."

Fariba then continues: "I feel you have been through so much, Akrisios. You embrace me with the enormity of your love and the wisdom of countless lives. I feel comforted and understood when in your presence. But tell me, in all these years we have known each other, I never knew you had a child. Why did you not keep her?"

"Athene was taken from me when she was scarcely a year old. I was an addicted romantic, driven to drink. You knew I was an alcoholic, didn't you? Maurya was a proud Indian prince, so her blood is both Indian and Greek."

"Tell me of your love for him. How did the madness begin? Your story might help me now, in my sorrow."

Akrisios, who can never sit still for very long, shifts her large body and responds, "Let us go out to the garden. Few people are there in the afternoon." She leaps up and offers her hand to Fariba.

While they rush down and out to the garden, Akrisios warms up to telling her story: "Twelve years ago, when I was in the hospital, I once fell when trying to get out of bed. A nurse rushed over and tied me down. There I was, bound up, tossing and turning from the twisted pain of losing my lover. I would scream madly, and that brought up the memory of another pain—of when, as an infant, I was tied to the bed for crying in rage."

"In rage?"

"My father molested me. The experience of the detox ward brought me back to the pain of being victimized by his lust."

As they approach the enclosed garden, the air around them dances with the light scents of crocuses, violets, and nasturtiums. Their beauty pulls Akrisios to the present, and she says softly, "I used to get drunk on wine. Now flowers are enough to bring me ecstasy."

Fariba sits down on the grass and leans back against a tree. Akrisios stands and continues with her tale, gesturing all the while: "My father was an alcoholic. By the time I was a teenager, I was swearing I would never be like him. But addiction often runs in the family. Or perhaps my own hatred turned me into what I most hated in him."

"How did you manage to overcome your addiction?"

Akrisios holds her hands to her heart: "I felt love would do it. Maurya fulfilled my wildest dreams. He was handsome, clever, and dignified. He was fun and creative! Both my sorrows and defenses dissolved in his presence. I was lost in a sea of rapture and bliss, but I had no anchor within myself. I gave all of myself to him, until I hit a wall of darkness."

"What happened?"

"Shortly after Athene was born, he fell in love with an American woman. I found myself hating her, wanting to kill her. I tried to drown all my sorrow and agony and jealousy in drink. In my heart, I knew that a more expansive love could overcome this torture, but I was split in two. One half of me longed for our wild, sensuous embraces while the other half was bursting with rage. By the time I got to the detox ward, I was delirious and facing death."

"You were close to death?"

"Drink had drained me of my soul. I faced the emptiness of death, but I had not yet lived. In one of my delirious states, I involuntarily saw into past lives. I saw Maurya, standing erect like a guard, staring straight at me, his temples pulsing. At the executioner's command, he lifted his gun and pointed it at my bound body.

"I realized that through many lives I had been subject to him, sometimes a bloody victim. My soul dreamed of bliss but was drummed into hell. Then, all at once, I saw. I realized that *I* was doing this to myself, that *I* allowed it, that something in *me* made me afraid to live my own life. I lived first through my lover, then alcohol. The shadows that had obscured my soul finally seized my body."

"But how did you ever find the strength to create a new life?"

"I had no choice. I was at a crossroads. Either I would carry on the addiction of my family and destroy myself, or I would create a new life out of the threads of my heritage. I joined Alcoholics Anonymous, which proved to be very supportive. Soon after I made a commitment to recovery, I found that I could accept my father and my lover for who they were. I realized that they, too, had stood at the same crossroads. But I chose a different path, for I was determined to live my own life."

THE CREATURES WITHIN US

Body Systems
Red of red within black

Organs
of specific function
respond
through instinct.

Over vast aeons, the Creatrix prepares the human body to animate and ground the human soul, spreading mortality from realm to realm. Like Chinese boxes, one within another, the forms of the mitochondria, ribosomes, and nuclei are integrated into cells, the cells into tissues, the tissues into organs, the organs into the body. She fills the torso with wings of birds and the abdomen with guts of snakes. She folds the River's ascending stream of protoplasm into the secret recesses of the body. Heart, intestines, lungs, brains, and genitals all pulsate with the forms of the primordial creatures within them. Downstream, the Sun of awareness fades into the cool minds of nature spirits. Upstream, it shines between the eyebrows of the gods and goddesses.

The Creatrix gathers the two streams and shapes the human body system from the embryonic currents of the River within her. Etheric egrets wade and fish swim as the River rises over the forests. The secret names of the animals hide in the vibrations of the human body.

Looking into the darkness of herself, the Creatrix pulls forth the mirror of still waters and places it on the back of the human head. The brain is filled with the script of the River, the hidden language of the mystery.

The Creatrix rises from the River, and, with a single stretch of her spine, pours creatures from the Primal Waters into the human nervous system. Clusters of neurons suspend in its net, like stars forming flowers on the spinal limbs of the Tree of Life. She utters words of power into the ganglionic centers, where the dreaming human image lies awaiting consciousness.

As the surging light breaks over the horizon, mind enters into all of life. Creatures awaken slowly within the body. Receiving the images of the descending stream, the awakening serpent spews them back in his ancient tongue and rises through the brows of happily mating males and females.

The Creatrix stretches the nervous fabric so that the senses may discern between inner and outer. They emerge as volatile responses to light, sound, smell, and touch in the changing River.

She forms the eye as a mirror, reversing the outward light of the stars into the images of the spirit.

From an eddy in the River, she creates the human ear, its soft spiral membranes reverberating with the potential songs of birds, the calls of whales, the hum of bees.

Through the solar blood of angels and the celestial fire of her heart, the Creatrix infuses the body with veins, arteries, and capillaries. The primeval heart enfolds the brain and nerves like a holy crown until, feeling the compassion needed for the downward stream of the River, it submerges in its own blood and beats steadily, with involuntary devotion, from below.

The consecration of a thousand sylphs, the human lungs receive air and fold it back in resonant chambers of inspiration.

From tubes of protoplasm, the Creatrix shapes the human guts that will absorb and transmute cellular waste. With deep groans she releases the magic of growth into decay. Matter is prefigured in the sparks of stars and the feces of mortal creatures within her.

Now the Creatrix feels the separation from the Creator as a perfumed opening to her lotus love of creation. The humming harps of heaven meld into watery words where tongues lick the mouths of caves. The mating of fish, birds, and reptiles brings the chain of reproduction inside vegetal walls, where the fiery memory of the struggles of sex and hunger persist in the sensitive wounds of penis and vagina.

The Creatrix directs the animals to act and mutate, but not to choose their fate. As programmed forms, they innocently enact the divine plan through the instinctual urge. She channels their wild cacophonous cries into recognizable hisses, cackles, roars, and growls. Anonymously, they speak through the human. It is for the human to see their divine interrelationship and to speak for them.

In the new mythic universe, humans seek through gesture and sound to return to the original fount of the River. With gratitude, they call back the source.

However, bestowed with free choice, humans fall into confusion. Aggression separates the centers inside the body. It twists their connection to the creatures of the Earth. Still, the shadowy spirit of the wild cries out through the body: "We are your instinctual nature. Do not deny us. We are the cry of the raven, lion, and dolphin longing to express your soul. You are filled with earthly eros. To harm our body is to deny your own. Our suffering is real; yours is an illusion. We live in the libido of life, you in the separation of body from soul. Your mutilation of animals, your killing and torture, your rape and pornography, all spring from denial of your desire and your body. To reject the primal act is to scatter the members of your family over the face of the Earth. Help us to be whole in the web of life, and you will be whole also."

Gus and Anita

For several months, Gus has been performing experiments with animals in his research lab at the University of California, Berkeley. Since he himself suffers from skin disease and ulcers, Gus has a vested interest in further understanding the role of stress in such bodily reactions. He subjects hundreds of dogs to stress and demonstrates only that their gastric secretions increase. Not one dog develops an ulcer.

Gus decides to extend the experiment to monkeys, whose physiology is closer to that of humans. He restrains the monkeys at their necks and hips so only their heads and limbs can move. He sets up one test in which a monkey receives a shock on the feet unless it presses a lever within thirty seconds. The monkey is subjected to this for six straight hours, then allowed to rest for six hours. This experiment continues on and off for three weeks, during which time Gus returns to the lab every six hours. In response to the test, the monkey presses the lever every fifteen to twenty seconds. After three weeks, the monkey contracts ulcers.

Gus wants to see whether the ulcers developed from the effect of the physical shocks themselves or from the emotional stress produced in anticipating the shock. He uses another monkey as a control. This monkey is given a dummy lever. After a few days, the control monkey loses interest in the lever. However, it still gets shocked whenever the experimental monkey fails to prevent his own shock. After three weeks, the experimental monkey, who has to press the levers to prevent shock, develops ulcers and dies. Finally, Gus schedules a group of monkeys to receive a shock every few seconds, with rest periods of only thirty minutes. After three weeks, all of the monkeys in this experiment die.

Gus enters Anita's apartment feeling depressed, despite the clear results of his tests. He is dissociated from himself, and from his body, and he doesn't even know it. Later on, after dinner, he sits at the table, holding his head between his hands and moaning. When Anita parodies his groan, he looks at her and complains, "It's not funny, Anita. Here I am suffering from headaches and ulcers, and all you do is make fun."

She laughs aloud, throwing back her dark hair: "If you could laugh at yourself, perhaps you would begin to heal some of your pain. Don't you see? You are tearing yourself apart. I'd like to help you, but you must first help yourself."

Gus has heard enough and bolts out the door in a rage. He is so angry that he trips running down the stairs, striking his head on the concrete floor below. When he tries to get up, faintness overwhelms him, and he collapses.

Eventually, he becomes aware of Anita holding and stroking his head. He looks up into her eyes and sees something he has not been able to see before, something tender and nurturing, something that begins to change him. Helpless, his soul momentarily walks in truth: "Anita, I don't know love. I don't know how to give it or how to receive it. I'm successful in my work, but I'm miserable. I feel like I'm in hell."

Anita briefly caresses his face and chest, then helps him back into the apartment. Once Gus is asleep, she calls Beverly, a friend who works with healing: "I'm afraid he may have a concussion. Do you know what the signs are? Should I call an ambulance?"

"Just let him be for now. I'll come right over."

As Gus sleeps, he dreams he is a military man, madly in love with a woman who looks very much like Anita. He idolizes her. Ecstatically in love, they fly together above the Earth. Suddenly, his father's face appears. With trepidation, Gus asks for his father's blessings upon the upcoming marriage. No sooner is the blessing granted than his father's body transforms into the hairy body of a monkey. He *is* a monkey, screaming aloud from excruciating pain. Gus begins to scream himself and then abruptly wakes up.

His head throbs with pain, both inside and outside. When he becomes conscious enough to realize that Beverly is checking his pulse, he screams, "Get her out of here!"

Having looked Gus over to her satisfaction, Beverly gets up to leave. She tells Anita, who accompanies her to the door, "Keep him warm and still. He will be all right. I don't see any signs of concussion. The biggest bruise is to his ego."

Gus looks up at Anita as she returns to his bedside. Again, he feels a tenderness in her that helps him to relax. He speaks in a barely audible whisper: "I had a dream. You and I were intending to be married, but when I asked my father for his blessing, he turned into a monkey. He was screaming in agony."

"Do your monkeys at the lab scream?"

"No."

"No? Are they too afraid to scream?"

"Maybe. They are preoccupied with avoiding pain."

"What pain in you is not getting to scream?"

After a long silence, Gus answers softly, "The pain of longing for you."

During the three days that Gus remains at Anita's, she rarely leaves his side. One night he awakes feeling aroused and reaches over to fondle Anita's breast. He then draws her to his body and presses his hand between her legs. Anita, startled and sleepy, resists. But Gus feels only the surge of power that seems to overcome his divided body and soul, and he gives in to it completely. He takes her and thrusts his penis into her.

He falls deeper into eros, lunging over and over, trying to release his lifelong resentment and rage into Anita's womb. She cries and pleads for him to stop, but he ignores her, pushing on in a wild sexual rampage. Using every ounce of strength, she manages to briefly pull herself away, but he grabs her leg and forces her to her knees on the floor. Then, in a siege of bestial madness, he penetrates her from behind. She continues to scream and struggle, which only deepens his rage, and he strikes her full force across the side of her head. She falls limp.

The sight of Anita lying still, with blood oozing from behind her ear, pulls Gus into full awareness of what he has just done. He bends over and vomits, his gut twisting with her love and his hate. Terrorized, he staggers out into the street and runs into the black night, the screams of Anita and a hundred monkeys rampaging through his brain.

DOUBLE IMPRISONMENT

Intensity
White of red within black

Vital energy
of male and female bodies
creates
tension.

Intensity is driven into the body through the intermingling of logos and eros, remembered as an exalted and ecstatic harmony before the priests grew afraid of the Primal Waters. As a subtle life force, intensity enlivens the body and is felt in the feedback of pain and pleasure. When eros and logos momentarily fuse within the human spine, the perennial culture becomes a living stream of wisdom from the First World and flows directly into the human body. The scintillating beauty of the interpenetration of chaos and cosmos in the body brings the greatest vital experience.

However, when either eros or logos dominates, the intensity of pain wracks the body. For then the River cannot pass through the subtle plexuses and mix the cosmic and human energies together. The script of the River is then forgotten. If the eros channel is too passionately wild and driven by fecundity in fear of the logos, desire draws intensity into time toward death. And when the logos channel is too transcendent, the human image becomes a lifeless phantom.

The mystery of language is hidden in the body as it is in all things. Sudden metaphors between the worlds startle those with balanced channels as the burning waters surge through their spines, changing enigmas into panoramas that only an awakened imagination can behold.

Gus, Pahulu, and Tawhiri

Convicted of rape and assault, Gus lies in his cell at San Quentin feeling the painful confinement of his body. Most of all, he feels the agony of having viciously abused a woman whom he had begun to love. He knows what he has done, but he is only beginning to realize how inhuman he was long before he almost killed Anita.

Even sleep brings no escape—only the tirade of unbearable dreams and hallucinations. His mind is crowded with images of gesticulating bodies and the screaming faces of monkeys. Black mouths open with red gums and white teeth to devour him. He is dying in the pulp of his own grinding existence, the shadows of his past clinging to him like feces. He hallucinates that the hairs on his arm are ape's fur.

Now he lives as less than an animal, less than the animals he victimized. He struggles to accept failure, to accept that he has been reduced to a living mass of pain because of having inflicted it. His body stings with the shattered memory of the one true moment when, knowing he was helpless, he opened to Anita's love. He tries to find his way back through pain to discover the aboriginal justice that brought it about. The brute facts of his existence are not his own doing, he thinks, for he did not make himself willingly, and, once born, what else could he have done?

The voice of death steals into his dream and says, *I am the stream of matter pressing you into existence. What desire do you shape me with? Your desires are your own.*

He remembers his lust for scores of women whose names he has forgotten. But when he thinks of Anita, his heart is stirred, and he mutters to the phantom, *I loved Anita. All my life I have sabotaged or destroyed what I most valued. Why?*

Death offers no response but instantly transforms into his father. Gus, startled, shouts, *You alcoholic asshole! You started it. I'm not a drunk, but I might as well be. I'm still torn by your tyranny. I never asked anything of you, so why are you here now?*

The spirit of his father answers, *I am weary of existence. Now I am in the secret service. But I want you to see me for who I am before you die.*

There is a disease in the family. Here, beyond death, I can see what I was. I am truly sorry. Now I strain against annihilation. I have faced death, but I am still bound to my past.

His father's face again becomes hairy as it transforms into a dwarf, then an ape, then a monkey tormenting Gus with high-pitched chatter. In the monkey's prattle he hears his mother, whose tongue wagged constantly to cover up the loveless disease of her family. He sees his mother, martyred and repressed, babbling with the neighbors to vent her frustration and to cover up the hollowness of her soul.

Gus partially awakens to the memory of himself as a child, empty and unloved, yet with vital energy throbbing in his young body. In a rage, he takes off his belt and whips the trees and bushes. He sees his mother's face of false smiles, a lid to a caldron of shadows. She is erratic, sometimes speaking harsh words, at other times talking glibly. All the while his father continues to abuse them both. Deprived of the love he so needs, he turns in anger on playmates and animals. His memories flow on to when, as a teenager, he gets both recognition and the pleasure of destruction by dissecting frogs in a biology lab and so is encouraged to channel his addictions in the acceptable direction of science. Arrogantly denying his need for love, he feels superior to and remains aloof from alcoholics among his peers.

Gus falls back into unconsciousness. He dreams he is with a prostitute who will do anything he wants. A misshapen dwarf appears between them and lunges at him. They struggle until the dwarf, as strong as five men, reveals a hatchet in his hand, with which he slits the prostitute's head and then slaughters her like a cow. Gus is nauseated by the sight of her severed flesh, but the dwarf stares hatefully and commands him to eat it.

The shock of the image stirs Gus to consciousness. Truth lies within him. He knows he is a prisoner of his own pain, and he tries to blot out its intensity by recalling his sexual escapades. But these thoughts only provoke more questions. *What is life about?* he wonders. *Primal throbbings? Sex? I had no joy as a child, so how can I have it now? I feel smothered by my own desires. But I can't live without a lover, without sex. It's the only thing that takes away the pain, even if only for an illusory moment.*

Pahulu stands at the bus stop with her three-year-old son, Tawhiri. She has flown in from Kauai to see Anita, one of her closest friends, who was hospitalized for several days after Gus raped and beat her. Pahulu muses on the past and her own relationship with each of them, for, ironically, it was Anita who had given Pahulu's phone number to Gus when he had visited the islands. Gus had needed love, and Pahulu had given it willingly. Tawhiri was the gift of their union.

Pahulu could not have been more different from Gus. Her scale of intensity had been of another order. Daily, she had been nurtured by her parents, brothers, and sisters. She had lived on the islands in vast waves of rhythms, feeling at one with the stars, the very sea responding to the ebb and flow of the Creatrix's chant within her body. As mutable as the Moon, deep within her she had held the constancy of the deep.

Now, Pahulu loves to travel with Tawhiri and see through his eyes. Born in the salty sea, midwifed by dolphins, he is a carrier of light. He *is* light. Lured by the streams of mystery, he spends his days in playful delight in the sandy deltas. He reaches with tiny fingers toward the Sun and the Moon and pulls down the River's descending stream to nourish his soul. He digs in the sand and offers the treasures of nature's creatures back to the heavens. Pahulu, knowing that the only way to have anything is to pass it on, radiates light to him from the Sun in her heart.

Raised in the gentle atmosphere of Kauai, Tawhiri feels the harshness of the city, with its hard lines of buildings, jutting poles and wires, endless blocks of pavement, and the smell of carbon monoxide. His eyes run and his head hurts. People seem busy, aloof. He senses the stress in the barking dogs and asks, "Why do the dogs bark that way, Mama?"

Pahulu is deep in her own reverie, momentarily struck dumb by her memories of Gus. *Should I visit him? Will it do him any good, or me?* she asks herself. To her, Gus poignantly embodies all the world's sadness. She loved him like a mother loves a needy son.

"Dogs bark like that when they are afraid."

"What are they afraid of?"

For a moment, Pahulu feels caught in the net of her own fear: "Just a ghost. Nothing real. But big people make ghosts real. Then they become afraid. The dogs feel their fear and try to get rid of it by barking."

She drifts back in memory to the time when she surrendered to the waves of the sea to face her truth and was rescued by dolphins. *Again I must surrender, or I, too, will succumb to fear,* she thinks to herself as she takes Tawhiri's hand to board the bus.

She sits down on the bus with Tawhiri and leans back. The memory of the dolphins and the miraculous presence of her son at her side enable her to break through the fear and consume it in the flames of her own courageous heart. She feels the vibrations of the River splash through her crown and descend down her spine to her lotus root. She thinks, *I will see him. Maybe all that has passed between us can be released. May my heart be filled with compassion, and may the gods and goddesses help me to be with him in balance. May Tawhiri touch his life and not be harmed by his glance.* Pahulu's whole being becomes a living prayer that she relate to Gus from her deepest center.

"We're going to see your father."

"My father?" Tawhiri is confused, for Pahulu has never mentioned his father to him. "Where is he, Mama?" Tawhiri becomes restless as he tries to understand what having a daddy means.

Pahulu now feels flooded with purpose. She wants to surround Gus and the entire prison with the living loving waters in which her own life has been immersed. Like a hovering field of flowers, her aura blazes with compassionate intention. Little by little, she begins to see that Gus needs not only nurturing, but respect and love for who he is. Her heart weeps for him. She sees that his crime occurred long before Anita's rape—that it was born out of generational patterns of fear from which only love can deliver him.

When Gus sees Pahulu at the visitor's window, he is both amazed and fearful, for he knows that she and Anita are close friends.

"I didn't mean to do it."

"We came to see you, to tell you that we love you still."

"I don't understand." Gus clutches at his stomach, his thoughts breaking apart like beads of dew on a spider web.

"You're still suffering from ulcers?"

"Worse than ever." Then, noticing Tawhiri's little head beneath the window, he asks, "Who is that?"

"Your son."

Gus is flooded with dizziness and trembling as his entire being undergoes a shift. The pain begins to lift, and a river of sadness bursts through his dam of self-torture, carrying off the lies, the masks, and the hypocrisy. He sits down and cries uncontrollably.

After a few minutes, he collects himself and thinks, *I have lived such a cowardly life.* Aloud, he says to Pahulu, "This is my son?"

Tawhiri tries to feel his daddy in the desperate man before him. Hope now begins to penetrate Gus's body, dislodging the hurt and the hardness forged by his own hatred. He again senses the softness, the vulnerability, he once felt with Anita.

Gus looks diffidently at Pahulu, as if to say, *Is it okay for him to know that his father is a prisoner, a rapist?* Finally he looks directly at Tawhiri and asks, "What is your name?"

"Tawhiri."

"Tawhiri. That's a great name."

Pahulu reads the questions in the pools of Gus's eyes and nods.

"I am your daddy," he says, with a soft, yet radiant smile. The wonder of the perfectly formed human body before him, that of his own son, shreds any lingering misery.

The Song of the River reverberates through the prison walls and out the barred windows. Blessed with Pahulu's love and the presence of his child, Gus feels himself emerging from a well of negativity. All three, each in a different way, hear the body's Song of the River:

Primal Pair's Song of the River

I am the human image seeking to become a body.
You can find me in the fivefold mystery of the golden section.
I am the genetic code of humanity.
You can find me in the sine wave that creates periodicity.
I am the etheric flow of the River in blood and nerve.
I am the synchronization of body systems.
Look for me in the tissues of all that is sentient
I am in the worm and the deer as well as the human.
I am the bone and blood in the stars and planets.
I live in the intensity amidst the immensity.
I transmit feeling from every center.
I am the eye, ear, and hand of the divine.
You can find me in every sensation.
I am the Adam and Eve of every race.

Are you an error in creation, a fallen form?
I am deep. Plunge to the root and you'll find me risen.

THE TRICKSTER

Smoke coils in the pathways of the mind and clouds the once-still waters of the imagination as the Trickster beholds the sacred fire of the Priest-Seer. Setting traps for the Sun in order to capture the fire, the Trickster manifests across the Earth—as Loki of Scandinavia, Maui of Polynesia, Hermes of Greece, and Coyote of the Americas. Joker, fool, wise man, he plays tricks on the senses and mind.

He sharpens tooth and claw to sever the mind and body, spirit and soul. Like the Priest-Seer, he fears the mingling of eros and chaos in the depths of the River. He appears in archaic technologists sharpening their instruments on the whetstones of reason, filling the air with logic. These technologists deepen the wedge between inner and outer, creating tools to bridge the widening gap while the irrational chant of the artist drowns in the silence of the deep.

The division of human consciousness widens as the River tunnels underground, then founts forth into four great currents at the root of the Tree of Life. In the north, the human spirit shimmers in resonance with the Creator, while the Eastern stream churns with the turbulent Primal Waters. The Western branch carries the patterns of the body that resemble the orientation of the Kingdom. The south ripples with the Priest-Seer's convolutions of the human mind.

The Creatrix rests under the Tree of Life, wishing she could imbue the Trickster with memory of the perennial wisdom streaming forth from the Kingdom. The symmetry between the divine reality of the First World and the human metaphor of the Second World is cut and strung like beads on threads of need, a linear band of logic winding around the human brain. The strands fork into a network of cosmic intelligence, giving rise to thought.

As abysses fill with the shadows of the soul, the reasoning Trickster mind gains prevalence, and the burning waters cease to circulate in the subtle nerves and chakras of the human spine. However, the roots of the Tree of Life still flourish in the Land of Zar, beneath the wide Pacific where the waters divide. Deep in the Earth the River runs, stirring the ashes of ancient ways.

GLIMPSES OF A GREATER REALITY

Imagination
Gold of white within black

The mirror
of the mind
perceives
the many in the one.

Luqman

Luqman slowly regains consciousness in the alley outside the mosque in Anar, Iran. He watches the morning Sun shine on the hoof of the donkey tethered beside him, the light shimmering like angel's wings. Lying in the dust of the Earth, he beholds the world anew. He is bruised, but filled with grace, seeing Allah in everything. The horrors of his recent war experiences drown in the surge of the River. He imagines himself as a child, sharing the child's sorrow and hurt, then as an old man who flings memories like salt into a sea that blissfully dissolves his tears.

He lies in the dirt, the rhythm of his breathing becoming like a sigh from the holy mother. He hears the call of the water, wind, and fire that fashion the rocks of the Earth. With the eyes of imagination, he beholds the warlords' desecration of ancient fertile valleys and peaceful cities. The donkey kicks, and Luqman sees the past disintegrate in a flurry of dust, every fleck becoming a star, bright and fragrant in its core. Marveling at the beauty of each fleck, he thinks, *Everything is beyond me, yet everything is within me.* He passes the morning in this reverie, living in the moment like a child, living in eternity like a fool. The sky darkens, but the Sun will not set. Time stands still. Luqman laughs and rolls over on the ground, the elixir of the Moon, the subtle dew of the heavens, washing over his body. Something within him speaks through him: "I will shine with the Sun that never sets."

On his right and left he beholds his spirit's witness and the Goddess of Change. Barnabas and Lady Flux he calls them. Red and blue-black, they blend in a purple sheen that surrounds a golden star. In the star appears the perfection of his life's longing: a virgin's face—clear, light, and filled with compassion. The golden rays from her mouth pierce his heart:

"Speak. Your body is lightening. Gather your family together and your body will heal. Do not wait. There is no time."

"Who . . . who are you?"

"I am Mary. I come by way of the burning waters."

"Grant me the heart to speak to my fellow people. How can I find the words?"

"Your willingness to speak will show you the way."

What am I to do?"

"Awaken the sleepers."

As her visage expands into a golden light, Luqman feels eyes opening in flames all over his body. "Shining beast, shining stars, shining masters, bring sight to men and women." The words move like burning liquid between his lips. His veins flow with rivers of light, breaking the confines of his body. Waiting in silence, he stares at the stars until he feels Barnabas on his right turning toward him: "You have passed through death and can gather your bones, flesh, and blood into the crystal cave of your skull. All things can be known there as images in the darkness. Look through my eyes and behold yourself." Barnabas passes through the mirror of Luqman's imagination.

Lady Flux then spreads her hands over Luqman, transforming the wounds of the past into floating dreams. The echoes of bombs within him are transmuted into images of birds and animals, the images of war woven into a silken braid of innocence to adorn his new body and mind. From Luqman's frail form in the dust comes a thunderous laugh.

Luqman feels himself standing before his masters as assorted lights dissolve any vestiges of fear. One by one, they speak in sequence: "Like a knife you can tear asunder false alliances." "Still water turns to poison.

Move with the spirit of ecstasy." "Walk by day and pray by night." "Like a polished mirror, reflect everyone as they are." "Break the blue egg of knowledge and reveal the child."

Lady Flux passes her hands through his transparent body, flooding it with clear water: "The water flowing in the River is never the same, yet everything circles around. Go now, and never say the same words twice."

Luqman stands up in the darkness. No longer a part of the world, he feels the world in all parts of himself. Lifted by celestial music, he sees the donkey as if for the first time and strokes the bleeding sores on its flank. The animal nudges him thankfully with his nose, and Luqman says, "Azar. I shall call you Azar. We shall be friends."

The Sun will not set. Time stands still. Luqman mounts the donkey and lets it take him where it will.

Luqman rides Azar along the road to Isfahan. The strange pair break ground slowly. Azar starts and stops according to whim and need, whereas Luqman surrenders his will to Allah in the form of everyone and everything he meets.

Azar wanders away from the beaten road and treads west over arid land. Both man and donkey move with parched throats. Luqman sometimes groans involuntarily. His ecstatic visions fade into emptiness, the desert mirroring the vacancy of his soul as the shadows of the past reassert themselves.

After a week, Luqman is in a stupor, trudging on foot and holding Azar's tail. His mind is washed clean, a mirror reflecting the inner in the outer. The perception of his senses sharpened, the blue of the sky, the smell of his sweat, the feel of the hot sand seem new to him. Songs of the universe rise through him.

Azar plods on, searching for water. Whenever they come upon a tree, Luqman greets it, talks to it, and gives thanks for its shade. He sings to the grass and the goats, to the sand and the birds and the souls of men who speak no more.

One evening, when they are about eight miles from Lake Gavkhaneh, Luqman encounters a wolf. Mesmerized by the Sun, he thinks it is a dog and calls to it. The wolf senses that Luqman's soul knows no fear and approaches him, limping. When Luqman reaches out his hand, the wolf warily moves back, sniffing all around. Luqman mimics the wolf, sniffing and rolling playfully on the ground, the bright vortex of his aura calming the animal, which lies down. Noticing a thorn in the wolf's forepaw, Luqman wraps one arm around the wolf, who surrenders to his love. Luqman quickly pulls out the thorn.

Luqman mounts Azar and, chanting the name of Allah, rides off into the evening. The wolf follows as if to say, "Here am I." The three arrive, once again, at the road to Isfahan, where people riding in cars laugh at the sight of the man on the donkey, calling Allah to a wolf.

The next day the three companions arrive at a mine where a middle-aged man stands beside the opening to a shaft. By now Luqman has become totally reborn, freed of all vestiges of his torturous past. Remembering the master's words to mirror everything as it is, he says to the stranger, "The barb in your heart soaks up the poison in your blood. Your face twists in anger. Come walk with us through the hills of peace."

The man, thinking Luqman mad, shouts, "Get out of here!" But his words are drowned in the sounds of crashing rock and human cries. Part of the shaft's support structure has collapsed, trapping the men inside. Panicked, the man jumps into his truck and leaves for Shahriza to get help.

Through his inner eye, Luqman immediately perceives the souls of three young men trapped inside the mine. He sees them as messengers of Allah. He leaps to the ground and kneels before the mine entrance as if it were a sanctuary of the holy mother. As he rises, he notices a small opening in the debris and hurriedly pulls away some of the smaller rocks. Squeezing his body into the shaft, he lowers himself through the rubble in wonder, still chanting in praise of Allah. The wolf follows, pawing at the rocks.

Luqman is totally immersed in the living moment. Silhouetted in the light streaming through the small opening, the blackened man and wolf appear as devils to the astonished youths. Luqman sees the shattered wall of rock as a veil lifted between himself and the holy mother. He cries out, "I am at Mother Mary's service. I cannot bear being parted from her beloved face. Please guide me to her."

More afraid of being buried than of the strange devils before them, the young men scramble past Luqman toward the opening in the shaft. As they pass by, Luqman can see in the light of his imagination that one boy has the guardian face of an eagle, another the face of a leopard, and the third the face of a rat. The first one, having climbed to safety, calls back to thank Luqman. The last one gazes back down the shaft and asks, "Who are you?"

Luqman echoes himself: "I follow Allah. I am a servant of the holy mother." Inside the mine, he feels he has entered her very womb. The cavern walls shimmer with veins of copper and iron, which he sees as rays emanating from Mary's crown. Faint from the bliss of beholding the splendor of her face, he cries, "O holy daughter of Imram, have mercy upon me. I yearn to speak to my fellow beings, but have no words for the love I feel."

In the darkness he hears, "Awake the sleepers, and then follow the footsteps of your friend. Speak while moving backward to turn humanity around. Then Allah will lead you out of your restlessness."

Luqman sighs and prostrates himself, then turns and climbs out of the mine behind the wolf. Facing backward, he mounts Azar, who now is content to follow the tracks of Allah. For reasons unknown to themselves, the three youths feel compelled to join this bizarre procession.

That night, the group stops to make camp. While Allah howls at the Moon, Luqman learns that the eagle's name is Daquai, the leopard's name is Sadik, and the rat's name is Uwais. They all riddle the harmless madman with questions: "Why do you travel with no food or water? Where are your clothes? Why do sit backward on your donkey? Where did you come from? Where are you going?"

Luqman smiles: "I follow Allah, who supplies all that I need. I am filled with bliss. I face behind in order to see you. I come from the blood of ancient memories, but I walk ever toward the holy mother."

The next day they arrive at Lake Gavkhaneh, where they refresh their parched throats and skin. In the evening they rest by the lake and relax. Daquai, the eagle, circles the lake, then climbs a hill from which he can see westward all the way to Shahriza. Sadik, the leopard, traps some ducks and brings them back for a feast. Uwais, the rat, simply sleeps. Remembering Mary's words to awaken the sleepers, Luqman stirs Uwais and, walking backward around his reclining body, says, "Animals are happy even when in need, for their mind is undisturbed by imagination."

Uwais rubs his eyes and snarls, "Why did you wake me to say that?"

"For you I sing a song and light the night sky. For you I bring food. For you I dispel illusions. For you I walk backward and forward. For you I hunt dark stones on a moonless night."

"I don't understand. You are strangest person I have ever met."

"I am a candle consuming itself. At the end of my wick is Mother Mary."

Azar brays as Daquai returns from his ascent. Daquai announces, "Our future is death unless we travel west to Shahriza. We should eat well tonight and leave early in the morning."

Jesting and laughing, the three build a fire and roast the duck. When they offer some to Luqman, he refuses, saying, "I cannot eat my brothers and sisters. Everything returns to nothing, but it is not for me to hasten it." The three young men depart at dawn, leaving Azar and Allah asleep.

Luqman, who has renewed himself in prayer all night, is living in conversation with Lady Flux and Barnabas. Midmorning, he mounts Azar, again facing backward. Black and red clouds turn golden in the sky as the Sun beats down on the scrub bushes and a herd of grazing goats. One by one, Luqman names the goats, the words of love bubbling from his heart. Bleating loudly, the goats begin to follow the wolf, man, and donkey as though responding to the call of an ancient tongue.

In the afternoon, Luqman and his entourage encounter his three companions resting in the shade of a great sycamore tree. Uncertain of their direction, they have circled northward. They rejoin Luqman and all continue together. When the procession enters the town of Na'in that evening, the people can only stare, mouths agape, at Allah leading, Luqman second in line on his backward mount, and three dirty youths and scores of goats following them both. Even further back are some goatherders who are coming to repossess their straying flock.

Alarmed, and convinced that a madman has stolen the goats, the townspeople begin rushing about and shouting. Luqman smiles and responds, "Like a River flowing on, I follow Allah. The water that comes is the same everywhere. I can behold all in its stillness. I do not question what passes before me or behind me."

When a local policeman attempts to apprehend him, he smiles and says, "I will go with you, but my friends will come with me."

THE THEFT OF FIRE

Reason
Black of white within black

The sacred fire
in the human brain
explodes
in technology.

The old priests, having schemed to divide eros and logos, seek to control the cosmos. A single spark of the Priest-Seer's sacred fire enters the human brain, and a dream is shattered.

Fearful of imbalance in the human mind, the Creatrix beckons shamans and artists, imploring them to attend to the primordial divine plan that flares in the fire of the old Priest-Seer. Only the Tree of Life in her spine, replicated in the backbones of men and women, can connect body and mind and purify the complications of evolving rational thought. But the River rages over the heads of mortals, and reason rises to the surface, submerging the power of eros.

Humankind sifts through the River's dark currents with logic coiled in its Trickster brain. Old priests plumb the depths to retrieve the pattern of the divine plan, but most are swallowed in a vortex of narcissism and superstition. No longer do they guard the secret knowledge, for linear thought obliterates their circled cross. A new priesthood emerges, one that manipulates the outer world in categorical patterns mirrored in the nervous system. Master magician of camouflage, the Trickster works furtively with inner and outer, chaos and order, mystery and knowledge, to foster the illusions of separation. Appropriating the sacred fire for their own purposes, arrogant priests of technology split the atom and alter the magnetic fields of the River.

Yet the love of the Creatrix abides in the body. There, through the whirling wheels of the chakras, the Creatrix allies with immortal spirit and refuses to interfere with the Creator's gift of free will.

Horst, Toda, and Channon

Horst's need for self-importance and control increases as his world deteriorates. Erhardt still refuses to take over his business. Christa has not returned. His anticipated dealings in Frankfurt have fallen through, for his encounter with Petruska and the experiences with Channon's immortality chamber have only reminded him of the despair of previous lifetimes. He cannot face his failed responsibility in positions of authority. Once an ancient priest who used the sacred fire as a subtle flame of authoritative power, he seeks power now through accumulation of the hardened gold of the Earth. This obsession with power results in severe distortion, for what he wants to conquer is of another realm. He is like an army marching against a phantom. Blinded by the Trickster to his own desire for love, he seeks allies in domination. He is confident that he can amass great financial returns by preying upon the appetites of the consumer.

Horst goes to Tokyo to attend an exposition of new technologies. He completes a series of meetings with Toda Hashigawa, CEO of a large Japanese corporation that produces video and computer games. Reviewing the company's annual reports from the last five years, Horst finds the escalating sales impressive and decides to make a substantial investment. The two men feel a kind of comradeship, realizing how much better it is to be allies in business than allies in war.

Channon, still looking for investors for his chamber, also attends the Tokyo exposition. While strolling on the convention floor, he sees Horst in conversation with Mr. Hashigawa and immediately goes over to them.

"Hello Horst. Good to see you again. Might I interrupt?" he asks, taking Horst's hand and shaking it.

"Channon! Yes, I'd like to introduce you to Mr. Hashigawa. Toda, this is Channon Goldfield, a recent acquaintance of mine."

The two men nod at each other with reserved smiles.

"We were just discussing how to benefit from the world's increasing population."

Channon refrains from expressing his adamance about the necessity of curbing population growth: "Please go on. What do you see as beneficial about the rising population?"

Toda speaks at this point: "By producing and marketing computer and video games, we not only receive profits, but we can influence people to buy other products."

"How so?"

"Users of these products tend to exhibit repetitive behaviors, as do users of VCRs and CD players."

Channon realizes that Toda is alluding to addiction, but he remains silent.

Toda continues with an air of confidence: "By manufacturing video games that enhance a person's competitive characteristics, we also encourage natural selection of the most strong-minded human beings."

Startled by Toda's remarks, Channon tries to refute him: "But research has shown that the growth encouraged by competition will eventually reach a saturation point. In competition, one group grows only at the cost of others. You are speaking of exploiting a consumer's addictive tendencies. Do you feel business has no ethical responsibility?"

Toda's hands jingle the coins in his pocket as he arrogantly rocks back and forth: "It is up to the consumers to know what is good for them. Let me be frank. We want to distinguish the weak minded from the strong minded. Our games are designed in hierarchical layers that build from a series of choices. The more intelligent players will penetrate the deeper levels of the game. The less intelligent will circle on the surface, eventually lose interest, and move on to another game. People live vicariously through these games, which in turn reflect how people operate in life. To a heavy user, the virtual reality of these games becomes reality itself. The smart player feels a degree of control and power that he does not experience in the outer world."

Channon disagrees and tries to turn Toda's thoughts to his advantage: "Virtual reality may be similar to the experiences people have in my cybernetic immortality chamber."

Toda's eyebrows rise in interest: "Tell me more."

"Horst himself has experienced it. He has gone back into past lives and also viewed the regressions of others on video projection."

"Yes," says Horst, "it takes you through layers in the soul. But unlike virtual reality, you do not project what you want. You are shown the phantoms of the past."

"They are not phantoms, but reality," Channon corrects. "More importantly, you clear distortions of the past so that lucid consciousness is retained beyond death."

"What kind of hardware can enable such durability of consciousness?" Toda asks.

"The hardware is relatively simple. The key is the pattern of the circuitry that I have transcribed from ancient Egyptian glyphs. The Egyptian priests had more knowledge than we of the twentieth century can easily admit."

Horst, knowing that Channon is still seeking financial backing, speaks directly: "What we are looking for, Channon, are products that appeal to mass markets. Population growth is to our advantage."

"I feel the chamber could have mass appeal, but I must tell you frankly that I am very opposed to population growth on this already overrun planet. The exponential rate of growth burns up more and more energy. Our environment is becoming a wasteland."

Horst tries to explain: "The answer to environmental pollution lies in technology. You see, we cannot leave a matter such as energy consumption up to the impulses of the masses. We can influence human destiny with our own priorities."

"You say your games will separate the bright from the dull. What then?"

"The dull will be exterminated by their own addictions."

Channon is shocked, although the idea is not totally new to him. He decides to question the men further: "You want the dull-minded exterminated, yet you want increasing populations to buy your products? I agree that impulsive greed drives people to consume more, but the higher the catalytic rate of production, the more energy required. Where will this energy come from?"

"Let me try to explain," offers Toda. "My family and I suffered greatly from the bombing of Hiroshima and Nagasaki. My parents, aunts, uncles, and sister all died from the radiation. My brothers and I were spared only because we were attending school in England. Nonetheless, I believe in nuclear energy. It is a way of helping to counter the devastating effects of the atomic bomb. Solar power is too costly and fossil fuels are nearly exhausted. Nuclear energy is infinite. It requires a large initial investment, but once made, it is like the bomb—it multiplies. Just as the exponential multiplication of neutrons produces a massive explosion, the proliferation of atomic energy can power all our cities, our electronic media, and, yes, even our video and computer games. We are talking about a network run from the atom itself."

Channon senses a kind of Faustian pact among Horst, Toda, and the core of the atom. It is all about power. He tries briefly to continue his argument: "But all energy is transformed by heat that must be absorbed by nature. How can the environment take this on? Our three-dimensional world is limited in space. Only in the higher powers of the mind can you find infinity."

Toda decides to use Channon's own argument against him: "But won't your chamber, by lengthening life span, inherently increase the population you are so concerned about?"

"Yes and no. This device assures immortality of the soul and consciousness, not of the body. Yet the resulting peace of soul and mind *may* contribute to a longer life."

"People in our world today live in the body," Toda objects. "They are captivated through the pleasures of the senses. Let's not beat about the bush, as you would say, Mr. Goldfield. We are talking about capturing people's attention through pleasure, which they pursue out of their own free will."

"Haven't you observed that people who follow only the pursuit of pleasure become addicted, not free?"

"Consumers are already puppets," intervenes Horst. "We can pull the strings, Channon."

Channon is now adamant: "There has to be balance in the physical world. Nature will collapse if the addictions of the populace that lead to increased consumption of energy, especially nuclear energy, are not checked. I feel we need to go in the direction of inner awareness. I urge you to develop technology that enhances that awareness instead of catering to people's emotional and sensory appetites."

Horst smiles, revealing something of the ancient priest: "The explosion of population is based on an explosion of the use of fire by our ancestors thousands of years ago."

Toda looks intently at Channon: "Do you want to hear the truth? Only now can we tap the atom and enable the population to mushroom, become addicted to our products, and then devour themselves by collapse. In many societies, the disabled, lazy, and retarded receive social welfare that drains economic and human resources. This is a great waste of human potential. We want the smartest to govern. That is what Darwin's natural selection is all about."

Channon, now totally disgusted, bows politely and says, "I have another meeting to attend now. I think we see eye-to-eye, Mr. Hashigawa, but we are moving in opposite directions. Thank you for your time."

INNER AND OUTER RELIGION

Memory
Red of white within black

The records and projections
of past and future
unwind
in the eternal present.

Few remember the script of the River; fewer still behold it directly. Most have succumbed to the great dangers: distraction and apathy. Both ways lead to amnesia. The contentions of the Antagonists disrupt the human soul, and the illusions of the Trickster permeate the human mind. Together, they veil the erotic source of life and spirit.

Only by aligning the spine to the vibrations of the Tree of Life and by being open to the River within can the script be remembered. The Tree stands at the source of the River's four branches with eros and logos entwined around its trunk. There, under the Pacific Ocean, lies the Land of Zar, where hope is revived and healing is possible for those who enter the imaginal life.

The Creatrix leaps across the abysses below the four branches where her passion flows as the living Word. Aware that the union of heaven and Earth still resides in the human heart, she tries to enchant the mind by stringing leaves of the great Tree into melodies that recall the River's source. Though longing to guide mortals to Zar, she watches without interfering, knowing the mortals must follow their own free will.

Survivors from the old priesthood consult akashic crystals to perceive the script chiseled in stone millennia ago. Engulfed by memory, they wander to exalt the timeless one, the Creator, as they fold history back on itself, standing on the cooled magma of ancient volcanoes. They look for the script in the Platonic forms and the sacred alphabets of the Earth's heart and brain while the new priests search among the fossils, sediments, and igneous formations of her shriveling skin.

Pravin and Luqman

After two days of driving, Pravin and his Indian friend Sabah have decided to rest for the night in Na'in. On their way to Rome to attend a conference of world religions, they have taken a long journey from Kalat, through Panjgur in Pakistan, up through Anar.

As they pass a small newsstand on their way to dinner, Sabah's eye is caught by a strange picture on the front page of the local paper. He decides to buy it. "Look at this!" he says, showing the picture to Pravin. "Such bizarre things happen in small towns. They've locked up a beggar who rides backward on a donkey."

After ordering dinner in a nearby cafe, Sabah hands the newspaper to Pravin. The picture of a man sitting backward on a donkey, followed by young men and goats, makes him curious: "What is going on here? The man is obviously not forcing them to follow him."

Anything that appears as a sign of the living Word of Savitri ignites Pravin's heart. Savitri is a vision of a just and compassionate source that motivates him in all things. "I sense abused innocence here," he says. "Let's go to the prison and find out." Pravin jumps up, leaving his plate untouched. But Sabah, who is ravenous, bids him to wait and quickly gulps down his food.

At the police station, they have trouble getting any information at all and are told to return the following morning. Upon leaving, Pravin sees three disheveled youths sitting on a bench. He recognizes them as the three persons in the newspaper photograph and decides to ask about the prisoner.

"He is innocent. He's been good to us and we want to help him," replies Daquai to Pravin's inquiry.

"Where did you meet this man?"

Sadik looks up: "We journeyed with him. He saved our lives."

"How?"

Uwais is suspicious: "Why do you want to know?"

"I sense injustice, for it seems this man harmed no one. And I am very curious as to what made you all follow him."

Daquai, naturally trustful, decides to speak: "He is unlike any man I know. We were trapped in a mine, and he and his wolf freed us. He calls the wolf Allah. Can you get that? He says he saw the holy mother in the mine. He thought we were messengers to her sanctuary. We later set off to go west to Shiraz, but we got lost and encountered him on the road north to Na'in. I believe we were meant to be with him, but I'm not sure why. I don't understand him."

Sadik looks dreamily into the sky: "I am starting to feel like I live in two worlds—one of things manifested and one of things hidden. I will stay here until he is released. I feel devoted to him."

"Why did he ride his donkey backward?" asks Sabah.

Uwais is still distrustful and irritable: "We don't know any more than we've already told you. His wolf is behind that fence in the alley. Why don't you ask him?"

Uwais's response annoys Pravin, but he says nothing. He goes over to the fence and calls to the wolf, "Come, Allah."

Pravin's words draw the attention of a humorless policeman, who yells, "Another crazy man? Get out! You profane the name of Allah."

But Allah hesitatingly follows Pravin and Sabah to their inn, where he lies down under some distant trees.

Pravin and Sabah manage to visit the prisoner the next morning. Pravin is astonished at the man's resemblance to Luqman, but cannot believe in the possibility of such a coincidence. "We come as friends," Pravin announces, as Luqman looks up and beholds Pravin's radiant violet aura. "You have aroused our interest and we have come to hear your story."

"Blessed is the holy mother. Blessed is Allah. Blessed is Azar. Blessed are you. Welcome to my home. I have this bread to offer you."

Touched by such graciousness in such circumstances, Pravin simply says, "No, thank you. We just want to hear your story. You've created quite a stir. What happened? Why did the goats follow you?"

"The goats love to graze in pleasant fields. The Goddess of Flux cares for all things. Have you seen the eagle, the leopard, and the rat?"

"Who?"

"My three messengers."

"Oh, you mean the three young men?"

Luqman nods.

"Yes, we saw them last evening."

"I hope they are taken care of."

"They are waiting for your release."

After a long silence, Luqman sighs, "You look like someone I knew in my journeys through India. My memory often deceives me, but the grapes ripen and I ferment like wine. I am flooding with the living waters of the holy mother. She purifies me each day. I am so blessed."

"You look familiar also," says Pravin, astonished at Luqman's words. "Your voice too. You remind me of a man I knew whose name was Luqman. Could you be the same?"

"O, ray of the Sun! I see now. Pravin, is it you? You are my father, my elder brother. You opened my heart to courage. Now I am happy. Now I remember."

After claiming Luqman as a family friend and persuading the police to release him, Pravin and Sabah travel on through Turkey to Greece, finally taking a ferry from Kerkira to Italy. His reunion with the ecstatic Luqman leaves Pravin hopeful that he may yet find Savitri. Luqman's vision of the holy mother was enough to fulfill his longing for his beloved. Why could not the same occur for himself?

People from the world over are congregated in Rome. Old souls gather in hope of recalling the divine plan—to gain some perspective on why individuals, families, and nations contend so destructively with one another. Most have come with the belief that the rediscovery of religious sources can empower the human heart and mind to dispel illusion. The conference has attracted Taoists, Buddhists, Jews, Muslims, Christians, even Gnostic sects and New Age orders based on ancient Greek and Celtic mysteries. About two thousand people are gathered in the arched assembly hall. The air is electric, yet infused with receptivity.

Maria and Raphael

Maria, too, journeys to Rome, leaving Ariel in the care of his grandmother in San Diego. She makes the journey primarily to hear Pravin's address. However, she is not prepared for the experience of seeing Raphael. It has been nine years since they were together. Their child, Ariel is now eight years old. With his bright aura and golden beard,

Raphael stands out in a crowd of people. Startled, Maria is deciding on whether to approach him when Raphael turns and sees her. He moves quickly through the crowd and gathers her in a long embrace. Maria speaks only through the welling tears in her eyes. Finally, she manages to say, "So, we meet in Rome after all these years."

Raphael motions to two seats nearby: "Will you sit with me?" Sparks of fire seem to radiate like stars from his forehead.

The moderator rings a bell for everyone to be seated. Pravin, in saffron red robes trimmed with golden braid, enters the stage and bows to the audience, then turns and lights a fire in a large caldron. He raises his hands in prayer.

"I invoke Agni, illuminator of darkness, dispeller of illusions, opener of remembrance. From light we come and to light we shall return. Let us offer ourselves to the white fire of the mind, the red fire of the body, and the invisible darkness in the depths of the soul.

"I invoke Savitri, the shining messenger, the beloved Word that is present in each of us. I ask now that we rise up and, filling our bodies with the holy Word, chant AUM together."

As everyone stands and chants together, the entire hall reverberates with the vibrations of the holy mantra. After a long silence that allows the beauty of the chant to be absorbed, Pravin begins his discourse on the laws of reincarnation and karma.

Pravin ends his talk with the statement: "The law of karma binds us to the past. It chains us in endless rounds of reincarnation until we transcend the illusion of the world and come back to ourselves through the divine Word of Savitri. After many cycles of forgetfulness, we can shed illusion like the skin of a snake and realize we are as the gods and goddesses." He bows to the audience and to the fire.

A tall German youth approaches a microphone and asks, "How can this vicious cycle of karma be broken so that we can be liberated?"

Pravin unhesitatingly responds, "Through devotion to Brahma, the absolute, or one of his manifestations as a god or goddess. The path of knowledge leads to a realization of *sat, chit,* and *ananda*—being, consciousness, and bliss—as remembrances of Brahma."

A stout man from Czechoslovakia asks, "You speak of gods and goddesses. How can there be an absolute, supreme God such as Brahma, and yet many gods at once?"

"When you are devoted to a god like Shiva or Vishnu, or a goddess like Parvati or Lakshmi, your whole being bursts through consciousness to bliss. Then the many are realized to be one and your karma is destroyed. You realize you *are* one with Brahma. This requires devotional practice and often much suffering as the mind is purified of attachments. Agni, the fire of truth, burns through the obstructions of returning to Brahma when you cease regretting the past and longing for the future."

When the discussion is over, Sabah, Maria, and Raphael all gather around Pravin. Raphael knew Pravin when they were both students at the University of London, but Pravin grew angry with Raphael for declaring truth without either substantiation or a way to experience the revelations of which he spoke. Now Raphael, after being with Zapana for four years, is a little humbler, and Pravin, though a scholar, is trying to immerse himself more fully in devotion to Savitri.

As the group gathers around Pravin, Raphael suggests, "Could we have lunch together? I'd like to discuss your talk in private, among friends, if you don't mind."

Pravin agrees, and they all proceed to a table in the courtyard where flowers and birds abound. After they are seated, Raphael grows very serious: "I feel you hold the secret of existence within you still, Pravin."

"What do you mean?"

"Like a flower that won't emerge from the bud, there is something you've left unsaid. You can unfurl it when the Word of your beloved explodes inside you and you remember."

"Remember what? I have searched the stars and the folds of the Earth in quest of Savitri. She consumes my devotion like a Sun. I will admit that Brahma is but an abstraction to me, but Savitri is a living reality."

"Then why haven't you found her?"

"If I knew, she would be here with me now. I burn with love for her, but I still live in an abyss."

Pravin looks over to Sabah on his left: "Luqman's devotion is complete, don't you agree? He sees his beloved in the hoof of donkey, the face of a wolf, or the blackness of a mine."

"But he is mad," Sabah counters.

"Is he? I wish I had his madness."

Maria tries to soften the conversation: "I was impressed with your depth of thought and scholarship, Pravin. Your sanity may enable you to overcome the darkness of the abyss you feel you live in. Remember that, when we were together in India, Luqman was very wretched. You see how things can change." Sparrows pick at the crumbs on the ground as the waiter takes their order.

Raphael is not finished. His brightness brings Pravin's anguish to the surface: "The eternal return of reincarnation has no end until you dance on a flame, until you rise like a phoenix out of the ashes of the past and renew your love. You have suffered for millennia from the purple illusion of Savitri as a mere memory. Where is she in life? How will you find the empyrean perfection in the flesh? Memory can be a living presence or a bolted door that keeps you trapped in old fantasies. You yourself said it: *The fire of truth burns through obstructions when you cease regretting the past and longing for the future.*"

Pravin bolts upright: "I have no fear of the pains and terrors of my mortality, Raphael. I am willing to go through any fire to find a living Savitri—if she is in the flesh."

Raphael's light is so clear that even the erudite ancient priest in Pravin is open and listening. Raphael speaks to the heart: "The transformation from Word to flesh may seem unbearable, for the abyss between the invisible logos and the visible eros is vast, but change is necessary if you would dispel your own karma. I have burned to ash in my wanderings, and only now, when I released all longing, did I find Maria again."

Raphael looks at Maria, then continues: "I went through the fire in Peru, where I had to go to destroy and re-create myself anew. For this impelling reason I left you, Maria: to wake from the ceaseless cycle of births and deaths that no longer had meaning to me. Through labor for a brother I was humbled. My friend, Zapana, is a kingly being who has rejected the world because he was rejected by it in past lives through the course of history. Yet I am impelled to bring him back to his kingly estate—not in this world, but in his self-respect and honor. Why? Because I knew him before in the French Revolution and we vowed to be brothers forever—to change the corruption of revolutionary values into a manifest utopia. No matter how far he falls into debt or confusion, I will stand by him. By laboring for him and his family I suffered, but I was released from some of my arrogance and aloofness. During that time with Zapana, I gave up hope of a reciprocal relationship with a woman."

Raphael smiles and presses Maria's hand: "Now I find you again. By surrendering my need for my idealized woman, I find the reality of Maria. I know the fire of eternity can shine through any face, but for me Maria's presence is a splendor that dispels all doubt."

Pravin feels the discrepancies amongst his ideals, the memories of his experiences, and his need for knowing the feminine within. His brow furrows as he hears Raphael's story. How can he be healed?

Raphael continues: "You are waiting for eternity, Pravin. It is here. You know the gods and goddesses you speak of are within, yet you act as if they dwell only in the world of time. I speak as a brother who has passed through the strife of ancient memory. Eternity is in this moment."

Pravin's dark eyes flash as he says in a low voice, "I am a babe in the throat of Savitri. The true Word within me longs to speak through her. Though Savitri is within my heart and between my eyebrows, I cannot birth myself. Though I imagine myself renewed, my memory quests for the vow to express the truth of Savitri I had before the eternal cycle of reincarnation began."

Raphael's face brightens: "You cannot find her by going back. Live the past in the present, and she will express within you here and now."

Sabah and Maria feel a new possibility in the air. Everyone has finished eating except Pravin, who has left his lunch untouched. He feels pulled to the center point of a vortex from which he can inwardly see his multitudes of selves circling in the wheel of creation. Lost in a moment of confusion, he asks, "Where will I find her?"

Raphael speaks like a master because of his love for Pravin: "Return to the source of the River of life. You must cross the abyss between intangible memory and tangible life."

Suddenly, the fire of Pravin's spirit consumes the veils of separation. He declares in a sudden revelation: "I will not rest until Savitri is one with my breath, until she beats in my heart. I will leave the dark world of memories and open myself to the red fires of suffering. When I think of Savitri in the flesh, I fear being scattered like a sacrificed god to the Goddess. Yet I ask Brahma to submerge me in the torrential living River. Philosophy will never imbue me with purpose. Thank you, Raphael. Your passion will glow through my sleep. For too long I have dwelled in conceptual abstractions. Whether I find Savitri in the flesh or not is up to fate. I move on in the present."

THE DIALECTIC
OF RELIGIOUS HISTORY

Thought
White of white within black

The inner reflection
of polarized ideas
synthesizes
paradox.

Henshaw

Professor John Henshaw stands at the podium, about to deliver the evening's primary lecture at the Conference of World Religions. He is of tall stature and has a distinguished head. He takes off his glasses and begins thoughtfully: "My profession, the history of religions, is but a trace through the flowering orchards of ancient knowledge, the perennial wisdom. I string gem beads of ideas on the chain of history. Try to bear with me as I touch upon what I consider to be momentous turnings in the history of religious thought. In this lecture I can only highlight the sequence of these turnings. Their deeper, underlying causes are discussed in my book, *The Dialectics of Western Religious History*."

Henshaw moves away from the podium and seems to relax more: "We must realize that we live in a unique time of change. Though I long for the purity of past traditions, I remind myself that we live in a cross-cultural melting pot, a global crucible of ideas, and not one of us can escape their fires. Yet these fires burn from the karmic laws that Pravin

Cuteswar discussed so thoughtfully yesterday. As we have sown, so shall we reap. In the past lay the seeds of our present living. In the present we face the jungles or gardens of our past actions and thoughts. In the future we shall reap whatever is our due. I believe in the justice of karmic law that is an outgrowth of the concept of eternal return. This is the first concept I will discuss. Later, we shall see how the past and future can awaken creative actions within us.

"In this discussion I want you to consider an extension of the dialectic of Hegel. Not only is there a thesis and antithesis that need reconciliation in a synthesis, but there is also a fourth phase that I consider the most regenerative part of the whole cycle. I call it the antisynthesis or paradox. The paradox goes beyond synthesis, beyond the mergence of the opposites of the antithesis. It is embracing even that which opposes it by *becoming* the opposite. In this way, a new thesis is born within the paradox. You might call the four phases *event, polarity, sharing* and *paradox.*

"Regeneration doesn't happen until the fourth phase of paradox. The thesis is like a seed, the antithesis is like the soil, water, and sunlight through which the seed is both destroyed as seed and born as a new entity, a sprout. The synthesis is like the growth of the tree from the sprout, including the roots, trunk, branches, leaves, and flowers. The fourth phase is like the fruit of the tree. There are seeds within the fruit that can regenerate the whole lineage of the tree and perhaps even create mutants. Let us take this analogy into Western religious history.

"As I indicated, the first concept I'd like to discuss tonight is that of the eternal return. The awareness of time as a cycle was prevalent not only in the earliest documented civilizations of Sumeria, Egypt, Greece, and India, but also in the entire Neolithic world that preceded these civilizations. The agrarian culture of the matriarchal Neolithic villages depended on seasonal cycles for the cultivation of food. The concept of the eternal return likely emerged around 9000 B.C. with this agricultural revolution, but its spiritual dimension was defined through the human experience of birth, death, and rebirth. This aspect of the circle of the eternal return is divided into the two halves of 'after birth' and 'after death.' The ancient awareness of reincarnation was an inherent part of the concept of the eternal return."

Henshaw raises his index finger and continues with feeling in his voice: "The cyclic eternal return of the ancient Indians, Greeks,

Sumerians, and Egyptians was built on the earlier matriarchal mythologies of birth, death, and rebirth. But the whole concept of the eternal return died among the Hebrews, who conceived a unique beginning for a unique people. The thesis of the eternal return was broken by the Jews through a projected beginning and end that became the antithesis of our dialectic of religious ideas. Yahweh was invisible, absolute, transcendent, and the ground of all identity and all history. The divine 'I am' was the absolute source that silenced natural origins and diminished the cycle of birth, death, and rebirth.

"In the antithesis of history, the Jewish priests must have asked, 'How is Yahweh's authority to be known?' Their written scripture became the authority. The divine Word of the Torah superseded the Greek mask and theater, which expressed the myths of the God sacrificed to the Great Goddess. The Word of Yahweh was an antimythical, prophetic revelation. After the Jewish prophets, both Christianity and Islam canonized scripture, lending weight to the antithesis of history against the background of the ancient eternal return. According to the Old Testament, all laws were derived from the authority of the Creator, and history was conceived as beginning at a specific time."

Henshaw pauses and looks around the conference room with his steel-blue eyes before offering his next thought: "The positing of an absolute genesis to history paralleled the concept of a single supreme God. Monotheism sought to dispel the Egyptian, Babylonian, Sumerian, and Greek pantheons that emerged from and were part of the thesis of the eternal return. The richness of theater, dance, and art sprang from the ancient mysteries of the eternal return. In polytheism, the pagan gods and goddesses reflected the many aspects of God, depending on the phase of the cycle invoked. These gods and goddesses were subdued or destroyed in monotheism. Iconoclasm, or the breaking of idols, became prevalent with monotheism and the birth of linear history. The antithesis is always opposed to the thesis. Both Judaism and Islam became iconoclastic."

Henshaw paces the floor as if looking for a thread of thought, then stops: "The eternal return, wherein the phases of time are congruent with a more polytheistic myth and ritual, contrasted strongly with monotheism and the genesis of history and linear time. The tension of these polarities has ramified throughout our Western religious history, for when poles are not unified in a circle of the invisible and visible, transcendent and existent, they conflict."

Henshaw gazes directly into the eyes of those in the front row before he goes on: "Now I want you to consider what happened in the Christian tradition. The dialectic of the antithesis that began with the Jewish absolute genesis was tensed into the greatest polarity attainable by mortals. Monarchic Israel sought to find the king as Messiah. When Jesus appeared, one group saw him as the Messiah while others found such a view heretical. During this time, the circle of the eternal return was extremely repressed, but it was alive among pagan Romans. The crucifixion of Jesus mirrored the conflict of doubt and belief represented by the pagans and the orthodox. In the crucifixion, the spirit and the flesh became totally opposed. The spirit and flesh were cleaved apart on the cross, which symbolized the polar tension resulting from a linear sense of time shattering the eternal return. But Christ himself ended the old aeon with a grace that was totally positive.

"Christian history was continued by Paul, in whom there existed a great dichotomy between the personal, self-conscious 'I' and revelation. In Paul the subjective 'I' became guilty and sinful when identified with the personal ego and the flesh. For Paul, self-consciousness was hostile to God. He lived in the dialectic that simultaneously knew God as the God of both salvation and judgment.

"Christians subsequently lived on the cross of the guilty and the righteous. The supreme God that the resurrected Jesus knew was projected as judge. The resurrected were to be free of death and guilt. As I understand it, both history and selfhood were totally negative for Paul. What the Jews started as an absolute beginning of history, Christ was to end.

"The passionate longing for death that the early Christians experienced was transcendental, yet it was intensified by persecution. It was wholly different from the Egyptian longing for immortality, which was absolute and universal, a return to the source. The Christian immortality was a self-conscious longing for an end, albeit an end in a transcendent heaven of reward or hell of damnation.

"It is interesting that the crucifixion of Jesus does not appear in art until the fifth and sixth centuries. Art attempts to be a synthesis, a way of reconciling opposites. During ancient and medieval times, art was a crafted transmission of religious experience, articulated by priests and theologians. A synthesis was needed to heal the antithesis between spirit and flesh, God and self-consciousness, represented by the cross. So the dying and resurrected God of Jesus replaced the earlier Greek Dionysus and Egyptian Osiris. Through the image of the Pieta, with Jesus lying in the arms of the mother, we touched again on the eternal return, where the cross is embraced by the circle. Among Christians, only the Celts depicted this greater wholeness of the cross inside the circle."

Henshaw takes off his glasses and smiles, then takes a sip of water: "What a journey we have made! These were momentous events that affected us all. Each change in the dialectic was a change of heart and attitude, a change of how the world was seen and grasped. Now I'll ask you to follow my thoughts some more.

"It was left to Augustine to begin the theological synthesis. During the fourth and fifth centuries, the self-consciousness expressed in Augustine's *Confessions* was completely alien to both the teachings of Paul and those of the Eastern Byzantine Christian church. Augustine saw the statement of Moses, 'I am that I am', as Plato's eternal ideal. In this view, Neoplatonism and catholic Christianity were compatible. Augustine said something that Plato would have concurred with—that truth was unobtainable by the senses. At first Augustine knew reason as the way to the knowledge of reality, but gradually he despaired of reason and saw that revelation was the way to truth.

"Like Plato, Augustine saw the contrast of time and eternity. With the Neoplatonists, he saw that only God, the eternal, was true and good. Augustine was the first to see time as subjective. He saw God's power as absolute will. According to his interpretation, God permitted sin and evil so as to exercise justice and mercy.

"Though Augustine belonged to the ancient world, it was due to Augustine's theology that the classical notion of man as the center of the universe, gave way to the medieval view of God as the center.

"Augustine's doctrine of predestination implied that the number of the elect and the damned was fixed. Yet salvation was possible in a future by God's grace. Grace aroused faith. Faith was an act of will, and the intellect must be subjected to will. Faith was followed by forgiveness, not as a reward, but as God's free gift. Love for God then became the prime motive and directive for life.

"For Augustine, the unity of will and being became immanent and transcendent at once. Free will was the realization of being a simultaneous embodiment of sin and grace. Through embracing immanence and transcendence, Augustine attempted a synthesis. He consequently laid the foundation for the thought and way of life that formed the basis of Western culture for over a thousand years. But the polarity of the antithesis remained, for the synthesis attained within was projected out into history at a time when humankind was not prepared to receive it.

"Augustine transposed the apocalyptic vision of Paul into an ecclesiastical vision by seeing the city of God as the Catholic Church. The irony that we must realize is that the church arose during times of social horror. When Gregory the Great founded the Papal States in A.D. 590, making the Roman Papal State independent of the Eastern Byzantine Church, external authority was dropped. Soon after, during the reign of Charlemagne, the population of the Roman Empire dropped from 250,000 to 20,000 people! Rome became the new Babylon. It seemed that God's plan was to conquer the world and impose peace. The result was not a stable synthesis, but a regression to the polarity of antagonism.

"Charlemagne's time led to the medieval Dark Ages that were at once clerical and militaristic. At that time there were only two classes: slaves and nobles. Both the clerics and leaders of the military were of the noble class. The rulers and the ruled were now the antagonists. The Carolingian Empire was followed by a dragon of chaos overturning all sense of order and control. Chaos burst forth in invasions by Vikings, Saracens, and Magyars. The pagans, representing polytheism, attacked the Christian monotheists because Christianity sought to rule the pagans. By the ninth and tenth centuries, Europe was entrenched in a feudalism in which war was the raison d'etre for every position of authority. This was the result of the incomplete synthesis to which I referred earlier.

"There was a voice of synthesis and even paradox at this time, but it went unheard: the voice of John Scotus Erigena. Writing in the darkness of the ninth and tenth centuries, Erigena was ignored and later condemned."

Henshaw pauses, looking out above the heads of the audience, in which he senses both openness and puzzlement. Some people have their eyes closed as if hoping to receive a vision of his meaning from within. He glances at his notes and continues.

"I want to tell you something of the thought of Erigena even though it was not received by his contemporaries. For, by examining syntheses, we can try to reconcile opposites within ourselves even though people in the past could not.

"For Erigena, God was both transcendent and immanent. Spirit and nature were not separate. God was, in fact, universal nature. Erigena's major work, On the Division of Nature, brought divinity and nature together in a dynamic evolutionary scheme that included the creation both of divine essence and of phenomenal existence, the purpose of which was to return to the source from which it came. God does not know phenomena because they exist; phenomena exist because of God's thought.

"The point of synthesis in Erigena's thought was that the fall of creation was part of the divine plan from the beginning. Consequently, being in a body was not sinful. All of creation returned to the source—not only humans, but also angels and beasts, including the so-called sinful. And here Erigena reached a point of paradox, the paradox being that evil was but a temporary state. Within paradox lay the compassion to love the sinner as Jesus did. Mistakes of the past could be rectified because the power of love dissolved all evil."

Henshaw shakes his head thoughtfully. "It is ironic that people often cannot receive what will heal them, even when the agents of healing are present. Erigena's De Divisione e Naturae was forgotten until the twelfth century and officially condemned by Pope Honorius III in the early thirteenth century. It was not really known until it first appeared in print in the late seventeenth century.

"In Erigena's time, the course of history ran according to the antithesis manifested in the sinful and the righteous, the poor and rich, the slaves and nobles. Plague, famine, and the destruction of commerce prevailed until the European bourgeoisie arose in the eleventh and twelfth centuries. The nobles and rulers could not ignore the growing middle class. The emerging bourgeoisie embodied a fortuitous social response, an attempted synthesis to the terrors of war, plague, and slavery. Their embrace of monasticism was an effort to synthesize the inner and the outer through a cloistered way of life."

Henshaw breaks into a broad smile: "Then an amazing thing happened. Christian scholasticism emerged in one generation, between A.D.

1255 and 1274, through the integrated thought of Thomas Aquinas. His revolutionary claim that the world itself is a new world, knowable by revelation, constituted a true synthesis. This synthesis wed Christian theology and Aristotelian philosophy. According to Aquinas, the act of creation itself could be known through revelation. There was no dichotomy between natural and revealed theology. The human contact with the divine was a way that embraced time and eternity simultaneously. This all-embracing synthesis gave birth to Gothic art, which touched the sublime heights and depths of paradox. The ecstatic experience and immediate vision of God was expressed in the Gothic world as its own proof."

Henshaw pauses to take a drink of water, then removes his glasses and closes his eyes. The audience remains still. He looks up and speaks, his glasses lying on the podium: "The birth of paradox is one of the hardest things for history to initiate. Where does the paradox emerge amidst the synthesis of the human embrace of time and eternity in Gothic art?

"Let us examine the thought of a German mystic who studied the thought of Aquinas thoroughly. Meister Eckhardt was radical in the depth of his imitation of Christ. He said humans are to become God, not merely worship him. Burning wood does not become wood, he said, it becomes fire. Eckhardt declared that pure being is a divine abyss or ground, but unlike the ancient pagan Neoplatonic idea, Eckhardt expressed a ground that was to be inwardly experienced in each individual human soul. This was the paradox in the dialectic of Western religious history. Freedom, for Eckhardt, came from the *selfless humility realizable in every human being*. Both creature and Creator were destroyed so that each could become fully itself. This mystical paradox was unacceptable to the papal authority, which condemned Meister Eckhardt for a vision that was revolutionary in the West.

"This conflict between the divine and human centers peaked during Eckhardt's condemnation in 1329, when Dante's *De Monarchia* was also condemned. Eckhardt's paradox was contained inside the synthesis like seeds inside fruit on a tree, you see?"

Henshaw looks around the hall trying to feel if his audience is comprehending: "But Eckhardt's paradox needed a ground in which to fall and draw nourishment, so that it might flower into history. The orthodox church could not receive it. Even other mystics like John Tauler, Henry Suso, and Ruysbroeck were less extreme and paradoxical than Eckhardt.

"By the time of the Renaissance, the divine presence and human presence were brought into art through Cimabue and Giotto, but already the vision was turning away from the divine toward the human. Giotto developed three-dimensional perspective and the use of light and shade, creating a realism not known before. Nature and man were becoming a tangible center of focus. God was now seen as born in the human, rather than the human born in God. In the new epiphany of the emerging Renaissance, Christ became incarnate in the three-dimensional world of each human being.

"Now individual artists became the harbingers of the message. The Renaissance masters—Giotto, Cimabue, and later Leonardo and Michelangelo and others—created a pattern wherein individuality emerged bearing the synthesis of the divine in the human, a union linked to ancient Greek ideas. This tendency first culminated in the fourteenth century with Dante. But Dante did not fully embrace Eckhardt's paradox of freedom coming from a selfless humility that arises within each person. This mystical paradox broke apart as soon as the papal authority interpreted it as a quest for freedom *from* orthodoxy. No society formed around Eckhardt's mystical paradox.

"After the Renaissance, the antithesis of the polarity between orthodoxy and the individual burst forth in a series of religious revolutions, stirred more by artists than theologians. These revolutions still sought a synthesis that would heal the old polarity of spirit and flesh, eternity and time, but the gap between the artist and society widened as history proceeded."

His mind racing, Henshaw begins to speaks faster: "Dante's thought opposed the orthodox Catholic Church by demanding two rulers—one temporal and one spiritual. Dante declared that nature, being God's creation, is perfect and therefore inherently 'chooses' the right means for its fulfillment. His synthesis of purpose and intention in nature contained intense messianic hope. According to Dante, humans were created to realize goodness that could be fulfilled in the present temporal realm. This goodness was an act of compassion inherent in the universe, a compassion that was born within the paradox of history being evil as well as good. When Dante said goodness was possible in the world, he achieved the phase of paradox. Dante's *Commedia* was at once a resurrection of the ancient world and a foretelling of the new."

Henshaw puts on his glasses and turns to the moderator, who announces, "We will have a fifteen-minute break and resume the lecture at 8:30 p.m.. Please return in time so that we may begin promptly. Thank you."

Henshaw descends the steps from the stage, where he is greeted by Akrisios and Fariba. Happy to see them, he smiles broadly and kisses them both on each cheek: "I did not know you were coming. How wonderful to see you here!"

"You are really trying to cover a lot in one lecture, my friend," says Fariba.

Akrisios is more affirming. "What a relief to hear the sweep of truth in your ideas. I only wish you had time to give more concrete examples. I understand these abstract ideas only vaguely."

Henshaw gently squeezes her arm: "In reality, what I am saying is not abstract, but born of the flesh and blood of people who sought to live their truth. We can learn from a history of religious thought. It reflects the inner struggles that underlie both the rise and fall of civilizations."

They converse a while longer until the bell rings, signaling people to return to their seats.

"Might we have breakfast together tomorrow at the cafe? About eight o'clock?" suggests Fariba.

"I'll be there."

As he waits for the audience to quiet down, Henshaw looks directly into the eyes of as many people as he can. He speaks slowly as he begins again: "When we look at the dynamic course between religious ideas and history, we are looking at the power of humans to pose a worldview and to integrate body, mind, and spirit. We are able to see that humans can become so humble as to be filled with the holy spirit, with divine influx. The points of paradox are hard to sustain, for they imply a nullification of the self, of experience, and even a temporary annihilation of the integrity of any synthesis achieved—so that a complete surrender to the divine influx becomes possible. No wonder that people like Eckhardt and Dante are few and far between!"

His speech becomes faster and more energetic: "As history proceeded, there remained a need for comprehending all four phases of the dialectic cycle, although this need was not fully conscious. Individual artists, like Dante, emerged seeking to embrace the whole. The mid-eighteenth century saw the birth of another artist, a genius who sought to comprehend the entire cycle within himself. This was Johann Wolfgang Goethe.

"Goethe attempted a synthesis in *Faust* as well as in his scientific research. The widening gap between the mystery of the divine sources and the emergence of the self-conscious, controlling ego was represented in *Faust* by opposing the archangelic powers of the *harmonia mundi* to the dreaded force of Mephistopheles. The pact made between Mephistopheles and Faust was a wager with an unknown fate. All that was known was that Faust, bearing the antithesis of the whole of human history in his breast, defied predetermined fate in his dream of a seemingly impossible love. Conciliation between the two opposed images of the universe—Faust, the idealist, and Mephistopheles, the trickster—seemed impossible. Mephistopheles regarded the angelic awe of God's wisdom as ridiculous. He was skeptical of and indifferent to order, harmony, and felicity.

"The pact between the forces of good and evil represented an agreement within Faust to share the blessings and misfortunes, loves and hates, joys and sufferings, of humanity. His dream was to rediscover the harmonious connection between himself and universal nature. In Goethe's drama, Faust left the books in his Gothic chamber for the vitality of nature's transformative reservoirs. Being so passionately alive, Faust was bound to meet with his opposite. His encounter with Mephistopheles was an encounter with the primordial Satan.

"But the pact between Mephistopheles and Faust, who sought to break through the limits of human nature, embraced all the good and evil of both the intangible and tangible worlds. The division and doubt that dwelled in Faust's soul were a necessary part of the unfoldment of his soul.

"In writing *Faust*, Goethe gathered the threads of the ancient eternal return and repeated the dialectic of history through the masquerade of nature spirits, angels, and the interaction of mortals with mythic beings. A polytheist, Goethe saw nature as a whole, both in her spiritual and her material aspects.

"When Mephistopheles revealed to Faust the mystery of the

Mothers, Faust at first was terrified, but his love for Helena drove him on. In the underworld of the Mothers he hoped to find her. When he asked how to reach the Mothers, Mephistopheles replied, 'There is no way, no path to the unreachable.'

"Upon questioning further, Faust learned that, in order to reach the Mothers, he must descend into the void of the underworld to obtain semidivine powers. Mephistopheles told him, 'Stomp and descend: by stomping you will rise again.' His struggle in the underworld was a quest to recover his beloved Helena. In the darkness he spoke with ugly griffins, sphinxes, and sirens—beings that he formerly would have scorned. He entered into the shadow side of nature and humanity. Beauty and ugliness were no longer polarized for him. He grew by moving *through* the shadows, not *away* from them.

"His descent to the Mothers, his summoning of Helena, and his quest for the forms of the past, were all attempts to obtain great perspective. He was comforted by a hope that flew beyond existence: a future that transcended human limitation. Yet this future was suited only to Faust's spirit, not his body or soul.

"A dedicated artist and scientist, Goethe was one of the last individuals to attempt to embrace the dialectic of opposites within himself. Through the character of Faust, Goethe sought to redeem nature by invoking the rebellious elements to obey the gentle laws of cosmic harmony. Faust dreamt of pacifying the violence of the oceans. In the end, Faust neither feared the darkness nor needed to dominate it through violence. Before his death, Faust said,

Oh, that I might see such teeming and living
and tread a free Earth with a free people.
Then could I bid the passing moment.
Halt here a while, thou art so fair!

"After Faust's death, Mephistopheles stepped forth and insisted that all Faust's dreams were doomed to failure, that the 'free Earth with a free people' could never be actualized. But Mephistopheles complained about the change in history. As the Satan of primordial times, he was clearly opposite from God. The infernal city was strictly his. But once good and evil got mixed up, Mephistopheles himself became confused.

"So that there would be no dispute about his ownership of Faust's soul, Mephistopheles produced the parchment whereupon their pact was signed in blood many years before. The ultimate outcome of the wager between Mephistopheles and Faust is still unknown. It depends on the tribunal of the present. But one thing is certain: By the end of the book, Mephistopheles has changed as much as Faust has. At the end of Goethe's drama, Mephistopheles wanted the angels to descend closer and grant him a single, tender glance, for love had entered his heart."

Henshaw's words seem to affect everyone in the great circular hall. He continues: "The perennial opposition, once embraced, momentarily became a free power of the love that moved the universe. Mephistopheles' conversion was as large as Faust's embrace of the shadow. Love entered the shadows and the shadows entered love—this was a true moment of paradox.

"Such moments of paradox do not last long in time. Mephistopheles still reigned as the lord of pranks, the Trickster that triumphed on Earth when consciousness identified with the objects of the world. He not only knew the abyss, but he navigated oceans, fought wars, and built dikes and canals to control both men and nature. The Trickster in him engineered roads and buildings and printed money to spread the illusion over the Earth of the possession of wealth.

"Yet Faust's immortal soul rose to heaven through the spheres of the planets. The final words of the *Chorus Mysticus* are a formula for the mystical paradox that Goethe embraced:

All that passes
Is only a comparison;
The inaccessible
Happens here;
The indescribable
Fulfills itself here;
The eternal feminine
Draws us on high."

Henshaw paces a few steps and then stops and puts his glasses in his lapel pocket: "Though Goethe was not a theologian, his work embraced religious ideas, for in the nineteenth century, art, science, and religion were torn apart due to the failure of a lived historical synthesis and paradox. Individuals who sought to embrace the whole worked in many fields at once. Goethe, like Leonardo, was a man whose life and work delved into the essentials of art and science. Matters of the spirit that usually belonged to religion were revealed through their capacity to penetrate to source archetypes.

"Goethe embodied the concept that laws of nature are one with the harmony of the mind. His science was empirical and archetypal at once. He refused to place the ultimate reality of the universe in the fundamental particles of physics or in the laws governing them or in theologies. He saw the archetypal substrata of life that applied to science, art, and society. According to Goethe, to apprehend archetypes, all of our faculties must be developed. Scientific training for Goethe meant developing powers of insight into nature and powers of cognition that were inseparable from spiritual insight. Only through direct cognition could the scientist experience the reality of archetypes as active forces in the living being of nature. The mechanical, reductive approach to nature that prevailed in his lifetime has led in our own day to both technological expansion and the destruction of the nature we need for support."

Henshaw returns to the podium as a few members of the audience leave. He takes his glasses from his pocket and puts them on. Glancing briefly at his notes, he continues: "The new science of Goethe's day followed Newton instead of Goethe. What I want you to realize is that the difference in the two views is tantamount to a difference in religious ideas.

"Goethe, as scientist, relied on observation as much as cognition. He found that color resulted from the interplay of light and darkness, not that white light contained colors, as Newton believed. Goethe contended that the polarity of light and darkness created the whole color spectrum that is experienced *qualitatively*. On the contrary, Newton saw light as an isolated emission of particles that could be measured quantitatively.

"Observation, to Goethe, was a religious experience because he regarded perceptible qualities like color, form, and sound not as accidental but as part of the divine plan. To take the qualities out of experience and objectively quantify them, as Newton sought to do, was to shatter human experience for Goethe.

"To understand our present modern-world predicament, we must understand the religious and spiritual ideas behind history, the ones that did not take root as well as those that did but failed to bring harmony into life."

Henshaw continues with renewed inspiration: "Another genius who opposed the Newtonian worldview was William Blake. An Englishman, he was the first to envision the unity of the American and French revolutions as the advent of a new social world. Blake's apocalyptic vision embodied the idea of the end of history. This vision was prophetic of our times. It shattered previous realities and propelled us toward a truly modern revolution.

"At the center of Blake's vision was the concept of the death of God that Nietzsche also promulgated. With the death of God, there was a deep disruption of every center of belief. This new thesis was as paradoxically distant from the ideology of the nineteenth-century Enlightenment as Goethe's greatest insights were. Blake was a radical political poet, whereas Goethe was a universal nature poet, a holistic scientist. Blake's and Nietzsche's vision represented a new thesis that emerged from Goethe's paradoxical embrace of opposites.

"Nietzsche rediscovered both the ground of Greek tragedy and the ground of inner, individual consciousness, a subjectivity that represented the fall from a primordial state of bliss. Yet the death of the Christian God, for Nietzsche, was not a transcendent saving act of grace but a subjective death in the soul. Belief in a transcendent God died for Nietzsche. In a world where the death of God divided the individual from his ground of being, Nietzsche gave birth to a Zarathustra who proclaimed the ancient thesis of the eternal return. Yet Zarathustra offered redemption, not by way of the past, but by way of the present and future. The eternal return was, in Nietzsche, born in a pure immanence of the present actual moment. 'Being begins in every now,' he said. Nietzsche knew that subjective consciousness represented a 'fall,' but he changed *what has been* into *what will be*. Redemption was through the re-creation of the Dionysian birth, death, and rebirth. Therefore, the archaic thesis of the eternal return entered the paradox in the premodernism of the late nineteenth-century world."

Henshaw paces back and forth twice and then resumes a former thread of thought: "Like Goethe, Blake opposed the rational, quantifying methods of Newton. Newton analyzed a fallen nature, isolated and apart from the divine source and the natural qualities of direct experience. Not only did Blake criticize the dissection of nature, but he also saw the absolute authoritarianism of monotheistic religions as a curse that consumed life under one monarchic law. The deism that became the established religion of the French Revolution, and that celebrated

God's laws as a way to freedom, Blake felt as a crushing weight.

"Deism was dedicated to the revolutionary transformation of the world. But such a deism could not be received by the people, and, by replacing the state church, deism made it impossible for the people to practice *any* form of religion. The deistic ideology transformed the cult of reason into the cult of an autocratic Supreme Being that suited the monarchies well. Robespierre, the high priest of the French Revolution, imposed God's law as but another form of the Jewish prophetic antithesis. The deists projected the kingdom of God, but they manifested its infernal counterfeit in the French Revolution."

The audience receives Henshaw's words with deepening insight. "Hegel, who was Blake's contemporary, created a modern analysis of history that is at the root of the historical dialectic we are using. For Hegel, as for Blake, the freedom promulgated by the French Revolution was a cold and abstract universality that actually destroyed all human and historical tradition and reduced the individual to slavery.

"Hegel's totality was not complete, though it had a real historical ground. Hegel's dialectic posited spirit's other as its direct opposite, as a fallen world. But the spirit became alienated from life in Hegel's mind. Self-consciousness became the antithesis of spirit and universal consciousness. Hegel called the self-consciousness that lost all essence of itself the *unhappy consciousness*, one that realized that God is dead. In this state, pure subjectivity became isolated and alienated from its spiritual ground. The authoritarian antithesis of Jewish scripture, in which Yahweh established an absolute beginning of history, here reached its own antithesis: If Yahweh was absolute, the subjective and empirical experience of the individual was denied and God was projected as an authoritarian principle that could not be experienced. Therefore, God either had to be believed in or denied. Absolutism of God as objective reality therefore polarized into its opposite, leading to the death of God."

Henshaw emanates the electricity of his thought: "It is of interest to note also that Goethe's direct experience of the French Revolution turned him away from all idealism. Goethe renounced the utopia that the revolution had sought to manifest, but he defended its essence. Although his aspirations and impossible loves remained pure and vivid, he could not support the means used by the revolution to attain them. Goethe accompanied Karl August, commander of a Prussian regiment, into the battles of the French Revolution. For two months, Goethe directly witnessed the foul conditions of war. He wrote of his experiences, 'Amid mud and misery, worry and discomfort, danger and torment, amid ruins, cadavers, carcasses, and piles of excrement.'

"Blake referred to Satan, the god who died in a reaction of subjective self-consciousness, for he was a solitary, infinitely transcendent mystery. Blake's own mythology spawned archetypal characters who entered increasingly complex multidimensional realms that were subjective yet transcendent, cosmic yet historical, psychological yet political.

"In a sense, Blake reenacted and embodied Milton's *Paradise Lost* by creating an apocalyptic epic whose end was a New Jerusalem that issued from the union of Milton's Satan and the Christ. Milton was dedicated to the restitution of the primal order that existed anterior to creation, before chaos, eros, or the Mothers existed. But, paradoxically, he was also dedicated to an absolutely sovereign order that transcended the existential and human order. He believed that Christ freely paid ransom for our sins. In his view, by accepting death, we can cease clinging to the immortality of the ancient Egyptians and accept the resurrected body of Christ. Milton looked forward to the freedom of the New Jerusalem rather than backward to the immortality and eternity of the ancient Egyptians. Freedom as the goal inaugurated the modern world, a turbulent world that shattered tradition and history as well as an absolutely sovereign order."

Henshaw's face is relaxed, yet open and animated: "For Blake, the reversal of the fall from Adam into Satan was through the human imagination, identified with the mystical body of Christ. At the end of Blake's *Jerusalem*, there was a profound interpenetration of Jesus and Satan wherein Jesus was identified with Jerusalem and Satan became the God, the Creator, the egotistical selfhood that was also identified with sin and death. The contradiction here was the all-embracing paradox of Blake's own thought."

Henshaw seems to transform from a retired professor into a fiery revolutionary: "In essence, Jesus as Jerusalem embraced Satan as a deceitful selfhood embodied in the biblical God. Uniting the contraries brought vibrant and ecstatic energy as a movement through death and darkness.

"The visions of Blake, Nietzsche, and Goethe led to a historical advent of apocalyptic hope for humanity at large. Poised over an abyss that was also a creative wellspring, Nietzsche's vision of re-creation sprang from his struggle with nihilism, the evacuation of all ideals. Zarathustra's *yes* was inseparable from the totality of saying *no* to the internal, subjective consciousness that was birthed in the split from God, which simultaneously declared that God was dead.

"Blake found this creative wellspring through a transformation of the center of self-consciousness into the divine imagination. Goethe found it through a descent to the void and an embracing of the shadows of the underworld. Blake, Goethe, and Nietzsche all embraced a humanity that is only now passing through a cataclysmic change paramount to the death of egotism.

"The objective universality of science in the modern world, coming out of the death of God, was the same as Goethe opposed. The analytic expression of human beings divided against themselves deadens individuality and the powers of the imagination to penetrate to the archetypes. Goethe's harmony of the world cannot be heard in such an existence. Yet, by embracing the trickster Mephistopheles, modern man has changed.

"Now we live in a shattered world, a world that can no longer look forward to the freedom that Milton conceived. Nor can we look backward to the freedom of immortality and eternity that the Egyptians proposed. We are not in a state of simple polarity of the antithesis. Rather, we are in a fragmentation of the polarity that emerged when linear history superseded the eternal return of the primordial Goddess. And we cannot go back, however adamant the feminists become."

Breaking out from his intense seriousness, Henshaw laughs with ironic acceptance: "The effects of Mephistopheles and all the tricksters are present in any mind that participates in technology and the new web of electronic media. But, as we have seen, even Mephistopheles is being changed. Reductionist Newtonian science has already been changed. Some physicists see mystical or implicate forces in the workings of subatomic waves and particles. Religious traditions of all kinds are being broken and transformed. We are here together in a great melding at this conference, using electronic tape recorders and microphones. We are together in a synthesis, seeking to find a way to sustain the paradox of compassion in a world shattered by evil—an evil that, like Satan, has its roots in the absolute good. We can see from the dialectics of religious ideas that absolutism in itself creates its own pole of the death of

God and the emergence of a scientific worldview that believes in an objective world.

"While the scientists have a consensus of empirical and statistical methods, the Fundamentalists cling to scripture and New Age cults run on in a rampant polytheistic syncretism. The Hegelian irony of history is that we are witnessing a new Epiphany, one that promises the end of history itself. There is something that wants to be birthed within and through us—we who embody the essence of compassion and love in the substantiality of existence itself, including the paradox of all its painful and blissful sides. No longer can the world go on divided from our interior consciousness, nor can our consciousness be divided within itself. Only when love is immediately present can the original abyss be filled with a chaos and a cosmos simultaneously. The new thesis may come out of the Trickster's own mouth if we listen intently to the paradoxes circling in our own minds.

"In conclusion, I have a poem about the Trickster. Thank you very much."

Trickster's Song of the River

I am the River in the mind that creates the many from the one.
You can find me in every hiding place.
I am the camouflage of butterflies and soldiers.
Look for me in disguises and projections of your thought.
I am the mask as well as the face it conceals.
I am the logic of sequential thinking.
I am the flash of imagination in a mirror.
I am the serpentine path that creates time in the mind.
Look for me in theories, lies, calculations, and illusions.
I am the fire of knowledge stolen from the gods.
You can find me in the rationalization of humanity.
Look for me in the rings of Saturn and in magnetic tapes.
I am the memory of the ages that seeks new beginnings.
You can find me in the play of shadows and the light of day.
I am thought creating the hologram of the world.
I am the separation of I and thou and the myriad forms.
I am the circle that has no beginning or end.

Are you true or false?
I am the truth of each moment.

THE THIRD WORLD

The Creator conceives of the Third World, realizing that the plans of the spirit, soul, body, and mind are templates requiring the fire of starry beams to bring them life. Through the laser beam of eternity and the intention of spirit, he creates the swirling vortex where the draconic powers dance.

The Trickster wanders with the sacred fire to the stairs that lead to the underworld. Descending into the darkness, he comes to the edge of the vortex where nature has its inception. There he beholds the swirling forms of archangels, dragons, devas, and nature spirits. Though these intelligent beings are the silent source of the galaxies, the Trickster is surprised and horrified. He feels the heat of change in his own mind and combats it with the fires of his imagination. Out of the vortex he seeks to deny the rotation of the Heavenly Powers.

Ignoring the Creator's intention, the Trickster grasps at reason to banish the draconic forms from his mind. When ensconsed in denial, he can perceive himself as ruler. But when the forms reappear, he becomes possessed and enraged, beholding illusions bred from the desires of the soul.

Still residing in the Second World, the Creatrix is humored by the

179

Trickster's wish to create an illusory realm within his mind. However, the Creator grows impatient and makes his will clear: "The human form must pass through matter and come to life or our sacrifice will be in vain. If we are not recognized, how shall the people know themselves?"

"Let us draw them through the vortex in the order of their creation," replies the Creatrix. "They are now like wax figures that will melt in the fire of the First World. We must slow and cool the currents descending into their Third World home."

The Creator is pleased with her suggestion: "Yes, humans aspire to our glory, although their souls have fallen into the darkness of desire. For redemption they must either return to the higher octave of the spirit or descend into incarnation. The elements that can make their bodies glow lie in the shapes and sounds of the River."

From the soul, the imaginal realm of the Shaman arises like a dream, a vision of new forms to be infused with matter and life. The Shaman renders the imaginal forms invisible with the wind of his breath. Yet these forms are to become the crystals, plants, and animals of nature. The Creatrix is fully aware that the plants and creatures cannot manifest until the cosmic vortex is imprinted with the innocence of the human body.

The Creatrix unveils the dream and watches the human image in the body give birth to nature. She replies to the Creator, "You yourself know that the mind will have to follow the spirit, soul, and body or else dwell forever in a self-authored mirage. Let us pray that humanity cooperates with the draconic forces, or we shall have war instead of praise."

"I will open the vortex through the turquoise realm of emptiness," utters the Creator in his final Word of intent. "The doorway through the dark abyss is forever open to those who can empty themselves of the Antagonist's desires and the Trickster's contriving thoughts. Humility is the path between the worlds."

However, the Antagonist and the Trickster, dashing their desires and thoughts against the vortex, try to prevent the birth of the Third World. From their resistance arises the realm of matter, the Death Dance. The Antagonist's desire descends into the body by passing through the imaginal realm into the density of matter where the Death Dance moves. The Death Dance creates the rippling patterns of subatomic particles, atoms, and molecules across the whole sky. As matter arises, the draconic powers enter into the harmonic patterns of matter's substance and create overtones with the waves of Death's Dance.

The Creatrix dances to enliven the draconic powers, pulling the moonrise, sunset, and flood of her memory into congruent streams. "Humility is the path to compassion," she reflects back to the Creator. "The River brings the burning waters into every stone and creature. The Tree of Life can grow in every human spine. Let the souls swirl past the gods and goddesses of the Second World and into the ethers where your turquoise windows shine. I will hold the power of the body until it stands as firm as the backbone of nature."

The Creator commands the souls to awaken. They spin and twist to the eternal rhythm of the River, beginning the natural world with the blessings of the Life Mother. Immersed in the power of truth, their vows become clear: To nurture nature. To tend the family. To protect the Goddess. To be of service. To speak the truth. To dance and sing the joy of creation.

However, the Trickster contrives against the mystery of the draconic powers. He tries to enslave the body to the mind and tries to bind the living now to thoughts of past and future. Those who can live in the eternal now bypass the Trickster's thoughts. Lost in his own nightmare, the Trickster resists the swirling course of the River. Yet involution's fall is full of fraternity, the symbiosis of the spirit and the stars, the body and the elements. Gold falls into the darkness and emerges blood red to build white bone and pink flesh. The spectral colors of the people flash in the draconic darkness.

HEAVENLY POWERS

Like an hourglass, the cosmic vortex opens to the human mind on one side of the River and to the draconic powers on the other. Born of the burning waters, these powers design the metamorphic patterns of nature. They are magnetic dragons holding the range of probabilities in subatomic patterns. They are devas fusing divine intelligence with emerging life forms. They are nature spirits who stir the chemical elements with fiery ignition, watery cohesion, airy expansion, and earthly contraction.

Moving to the wailing wind, the draconic powers coil and ripple like magnetic snakes attuned to the resonance of the cosmic language. Now the Trickster perceives the snakes as electromagnetic waves with which he can invent a machine that resembles his thought—a computer that will quantify time and run the programs of soul, body, and mind through the wheels of the heavenly vortex.

On the other side of the vortex, devas and nature spirits weave the vibrations from the harp of the Creatrix into different patterns of time. Her music resounds inside the atoms of the body, intoning the resonant patterns of the human image. The essential rhythms of life burst forth as stars spinning at diverse angles. Time thus becomes light, bearing the intentions and aspirations of each soul who walks across the abyss toward form. The night burns with the glow of ether as they proceed through the Heavenly Powers crying for sight, speech, and the heart of a beloved. Each one is showered with colors and tones that will maintain health in the body and wholeness in the soul.

The sight of humans passing through the vortex frightens the Trickster and Antagonist in the human psyche, for they know that their emergence from the draconic hourglass will subject them not only to limitation, but also to the inner-directed empowerment of nature.

The Journey to Dragon Hill

Vortex
Gold of gold within red

The center
of every action
spirals
from within.

Kau Chiang

Kau Chiang is still recovering from his work in the refugee camps in the flooded south river country. Now that same area is scourged by drought. Partly to heal himself, he decides to take his wife and daughter to visit his aging mother, Shu Lao. Though eighty-four-years old, Shu Lao is sprightly and active in her village in the Shensi province. As their train makes its way through the mountains and valleys of the Hunan province, Kau Chiang and his wife, Heng-O, reminisce about their childhood. Their daughter, Ho Liu, who hasn't been to her grandparent's native village since she was three, peers out the window in awe of China's vastness.

Shu Lao's village lies outside the city of Ankang. As Kau Chiang stumbles up the pathway to her small house, he grows wistful. A man's thoughts and actions become his fate, he thinks. His soul still struggles with the pain of Hypatia's death, the death that split him off from his Western stream and confined him to the obscure, mysterious life of an oriental mystic poet and herbalist. Something in him longs to make public his deep insights, but his introverted nature denies this worldly connection. Periodically, sickness still overcomes him, for though he can heal others, he cannot heal himself. He is returning home both to find the root of this pain and to see his mother before she passes into the infinite beyond of heaven.

He sees his mother's small frame outside the house, her wrinkled face shining in complete happiness. "You have come home, my son," says Shu Lao after they embrace. "Come inside. I have tea and cookies for you." Then, looking around, she asks, "Where is Yu?"

"He is still studying in America. Like the Sun, he is a light that moves on, while we return to the ancient things."

While they are settling in, Ho Liu helps herself to several rice cookies and goes outside to wander in the fields. After a while, Kau Chiang asks his mother, "Do you remember when I was sick as a child, that I would soothe myself by playing the *kin* harp, and when, about forty years ago, the music stopped healing me?"

"Yes, you were Ho Liu's age, and I was afraid you would die. How could I forget that? Your father brought home an old exorcist. He thought the man saved your life."

"But I know it was your herb-soaked towels and your love that healed me, Mother. Recently, when I was helping refugees in the flooded plains of Si Kiang, I entered the same frightening state of consciousness I did back then, when I was so young. My illnesses are seeded from the same fear. I am still seeking something to release me from the fear, but it is hard to grasp, as elusive as a silk thread."

"What can it be?"

"Every morning I give thanks, and yet my body trembles with an awareness of shattered fragments of past lives. Do you recall any past lives, mother?"

"Our family knows the terrible truth of reincarnation, but I seek nothing more than what comes to me in daily life. The Tao is as vast as the River, my son. I cannot hope to know all its movements."

"But if one is limited by the pain of a previous incarnation, should one not try to find its cause?"

"Yes, I would bless the darkness, the unknown, if you need to travel that pathway. I am but an old withered leaf through which the light shines. Why do you speak to me of this?"

Heng-O dares to comment, "He wants to hunt dragons."

"Ai! Best leave them alone," Shu Lao responds, raising her hands as if to ward off danger.

Kau Chiang persists: "Not to hurt them, but to ask of their wisdom, to receive their medicines as was done in the old days."

Shu Lao leans forward, considering what it might mean for her son to encounter the dragons. Then she speaks sternly: "I've heard that the dragons are enraged in these times. Too many machines disturb the air, water, and earth. I know the facts of life. The dragons have to clear and transmute all the human disturbances. Even the magician, Fu Tsing, cannot contact the dragons anymore without earthquakes, floods, volcanoes, and pests descending upon us. Don't you know they are the cause of the cataclysms of flood and drought you've been trying to heal?"

Kau Chiang looks down at the cracked wooden floor, appreciative of the truth of his mother's humility: "I do know, Mother. I am called from my fields and my work, called from every duty or wish, to do this. I need your support. I've lived through the nightmares of this old pain for too long. I feel I can serve this Earth more fully if I am healed, and I know that only the dragons can heal me."

Shu Lao listens intently as Kau Chiang continues: "And you know the passage to Dragon Hill. I no longer know the way. If you and Heng-O support and guide me in this, I feel I can pass into the ineffable Tao before my death. I long to heal my soul's split and to make peace with the dragons so that they no longer bring destruction. I must ask them to stop shaking the Earth. All my life has returned to this single point."

The evening breeze fills the air with the scent of peach blossoms. Shu Lao sits in silence and contemplates her son's sense of purpose: "In the morning I will draw a map of the way to Dragon Hill," she says, her face donning the knowing smile of an ancient immortal. "But there are more than dragons there. I've heard that spirits controlling all of life dwell there."

Kau Chiang rises before dawn to meditate before the Taoist altar in his mother's house. The Sun and Moon shine in his eyes as he turns to greet Shu Lao. As the first rosy hues appear in the eastern sky, Shu Lao speaks: "Dragons coil around themselves when humans do not know the sacred members of their own bodies. Then water churns and clouds billow. If you do not ally with nature, the dragons tighten their coils until the very atoms of the air, water, and earth spin back toward fire. Then you can only tremble in powerlessness. Storms and quakes will burst from your cells when your thoughts scatter like rain. On your journey, take notice of the clouds and wind and any change in your body. A dragon or spirit is near. Stay in your body then, my son. Here, this stone will help you ground yourself when the whirlwinds toss everything around you."

"Thank you, Mama. This stone will touch both the skin of my hand and the breath of the dragon. Will you keep vigilance with Heng-O until I return?"

"The spirit that touches all things will be with you. My daily living will be enough support. That is all I can give. Here is the map to Dragon Hill. Even now the dragons know you are coming. Stay in your center, my son. We'll await your return."

Kau Chiang sets out, passing over the Ho Ling mountains at Chung-Nana. Holding the stone, he catches a glimmer of a dragon coiled amidst the clouds. He prays to the spirit who surrounds him, "Help me walk on clouds as in the old days!"

The counsel of the spirit dances in Kau Chiang's undulating thoughts: "Befriend the Green Dragon of the east. Then you can face the demons that hold you in fear."

The spirit speaks in a mysterious language that Kau Chiang can only intuit. Open and receptive from the long trek through the mountains, his mind translates the formless ethers of the River's message: "Dangerous Moon over moist mountains, daring you to face the Green Dragon. Step in the steepness of your holy intention and travel the long silken road to your true nature robe."

Kau Chiang feels elixir hormones dripping down from his pineal and watches the dragon loosen its knotted grip on the wind and water. He crosses the boundary of the eastern country where the elementals of wind and wood move. He bows to the ground. A great whirling cone forms over his head, anchored by four great invisible beings: his spirit, the dragon of the eastern country, and the elementals of wind and wood.

"Drin, dtin, djiin!" The Green Dragon sweeps up Kau Chiang's anguish while a hummingbird suspends itself over his prostrate body. His soul enters the crystal fire, plunging back through the events that led to this inexplicable pain of death and the division of the Eastern and Western ways of the Tao. He sees himself as Hypatia in Alexandria, before her death.

Kau Chiang sees the streets of Alexandria filled with Jews, Greeks, Christians, and Egyptians. His soul is the soul of Hypatia. His vow is her own. Yet the painful split of East and West separates him from her. Riding in her chariot on that fateful day, she became precognizant of her own untimely death. Yet to prevent it she would have to swallow her light and stifle her truth. This she could not do. As one who communed with the dragons and archangels in her former archaic lives, Hypatia knew both the precise mathematics of the vortex of heaven and the subtle natural laws that the Christians saw as miracles. She lectured and wrote on conics and astronomy, and the lineage of the perennial wisdom through pagan Neoplatonic pathways. She knew the truth when she saw it. The Bishop of Alexandria feared her light. Their purposes clashed like swords. Hypatia chose to not strive against fate. The bishop designed her death.

In his trance, Kau Chiang sees a wide-eyed Christian monk whom he recognizes as Peter. The man is leading other monks toward Hypatia's chariot. She is dragged to the Caesarean Church and beaten to death. But her soul hovers above her body in a fierce but beautiful love, watching the mutilation and burning of the bone and fleshly remains. Rising through the cones of the heavens she had so meticulously studied and known, Hypatia's soul still radiates her spiritual vow: *To know the laws of creation and redemption and to speak the truth.*

Out of the clouds above the Ho Ling mountains spin the akashic crystals, revealing precise answers to Kau Chiang's quest. Even though he knows the answer, Kau Chiang cries out to the Green Dragon of the east, "But what *within me* made the bishop and Peter so vengeful?"

He has only to think of a question before the answer emanates from the etheric vortices that link the dragon, Earth, and memory. The dragon speaks in riddles: "Weep no more. The spirit of my wind is in your lungs. My teeth are akashic crystals reflecting the fire of mortals' vows. You cannot fully live your vow until you meet the Red Bird of the south. To find her you must release Hypatia's death as a voluntary sacrifice. Nothing can be taken that is freely given. Peter's soul wanders in the darkness. Have no vengeance."

Kau Chiang's memory turns back to his fear: "But why am I split into two souls?"

The spirit slows its vibration to speak clearly to Kau Chiang: "Your road of life did not begin in Alexandria. It only stopped there momentarily. Your light beamed too brightly amid a world plunging into darkness. The one who killed you was an old nemesis. Those who have fallen cannot bear that others see the light of heaven. Even from death, you came forth a shining one, your bones white with the divine plan of old priests and priestesses. And, since you were a woman in a world already subdued by men, envy waxed too strong for you to survive unchanged."

Kau Chiang understands, but his soul cries in pain: "How did the perennial wisdom become lost? Why must the Western way dominate nature? How can I find and heal my Western soul and bring it back to the old wisdom?"

His own spirit speaks clearly: "The winds of time and history were turbulent then. What is lost is unreal. Stay with truth and your Western soul will eventually learn the Eastern wisdom that you know. The old temples stand empty that they may be again filled with a beauty that will banish doubt and fear forever. How can fear be released if it is not felt? Fear drives those who have no light between their eyebrows, no warmth in their heart. You yourself feared your light would be swallowed, but now you can move into the light beyond heaven."

"But I want to manifest that light on Earth."

"And so you shall."

In a turning of his consciousness, Kau Chiang announces, "May I be humble, yet not fear my own light. For sixteen-hundred years I have lived in obscurity. Help me to forgive all those who have striven against me or have fear on my account. Help me to ground the truth on Earth and to heal the split between East and West."

Once Kau Chiang has fully embodied his vow, he enters through the turquoise realm into the eye of the cone. Before him are images of heavenly landscapes where he beholds the circling spheres of archangels, angels, and spirits of the stars. He has not seen them since the time in Alexandria, and before that in Atlantis and Lemuria. Gradually the clouds disperse, and he enters the vortex around the Green Dragon. His communion with the Green Dragon washes the evils away from thousands of souls in the floods of time. The cone of stars turns to diamond. Before him now is a pure lake of paradise.

In his vision, three Immortals appear. Resonating to the sounds of the pentatonic scale, they fly with him over the pyramids of Shensi. Kau Chiang beholds the ten pyramids as they were before the city of Sian-Fu existed, when they powered all of southeastern Asia. As he rides on the top of the pyramids' etheric vortices, he hears the counsel of the three Immortals: "Your work is to heal the Earth by uniting the Eastern and Western streams."

Kau Chiang's spirit, now at one with him, speaks from within him: *Something in me remembers the origin of the universe. After Lemuria crystallized, I thought my way to the mainland of China. I went from the wild waters of chaos to the holy waters of peace. My spirit soared to the four directions over the Shensi pyramids, where the holy lake reflected the Silver Net that even now links all things. Oh, wonder of wonders! The net is so fine that nothing can measure it, for it is the measure of all things. It surpasses even the cone of heaven.*

Kau Chiang stands free of all desire and will. The wind grows stronger and the air swirls with dust. The holy lake ripples, as if speaking for the first time in aeons. Feeling the tension of the wind in his spirit, Kau Chiang descends the ridge to the valley, where Dragon Hill rises in a bowl of moss-covered cliffs.

There he beholds the lake he saw in his vision only moments before. He takes some water and drinks deeply, his body breaking into a cleansing sweat. Suddenly he realizes what before he knew only as a spirit: *No one has drunk from these waters since the holy warriors fled the*

Atlantean cities. Set free, the demons of Sian converged on the yellow Earth from the highest pyramid and blocked all access to the holy lake country.

Kau Chiang climbs Dragon Hill with his stone in his hand. He can feel the support and strength of his mother and Heng-O. *I open my heart to the silence of the stars. May I be filled with the holy waters and the messages of dragons. Here and now I invoke the vortex of heaven to help me heal the division of East and West.*

The four divine beings of the four directions fly toward Dragon Hill where Kau Chiang stands. The overlighting intelligences of the landscape swirl into the vortex that surrounds him. As the holy waters flush the ancient torment from his cells, he grows ecstatic. There in the glow of descending twilight, he beholds the Red Bird of the south.

THE WIDE PACIFIC

Resonance
Black of gold within red

Interference patterns
of divine thought
ripple and spread
through the darkness.

The Creatrix spreads the vibrations of the heavenly vortex into resonant fields where human souls scintillate like flowers in the Sun. The Antagonists of the soul, bewildered by her quivering harp strings, behold the shadows of their unlived vows and unfulfilled desires, lying idle in the abyss between worlds. The golden immortal spirit slips through the heavenly vortex without a whisper, in sharp contrast to the black turbulence of the soul. Although the Antagonists resist entry into the Third World, the genetic code already spins a prenatal etheric mold imprinted with the soul's desire.

The play of vibrations floods the sky with the akashic records of the human souls. While each soul spins through the vortex, its colors, tones, movements, and forms resound on the harp strings, vibrating to those patterns in the River's script that hold the fulfillment of its vow. The Creatrix acknowledges the name each has chosen through the intensity of its dedication to the whole of creation. The River undulates with individual harmonics while providing the great flux that connects all in a buoyant stream.

Divine immanence, the central channel of creation, links the involuting people to the Tree of Life in the spine of the Creatrix. As their causal bodies flow toward their astral bodies, the shock of uniqueness ripples from the River to the shore of existence and back again. Not yet in body, the human souls feel already how life is created through the music of resonance.

Zoa, Mujaji, Nummo, and Fa

Breakers crash over the reef that protects the island of Tahiti. On the beach beside a placid lagoon, Zoa is working hard on his boat. He glances up occasionally to check on his son Nummo, now ten, who is gleefully playing in the waves with Tahitian youths. Nearby, in the shade of tall coconut palms, stands the small thatched hut Zoa has built for his family. His friend Paloa, who taught, or rather helped Zoa remember, the old crafts, works beside him. They are milling a pole for a doubled-hulled canoe, the type introduced by the 'ari'i, the Polynesian conquerors who came to the islands around A.D. 600. Zoa feels happy. The crafting of his own canoe and house have brought his hands alive. As he relaxes into his new life, the resonance of the vow he made before his birth shines in blue tinged with pink.

Although there are few black people on the island, Mujaji's loving radiance has helped to allay any wariness among the natives. Mujaji, Zoa's wife, teaches African dances to the village women and has become friends with Ohah, a priestess who is instructing her in the sacred dances of the Tahitians.

Mujaji likes to weave her way through the Tahitian jungle. Its lush green helps to dissolve the sounds of the city—the traffic, the sirens, and the blaring music that even now vibrates in her cells. Although the blue Pacific waters are gradually dissolving the anxiety she felt in New York, she feels troubled as she walks to Ohah's house near the village temple. She needs to confide in someone her worry about Fa.

Ohah waves to Mujaji from the stone platform outside her home.

"I'm glad you're here," says Mujaji.

"What is it, Mujaji?" asks Ohah, who can see the worry on the face of her friend. "Come inside." They enter a matted room, where a single lotus flower casts an aura of peace.

"Would you like some guava juice?"

"Yes, thank you."

Ohah's brown eyes seem to turn to amethyst.

"I'm worried about my daughter, Fa," Mujaji begins. "She wants to leave New York, but instead of joining us here she wants to go to Africa."

"Fa lives in the dream of a future beyond our ways," says Ohah, from a caring yet distant place. "She has a mission, Mujaji. Her life vow is different from yours, yet the same."

"How do you mean?"

Ohah has observed Fa clairvoyantly: "Her will is with the old spirits of your people. She wants to learn from them, and she will offer them something about the Earth that she already knows. Doesn't she love to garden?"

"Yes, her school interests were in agriculture and biology. She wants to make the whole Earth a garden. Her letters tell of a mission to help the starving people of a village in Africa where a friend dwells. With such an impossible dream, how could she not be disappointed?"

"Mujaji, my friend," responds Ohah compassionately, "I feel you've reached a knot in your own soul that needs untying."

Mujaji looks up and asks, "What is it?" Then her head drops: "Am I to lose my daughter, my baby?"

"Perhaps you can find her as she finds herself."

Mujaji sighs and rises to go. Ohah walks with her to the top of the hill above the northern shore and then returns to her own hut in the heat of midday.

Mujaji weeps as she walks down the forested slope toward the northern shore. On the long walk back through the forest, Mujaji realizes how her own mother's possessive love made her react and rebel when she was younger. Now that repressed selfish love still resides within her and clings to Fa. She inwardly declares to herself, *I am trying to hold on to Fa just like Mama held on to me!* As she begins to release her expectations and possessiveness, she sees the gold-green light flicker in the leaves. She begins to feel diaphanous, permeated by the mystery of the forest. She renews her inner vow: *I will try to let Fa follow her own loves and interests.*

Feeling lighter, she can faintly see the devas of the valley who were invisible to her sight before. Her step becomes agile as she begins to dance in the forest between the twisted vines. New dances spin from her soul, casting her into a spell of rhythm and gesture that breaks through the clinging knot in her heart. She sees the blue of the Pacific shine through the vines. Waves whisper and birds call in a tongue that her soul remembers. Reaching the beach, she moves in song and dance and begins to reclaim peace.

On her return to the village, she sees Zoa and Nummo carrying the new outrigger across the white sands. The excitement of the fishing launch vibrates across the shallows. Brown and black feet splash through the water and vault into place along the gunwales. Filled with the resonance of their own souls, Zoa and Nummo laugh as their paddles dip in unison. The canoe moves at one with the music of their hearts, through the break in the reef and out to the open sea.

Turning Back Heaven

Time
Red of gold within red

The circles
of heaven
turn forward and back
through the Earth.

Again and again, a soul lives and dies to release unspent desires into creation. The fiery power of the First World flashes through the spirits and into the souls of mortals who ever press against eternity toward time. The movement toward incarnation begins with fire, then passes through desire and falls into existence.

Appearing to advance in the straight path of the arrow, time circles among intersecting lives that push through darkness into the red flame of life. A mandala of creation, time circles backward and forward in bodies whose cellular eyes behold the mystic center of the twelve-jeweled wheel. The twelve knights of the Round Table, the twelve gods of Egypt, the twelve kings of Madagascar, the twelve saints of Georgia—all reflect the zodiacal circles that mirror heaven on Earth. The rulers of the twelve tribes migrate across the Earth, each bearing the breastplate of twelve gems attuned to the heavenly zodiac and the cities of an unknown future.

Zapana and Raphael

Having crossed the ocean from Europe to reach Zapana's village in Mexico, Raphael remains immersed in the ocean of his own thought. He reflects on how time both unites and divides people. Even though he and Maria have parted once again, he feels the eternal love that liberates them both from time's illusions. Carrying this sense of eternity in his heart enables him to greet trials with compassion as he works again in Zapana's village.

The poverty in the village staggers Raphael. The streets are filled with homeless children who wander and beg and sometimes eat garbage. Raphael dreams of Maria as the children's mother and reflects on the contrasting prosperity of his son, Ariel. Maria inspires him. Her power is that of the mother within him whose compassion is boundless. Turning his own love into charity, he works with Zapana to find families who will take in abandoned children. Behind every child's cry he sees the innocence of a soul trying to distill goodness and love from the dregs of fear.

As each tomorrow becomes today, they create a park where the children can play and run, where their cries change into song. The two men search for the streams of work and play where the River runs deep, renewing them with the burning waters of love.

After a day's hard work, they nurture each other in small ways. Frequently they retire to their room, next to the one shared by Zapana's sisters, and read poetry to each other by candlelight. Although they sometimes feel a tender nostalgia and a harmony that transcends time, there remains a strain on Zapana's soul that consumes him. Like a burning house, he feels his attachments to the past being peeled back and burned, revealing a painful yet ecstatic core. His illusions are being shattered. Though he no longer yearns to resurrect the ruins of his royal history, something obstructs him from giving himself wholly to the present. He has experienced many lives, yet time seems to slither away like a snake. Already forty, he is nevertheless very wise. His work with the children continuously opens him to himself and to the love of Raphael. But it is hard.

Zapana is like a serpent that devours itself in circles of circles, wheels within wheels. His house is filled with objects reflecting the old sacred calendars, for he feels that improving the social world is reliant on the rhythms of the heavens. In the evenings he sometimes studies the meaning of the ancient glyphs.

Zapana feels ignited by the presence of Raphael, whose energy is even more radiant since returning from Europe. Zapana's own kundalini energy has become so powerful that he is rapt in a continuous waking communion that alternates between ecstasy and pain. Were it not for Raphael, he might run madly through the night, for he cannot sleep. He lies on his cot and breathes the air in inspired prayer with the silent current flowing up his spine. Tormenting sensations and thoughts from long ago flurry through his being until they melt in the fire of his soul. He seeks to conquer time and live in the eternal now.

Zapana's constant stirring wakes Raphael on a cot next to him. Raphael speaks plainly as he passes from dream to consciousness: "You are restless, my friend. Would it help to talk?"

Zapana sighs: "My heart is heavy. There is some orb that moves through my stream of incarnations that I struggle to remember and heal. I lie here burning in a strange water that awakens struggle within me."

Raphael rubs his eyes: "Just talk, and the essence of it may be revealed. I believe in you."

"Let's walk to the river and talk there. I don't want to wake up my mother and sisters."

They walk under a full Moon in silence, the air full with the sound of crickets and fragrant with night-blooming flowers. Raphael carries his drum. At the river bank they sit down and look up at the Moon, which seems to rush through the clouds.

A certain tension vibrates between them. Finally Raphael tries to comfort Zapana: "I float content, and I can hold the restlessness of your soul. At the core of pain and ecstasy is a vision that can bring you peace and freedom. Now, if you wish, I will help you enter a trance in which you can explore the root of your pain in time. I will be with you anywhere you go."

Grateful for such a friend, Zapana feels the tension beginning to dissolve inside him. Raphael speaks softly and begins to drum: "Merge with the sound of the water. The River knows everything, and in its depths you can turn back the pages of your incarnations and bless the darkness. Eternity loves the myriad forms of time that die and are reborn. Through the past you can find the eternal present. Just listen, and when you touch depth, let your eternal soul speak."

Zapana feels an emotion of soul that cannot be spoken. Time rotates in a whirlwind of passion as he enters the dark secrets of his heart. He longs to play the music of his soul, but there is an obstruction. The more he relaxes, the greater the vigilance of his mind and the greater the inner tension. The words of Raphael seem to float around him: "Allow yourself to go deeper in the River. Down, down into the depths."

A concentrated dilation opens Zapana to visions of a former life in the tenth century. He begins to speak, faintly at first: "I am Mixcoatl, the chief of the Chichimeca tribe. I am dressed in full warrior regalia. There is a scent of weed. We are marching in intense heat toward Cuernavaca."

His words become clearer as the scenes unfold before him: "I am seeking to establish a center for our people. Just as the shadows grow long toward the east, a woman leads a band of fighting men toward me. She is dressed as a warrior and I am stupefied by her beauty. She throws her spear toward me but I leap aside, the spear just missing my flesh. Her eyes speak of her defense of Cuernavaca. I read her soul as if it were my own, yet I feel alone. She is a ball of fury. I realize I must fight her or die myself. I see an ominous darkness in the sky, but behind it is a feeling of the music of my soul. The fragrance of roses comes to me though none grow in this rocky plain.

"My soul questions whether I am to kill her, but I have no choice. I thrust my spear. She fends it off with her shield. We battle with clubs edged with sharp obsidian blades, poised like hungry snakes ready to devour each other. She rages, then strikes me and leaps upon me. I use the magic of my God against her, but she is protected by some invisible power. Stumbling up again, she curses me as I strike her feather-covered shoulder. Mindlessly, I watch the blood flow. She surprises me with a quick move and throws me to the ground again. I feel both elation and dread. I grab her arm and pull her down. Our bodies roll together in confusion. Two of her men descend upon me as she gets to her feet. She stands still against the sunset, holding a feathered sword, and orders them not to kill me.

"Thunder rolls from the sky. I am enthralled by her magic, by the wonder of this warrior who shows her enemy such mercy. Then she speaks: 'Let us make a truce. I will allow you to come to Cuernavaca if you give me your soul.'

"'Who are you?'

"'I am Chimalman.'"

Raphael watches Zapana stare into space as he breathes silently. He feels a change in him. The warrior is dying and the lover is being born. Raphael sees Mixcoatl consumed in flame, becoming one with the light of the stars.

"I see your heart is a river of fire, my friend," says Raphael clearly. "Lead me to your desires. Let the River carry you. Bless me with your words."

Zapana finds it hard to speak: "My fear of Chimalman has changed to desire. The Sun rolls from east to west as we lie in bed together for the first time. The Moon rises and sets through our kiss. I have never felt such love. Our breath, our blood, sing in midair as if one. We vibrate in unison to the pant and thrill of serpentine rhythms, longing for eternity within each other. I enter the mysterious fragrance of her body and together we plunge to the depths of the cosmos. I dive like a serpent and rise like a quetzal bird. I feel all of heaven within me."

Zapana pauses as if in awe of some unknown beauty: "Now her belly swells like a ripened fruit. Her lips are soft. The Sun and stars move through my pores like eyes beholding the colors of flowers. We find we are warriors of a single resolve: to open the gates of heaven and flood the Earth with the waters and fires of the gods. She is pregnant both with child and with purpose. Chimalman and I are one."

Zapana becomes silent and seems to sink into unconsciousness, but his soul emerges like a ribbon of blue smoke: "I see who I am. I am the father of a child, a being of great destiny. His aura billows out like a plumed serpent. But my sorrow is as deep as the abyss, for Chimalman has died in childbirth, the blood spilling from her womb like a river. My soul is hers. She has gone into the matrix of the lord of death. Where is she now? I cannot find her. I am a feathered warrior, thirsty for her love."

Zapana weeps and seems lost in self-absorption until he says, "The pain of her loss overwhelms me. I rule Cuernavaca for many years, but I grow angry and bitter. Tigers of wrath prowl in my soul. Only chanting the teachings of Quetzalcoatl changes my sorrow into hope. Chimalman's voice resounds from heaven. Through chanting I rise to her. She gathers up my soul in the vibrancy of spiritual fire. Invisible light radiates from the netherworld. I struggle for her love.

"Sometimes I forget my sorrow and move beyond memory while our son grows in stature. His name is Ce Acatl Topiltzin. Chimalman speaks power into him from the heavens and teaches him the sacred ways of Quetzalcoatl. My soul ripens through love for him. He embodies the ancient ways. His brow pulses with the knowledge of the Sun and the planets. His heart carries the wisdom of the one spirit, turning through the vortex that unites heaven and Earth. His hands learn the skills of the spear and the pen. He knows the symbols. For this I am grateful."

Zapana lies by the riverbank in another time, another place. Chimalman glows in the stars above him. His soul is caught in two parts of one whole whose body extends beyond the turning of the planet. The oneness of his love lifts him from the hungry faces of the orphans. The sad music of humanity only charges his intent.

As the Moon descends toward the west, Raphael speaks gently: "Cast off all that is false. Conceal nothing from yourself. Tell all to the River and you shall be free."

Zapana feels the magnetism of the two parts of his soul drawn toward one source: "I am lying awake on my bed, feeling the power of Chimalman nearby," he murmurs. "Suddenly a man enters my room. I recognize his profile against the moonlit windows. He is the rival of my son. Without warning, he plunges his dagger into my heart."

Zapana screams the scream he could not scream before. He feels a double destiny, drawn both toward life and toward death, where Chimalman dwells. He is transported by death in a silver phantom boat from the eastern to the western horizon:

"I feel Chimalman gather my soul into hers. Now we are one again.

Her compassionate face opens to me. We meet in a realm that is neither dark nor light. I count my breath forward and back until time ceases. I face the serpents who held me in their power. I see where my flesh burned with war. I die for every man I sacrificed and vow to never kill again. Chimalman and I have one purpose. We return through a turquoise hourglass to a realm of gold. I long to rule a kingdom in peace, but my kingdom is seized by my assassin."

THE BIRTH OF A STAR

Star
White of gold within red

The radiance
of the soul
shines brighter
in the darkness.

Petruska

Petruska is neither alive nor dead. Her body left Channon and Horst in hatred and rage, but her soul still wanders in other worlds. She frequently hallucinates. Over and over she has the same dream of being refused a new incarnation. She wanders Siberia this summer, seeking a way through her madness. Dozing in a Siberian inn, she begins to dream again:

Petruska's soul casts no shadow in the abyss. For another thousand years she walks with her heart entangled in thorns, severed from the ways of immortality and mortality. Her mind watches her soul falling— falling into nothingness like a meteor dropping in the sky. Her passion is spent. Only a thin ribbon of vital essence remains in her desperate appeal to the gods to call her soul back. In fear of total annihilation, she wanders as a hungry ghost, drifting endlessly in a vortex of backward-turning cycles.

She circles the zodiac of beasts with unexpressed longing. In the faces of her sister, and of priests and priestesses, she projects enemies that conceal her from a shaft of light. With twisted reasoning, she asks, "Haven't I given everything for my soul?"

"No, you have given nothing for your soul," replies a forbearing angel, who wears a tiger skin to shield herself from the thick images of the astral realms where she descends when Petruska calls.

"I will not be annihilated," cries Petruska's ghost.

The angel is stern, yet compassionate: "I will cover you with the darkness of the abyss until you can walk home yourself."

"What can I do here? I am tired, even without a body. My arms are heavy and my back is bent under the weight of my past."

"Those sensations are mere phantoms. Lay down your burden. You are a star. You have the power to go through your fears."

"What strength is left in me to be born? Every time I enter a body, I become enraged and my blood turns to poison. I tremble before birth and have no chance of rebirth. Yet I will not pass away."

The angel disappears into a star while Petruska's ghost drifts as aimlessly as smoke throughout the abyss. She sees her sister as a nun, praying before a medieval altar, her knees calloused from the stone church floor. Petruska inhales the prayer until it stirs within her, becoming an urge, a portent of possibility. Gathering her feeble essence, she tries to walk between the giant pillars of heaven. Yet when she approaches the tall columns of truth, she encounters the hideous faces of her own demons and draws back. She tries to fight them, once again wasting the precious fluids of her soul essence. She falls back, away from the pillars, and weeps helplessly. Angry mists weave knots around her heart. Although hundreds of years pass in the darkness, time stands still at the River's edge where waves of possibility pass by.

Looking into the abyss, Petruska's ghost beholds the face of Horst as Manesis. He is a magician in the sixteenth century, mixing earthly elements and spells in an attempt to steer the stars. But his efforts at control only reverberate back to him, for he is tangled in fate, pressed into a density where the freedom of his destiny is lost. Horrified at the vision, Petruska spits out darting flames of hatred from the last coals burning in her heart.

Memory still churns within Petruska. She recalls the language of the gods, but fears the emergence of truth. On another night of dreaming, again the pillars of heaven rise before her. Purple dreams float by as she puts all her hope in her heart. This night, Petruska's dream changes. Looking toward the horizon of potential birth, she spins a cocoon of her original purpose and reaches back to the source of her soul. *I shall not fall into oblivion,* she cries. *I am filled with rainbow colors. I am fire becoming light. My deliverance is within me. I create myself anew. I spin my destiny and part the waves of terror and madness to live in truth. Help me!*

Petruska's affirmation and prayer enable her to hold the fire within her heart long enough to pass through the pillars of heaven with the veils of illusion pulled back. She momentarily dies to the phantoms of the past, the debris of illusory projections consumed in the burning waters of the River. Having passed through the pillars, she beholds the Tree of Life. She reaches out and touches it, instantly sliding into the womb of her mother.

Curled up around the umbilical cord of life, she dreams of the universe forming out of the darkness. She beholds the giant lotus emerging out of the chaos of the First World. Pulsing with primal vibrations, the flower of the world opens and closes amid galaxies swirling out of the abyss. She sees her soul's longing as a blue snake that winds back and forth between her immortal spirit and her changing bodies. It moves between the lotus petals and weaves the elements into growing cells. Her flickering light steadies as she rediscovers the meaning in the speech of the ancient gods. The cells of her embryo remember the symbols, the spells, and the ancient names.

Circling in the flux of time, Petruska's light forges a new body, molded from her longing. Her spine stretches, blessed by the Tree of Life she touched with her heart. Her brain fills with the white heat of her phoenix power of regeneration. She remembers. When the faces of her demons appear, her tiny fingers burn holes in the phantom of their forms. Descending on a silver cord rooted in the immortal spirit, her angel appears and proclaims, "Awaken. Open your heart before you are born, or you shall be pulled back into the darkness. Your mind turns back on itself. Your soul cannot find its home as long as your heart is fearful. Your eyes are double. Align them into a single vision of the heart."

Still terrified of existence, Petruska trembles, afraid to open her heart in a world of change. Her embryonic body begins to contract as the ripples in her heart rebound in her mind. But the prayers of her sister course through the sweet ethers and sweep aside the fear. Filled with unseen light, Petruska unwinds the scroll of her destiny and calls out the spells to the gods. Now linked to all of life, her heart is full, throbbing with a crystalline light that mirrors the light of her soul.

A star is born, and all of heaven rejoices in a song.

Heavenly Power's Song of the River

I am the heavenly vortex that spins all worlds.
I am the spiral that curves in cones, shells, and the human ear.
I am the sound of the wind changing tone at every front.
I live in the tides and rolling surf.
I am the stars and planets rotating in heaven.
You can find me in the spin of every galaxy.
Look for me in all resonant waves.
I am the wave-field of all tonalities.
I am the light that geometrizes in constant motion.
I am time as a cycle of rhythms.
I am growth and decay, birth and death.
I am the mirror of God in nature.
Look for me in the helical unfoldment of water, plants, and bones.
You can find me in shifting perceptions.
I am the radiant expression of every star.

Are you the source of movement in the world?
I am the arrow of time in the bow of the ages.

THE SHAMAN

From the turbulent Primal Waters and the unbridled feelings of the human soul, the imaginal world of nature is conceived. Astounding in its immensity, driven by the force of the Creator and the blood of the Creatrix, Creation falls from the triumphant tide of the waters into the imaginal realm of the Shaman.

In this way, the soul of Creation proliferates from the Second World. Nature spirits spread canopies of elemental wonder in hidden pristine landscapes. Beauty blooms fresh and full in the fellowship of simple things. Nothing is lost in the imaginal wilderness, for all is a revelation where nothing is possessed. The Shaman owns nothing, and thus the wild responds to his song and his drum. The spectral colors of his feathered headdress ripple through flowers and fields.

Emerging from the underworld of the Goddess, he lays out a medicine wheel, the sphere of wholeness and potential that permeates all things with the immanence of spirit. He forms the wheel from the body of the Primal Pair, spreading it into four directions that become dimensions of the imaginal world.

In the north of the wheel he places the human image. It carries the power of the spirit that defies mortality. In the east he places the genetic code, transmitting the qualities of the soul into physical dimension. In the south he arranges the flesh and blood of body systems into patterns for the entire substance of space. In the west his mind quickens with the vital intensity of the body. Now able to perceive the forms of things, he empowers them with magic and arranges them in the imaginal landscape.

Looking for a place to settle, the human souls pass through the dimensions of the medicine wheel and cross the depths of innocence. They behold a vast space filled with images of possible natural forms. They follow the sinless paths of nature where the Shaman journeys inward. Neither vice nor virtue is known here. Neither aspen nor ash, neither oak nor elm is felled here. The axe is aimed at matter, not the plumed inner linings of the River's imaginal forms. Here the trees speak in wondrous pastoral elegies that poets will try to capture. Here the auric fields of all beings radiate.

From inside the wheel, the souls seek to understand the designs of the *wilderness that cascade down in the script of the River. Even now, they behold the work of the Shaman in the beautiful realm of form. Although dragons and devas tell the dreams of nature through flame, fluid, vapor, and Earth, their deep language cannot be fathomed by ordinary consciousness. Realizing this, the Shaman picks up his blowpipe and shoots the souls with darts of dreams. Soon they are asleep, dreaming in the wild while rapt dragons sing.*

THE LANGUAGE OF THE TREES

Sphere
Gold of black within red

Opening
to the wounded Earth
caresses
the inner child.

The gods and goddesses of the Second World circle in the sphere of the medicine wheel, the natural mirror of heaven. There, the Shaman's darts of passionflower put the human souls to sleep. The north is now dark with unconscious dreams.

The Creatrix tempers all with the faultless fluid of her blood. She brings menstruation through the heart of nature, linking women to the Shaman's dreams through the release of their blood to the Earth. Rising barefoot, they respond to the magnetism of the Moon and the language of the trees. The dreams pulse with expansion and contraction, chaos and cosmos, as the Moon waxes and wanes with the waves of the River.

The skin stretched tight over the sphere of heaven reverberates with each beat of the Shaman's drum and awakens the human souls. Moving through the medicine wheel, they resonate with the vibrations of the Earth. The course of the River spins anew, into and away from the heart and womb of the Creatrix. The resemblance of the inner and outer life trembles in the fervor of desperate eyes, seeking to behold the plan of the First World in the forms of the imaginal.

Christa and Karl

Christa awakens in the forest with nothing but the owl feather and her great inner strength. She knows she will never return to Horst. Now that she has awakened to the world of nature, she vows to live in it until she is healed. Her spontaneous vision quest weaves its own reality. She is distressed to see the trees blighted with disease. The new experience presses upon her consciousness as a continuous prayer, and she searches for the hidden charge of creation that can heal her soul as well as the Earth.

As if in answer to her prayers, she comes upon a field of buttercups drinking in the dew of dawn. Although open to nature's mysteries, she recoils from the contorted, diseased trees that remind her of Horst's grasping possessiveness. She seems to reflect everything that appears as a manifest form. Yet she shines from within, gathering her own power from fleeting steams of inspiration. When Horst railed in anger at her pursuit of her own interests, the forms of nature inspired her to draw and paint. Here, with no materials for art, but freed from the bonds of marriage, she gathers nature's ingredients in her soul.

Christa sees the owl asleep, high in the branch of an elm tree. Below, a rainbow refracts in the down of a thistle, its glitter drawing her on toward the light of a new day. The rainbow beauty also shines through the owl feather she holds up against the rising Sun. Looking through the feather into the fans of color, she is reminded of a fragment of last night's dream in which a man appeared and spoke to her: "Now you can see, where before you were blind. When you enter the sphere of nature's soul, the language of the trees will be revealed." She recalls his soft but overwhelming beauty, feeling she once knew him, but with no memory of when. She senses the dream is about a new beginning.

Not having eaten since the day before, Christa feels hungry and slightly light-headed, but she is distracted by the sound of rushing water and decides to walk toward it. Soon she comes to the great Rhine River. Its rhythmic waves lure her into a trance in which she sees herself as a medieval nun, garbed in a drab brown habit, standing in the exact same place. Her pain is deep, but it is dissolved with the divine balm of the

Holy Spirit. Christa's body fills with the joy of divine love as she looks between the worlds.

When she regains her consciousness of the present, she feels the pulsation of life all around her. She walks northward along the river and stops to eat some berries amidst the dying trees of the Black Forest. Feeling revived, she walks on and comes to a meadow spreading out from the river bank. Following her impulse to walk in a circular path, she softly hums to herself, her voice resonating with the vibrations of the plants nearby. Gradually, this attunement begins to melt some of the pain of her marriage. As she hums, her chakras begin to whirl, and she becomes aware of atoms spinning inside her cells while the Earth spins on its axis. Spheres within spheres, wheels within wheels, she begins to feel the deep connection between Mother Earth below her and the point of purpose above. All through her body the subtle energy begins to flow.

Still, she cannot remove Horst entirely from her mind. In her highly sensitized state, the mere thought of him brings a rash to her skin. Remembering the experience of the nun in her entranced vision, she begins to recite "divine love" in an effort to transform her anger. The chant brightens her, and she circles on, recalling the medieval songs of a former life.

She moves into the center of her circular path and sits down. Breathing deeply, the air flowing into her throat, chest, and belly, she sways rhythmically back and forth. She does not realize that her entire being has reached a level of relaxation unknown during her marriage. Now deep, deep pain becomes accessible, and she groans in grief as the accumulated tension from years of confinement begins to flow out of her. From the deep drone of her moaning comes an upward whine, a sound discharging sorrow. Yet over and above her wails she can hear the trees themselves crying. Christa feels horror and sorrow, for she sees how human thoughtforms have assaulted the noble trunks and changed them into knarled burls. Faces scream within those burls. She looks up at a twisted oak tree, its branches still reaching for the Sun, and sees it as a sign of hope. Many starved conifers have lost their needles.

She leans over and picks up one of the many acorns scattered on the ground and studies it, transfixed. One who has always been able to see essential patterns in the wild chaos of life, she now ponders the formless infinitude of potency within the hardened sphere of the shell. The deep contemplation transforms her pain. She feels that she herself is like a seed, that her confinement has been preparation for a new life. Scooping a handful of acorns into her pocket, she holds onto one and reflects, sensing that it might reveal the language of the trees.

That evening, she comes upon some berry bushes and spring violets that cover the forest floor. Feeling especially graced, she eats with reverence, then peacefully lies down to rest when she is startled by the sound of flapping wings. The owl has come to accompany her night journey of the soul. Alighting in the middle branches of a tall fir tree, it pulls its wings inward and blinks. Darkness descends through a long spacious silence until the owl's quiescent hoot brings a glimpse of truth and peace to her soul.

The following morning, Christa awakens feeling the air crisp with expectation and decides to wander among the flowers in the meadow. The song of a nearby thrush is so clear that it seems to cleanse her own throat.

She begins to move in the simplicity of being one with the innocent mind, and she tethers her soul to nature. Still musing upon the language of the trees, she gazes upon a grove of alders and feels their patience. In the bright patterns of plants, insects, and birds, she finds the threads of a story. *These, too, are paths to and from God,* she reflects to herself, seeing the symmetry of the leaves as an oracle that unites the sundered sides of right and wrong. She wonders how people can return to the innocence of nature.

Examining the sibylline patterns of root and shoot that pierce the hardness of rock, she realizes that gentleness can overcome rigidity if one has the silent constancy of the plant. She reflects on how the seed dies to become both a root reaching down for the darkness, density, and depth of the Earth and a shoot stretching upward toward the light, air, and height of heaven. *Everything in life expands and contracts in rhythms,* she thinks. *Light and darkness, spirit and flesh, fire and earth, are not good and evil, but the natural innocence of opposites.*

Her intense reactions to Horst change. Atavistic images swirl within her mind until she calms the pain of human abuse of nature and other humans. Slowly she disengages from identifying with her own pain. Instead, she transmutes the pain into a stimulant that charges her nerves toward exploration.

By seeing pattern in chaos and finding the thread of similarity in the diverse forms of trees, she begins to rediscover her own spirit. She beholds in nature the rays, spirals, circles, and whorls that characterized her art. *Chaos is full of possibility*, she muses, recalling the wild flurry of energy in the turbulence of the river's whirlpools. *Without chaos there can be no form. It is part of the process of the spiritual becoming material.*

Christa observes how leaves climb stems in rhythmic spiraling alternation until they flower at their apex into a star or cup. *Leaves long for light and become chalices when they flower*, she thinks. *Their desire blooms into a colorful, scented essence that lures insects for pollination. Then, as though pregnant, the berry begins to swell.* Recalling the acorns in her pocket, she ponders how the spherical form begins in the seed and reappears in the fruit at the end of the cycle.

As she meanders lost in thought along the banks of the polluted Rhine, she sees the great river as it was in medieval times, relatively pristine and pure, bubbling with blue waters. Medieval chants again emerge from her heart. She breaks into song in praise of God, the joyful melodies drawing her spiritual intention to a peak.

Karl hears Christa's voice in crescendo above the rushing sound of the whitewater and is stirred by its beauty. The contrast of pollution and purity beckons him. He continues walking along the river until he sees her, standing and singing as if drawn toward some mystical center. He stops and listens to the loveliness of her song, not knowing whether to withdraw or to approach her. When Christa turns and sees him, she flinches, startled by the sudden appearance of a man in the woods.

"Don't be afraid." His gentle voice at once puts her at ease. Slowly he walks toward her.

"Who are you? Where did you come from?" she asks.

"I used to live near here, in Karlsruhe. I walk out here whenever I get a chance. My name is Karl." He plucks some shepherd's purse to combine with the prickly lettuce and other herbs he has been gathering in a knapsack. "Would you like some herbs?"

"How do you know what is edible?" Christa is hungry, but feels cautious.

"I lived entirely on plants and animals in this forest during the Second World War. As a child I slept in the thick boughs of these trees. But now they are diseased and suffering. A human wasteland is encroaching upon the virgin forest."

"Yes, it seems that our pollution has affected the entire Earth. It saddens me as it must sadden you, who knew this forest when it was pristine. Why have you returned here?"

"To see if I can recapture the mystery of nature I knew in childhood. I am amazed that Mother Earth supports us all despite our abuse of her."

Christa nods, pondering briefly a sense of familiar alliance with this stranger. Suddenly she realizes he is the man who appeared in her dream during her first night in the forest.

"Odd that we should meet here in the forest," she says, hesitant to reveal her dream. "I didn't expect to see anyone." She decides to try some of the wild herbs.

"And what is *your* name?" asks Karl, sitting down on the grass. "Why did *you* come here?"

Christa sits down across from him. "My name is Christa. I have yet to discover why I came here," she replies in a serious tone. She looks into Karl's face and decides to be totally frank. "I have run away from my husband. I am trying to recover from that, to heal myself. You may not believe this, but I recently dreamed of you. I'm sure the face was yours. You told me to enter the sphere of nature's soul—that there the language of the trees would be revealed."

Karl listens intently, but pauses a long while before speaking. He has recognized her from a previous lifetime. "Destiny has brought us together. I have lost my way many times and have waited through many long nights. Now I have found. . . ."

"You have found what?"

"I have found . . . formless mystery."

He tries to make a more tangible metaphor: "I want to fathom the relationship between chaos and form. I want to surrender to the formless so that I can find a new form, a new way of life."

Christa hands him an acorn: "There is possibly something within a seed that can reveal the mystery. I am looking for it also." She pauses and looks deeply into his eyes.

Karl silently studies the acorn, then looks up and gazes at Christa. Their eyes stay fixed upon one another until Karl is distracted by something in the bushes. He goes over and plucks a cocoon from a tree limb: "Look at this! Have you ever seen the emergence of a butterfly from a pupa? Metamorphosis from a crawling, devouring larva into a free-flying butterfly is through a kind of chaos, a protoplasmic decomposition."

"Do you mean the insect regresses?"

"Yes. It returns to chaos to grow into a higher form of life. It goes inward to find a new outer form. Perhaps we are both looking for the same things in different ways. It seems that a chaotic formless state often takes place inside an encapsulated sphere—a seed or egg. It holds the greatest possibility."

Christa, recalling her own similar insight with the acorn, is excited by Karl's statement: "Maybe what happens in the seed is reminiscent of the emotional turmoil I feel. The river's polluted, swirling waves mirror my own state of being. I have no idea what will emerge. I'm amazed that the forces in a tiny seed can transform it into a tree." She hands another acorn to Karl.

"Perhaps we have not been planted in the right soil. I have returned here from the United States to rediscover what I knew in childhood. The scientific work was challenging, but it left my soul unfulfilled." He munches on the herbs and offers more to Christa.

"I love nature, but I don't understand science," she responds, feeling very animated. "Science has not brought healing to nature."

"And what fulfills your soul?"

"What saved my soul in my tormenting marriage was my creativity. I tried to express chaos through art, to discover some universal patterns in the wild stream of life. I don't know what soil I will be planted in, but I do know that I will never go back. I prefer this wilderness to the stifling show of aristocratic society."

Immersed in a powerful resonance, Karl and Christa reflect upon their own deepest longings. Each aura expands to include the other, merging the polarities of their souls into a great sphere of golden light filled with eternity. Their imaginations glow with visions of a possible future.

Unable to remain in the vastness of that sphere, Christa leaps up impulsively. She picks up a bundle of fallen leaves and needles and flings them at Karl. He jumps up to chase her, and they playfully dart in and out of the shadows of the trees. Christa manages to hide behind a thicket of blackberry bushes and shrieks in delight when Karl passes her by. He feels the power of life pulse between them. She bolts away and runs as fast as she can back to the meadow, where she tumbles laughing into the grass. Soon Karl is beside her, and their bodies surrender to the Earth and to each other.

THE GAME OF LIFE

Dimension
Black of black within red

Perception
of self and others
builds or collapses
world views.

To be loving and lovable, mortals must stretch out into distant dimensions and down toward death. Without tests and temptations, the soul is all too apt to fly away. The Creatrix knows this, and from her vibrant heart releases the twelvefold genetic code as an imaginal pattern for nature's unfoldment in matter. Although skeptics will later ascribe the code to chance, all of life evolves from this single origin, streaming down through the cycles of time.

Through helical chains, human love becomes bound into desire. Not yet clothed in matter, the soul holds its power poised in pure genetic possibility. The spiraling messages spin through the River as burning witnesses to the wanderings of the human souls. Desiring to feel, and then feeling, the souls long to survive in the imaginal wilderness as bodies with dimension.

The body calls forth the River and sings with the pleasures of the Earth as the human embryo passes through the cosmic flux of evolution. The spirits of the ancestors, longing to be recognized, cry passionately within the organs. Nostalgically seeking the source of the River, tribes embrace the totems of the jackal, the bear, the spider.

The labyrinths of the jungle and bush mirror the brains and ganglia of the hunter. Animal wisdom climbs the human spine, emerging as the language of the power animal, transforming hunger and predation into rites that recapitulate the brain's unfoldment.

However, the Antagonists still rage in the human soul whenever love is seemingly lost. In the struggle for love that divides and yet drives people, innocence stretches at right angles to experience. The draconic powers twist violently when the people forget their vows. Joy abounds when they live who they are, for the course of the River holds no enclosed goal.

Starlie

In the vast arid plateau of the Four Corners region of the American Southwest, the land of the Hopi Indians lies surrounded by the Navaho domain. The dust has settled from the whirlwinds of battle, when the white man broke up the communal tribal ways and the elders hid the sacred tablets. Here, on the Third Mesa of Oraibi, Starlie first heard the stories of creation and the emergence of his ancestors into the Four Worlds.

At first he did not not like being in *Tuwaqachi*, the Fourth World. In this world one could choose what one wanted, but the choice determined whether the plan of creation would continue or end in destruction, as had the previous three worlds. A prophecy told of a Fifth World that would emerge when a blue-star kachina danced in the plaza, but the thought of the disappearance of the Fourth World frightened him. Some said the Fourth World would be annihilated by nuclear bombs and radiation, an invisible fire that would instantly sear the flesh. As a child, he restlessly wondered why such a fire had to be.

His father, Wickvaya, had told him that everyone had a star. And Masaw, who became the caretaker of the Fourth World, had said that all people should look to their star for guidance, for they must migrate to find their true home and emerge into the Fifth World.

Starlie's mind and heart were strong. Until he went to the white man's boarding school, his thoughts and feelings shone like the star he knew was his. But at school he was punished when he said how he felt, so he learned to remain silent. He could only talk about his feelings to his mother, Nesaru. She had taken a job in the city, and learned the ways of the white people when his father was sent to jail.

Migrating as he did between his native ways and the white man's ways, Starlie had to follow his own star or go crazy like some of his friends. Many of the Hopi had lost their stars to alcohol.

Whenever he accompanied his mother to Winslow or Flagstaff, he would stare in amazement at the maze of railroad tracks, freeways, and jetways. Roads and wires sprang up in straight rows, like the white man's gardens. As a child he felt the power of the wires, the electronic pathways. Through the singing wires, he could hear people from far away. And he could see lights that glowed like stars inside dark buildings, where neither Sun or fire burned. These things made him wonder about the prophecy, and he would walk the streets asking himself if he was in the Fifth World. He wondered if all the technologies he encountered were part of the migrations and the plan of creation, or, as his father had said, just signs of the white man's aimless wandering.

When Wickvaya returned to his family after serving his term, he spoke sharply: "The ways of the white man will destroy the Fourth World with violence and the rain of fire. Our way is simple, gentle, one with the Earth. We must help the Fifth World to emerge gently."

However, life was not a single way to Starlie. It was a tangle of possibilities that often confused him. When he was fifteen, his father taught him how to control his star with prayer and fasting. Through the sacred ceremonies, Starlie's heart became pure and etched deeply in his soul. But he remained bored at school and found the cities exciting. Whenever he was irritated or restless, he would go to a local arcade and play the pinball machine under the dazzling lights. By pushing and jostling the machine, he could make the balls go where he wanted. His playing pinball angered his father, but it brought Starlie a certain peace. Playing the games changed his thoughts and feelings and put him in touch with his star again. He loved games of all kinds—mazes, board games, and card games.

When he first used computers at the reservation school, Starlie felt they were alive and intelligent. They had colorful displays that he could magically change by punching a few keys. He would lie in bed at night and wonder what the computers were thinking when no one was using them, for they seemed to think. Did they dream? He felt computers were his friends.

As time went on, his affinity for computers conflicted increasingly with the views of his father. Starlie accepted the white man, but only on his own traditional terms. Starlie remembered his father's warning: "When the Earth trembles and quakes, the white man will have to change back to the old ways".

Sometimes, filled with pent-up energy from the clash of different values, Starlie hitchhiked to the city to play the craziest video game he could find. He would pour power and passion into firing a laser gun at a whole fleet of jets. Controlling the game transformed his anger, for when he was angry, he lost sight of his star and became confused.

Starlie was angry for many reasons. He was angry with his father for being away in jail during the four years he needed him most. He was angry that his father, though struggling to accept the white man in his own way, refused to use modern technology. He was angry at his people for losing the Hopi way of life. He was angry at the white man for making things complicated. But when he played the video games, he *became* the laser fire. Then his star would shine and bring him peace again. His father didn't understand. Oh, how he wished he would understand!

He dreamed of using the boring stuff of the classroom to make games: words, numbers, personalities, objects. At night, looking up at the ceiling of his small room, he imagined a dream machine in which everything that was chaotic and unpredictable could enter into a game personified by monsters or allies. His shadow emerged in these wild dreams as his explosive inner life danced toward both creativity and craziness.

The computer programming classes at school were the only ones that held his interest. Through programming, he could make his dreams real. His allies and monsters could fly, shape-shift, and disappear, limited only by his imagination. When he was creating his own video games, his heart and his mind ran together, and his star shone brightly. In the classes where his energy was stifled, his star grew dim. Through the games he began to find the pathway of his own migration toward "home," the Fifth World. His father could not understand how his brilliant son had lost the sacred ways. But to Starlie, the games expressed his star and his sacred inner life.

When Starlie finished high school, he received a scholarship to the University of California at Berkeley and continued his migration further into the white man's world. In the hub of the San Francisco Bay area, he encountered many kinds of people and many ways of life.

Now, at the university, Starlie struggles to reconcile his people's creation myth with the modern world. He finds an outlet for his inner strife by conceiving a new kind of video game—one in which people can have superhuman powers, and in which time can go forward or back. The kachinas can come to life in new ways, with new faces. Red people can be reborn as white people and vice versa, learning how it feels to be in another's place. In his imagination, entire worlds can be created or destroyed.

As Starlie's care and understanding increase, so do his thoughts: *Games can be used to pre-figure actions in the world. If enough people act out their migrations in games and see the consequences, then perhaps the Fourth World will not be destroyed as in the prophecy. The Fifth World can emerge from gentler, more creative ways, like father said. There are those who know nothing of their stars, but perhaps they can learn by seeing where they stumble and where they grow strong. In a game, one can choose when to stop the wheel of life. Poison and rage can be changed. Perhaps, if people see the effects of their actions in a game, the chain of destruction can be broken. How can I create a game that mimics the feedback of real life?*

Starlie is eager to discuss his ideas with his friend Frank, a psychology major who has emerged from many stresses in life with his humor and sanity intact.

Starlie shares his thoughts as the two walk across the campus: "I haven't mentioned this before, but I'm creating a game in which the players can perform acts of love, anger, and violence—and then see the consequences of their thoughts and actions. I'd like to talk to you about it."

"Shoot it all out, man."

"I've been thinking how everyone wants fulfillment in their life, but how there are many different ways to go about it."

"Hey, Starbright, tell me about it."

"We are all on a migration looking for home, but there are many paths, and some are dead ends."

"Lots of dead ends," says Frank with a knowing laugh, as they come to a cafe at the edge of the campus.

"Do you think there is a plan of creation? I mean, what divides one path from another? How can we understand these differences and what they will lead to? And how can we reconcile them?"

"You're asking awfully big questions, Powers. I have to sit down for this." His curly hair springing in all directions, Frank seats himself facing the back of the chair and perches his chin on his folded arms. "What divides paths? I'd say different perceptions, different worldviews. Coming from different races, cultures, religions, political beliefs, everything. Some views are opposed to others."

"Yes! And what you've said gives me an idea. Different views can be expressed as different dimensions in my game."

"Dimensions?"

"The Hopi people believe we are all on migrations to our 'home', or Fifth World, where the people of all races and nations will become like brothers of one family."

"Does that mean they will fight?"

"No, it means we care about each other, that we are aware of each other's needs. Can you imagine a world where we live by our stars in harmony?"

Frank shakes his head in disbelief.

"I mean, where we realize our common humanity, and, in generation after generation, we wage battle with our own shadows instead of with each other. Can you imagine that?"

Their conversation is interrupted by the sirens of two police cars that have pulled up to a store across the street. Starlie and Frank watch as the police drag two leather-jacketed young men into one of the cars.

"See that! I've rubbed shoulders with many types, Powers. They don't change easily."

Despite the interruption, Starlie continues his stream of thought: "I've noticed that it's not only race, culture, or religion that divides people, but something even more fundamental. We live in a time when everybody's worldview is being broken up and shattered. What divides people is the dimension through which they see. What they really want is freedom. When there is freedom, one's star shines."

"Star? What do you mean? Give me an example. What happens to a singer when he's singing? Isn't he free? What dimension is he in?"

"It depends on his sensitivity and openness to his innermost creative voice. But it comes through a dimension in which we're all connected—I've heard it called *psi*."

"Psi? Sounds like you're getting spaced-out, Starbright. What about logic?"

"Yes, both psi and logic. It takes both in tandem. Then one's star shines. You see, if the singer only works in one dimension, he's on his path to his goal, but it's limiting. Say he wants money or fame. These goals stimulate him, but a one-dimensional worldview keeps him from being open to creative improvisations, because he's catering to what he thinks the public wants. His star shines with only one ray, the ray of his goal. He's following his logic of becoming famous, but he's no different from a car salesman whose only goal is to sell cars."

Frank's blue eyes grow round: "My goal is to psych out the world and get rich doing it. What dimension am I in?"

"To psych out the world is one thing and to get rich is another. Expectation leads to frustration and anger. What do you think underlies crime, riots, and disease? A one-dimensional worldview often leads to addiction and violence. To psyche out the world you need psi, you need to be open. You *are* open, Frank. That's why I can talk to you."

"But it's good to have a goal, Starbright. Where do you think people would be without goals?"

"We need goals, but we need a multidimensional worldview that is more than a one-way track to a goal. It's like a playing field, a board game, a plane where you can explore. The more dimensions, the more freedom. The more your openness to psi and step-by-step logic are combined, the brighter your star."

"Isn't freedom a goal?"

"People often try to make it a goal, but freedom is liberation from a limited goal. It is being open to new possibilities. Psi. It's going into higher dimensions at right angles to anything you've ever done before.

That's what it will take to follow one's star to the Fifth World, the global New World."

Starlie feels inspired as he gets up to leave. "I need to get back to the computer. Thanks for listening. You've helped refine my ideas."

In the computer lab that has become his second home, Starlie begins drawing conceptual flow charts to program what he calls the Game of Life. He maps a star that will appear on the computer's display screen. The star represents the player's soul and will change color and intensity according to the player's resonance. If the star grows brighter, the player is choosing the direction of greater psi. If it grows larger, the player is taking logical steps to achieve the goal. More colors indicate richer interactions.

Starlie's absorbtion is total as he lays out a game with four dimensional analogs. He calls the first three dimensions Goals, Playing Field, and Pyramid. Goals concerns the acquisition of wealth, marriage, power, or certain skills. The player sets a goal and creates a path to attain it by answering questions about motives and means. Starlie realizes that a player's tendency to *grasp* is a major problem with the pursuit of one-dimensional goals. Grasping without openness to the flux of life leads to tunnel vision, in which case the player is diverted from the chosen path and his or her star fades.

Starlie displays the second dimension, Playing Field, as a maze. In this dimension, the player has to give and receive something: sex, money, food, jewels, art, and so on. The exchanges with others enable the player to move into as many places on the field as possible. New choices branch out from each selection. Food, for example, can be used for nourishment, but it can also lead to indulgence and addiction.

In the Pyramid dimension, Starlie structures the world as a hierarchy of leaders with a supreme ruler at the head. There are goals and exchanges that work only via interactions with a series of "bosses". Everyone can choose a place. Starlie works laboriously with his own logic to develop the series of questions that the player will face—questions he has known people to have. For example, one question is "Do you want to be a leader in order to have power, or in order to more effectively serve the needs of society as a whole?" Another is "Do you want to panhandle in order to shun responsibility, or to live in the freedom of humility?"

When he finishes programming the Game of Life in three dimensions, Starlie feels he has built a model representing the values of the past, the Fourth World. But what about the Fifth World? It seems that everything in the modern world is being leveled. Even the pyramids can't stand forever. He knows that the traditional views of many cultures are breaking up. The Fourth World of his own people is being destroyed, as is the world of the white man. Deep in his heart, he feels both sorrow and anticipation in wondering what kind of world will emerge.

For Starlie, all events converge on this single question, which he ponders during the week. In his classes he is distracted and sullen, a change quite apparent to Frank. "What's going on, Starbright? Want to talk?" he asks one day after math class.

Frank follows Starlie out the classroom door. They head up toward the Berkeley hills in silence and finally stop at a place where they can gaze out toward the bay and the Pacific Ocean. Starlie contemplates the electronic network of satellites, computers, and telecommunications devices that encircle the globe. "Values are crumbling, yet the entire world is linked by wires," he says finally. "It's as though electronics have become the nervous system of the world in which traditional hierarchies and means of exchange are being destroyed. Goals are not clear. To have a nervous system without a foundation of meaning is dangerous."

"What is the meaning of meaninglessness?" Frank asks, trying to lighten the mood.

"It means one's star has gone out."

"What *is* one's star, Starbright, really? Tell me."

"It's finding your guts, heart, and mind all at once. It's finding your joy."

"Where's your joy right now?"

Starlie laughs, realizing the irony of Frank's question: "My star is in my heart and guts, but I haven't found the fourth dimension for the Game of Life. The whole world is linked with electronic media—cables, transmitters, receivers, computers, modems—but without our stars, life is meaningless. That's why people fall into addiction or become violent."

"Maybe the fourth-dimensional worldview is the inside of the three-dimensional worldview," suggests Frank.

Starlie is silent for a few moments, then bursts out, "Inside-out! That's it! One's inner life must be revived! Our stars shining in the network of media—that's the fourth-dimensional world."

"Didn't some guy say 'the media *is* the message'?"

"Yes, but that's wrong. It's what a person *does* with their life that has meaning. To be who you are and put *that* message into the media is the Network."

Back in his room, Starlie spends the entire night creating a grid that represents the fourth dimension. His mind races ahead: *Reaching a goal is hard, exchanges are risky, and the pyramid can easily become rigid, but the fourth-dimensional Network enables everyone to have a voice.* He builds networks for people who share mutual concerns and interests—the environment, politics, housing, music, film, literature, metaphysics, and so on. To join the Network, the player has to be able to give and receive and has to keep moving. As Starlie works, he thinks, *The plan of creation is not to go back, but to go on. The question is not where we have come from, but what we can become.*

When Starlie returns to the Hopi reservation during the winter break, he describes everything he has been working on to his father. Wickvaya listens quietly, nodding. When he has finished, all seems tranquil and still, and Starlie feels at last that his father understands him, that he accepts his new way of life.

Old Wickvaya's clear eyes shine out of his wrinkled skin: "What about zero dimensions?" he asks.

"What do you mean?"

"In zero dimensions, there is no goal, no one-way track to a goal, no playing field, no pyramid, and no network."

"What, then, is there?"

"To shine as a star is to follow the plan of creation. To follow the plan of creation is to emerge into the Fifth World. The Fifth World is a single point, the point of the original fire, the blue star. Time is a liquid that circles around. The fourth-dimensional network returns to the center when the violent, the useless, and the diseased are consumed in the flame of each person's heart. The Fourth World is on fire within us all—white, red, black, and yellow. Think about it, my son."

A SHAMANIC
DEATH AND REBIRTH

Space
Red of black within red

The pollution
of the atmosphere
can be cleared
by spacious hearts.

By following the geese, the clouds, and the oracles of stones and
bones, the human souls knew the River before they donned material
bodies. Now they see space, spreading like spider webs through the
branches of the Tree of Life.

Their rainbow auras fan out into that space, expanding and contracting according to their trust in the flux of the River. Photons of light
follow lives of thought and feeling: the red of intensity, the orange of
power, the yellow of brilliance, the emerald of balance, the turquoise of
truth, the blue of aspiration, and the violet of intuition.

Sun, light, spirit, and seed mingle in the creative energy of the
Shaman until the colors pass through each other and separate from the
light and darkness. The solar seed rays from the Sun behind the Sun
crystallize as gems in his drum, each gem transmitting a color, tone, and
quality for a soul to ignite within itself as it defines its own auric field.

The Shaman performs sacred gestures to bring alignment with the
dragons, devas, and nature spirits. He knows that to acknowledge these

powers is to take real action in the world. One by one, the souls awaken and ride the draconic powers back across the abyss, where the Trickster shudders at the transfiguration of the soul and body in nature.

Like arrows from heaven, the colored rays of the Shaman's halo enter the crowns of mortals and vibrate through their spines. Gathering the five luminous elements in their imaginal bodies, the mortals radiate their auric colors back to the universe.

The dragons, devas, and nature spirits offer a spirit dawn to help mortals find their way back to the Creator and then on—on forever in the ever-new creation.

The Shaman, Bear-Looks-Twice, and Petruska

The Siberian wind sweeps snow across the open tundra and beats tirelessly against the skin wall of the yurt. Inside, Bear-Looks-Twice throws branches on the fire, then moves his drum up and down through the smoke, invoking the spirits with shouts of "Kam! Kam Kam!" Drawn by the motion of the drum, the spirits appear as gems of diverse colors to those who can "see".

Petruska lies on the ground beside the Shaman. She has found a Siberian Shaman out of desperate need to purge her soul of negativity and to cross the abyss, even at the risk of her life. Sasha sits next to her, the shadows of the fire flickering on her face.

Bear-Looks-Twice offers tobacco to the Black Bird that eats ghosts as he prepares to journey with Petruska's soul. They will pass through all the realms to find the source of her spirit in the highest heaven. He shouts blessings through his nostrils and flaps his arms like the wings of a bird. Then, beating steadily on his drum, he summons the spirits to enter Petruska's soul and carry it aloft. Her soul rises out of her body and, with the spirit helpers, alights on the Shaman's back. Carrying Petruska, the Shaman's soul flies upward and, protected by the radiation of the gem elixirs, slowly ascends the birch pole of the yurt. Finally, the Shaman reaches the top of the birch axis. There he speaks with the Creator on Petruska's behalf:

> Oh Lord, to whom all ladders lead!
> Oh, unattainable One! Listen to me!

I have come here to speak truth.
You know how hard it is to come this far.
I have sacrificed my own life-blood.
This one, who has contortions in her soul—
    who dims her own colors,
    who sabotages her spirit allies,
    who kills her own ancestors,
    who refuses to fill her own space—
    on her behalf I speak.
I pronounce no judgments.
Hear me! She has lost her way,
    but now is ready to fill her space.
Have mercy!
She has tried to pass between the two columns of heaven,
    but without you falls into oblivion.
She has no footing on the bridge to life.
Command that the dragons she has turned to demons
    hold no malice against her.
Let her try once again.

The Creator looks down with his divine eye upon the Shaman, laboring in harsh conditions with such great spiritual energy. "Your sacrifice is great," he says, "but you do not see that poison still lies in the fruit of her desires. You must take her soul down to the House of Death to face the sharp-toothed scaly ones who suffered from her past deceit. The evil ones are easy to recognize, but if she lies to herself, she will not even know her own true colors."

The Shaman implores the Creator: "She seeks to make amends and will labor for many lifetimes to bring life and glory back into the dragons. She knows she has become a shitting ghost, but now she has vowed to fill her place. I ask that she be given another chance."

"The dragons have grown dark and embittered from lifetimes of human confusion," roars the Creator in response. "Their space is inhabited by demons that fly out from the confused souls who refused to live according to the plan of creation."

Bear-Looks-Twice can do nothing but accept the Creator's words.

His effort is great, for Petruska's soul is heavy. When he turns to descend the birch pole back through the celestial realms, the Creator's voice calls him back: "Take this crystal that has been refined in my spiritual fire. When you beat your drum, it will protect you both from the demons. Go now to the Land of the Dead. If she can face her demons, her fate will be changed by her own free will."

After the spirit allies insert the precious crystal into the Shaman's heart, they all descend the pole to the middle world, where Petruska's body lies in the yurt. Bear-Looks-Twice emits a sharp yell, then begins intoning a song that is echoed by his spirit allies. Exhausted from climbing and descending with Petruska's soul, he breathes deeply. With each breath, more of his truth returns until it fills not only the space of his body but even the yurt and the snow-covered hills.

The Shaman stands and prepares to descend to the Land of the Dead, bearing still the ghost of Petruska on his back. He also carries gifts of beer and polecat skins for the dragons who guard the black mouth to the underworld. He dances to the beat of his drum and the rattle of metal amulets and sings a formula to ward off evil. Passing down to the subterranean rivers, he beholds the great dragons that bar the mouth to the underworld, their scales colored with the auras of human souls who have feared living their own lives. Petruska's colors vibrate within their bodies. When the dragons see the Shaman, they snarl and hiss hot fire. One very old dragon bellows in a deep voice, "What do you want here? Go back! All who pass by here sink into oblivion!"

Bear-Looks-Twice offers the flask of beer to the old dragon, who inhales it instantly through his fiery nostrils. Holding out the polecat skins, he cries, "O Great Ones of the deep! I offer these as a token. I speak on behalf of one who, having refused to live her true life, now wants to face her demons and make amends. She is sincere. Please let us pass."

The dragon spits a rotten tooth into his hand and says, "Our teeth are decayed from human transgression. She has broken the ley lines of the Earth with her hatred."

Bear-Looks-Twice touches his drum to his heart, where the Creator's crystal iridescently shines. Knowing the signs of power and protection, the dragons undulate in retreat from the dark mouth of the underworld.

The old dragon shouts, "You may pass if you can return this rotten tooth as a gem." The spirit allies present the tooth to Bear-Looks-Twice, who swallows it at once and descends into the underworld.

Inside the yurt, Sasha throws more wood on the fire, for the night is bitter and the wind is wild with the forms of hideous entities. Even Sasha can see a two-headed monster confronting Petruska's ghost with one face of malice and one face of false charm. All night the Shaman must hold the terrified ghost within his body, summoning the light and fire to change the very nuclei within her cells. Sasha watches in horror as the shadows of his writhing body ripple against the wall. At last, toward morning, the Creatrix enters his spine as the Tree of Life. He becomes as a goddess, able to rebirth Pertruska's soul as her breathing becomes stronger.

Through her own soul, Petruska beholds Manesis as a wise magician. But as the fire glows within her from the crystal in the Shaman's heart, she sees that Manesis is nothing but a mask of herself. She tears off the mask and shouts through the mouth of the Shaman: *I shall not fall into oblivion! I am filled with rainbow colors. I am fire becoming light. My deliverance is within me. I create myself anew. I spin my destiny and part the waves of terror and madness to live in truth. Help me!*

Her prayer intersects the prayer of her ghost, her possessed self, and draws it into reality. At that very moment, the Creatrix pulls the veils of illusion away from the mouth of the underworld, revealing it to be the pillars of heaven. Emerging through the pillars, the Shaman returns the dragon's tooth, which has been transformed into a brilliant emerald. Now the true colors of Petruska's aura fill the space. The Tree of Life quickens within her spine as the Creator sends his blessing down the birch pole axis. Bear-Looks-Twice stops his drumming and slowly emerges from his trance, then sinks into his place in the west of the yurt.

Petruska kneels. She realizes that her experience was real, that she has been reborn as a star. She stares at the ground, feeling the great sacrifice of her sister and the Shaman. Her eyes glisten as she turns to Sasha: "I am born of light. You helped me. I didn't know."

The glow from Petruska's journey sends arrows of colored light throughout the yurt. The Shaman rests quietly in the west, while Sasha sits beside her sister. Shadows move inside Petruska's eyes, and her whole body trembles as elementals burn and reweave the debris of her age-old fears.

"I don't understand how, but I have been seeded from a star. I feel fresh, unchristened, like a newborn babe."

Petruska's ghost was but an imaginal dream of lives from long ago. Although the air still whirs with lingering demons that seek to reestablish the habitual ways of unlived life, she knows she will never go back. Her heart remains filled with the purging light of the iridescent crystal in the Shaman's heart.

"It is the Tree of Life that heals," she says knowingly. "I am not just a person. I am the space between the atoms of my body, the feelings of my soul. Yet, for fear of dying once, I almost died forever."

She looks into the eyes of Bear-Looks-Twice: "You have saved not only this life, but all my lives."

The Shaman shakes his head: "Thank the spirits and dragons." He gets up and, with a sigh and a belch, goes out into the winter night.

Tears return to her eyes as she watchs him depart. Turning to Sasha, she is able to say, "No longer will you need to pry my fingers from what I grasp, nor scold me for being so stubborn. Space lives inside of me—in my breath, in my blood, and in every cell. My soul is alive!"

Her true colors dance to greet the dawning day as the elementals of fire, earth, water, wind, and wood chant her true song. They grind her fear into the earth and return her feelings to the cleansing waters. Trusting in the spacious flow of the River, reborn to a whirling new world, she lies back and falls into a peaceful sleep.

INCARNATIONAL FORMS

Form
White of black within red

The boundary between
spirit and matter
teems
with turbulent forms.

The human souls move out through the western gate of the medicine wheel to see vast fields of weeds bursting from the decaying ground
of death. The weeds reveal beauty, for nothing in the wilderness is unwanted or truly dies. Washed with the mercy of the Creatrix, the imaginal field entwines all of existence in vines of blossoming forms.

The River teems with the patterns of the Shaman's inner perception, which the human souls seek to know directly. Layer upon layer, the
River changes, its tributaries moving toward crystalline forms as it cools
and falls further from the Creator's spiritual fire. The exchanges of eros
and logos become limited, and yet expressed, by the boundaries of form.

Form is seldom attained without struggle, and each heart contends
inwardly before its vision appears in the Shaman's sacred art. Form precedes substance as desire precedes action. In this way the Shaman main-
tains the energetic flow of the River, and his medicine of herbs, colors,
tones, gems, and animal forms connects the whirling chakras of the
human to the energies of the cosmos.

Christa and Karl

Since ancient times, Christa and Karl have known the script of the River through the language of the trees and the laws of mathematical forms. But in this life, each has been blocked from speaking and living truth: Karl by the limitations of empirical science, Christa by her marriage and a society scornful of visionaries.

Afraid of her power as an artist, Christa imprisoned herself in her marriage as a test of her own anonymity. For Horst, who could not deal with the reality of chaos, controlling Christa meant controlling the Primal Waters themselves, triumphing over the power of the River running through her.

Having entered a new life, Christa now flows like the River itself. She and Karl share a home bequeathed to him by German relatives in Karlsruhe. For almost a year, they spend their days along the Rhine or in the Black Forest, rediscovering both the universal patterns of life and each other. They want to do something about the pollution of the river and the death of the forest, but for now they are too absorbed in each other to do so.

Never has love pierced Christa's soul so deeply. Her body flames for Karl, and the fire in her heart illuminates lifetimes. Day by day, their chakras whirl brighter with clarity and truth as they examine and draw the forms of nature. Filled with the rhythms pulsing down from the Creator through the Creatrix, they meditate together and find the luminous forms of vision within. Through their love, the signs and symbols in nature and art radiate a meaning lost to human consciousness, except for the shamans of old.

Christa now understands her enduring attraction to sacred books and art, to the language of symbols and nature's forms. During those years when she was raising Erhardt and dealing with Horst's oppressiveness, she developed the stamina to paint at night while husband and child slept. That dedication enabled her soul to live. Now her art dances with the whorls and heart-shapes, the dots and crosses, the precise waves and chevrons, that issue from her inner life in wave upon wave of energy.

Sustained by an inheritance, Karl withdraws entirely from an established way of pursuing his scientific career. His love for Christa reveals his own mystical side, and he begins to see the symphony of life as one great whole. He discovers the missing links between chaos and cosmos—the patterns that meld together the platonic forms, the organic forms and the forms of chaos theory. He sees the patterns of diverse realms that enable the true explorer of form to travel from the pure light of the unmanifest, through chaos, and into manifest order.

Through his study of magic and mysticism, Karl realizes that, over the centuries, humanity's increasing isolation from the intangible forms of imaginal reality has made the occasional encounter with these forms seem miraculous. As the outer technological world grows more estranged from the inner world of intuition and vision, the forces of nature become increasingly threatening to those who want to control this inner world. And Christa sees that the estrangement of religious authorities from the real spiritual life of the people only widens the divisions of a deteriorating civilization.

Therefore, Karl and Christa withdraw from a society that, faced with increasing crime, drug abuse, and violence, strives to maintain law and order rather than address causes. The more nature propels her tides of change before the controlling mind, the more the political and legal authorities try to strangle the currents of the River running through the hearts of the people. Finally, the currents burst forth in volcanos and earthquakes that reshape the face of the Earth.

Now, sleeping beside Karl in their room, Christa is stirred by the hoot of an owl. With the hoot comes a high ringing in her ears . . . and her mind becomes a mind beyond space. She enters a great ecstasy and beholds a great vision.

She returns through incarnations to the twelfth century, when she is a young nun. Her convent, administered by the abbot and monks of an adjoining monastery, lies near the confluence of the Nahe and Rhine rivers. The repetition of the psalms in the early morning hours sinks them into her soul. As symphonic sounds fill the cell where she fasts in solitude, she receives a vision of a great light and angels dancing on flames. After the vision subsides, she is left almost blinded by shimmering lights. Christa becomes aware of a headache and extreme fatigue, yet her spirit seeks to transcend the pain by remembering something even deeper within her.

Searching for a sign of the mystery of her purpose, Christa returns to the same century. Now an older abbess in charge of the nuns, she is addressing the abbot and his council, charging the monks with appropriation of the nuns' dowries for their own use. "We will go to the buildings on the hill," she tells them. "No longer will you adminster to us." The anger in the abbot's face and his threatening presence seem astonishingly familiar. Among all the monks, only Gernot, her friend and teacher, supports her decision.

Besieged by illness and headaches, she succeeds in moving the nuns despite the abbot's attempts to thwart her. The new location is barren, devoid of the fruit gardens and comforts of their former home. But she has turned to the stream of her destiny, and she establishes the new convent in the name of the Mother of God.

In her waking dream as the abbess, Christa hears the antiphony of her life call. She is lifted into great ecstasy and great pain. Visions open the veils between the realms where angels conduct her ascent into the First World. Heavenly revelations in image and song flood her being. She sees the circles of stars behind stars move like chariot wheels as death slides like a shadow beneath the Earth. She sees people fall back as their chakras cease to turn. The wisdom of the stars, the blood of Christ, the divine egg, the Creatrix as Sophia, the deserts of sin, the sword of purification, the cosmic wheel—all shimmer through her cells in an ecstasy filled with evocative aromas, colors, and forms.

Her vibrating cells become imprinted with the story of creation and regeneration, and she beholds the many paths of mortals journeying away from and back to the Creator. She sees the red of the Creator's throne, encircled in white as if from a light beyond the Sun. She cannot fathom the fullness of the white light, though it outlines the edges of the dark abyss. Melodic lines of eternity spin down in the *Kyries* and *Alleluias* of the Mass as the Holy Spirit washes away unknown fear and pain. Throughout the entire vision, the blood and body of Christ sustain her.

Now Christa sees herself as the abbess return to the monastery, where she meets her old friend Gernot. She tells him of her visions, and also of the blindness and pain that follow. Then, in a moment of still silence between them, she beholds Christ's cross as the Tree of Life in Gernot's spine. When Gernot encourages her to write and paint what she has experienced, she sees, deep in his eyes, the soul of Karl.

Christa feels the River shatter into darkness and dread as the burning waters, crystallized by the moments of death, turn in her veins and nerves. In her vision, her soul finally reaches the point of white heat that dissolves the crystals. The force within her leads her back toward the point of pain when her soul was severed in two.

She goes back to the tenth century in Mexico, where she is Chimalman fighting Mixcoatl. She cannot kill him without killing herself, for war and love lie close together in a battle that is whole-hearted and beyond betrayal. Her two halves vibrate in the night with the power of love. She remembers the scenes experienced by Zapana, and she becomes Chimalman crying out in the midst of childbirth.

Karl awakens in the moonlight to find Christa in a breathless trance. Entering the umbra of her shadow, he walks in vision with her, watching her die in childbirth as Chimalman. Her breath is faint, then erratic, for she reexperiences her longing for Mixcoatl, her longing for a union with another part of her soul. As Karl attunes to Christa's being, her breath turns sweet with the scent of lavender. He enters her sweetness to know the unknowable and beholds angels carrying her toward a shaft of light.

Karl sees her soul entwined with another on a column that reaches upward to heaven and downward to a single life on Earth. An incandescent light condenses her soul until, reaching the heat of white fire, her soul fuses with the soul of Zapana. They become one: the seventh-century, astronomer-priest Huemetzin, the scribe of the ancient American *Divine Book—Tecomoxtli*. She sees her tribe crossing the Bering Strait.

Christa slowly emerges from her trance to an awareness of Karl beside her. All that she has seen in her vision, he has dreamed. Again the owl hoots. After a long silence, Karl speaks softly: "I saw you in a world filled with wisdom and beauty. We will live again and again until the blindness in this world stops."

Through the open window, he watches the Moon stride among the stars. They can hear the stars singing, but Christa sees nothing, for her body tingles throughout. She is aware that the white fire from her visions of that other life has left her eyes sparkling with iridescence but temporarily blind to the world of the senses.

After three days, Christa regains her eyesight and her strength. She at once begins to draw. Karl watches in amazement as the forms seem to vibrate out of a light in her hand: "You have shown me the key that opens the passageway between the ineffable light and the world of form," he says. "Now the cosmic octaves sound clearly in the chaos. The new geometry has no angles, only angels."

After he speaks, they both hear the chant of an ancient tongue:

Shaman's Song of the River

I am the seed idea in every form.
I am the sprouting into dimensionality where space embraces all.
I am the soul of nature running deep in underwater currents of dream.
You can find me in the hologram of nature.
I am the spider web that hangs on the Tree of Life.
I am the length of desire longing for expression.
Look for me in the inner realm of vision and the outer realm of form.
I am in every projection of imaginal light.
You can find me in the finiteness of a cone and the infinity of space.
I am in your true cognition of how nature grows.
I am the law of love in touch with Source.
I am the blueprint of nature in the Goddess.
I am the beat of the drum in your blood.
I am the thought that rides on your breath.
I am the image that goes beyond thought.
You can find me in the vibrations of sacred art.
I am in the rattle of dried leaves and underwater pebbles.
I am the virtual reality lying behind all form.

Are you a conductor of nature's blueprints?
I am the superconductor that is transparent to all things.

THE DEATH DANCE

As the waters rush in torrents toward matter, the Creatrix places the pattern of the human body in a coffer. She then releases the coffer to the River, where it floats studded with gems, infused with incense, and embroidered with flowers. Within the body flows the script of the River, its signs mysterious, but its meaning clear: "The Kingdom is within your own temple. Make death your friend and you shall rise like a column of gold. Death delivers you beyond the shadows when you marry enmity to empathy. The serpents of change will respond when you allow yourself to be scattered over the land and then gathered together as one power of life."

Lives given and taken flow in the red blood of the Earth. Women water the soil with tears for husbands and sons. Men cry for wives and daughters. Serpents within the waves twist to unheard music, the vibratory pathways of electrons and neutrinos. Matter and antimatter bind in the erotic charge of the Death Dance. She is the dance of energy, of chance and change and release from form. She buries the dead and makes them of use. She mixes the dreams of existence in the vessel of the body. She fills the realms of space with the magnetic fields of quartz, carnelian, and amethyst.

Death drones through vibrating strings, oozing chaos from the River's tides that pound the shores of gravity. The vacuous black hole sleeps on the other side of birth. Yet death embraces existence, dancing in every wave, particle, and atom in the cosmos.

The Creator observes light and dark forces in continuous oscillation. His pendulum swings with the contest of the Antagonist and the Shaman. Shall desire or dimension have dominion over death? Neither can claim victory, for each reflects the other in the human and natural worlds and deepens the interweaving of the soul and the body.

The Shaman descends to the House of Death and fills the darkness with dimensions. The solid is empty and the spacious full of resistance. The universe longs to sink into the eddying vortex, where the River rushes out of exploding electrons toward the cooling of lava into stone. Charged through the polar struggle, the pool of energy coagulates into mass.

241

However, the Antagonist opens the coffer and dismembers the human body, scattering it to the eight directions. Seeing the limbs pushed down by gravity and pulled up by light, the Creatrix implores, "Let death be revered and the plan of creation be known on Earth. Let inertia be the limit of the fall into matter."

The Antagonist feels the vacuity of his soul without love and declares that God is dead. But the Shaman proclaims, "The vision of God embraces even the lower world, where flesh and bone are bound by dreams that weave limbs into bodies, bodies into tribes, and tribes into the great God Pan. Here in the caves of death we shall be reborn through Pan!"

Yet the road is dark where passion is spent, and bodies fall in search of direction. Through her vibrational Death Dance, the Creatrix spreads compassion into the matter of the Third World, fusing the fire of the logos and the waters of eros in the burning waters of her blood. Holding the valor of the Sun and the passion of the River, she draws creation toward its destiny.

Some doors open, others close. The Death Dance tramples upon preordained purposes and melds them through the body into the chemical elements of matter. While leveling cities and moving mountains, she sings to mortals, "My body is a pool of vibrating forms, lifted by music into matter. Without my resistance, you could neither stand nor walk. I hammer you home! I refuse no one the red of my blood! I weave you all into one vibrating field of matter. I am a drop of rain, a crackle of fire, a whisper of wind."

Even now, death speaks the true language of transformation, plowing the field to mix the living and the dead, crushing the seed to bring forth oil, and grinding the grain to yield the bread of life.

THE MYSTERY OF THE BURNING WATERS

Energy
Gold of red within red

The dance
of luminous energy
creates
the blood of mortals.

Akrisios, Zapana, and Raphael

Akrisios grows restless in London. Fariba convinces her to try to find her only child. After months of searching, she locates her husband and daughter, only to have Maurya once again deny her permission to see Athene. Intensely hurt and frustrated, she decides to respond to Raphael's invitation to come and help the children in Guatamala. After taking a night flight from London and traveling all the next day, she finally reaches her destination late on the third day.

What she sees while traveling through the towns shocks her. The poverty and sickness of the native people press into her consciousness quickly. After opening to the possibility of seeing Athene, she feels particularly sensitive. Her mothering instincts are alive and responsive as she looks at the children wandering the hills and streets.

She arrives in the small village of El Cambio to receive an additional shock. She learns from Raphael that, for the past three years, his friend Zapana has been suffering from AIDS. When they come to

Zapana's hammock by the Rio de la Pasion, where the vines of the trees shade him from the hot Sun, she finds him gaunt, his finely molded bones shining through his weak muscles and taut skin.

The large brown eyes of the past Incan emperor greet her warmly. "I am so grateful that you have come to help," says Zapana, with apparent love and appreciation for her traveling so far. His transformation is toward pure light as energy, desire, and intellect all gradually diminish within him.

"We are torn from our ground like plants, to become fertilizer for others," Zapana says with a slight smile that reveals his detachment from his condition. He looks earnestly at Akrisios: "You must be tired. My sisters will help you." The spiritual light in his face momentarily lifts her out of her exhaustion.

Raphael picks up her bags and leads Akrisios toward the ramshackle house where Zapana's sisters are waiting. "Ria will show you where you can rest," he says. "I must go now and work with the children. I'll be back at dusk."

After she rests awhile, she returns to Zapana with some cool water. His dark eyes, blazing with light out of his ninety-pound frame, inspire her. "The sound of the river helps me approach death," he says, feeling a change coming. "When I listen, I hear the passing away of ancient memories." He drinks the water with appreciation.

Akrisios has only been at the village a week when she finds herself dying to her attachment to the comforts of city life—a life empty and torn from the roots of her spirit in nature. She spends her days by Zapana's side and comes to sense that devotion to him will help her on her path. One afternoon she asks him if there is anything that he still wants.

"Only one desire lives in my heart," he responds. "To plant the seeds of a new world where children have the power and love to be the light of the Earth. My lungs have only a few breaths left. My mind is empty of thoughts. But my heart is full, and I see that yours is, too. You can receive these seeds of trust. Raphael told me something about you."

Deeply moved, Akrisios feels change in her own blood. She senses a throng of energies in the atmosphere, for the spirit of Zapana is infused with the presence of the old Incan gods, the vision of Mama Ocllo, and the secrets of ancient America.

"I will do all I can."

Zapana sighs and gives her a long, penetrating look as he gathers his energies inward. Ria brings him some soup and implores him to eat, but he motions it away: "I can no longer eat the food of the Earth. My nourishment is the truth shining in the eyes of the children. The gods and goddesses are with us. I have remembered." His voice drifts off into silence. Ria returns to the house to get her sisters.

When Zapana closes his eyes Akrisios feels impelled to gather his emaciated body in her arms. "Do you mind if I hold you?" she asks.

He opens his eyes and smiles. She balances herself in the hammock and takes him into her arms, rocking back and forth to the sound of the river, sensing his total lack of resistance to death. She feels the eternity of Zapana's soul, yet deep within her she knows he will not incarnate on Earth again. She cradles his limp body like a mother goddess embracing a baby son. Her arms surround him, but it is she who feels enfolded by his soul as their energies meld and she is touched by the burning waters of his spirit. As he draws his last breath, she receives his fire—an aurora of something born from the crown of his head. She gives her love and vital energy to the beauty of his death. The spark of his soul flies out to the river below them and to the stars in endless orbit above.

Raphael knew when he left for the park that morning that Akrisios was the one to deliver Zapana's soul to the circle of stars. When he returns he finds Akrisios still holding the body of his friend. A perfume permeates the area of the hammock, wafting out across the river and back to the house where Zapana's mother and sisters mourn. Raphael reaches down and takes Zapana's boney hand.

"I'm happy you were with him," he says, beginning to cry.

"Only the thinnest thread held him here. He is finished with his work. Perhaps now mine is just beginning. What an inspiration he is!"

"Yes, it was time. He showed me how humility can clarify all incarnations like a thread through endless beads."

"You mean he cleared all his karma?"

"Yes. But there is one link I have yet to understand."

"Tell me all that you wish to share of his life. It may help me as I search for the roots of my own dilemma. Something obstructs my growth. I feel it is linked with growing up in an alcoholic family and with losing my daughter."

Raphael sits down beside her: "Remember, in Rome, when you asked Pravin for something to help your devotion?"

"Yes, I do. And you said to come and devote myself to the homeless children."

"Did Zapana give you any guidance before he died?"

"He said he had only one desire: 'To plant the seeds of a new world where children have the power and love to be the light of the Earth.' If you can help me to understand what led him to this point, I may understand my own work here better."

Akrisios lays the body of Zapana back in the hammock and rocks it like a newborn child. Raphael breathes deeply and looks up at the sky: "Zapana and I went through many incarnations together—as brothers, sisters, husband and wife, emperor and priest. I knew when I met him in the ruins of Incahuasca that we were destined to complete something in this life. Occasionally, when he couldn't sleep, we would go to the river. We would drum for each other and go into trances. It came to be that, when I drummed for Zapana, I could see and hear what he was seeing and hearing."

"How could you know?"

"After the trance we always shared what we had just experienced. We could remember everything. One time, we saw each other's souls in an incarnation fourteen-hundred years ago. We were migrating with multitudes of people across Asia. He was being trained as an Egyptian priest of Amun. I was being trained as a warrior, but it soon became clear that I was to be the tribal leader. My name then was Xumu, and Zapana's was Huemetzin. He communed with the stars and knew the sacred alphabets and calendars. He received the plan of creation directly from the gods and goddesses. I followed his guidance implicitly, for it was through his wisdom that I was able to safely lead the people. Some had done it centuries before, but we had a particular mission."

"What was it that drove you on?"

"We stood before masters who instructed us to transmit a new energy into America. Zapana was chosen because of the brilliant light he emanated as he cleared himself of past karma."

"What did he clear? Is that why he was able to die so easily, so consciously, and with such detachment?"

"Over a succession of lives he was attempting to clear a reaction to a sudden, unwarranted death in a yet earlier life. His slow dying process in this life is the direct antithesis of that one."

Akrisios furrows her brow: "Almost everyone is reactive to death. If it takes many incarnations to clear a reaction to an undeserved death, how will we ever become free of karma?"

"Most people do not even ask that question. It is difficult. People have fallen into unconsciousness ever since the burning waters were lost."

"What do you mean, the burning waters were lost?"

"If you really want to know, I shall tell you a long story."

"Please do."

Raphael continues: "Through our explorations in trance, I have come to learn that a soul can actually split when in a highly reactive state. It may split into two or more fragments, which incarnate in different times and places to learn separate lessons."

"Really? Are you and Zapana one soul?"

"I don't believe so, but our life purpose is very much the same. His soul was fragmented over many lifetimes. It is for that reason that he was so humble in this life, a humility I am only just learning."

"What is the life purpose that you and Zapana have in common? Does one's purpose change in each life, or does a single purpose run through all one's lives?"

"You are full of questions! I believe we have an overall life purpose resulting from a vow we made before incarnating for the first time— when we were stars, so to speak. In my and Zapana's case, we vowed to bring love and light down from heaven, to enable a remembrance of the Creator and the plan of creation. We both were born to enlighten and inspire humanity. To do this, we ourselves had to remain clear of the confused motives of the world."

"That must be why you assumed the roles of leader and priest four-teen-hundred years ago. What happened then?"

"As I said, we guided a band of people from Asia to the Americas. He received the guidance, and I then executed his vision among the people. Our suffering in that long journey was part of our test to be con-stant as leaders.

"I remember one day, when Huemetzin was old, he suddenly announced: 'I am the seed of the gods.' Soon afterward he began paint-ing the mystery of the innerdimensional matrix of the heavens and Earth. He brought the spirits of the animals into his images. The Order of the Eagle and the Order of the Jaguar emerged from his visions. The jaguar and serpent heads that cover the temple of Quetzalcoatl were taken from his images in the *Divine Book, Tecamoxtli*. He knew the Tree of Life and the rain god, Tlaloc. He knew how to prepare the sacred elixir from the maguey plant, for he learned the mysteries of regenera-tion from the Egyptian hieroglyphs and from the priest of Amun. At that time, the followers of the Egyptian religion were in secret mystery cults. Huemetzin held the keys to those mysteries. Were it not for his transmission from the gods, the magical secrets of the Egyptians would have been lost as a living tradition. When we arrived in Tollan, in what is now Mexico, we were among the first to behold the vision of what was to become Teotihuacan and Chalua."

"Are you saying that the ancient Mexicans came from Egypt?"

"No. When we arrived in the valley of Mexico, we found the native people already living peacefully in simple mud buildings. But they did not know the secrets of the burning waters. Huemetzin understood the transference of matter into other dimensions through magnetic reso-nance. We were Egyptians, guided by the stars to the Americas at a spe-cific time for a specific purpose. We employed the Egyptian secrets of concentrating and transmitting cosmic energy in a new method of using adobe whereby, all at once, we could create the massive bases of the pyramids of the Sun and Moon."

"I am astounded! Who would have known that Zapana had these powers? Yet, when I arrived, I was instantly transformed by his presence. I felt energized, even after three days of travel. All his energy seemed to be spiritual. Even now I feel it." She looks over at Zapana's lifeless body in the hammock.

"His energy became increasingly spiritual over the course of his long dying process. But when we met several years ago, he was living in the past, in despair over his lost empire in Peru. "

"How can that be?"

"He temporarily lost his connection to the gods. Only his spiritual mother, Mama Ocllo, stayed with him. She was patient and compassionate. Her love kept his vision alive through his despair. Though he had lost his connection to the gods, he could see clearly. That is why his despair was so deep. Otherwise he would have been just confused and apathetic. Our meeting energized him, I believe. Our relationship steadied him and enabled him to recover his spirit through his soul journeys. I will never forget when, in trance, he reexperienced the manifestation of the pyramids of the Sun and Moon at Teotihuacan. I believe Zapana's body would have been shattered had I not been present to ground his energy."

"What happened to you?"

"The burning waters scourged through us. I almost lost my own life in that moment. In reexperiencing the conversion of energy into matter through multiple dimensions, Zapana passed through the whole succession of his incarnations all at once. His soul phased in and out of different planes as it melded to pure spirit through divine fusion. Then, in his life as Mixcoatl, he realized that the soul of one named Chimalman was yet another aspect of his own soul."

Raphael looks up questioningly to see if Akrisios is following.

"You mean Mixcoatl and Chimalman were aspects of Zapana's soul that reactively incarnated in two separate bodies?"

"Yes. When Huemetzin died, his soul split and incarnated as Mixcoatl and Chimalman. Huemetzin had guided his people, written the *Divine Book*, and manifested the pyramids by the power of the gods, but he failed to do one thing."

"What was that?"

"He failed to calculate the Horus Eye fractions exactly. Consequently, he lost the power of regeneration from the blood of Osiris.

Those are the Egyptian terms. The Horus Eye is Polaris, the pole star, but it is also the center of the Ollin, the Mexican symbol at the center of the calendar stone."

"What does this symbol represent?"

"It represents the blood transmuted through the Divine Four. The Ollin commemorates the four epochs of world history, and its center represents stability and balance, the Fifth World of renewal through a redeemed humanity. That is what Zapana saw in the children of the world. Through all his lives he sought to receive the burning waters that energized the Earth. He often relied on me for balance and stability, for, in the past, without me, he lost his own center. When he lost the power of regeneration from the blood of Osiris, he lost the connection of the divine eye to the Sun, so his blood was not fully transmuted through the Sun."

"I sense mystery here that I cannot yet fathom. Did the miscalculation of the Horus Eye fractions lead to the Aztec's bloody sacrifices?"

"The later Aztec priests needlessly sacrificed victims to appease the gods. But the gods never recognized such sacrifices. Once the connection of the eye, heart, and Sun was lost, the gods could not be contacted. Losing this connection weighed heavily upon Huemetzin. As Mixcoatl, he tried to repay humanity, but he suffered greatly from the split in his soul. Reactions do not heal easily. He and Chimalman fought fiercely as warriors, then became lovers. When she died in childbirth, he grieved deeply. But part of his debt was repaid through their son, Ce Actl Topiltzin, who became the king of Tula and high priest of the teachings of Quetzalcoatl, the feathered serpent. He later came to be called Quetzalcoatl himself. His blood had been transmuted by the burning waters, and he was adamantly *opposed* to human sacrifice."

"No wonder I feel such powerful spiritual energy in Zapana's and your presence. There is something in your story of the Mexican gods that resonates with me. Perhaps that is why I am here, for my life is at a turning point. Tell me more about Quetzalcoatl. I don't understand why the practice of sacrifice ever arose."

Raphael brushes back his golden hair and remains silent for a while, then gently puts his hand on Zapana's body. He weeps silently, his tears dropping quietly on Zapana's heart. Eventually he reaches for an amulet hanging on his necklace.

"Do you see this symbol? It is the hieroglyph *Atl-Tlachinolli*, which means 'burning water.' It shows two streams uniting, one red, one blue—one fire, the other water. When the gods of fire, who are the gods of war, separated from the gods of water, a sense of victimization arose, resulting in the bloody sacrifices of the Aztec warriors and priests. This tells us why the concept of *sacrifice*, which once meant 'to make sacred', has become associated with victimization and martyrdom.

"The pyramids of the Sun and Moon were laid out in the shape of the great quincunx. It symbolized the four previous worlds and the possibility of a balanced new world, a fifth Sun. But the reconciliation of the fire and water must take place in the human heart, not just in stone. The ancient Quetzalcoatl, through penitence and self-sacrifice, ascended into spirit to redeem us, to rejoin the fire and water in our blood and energize our light bodies."

"Where is Quetzalcoatl now?"

"He was transformed into Venus, the morning star. His twin, Xolotl, is the fire that falls from the sky. Xolotl is born from water just as lightning is born from clouds. Xolotl is one with Tlaloc, the rain god."

"I still don't understand."

"Quetzalcoatl is the power of the burning waters from the Tree of Life within us. I know that Zapana created those burning waters in the vessel of his body before he died. The burning waters come from the transmutation of vital energy into the elixir of immortal life. In this process, all karma is cleared. The gods are with us. I feel it. Zapana even now is sending the burning waters through his blood to ours."

Three days later, Raphael, Akrisios, and Zapana's mother and sisters perform a simple funerary ceremony in Zapana's honor. While she watches his body burn on a pyre, according to the ancient rite, Zapana's mother murmurs a prayer for his soul: "Zapana, I loved thee and love thee still. I know, somewhere, head, heart, hand, and heel beat and breathe the power of the gods. Thank you for being my son."

Raphael then speaks: "My brother is with us all. We feel the fire of his spirit as his body turns to ash. Soon I will gather these ashes and entrust them to the river he loved so well. He told me that the river receives everything and mirrors it back to us. When he spoke of the power of the fire in the water, he once sang this song:

> I see eternity through the stars,
> a pyramid of crystal
> stepping down aeons to hours.
>
> My heart is the knot where two lives weave.
> Time turns in two directions of miracle.
> My beloved walks inside my dream.
>
> I see with the eye of the one,
> reflecting the truth of an oriental,
> I am Hypatia before the eternal Sun.

"This verse holds the mystery of a procession of lives that moves toward eternity. I know that Zapana dwells there now."

Aglow with wholeness, Raphael continues: "Zapana spoke and lived truth. His story is a story of fragmentation and the return back to wholeness. He inspires us to find our own wholeness. He has arisen from graves in Peru, Mexico, China, and Egypt. Those tombstones have shattered into iridescent light, and his bones are now turquoise like the vortex of heaven. He stands at the point from which time began. He shall not pass away. His soul is forever. I am grateful. He has shown us the way of the burning waters."

The next day, Zapana's ashes are gathered and placed in a golden pot on an altar to Quetzalcoatl. The children whom Zapana loved and helped have come, some with adopted parents and friends. Dressed in red and black, some wearing masks with mournful expressions, they form a great circle around the altar. Zapana had taught them traditional songs and dances, but also to be open to the ones that arise within them. The women's dark hair, usually braided, hangs free and loose. After Zapana's mother intones a ritual in a mixture of Spanish, Latin, and her native tongue, all dance and sing as if in celebration of a birth.

HOLOCAUST ROCK

Mass
Black of red within red

The fire
of the spirit
hides
in the darkness of matter.

In the Second World, the cosmic computer of the heavens is woven from lattices of light issuing from the Trickster's thought. The lattices are comprised of massless light-cones ignited from the fiery logos of the Priest-Seer and maintained in the burning waters of the Creatrix's blood. But the priests are still afraid, and without the compassion of the Creatrix, their fire and light would be sundered from the Primal Waters that revitalize all worlds, and the plan of creation could not go on.

In primeval times, the vibrating lattices of thought flung themselves out like spider webs and wove galaxies into space. Now the galaxies whirl through the Heavenly Powers, creating zodiacal qualities that radiate through the stars to all Earths. The imaginary quantity of time penetrates the lattices, causing them to curve back upon themselves. The swirling veins of dragons move in this curve through time, keeping the energy of the burning waters flowing throughout all universes.

Death dances below, spinning the lattices into twisters while the River torrents down. The dance draws energy from the curving lattices of light and torques them into magnetic and electrical patterns wherein each wave amplifies, resists, or cancels another wave in the creation of matter and antimatter.

Death dances faster and faster to increase the momentum of the appearing and disappearing twisters until the universe explodes from her wild gyrations and cools into millions of stars and planets. The Trickster feels the gravitational pull of the twisters in his mind and realizes that pure thoughts have no meaning without manifestation.

Time leads the Trickster on toward the vortex between the Second and Third Worlds, despite his revulsion of the dragons and devas who dwell there. The changing rhythms of the twisters contort the lattices and create massive matter that obscures the light. Passed on by the waves of the River, the distortions break into bubbling spheres at the base of the waterfalls where Death renews all of matter with her dance.

Martha

Martha is late for church because of an argument with Allen about Pete, who, after earning his way through college, has formed a rock band in New York with several friends. And even though she has begun to confront Allen about his abusiveness, her fear remains. By the time she arrives for the service with Melissa, Preacher Zain is already well into his sermon:

"We have entered the time of tribulation, my people. Look around! You can see the nonbelievers suffering the punishment of the Lord. Already the signs are here—the earthquakes, famines, and droughts. The end times are upon us, bless the Lord! Hold on to your faith. Just as he spared Noah and the animals, so shall you be saved from destruction, for Jesus will gather the faithful. All of your worries shall be eased, for the hour of fulfillment is near—the end of this world and the coming of the new. But be not deceived. We must endure a false peace before the Second Coming of Jesus.

"The evil world shall be destroyed, not by flood, but by the fire of the Battle of Armageddon. What is this battle? It is our endeavor against the Antichrist who appears in the guise of a world government and New Age beliefs. The Antichrist is on Earth right now with a false promise of a global religion and government. Hold fast to your faith, for in the final hour Jesus will come. He alone will bring peace to Earth.

"However, first there will be trials brought on by two very different agents of Satan. The first are the technocrats who seek to turn you into a number. I advise you all to cut up your credit cards and withdraw your savings from the banks. Keep your money in a safe place in your house, for bankruptcy will sweep the land and the banks that stay open will be run by the government. These satanic institutions will reduce you to a code of electronic pulses. Your social security, bank account, and credit card numbers will become the mark of the Beast on your forehead. Black magicians, cohorts of the devil, are in a conspiracy to enslave you to the international system of government. They believe in the progress of technology. Anyone using a computer might succumb to the devil, for black magic runs through all electronic systems."

Murmurs of voices rumble through the crowded hall.

"Everything against our Lord is satanic. The other side of the Beast is represented by the New Agers. I've see some of their books and even talked to them first hand. They profess a universal religion and carry a blind hope in a utopia where all races, nations, and peoples are one. But they are no different from the old pagan worshippers—only the names of their gods have changed. They combine physics with Zen, and pagan animism with astronomy. They perform tribal rituals and African drumming. Yet others mingle Jungian psychology with the black arts of alchemy. All of this is blasphemy! Oh, some of them are very smart, but they lack the faith in Jesus that alone can save. They appear as Buddhists, Sufis, or Hari Krishnas—the ones you've seen in the airports. And the worst ones of all are those who practice a new form of Goddess religion. They worship the Moon and wear images of faceless, big-buxomed Paleolithic goddesses around their necks. Idolatry!

"I repeat, only Jesus can save us. It is our duty to alert as many of our brothers and sisters as possible to these two signs of the Beast and bring them back into the fold. Some are naive and have been led astray. In Matthew 24:14 it is said that the end won't come until 'this gospel of the kingdom is proclaimed through the Earth.' It is we who shall proclaim it.

"Whenever you hear of our children being taught Darwin's theory of evolution, you have the duty to bring that teacher before us, that we may preach the truth of Creation and restore his faith. Creation is a fact, not a theory. The Bible is our testament.

"Brethren! We must fight the rise of secularism and paganism in this country. It is through our battle against the devil that Jesus shall know us. Our Lord and Savior, Jesus Christ, is with us now as we pray together."

As she bows her head in prayer, Martha is seized with fear. She thinks only of Pete, who has shown interest in some of these dreaded New Age beliefs. She longs for someone she can talk to about it. Worried, she puts her faith in Jesus and turns inward, her heart like a mirror that hides what is behind it.

Although uncomprehending of most of the preacher's words, Melissa is captivated by Zain's fiery energy. Seeing her mother's drawn face, she asks, "Didn't you like the sermon, Mama? Isn't it true that Jesus saves?"

Martha looks down at her daughter and strokes her hair: "Yes, but you heard Preacher Zain himself say that Jesus shall save only those who battle against the devil."

"No, Mama, I heard him say Jesus saves those who have faith."

"Your brother has lost his faith!" cries Martha as she bursts into tears.

Pete

Pete stands in New York's Central Park, where he is musing with his friends about past, present, and future. He feels fed up with a father who vacillates between oppression and apathy, and a mother who clings to Jesus. Ever since he decided to major in drama and music, Pete has felt rejected by Allen, who termed it all "useless fluff".

Mike, Rita, and Laurie sit on a park bench while Rob and Tarcher stand next to Pete, their lithe and powerful bodies singing with energy under bright T-shirts and multipatterned pants.

"The world situation is hopeless!" bemoans Mike, whose dark hair rolls over his shoulders. "More and more people on a wasting planet!

Sometimes I wonder why I was born! Who can live in a world like this?" He squats down, elbows on his knees and puts his head between his large hands.

"You've got such great talent, Mike. Don't let your own fire go out!" responds Rita, a savvy and beautiful black woman.

Laurie puts her arm on Mike's back and reproaches him: "Yes, if you let your fire go out, there will only be smoke curling up and dissipating into the ozone."

Mike looks up at Laurie, then brushes away her hand and stands up again. "The radiation leaking through the ozone hole will kill us anyway!"

Laurie tries to soften Mike's hard attitude: "If you love your Mother Earth and heal your soul, the ozone hole will be healed too."

"You're so naive and idealistic, Laurie!" protests Rob. He is Rita's brother, a large, gentle black man who is always moving. "Let's face it, Mike's right. We're in the breakdown of civilization and the planet is being polluted beyond repair. All we can do is escape into our personal stuff."

Tarcher, who has just come back from England, has his own solution: "The UFOs might be the answer. I've seen their signs in the crop circles. I believe they are connected with some miracle that will save us."

"The war in the Near East is affecting us all," adds Rita in her own confusion. "Radiation is everywhere. We're probably becoming mutants. I try to keep the faith, but sometimes it's too hard."

"Yeah. My dad's an M.D.," says Rob. "He doesn't say this to everybody, but he knows of research that shows the human DNA itself is changing. There's an extra hydrogen atom. We *are* mutating!"

"Into what? Monsters?" blurts out Mike cynically.

Pete listens to his friends in silence. His father's repression of his mother has affected him inwardly. But the fire in his spirit and the mass of contradictions in his soul emerge like explosive shrapnel in his music. Composing music offers him release from emotional trauma, a way to express the matter in his being. He knows that Western civilization has been breaking down since the First World War and even before. Although its inexorable momentum leads him to project faith in a New

Age, he vacillates between hope of a miraculous regeneration of the world and fear of its end. Too many times he has heard the preaching of Zain. Too many times has he felt the aggression of his father. He has become techno-tribal, his anger finally surfacing when the bombs were dropped in the Near East—bombs that exploded his own repression, bombs that split open denied sexuality. Passionate about Rita, Pete holds himself in check. He feels the fiery energy in his body. He feels his father's erotic desire for his mother and sees that they are both plated with defensive armor. He sees the armor around everyone, including himself. He feels like a living stockpile of cosmic energy.

Finally he says, "Defense, bombs, shields—they're a result of the inability to feel and express desire. It's all the same affliction! We need to create music that shows we're not afraid, that we're open, without defenses."

"You're nuts!" retorts Mike.

"No, listen," counters Tarcher. "Pete always has a reason for what he says."

"Let's produce a concert to expose the rigid orthodoxies of all kinds," continues Pete. "The self-righteous moralizing, the fear, the aggression, the stockpiling of arms. Don't you see, it's all the same?"

Pete grows charismatic, commanding his friends' attention as they feel their energy rising. He speaks adamantly: "If we *live* the holocaust and raise our spirits, the radiation polluting the atmosphere may be transmuted."

"You mean, like, *become* the fire?" asks Rita.

"Yes—a new art: *embody* the holocaust."

"I want freedom, Pete, but I don't understand," responds Mike. "How can we become free by embodying the holocaust? We're the ones who will get burned in the process."

"Freedom comes from the fire of our spirit, our expression," replies Pete, who has penetrated to his own depths. "Our music will inspire people to embody the holocaust by bringing them face to face with their desperation and holding them there." He pauses and then blurts out, "I've even got a name—Holocaust Rock."

"Rock, Rock, Holocaust Rock!" sings Rita, jumping up and dancing around the benches.

"But how will the people get it?" asks Rob, hopeful yet questioning.

"The people *have* gotten it," says Pete, his eyes gleaming. "They've had all they can take. Our music will shake them from their apathy. The war got their attention. Now we can direct it. We'll use the media."

Mike is still depressed. He senses that the masses have no consciousness and can't possibly awake. He even has his own theory about the world's excessive population density, which he sees as the fallout from reactive souls who have incarnated and now lie buried, unconscious in material bodies. "We'll never awaken the masses," he declares.

But Tarcher feels infused with hope: "Death is dancing on all rigid views, man—apathy, illusion, and two-faced politicians. Don't you see, Mike? The old world is coming to an end! We need *you* to drum it into them. I can get Tarz to record it and put it on television."

"That's it!" says Laurie, who jumps up and embraces Tarcher. "Let's do the concert to raise money for refugees, or to feed the homeless, or to help save the rainforests. We can put it to a good cause."

Mike is still skeptical as he stands up. "Entropy!" he says cynically. "That can be the first piece."

Pete pretends to biff Mike in the solar plexus, then embraces him: "You're right, Mike, the first piece *can* be called 'entropy'. Entropy is welfare programs, insurance, government and corporate bureaucracy, and drug addiction. It's every sanitized version of conspiracy against a free life. Holocaust Rock is the free life. The entropy of a mechanized life can emerge from our music as the breakdown of manipulation, credit cards, the false promise of world peace, and leisure through automation."

Mike beats a stick in syncopated rhythm on the bench: "You mean the breakdown of the ultimate repression—'defense' through the stockpiling of arms?"

"Yes, we'll explode it all!" says Pete. "The antidote to nuclear weapons is our own free spirit. Are we going to put it on the line or not? If we don't, we're just like all the other sheep—addicted, desensitized, and clutching to a false hope."

IN QUEST OF THE EMERALD RIVER

Inertia
Red of red within red

The great momentum
of matter
turns the blood
in the heart.

Akrisios

"I must go to the mountains and be alone for a while," Akrisios announces to Raphael at dawn. Her entire being surges with a torrent of energy. Raphael looks at her a long time: "I support you in your vigil and entrust your safety to the gods."

"It is a vigil and a journey in one," Akrisios says quietly. "I will follow the river upstream."

"The Cockscombs are steep. If you follow the hills beyond the source of the river to the northeast, you will enter British Honduras. Please stay along the headwaters of Rio de la Pasion. There you will find both protection and inspiration. If you do not return in five days, I will come for you. But wait here a minute. I have something for you."

Raphael goes into the shack and returns with a small pack: "Take this. It contains some seeds, nuts, and dried fruit. You may need it on your way down. Also take this jug of water. The river water is not safe to drink until you have gone two miles upstream."

"I'm grateful for your kindness," says Akrisios with tears welling up. "I feel this journey represents a kind of death within me. I've never had such support for a venture into the unknown before." She cries and embraces him.

From his pocket Raphael pulls two small sculptures hanging from leather thongs: "Here, take these amulets. Whenever you feel afraid, hold the jackal in your right hand so that you may be willing to have all false thoughts and desires devoured. Whenever you need inspiration, hold the dragon in your left hand so that you may re-create yourself from the receptive empowerment of nature. Then all inertia in your life will be turned in your blood toward the emerald waters."

"Emerald waters?"

At that moment a vulture swoops down and pecks at a dead rabbit.

Raphael gives her a light kiss: "Bless the darkness and the unknown and you will find where the path turns to emerald. Wait until morning unless the light of your desire shines bright enough to guide you, for the moonlight is waning."

Akrisios is agitated: "I cannot sleep, for a millennia of terrors lives in my cells. I shall not rest until the teeth of this jackal tear all fear and falsity out of my flesh. I hear the screams of future children being devoured by the jaws of our ignorance. I must find my own way to the burning waters. I know nothing, but I live in a spell of desires unloosed from ages of darkness. I must find my center and lay down my life on the altar of the mountain where the headwaters spring forth. Thank you, my friend. I'll leave tonight. Zapana moves with me. My blood is on fire."

Akrisios sets out with a mixture of doubt, denial, and desire driven deep into her bones. Her marrow mixes new blood as she walks by the riverbank, following the sound of the water in the darkness. At one point she takes off her shoes and places them in the small pack that Raphael gave her. Her feet seem to have grown eyes of their own. She is like a tiger, stalking the prey of her own doubts. The crescent Moon dreams. Looking through the trees to the stars watching her, she speaks to her higher self in a soliloquy: *We all come from starseed. How far we have fallen!* She falls to the ground. *The trees are in pain and can express it only through disease.*

She stands up and continues to walk as the river streams down tumultuously from the roar of desire. *Has anyone the power to go upstream?* she asks herself. She feels the weakness of her personal will compared to the power of the river tumbling like the word of God falling toward matter—words of water uttering the divine intention. In the moonlight she sees a branch stuck in the bank, bobbing up and down in the water. She feels like the branch, unable to be delivered of her sorrow until the currents turn or until she reaches the source. *What is it? How can I reach the River's source?*

As she walks, she becomes aware of the flow of her menstrual blood, which greatly increases her sensitivity. Naturally attuned to Moon cycles, she is now even more attuned to the meaning of every tree, leaf, and stone. As the blood is released from her womb, she beholds the blood of the ages—genocide, infanticide, and war—and feels the pain of the ages in the waves of the river. She wades into the water and gives her blood to its black depths. The river flows downstream as time, as creation. She asks, *Is this compassion? No! Passion! Passion drives us.*

Beholding a vision of bodies contorting to find pleasure amidst pain, she sobs and moans: *Oh, the bodies of trees and plants remain unseen! The human race is numb! We cannot even see the pain of one other, let alone the pain of nature that results from our abuse.*

Involuntarily, she doubles over and retches. She goes to retrieve the jug of water and drinks as if she were taking in new life, feeling enveloped in a warm velvet sky where the masks of ancient amnesia cover the faces of memory. She clutches the jackal in her right hand and prays to release all falsity.

Akrisios feels her own boundaries break with a shift of consciousness that brings the terror of all the gravitation of the Earth to the vastness of the sky. She dreams the dream inside her own belly. In a darkness that glows of other realities, she beholds vast lattices of light and scintillating dots inside geometric arabesques. Her astonishment is as great as her fear: *This is the womb and belly of Kali! It holds all that humanity has devoured in its unconscious craving. But it shines with the luminous colors of energy that are also within us. Our cells are eyes opening billions of times and closing to the blood of the ages.*

The river glistens in the faint glow of dawn. Now she begins a wild dance of death, her head moving involuntarily, her hair darting out in Medusalike coils—serpents of hatred and sorrow that writhe and fall to the ground to disperse into pure energy. *Old defenses, old ways, get out! Break the stony knowledge and memory of my mind!* Her hatred of Maurya, her jealousy of his lover, her bitterness over the loss of Athene—all race out of her body. The catharsis hurls her into the river where she feels one with the dark waters. Crystalline stars blink in her own body as she watches the morning Sun crest over the hills.

She gazes at the glowing reflection of the water, realizing that the river has been changed by her experience of Kali and Medusa. But bloody turbulence still rolls beneath the surface.

As she faces a great old pine tree, she sees herself as a warrior who refuses to be a victim. She embraces the tree, her old warrior self. *I have been an old warrior. Now I am a chief of peace. I am, in truth, a queen.* A flood of past lives unfolds to her inner eye.

The next morning Akrisios looks east to the Sun shining through the aspens and willows, their chartreuse leaves dancing like children. *Praise the Sun, alive and glowing!* Taking the dragon amulet into her left palm, she prays for inspiration and renewal.

She looks west into the forest and sees a circle of trees standing in council. She strips naked and walks into the river, her blood once again flowing into the water. She feels the nurture of nature, the dance of life, as eros is renewed within her. Stretching her arms to the treetops, she looks upstream and sees the river flowing from the mouths of goddesses. *Water is eros: eros is in everything! Open vagina. Va vagina, water, vater is her flow. Vater, father, come—vast open dawn. Resurrection of the trees!*

She sighs deeply, seemingly in concert with the fish, insects, and spirits, as if all of evolution shares her release and renewal. *Even dead trees shall arise! Corpses shall pass through their tombs. I embrace the angry, the hurt, the numb, the dead!*

She bends over, squeezing her gut and the dazzling womb of Kali. She sees that the Kali in her devours the dead so that new Earth can rise through the darkness. Her pelvis undulates, releasing eros into the river as life roars within her orgasm. She recalls the words of Raphael: *All inertia will be turned toward the emerald waters.* In her hands the jackal and dragon seem to come alive. She sees that one re-creates what the other destroys, that what appear as opposites are but part of a larger unity. She hangs the amulets around her neck and draws her palms together, the released energy guiding her hands to gesture in ancient sign language. What she now knows directly and intuitively astonishes her.

Growing quiet, she thinks of her seventy-eight-year-old mother who has spent a lifetime in erotic denial: *Oh, mother! I will nurture you awake until you die! You conceived me in pain, unconsciously denying the body and the Earth! Look at your wound, your hurt. Look for the Goddess in the matter of your body. Release your guilt and become a babe in the womb of all goddesses. I cry for my mother! Mother Earth and mother flesh. My anguish is ancient.*

Akrisios hears the trees speak in monosyllables of alternating light and shade as she continues upstream. Although their height diminishes with the altitude, their power increases. They stand short and gnarled, as though still struggling to reach the sky. In a hallucination, she sees her daughter Athene on the rocky hill where the source of the Rio de la Pasion issues from a spring.

Akrisios wades into the water and calls aloud: *Athene! Forgive me for passing on unconsciousness. Now! Come home!* She flings water over her head and revels in ecstatic dance, shouting: *The river is the saliva of Kali. It speaks of truth and wisdom, of eros and intimacy. Let it be! Let us love our mothers! Turn back and go forward. Help me turn away from running away.* The stones under her feet sing with her.

Now she sees Athene as Kali herself, dancing wildly through the wind-blown trees, the turbulent river, the spinning air, the groaning Earth. Akrisios looks into the river of her own blood turning emerald. *I will never cease loving you!*

Kali responds to her: *Don't mistake me for your own idolatry, your frustrated eros! I am emerald eros sublime. Show me your life through death! I am your mother and your daughter!*

Akrisios shouts through the forest: *Let the river run! Let passion flow into compassion! Ha! Thank you, Athene! Thank you, Kali!*

She circles the hilltop where the emerald water springs: *I watch the world from Kali's womb where poison turns to medicine. The tops of the pines and aspens and willows cry for freedom, along with all sentient beings of aeons past. No longer will I be hostage to the lies of my own fear and live in unconsciousness passed from generation to generation. I release anger and fear into the current. I flow through the rocks. I am gentle, strong, simple, and clear.*

In the crucible of her heart, the burning waters are renewed, and Akrisios' blood flows transformed as the Emerald River of Compassion. Sleeping that night beside the Rio de la Pasion, she dreams of emerald currents flowing into the hearts of children.

THE TAO OF CHANCE

Direction
White of red within red

The One
and the many
flow through
each other.

As the Trickster glides into the vortex between the Second and Third Worlds, he realizes the power of the dragon's spiralling energy to materialize his thought. Though frightened of dragons, the Trickster nevertheless fills the brains and nerves of mortals with spirals, activating their memory of the human image, focused through the spinning eye of heaven. The human body, previously scattered throughout the lattices, now congeals and forms itself out of the burning waters of the Creatrix. Suspended in her blood are twelve cell salts that vibrate with the qualities of the zodiac. While the lattices twist in the Dance of Death, the salts condense into minerals and create matter out of the matrix of light.

The burning waters crystallize the salts out of the dried mud beneath Death's dancing feet. Some of the blood of the Creatrix flows underground as the pure Primal Waters, while above, the starry elements are hammered into crystalline shapes. Forms congeal into matter on the cracked Earth.

The human souls are bewildered. Leaving one world to enter another, they see parallel universes in the vibrating waves of heat and drought. Every thought and action boomerangs back to them in the curved space of the Third World. A few discover that matter with mass holds the light within itself. But the sacred fire isolated from the Primal Waters explodes into radioactive infliction of pain and suffering. Even the Death Dance herself is amazed at the effect of the Trickster's thought within her matter.

Karl and Yu

Karl sits in a Munich conference room where he is watching an animated video about the Big Bang theory of the origin of the universe. Christa has remained in Karlsruhe, working on a painting and pondering the story of creation.

The video has been shown a dozen times during the physics conference, which has drawn scientists from around the world to hear the latest research on the four forces of physics, the Big Bang, superconductors, and string theory.

The video, generated by paired supercomputers, reveals startling arrays of transformation that make the chaos theories of the seventies seem elementary. New math models, involving pure cubes, extrapolate scenes of the cosmic fog that preceded the first seconds of the Big Bang. Astonished observers witness the slow-motion collision of free electrons and their interactions with light in multiple dimensions. Throughout the pregnant universe, an opaque, transluscent fog is created from the glow of feedback from the subatomic particles. In a dazzling depiction of the Big Bang, the video shows the phase transition from energy to mass through magnetic monopoles, which create cosmic strings that behave like superconductors. Bubbles of compressed matter intersect and create chains of galaxies swirling and drifting in the vast darkness of space.

Sitting next to Karl is Kau Chiang's son Yu, who cries out as he watches the universe explode from the primordial fireball. Karl looks over at Yu, who sits spellbound by the immense radial, expansive power on the screen. The video's narrator gives detailed scientific information:

More spacetime was created in the first millisecond than in all the spacetime since. It is estimated that the quantum fields in the early universe had an expansion factor of ten to the fiftieth or more. Then the driving force faded and expansion slowed. If the matter density is greater than 5×10^{27} kilograms per cubic meter, the universe closes and the gravitational force pulls it toward collapse.

Through the miracle of computer animation, Yu witnesses the initial rapid expansion attain a critical value that drives the spatial curvature out of the universe. Yu's mouth drops open as he contemplates the incredible possibility of a collapsing universe. The narrator continues:

> Our universe is on the borderline of being open and closed. In a compressed space the quantum uncertainties erase the distinction of space and time. Four-dimensional space curves back on itself. The theories of super symmetry posit that particle classes of fermions and bosons—normally mutually exclusive—relate to each other like vibrating strings in ten dimensions.

As the video concludes, Yu slides down in his seat and goes deeply within, closing his eyes to recall the breathtaking images. He reflects to himself: *Perhaps we may discover ourselves more readily in a collapsing universe than in an expanding one. Could it be that we on Earth have reached a critical threshold of expansion, and now we must face one another and find direction together?* He continues to sit for some time, stupefied by the video's beauty and in awe of its implications.

Karl has been observing and feeling Yu's response as much as the video itself. When Yu finally sits up and opens his eyes, Karl turns and asks, "Have you heard of these theories before?"

Yu turns his dark flashing eyes toward Karl: "Yes, I've heard, but I have not seen. I did not know physicists have seriously posited the idea of a collapsing universe. I was thinking the concept may be useful if it will lead us to facing ourselves." He looks over at the graying but vibrant Karl and asks, "Are you a physicist?"

Karl smiles, his piercing blue eyes as bright as if he were twenty-eight like Yu: "I used to be. In the seventies my specialty was chaos theory. Now I am doing independent research on morphology."

"What's that?"

"The study of form and the process of its transformation. Shall we go outside and talk?"

"Yes, thank you," says Yu, standing up. "I would like to understand more about transformation—morphology you call it. I have been studying in America for nine years. Now that I have my doctorate, I have come to Munich to understand more about the latest research in sub-atomic physics."

Yu continues as they stroll into the hotel's courtyard garden: "I believe it is at the subatomic level that what my father calls the harmonics of the universe work. I used to be skeptical of the old thought of China that he expounds, but I'm growing more respectful."

"What is your field?" asks Karl, looking into Yu's eyes.

"I observe solar flares and sunspot activity and their correlation to magnetic conditions on Earth."

"Have you researched the uses of solar energy?"

They sit down on a vacant bench. "Yes, but I hope to get involved on a more practical level now that I am finished with my studies. My research focused on the correlation of sharp changes in solar activity with the incidence of coronary artery disease and nervous disorders. Few people know that the peaks of solar activity are 179 years apart, the last peak being in 1960. I do not think anything happens by chance."

"Are you an astrologer?"

"Not really, but I watch the magnetic fluctuations that correlate with the angles between planets and between the planets and Earth. In February 1956, the greatest known cosmic shower took place when Mercury and Mars were again in conjunction. I have been researching the effects of these cosmic events on human health. Four years ago, I discovered Dr. Make Takata's research on the changes in human blood just after peak sunspot years."

Yu smiles wistfully: "As I said, I once thought my father's Taoist ways were old-fashioned, but the more deeply I research energy fields, the more I realize how true the Taoist wisdom is."

"Could you give me an example?"

Yu brightens: "Yes. Take the old Taoist concept of 'mutual arising'. Scientists call it correlation and say it is less important than causation. But everything is mutually arising: the flower with the bee, the wave with the shore, the air with our lungs. The original fireball contained everything that now exists. We mutually arise with the stars and solar flares."

Karl is stimulated by Yu's words: "Yes, when we see the universe as a multidimensional field rather than a linear track, correlation *is* a signifi-cant pattern." He muses on: "Correlation, to the linear mind, may seem like chance, but even chance is not without order or pattern."

Yu, too, is delighted to find a fellow researcher who is openminded: "I find that when we have a rigid orientation or direction, we can't see the patterns that are there."

Karl continues Yu's thought as if it were his own: "Yes, it may look like chaos to us. But from another perspective, chaos itself reveals amaz-ing patterns. I look at correlations between formless energy and formed matter to see new orders in apparent chaos. The craziness of our modern world has emerged because we have become fixated on one specific order and deny the many other orders that live within the chaos itself."

Yu nods: "There *is* a lot of craziness in the world now."

"In studying chaos theory I learned long ago that a linear process, given a stimulus to make a change, remains off track. But a nonlinear process, given a stimulus, returns to its starting point. You'd think that with all the human social disorder, the violence inflicted upon one another and the environment, plus the Earth's natural disorders—the earthquakes and droughts—that we would seek a return to balance, but it seems not so. Humanity needs to find direction. If our consciousness is linear, locked into specific ideas and habits, our life is monotonous and repetitive in a way that serves as an inertial lag to changes of any kind, good or bad. Direction does not appear to be found in the chaos of the world."

"Are you pessimistic? How do you see transformation happening between humanity and the forces of nature?"

Yu's like-mindedness invites confidence in Karl as he probes his own mind: "There must be some reversal of the monotonous deterioration of human consciousness. There must be a resonance between human con-sciousness and the harmonics of the universe, as your father calls it. The universe is a rich, multidimensional, complex web. We must see this richness and feel the connections, both inwardly and outwardly. Through resonance and nonlinear awareness, perhaps direction can be found."

Yu nods in assent as Karl continues: "I live with an artist who has helped me open my inner life. I believe that only by thinking in the flexible and intuitive manner of the artist are we likely to interact with nature in a way that leads, not only to homeostasis, but to higher evolutionary tendencies for both humans and ecosystems."

Yu's eyebrows rise as he speaks: "What really is the crux of the direction of our destiny? What determines the radical changes needed? I am very concerned about humanity's future. We've created a wasteland and don't seem to know how to go about changing it."

Karl looks hesitantly at Yu, but decides to speak his truth: "It is really a matter of changing our whole orientation from that of will and force to that of love and exchange."

Yu smiles knowingly, realizing that he has found a true friend and teacher in Karl: "Do you know *The Way of Life* by Lao Tzu?"

"I've heard some of it but not studied it."

"Lao Tzu said:

The great Tao flows everywhere,
to the left and to the right.
All things depend upon it to exist,
and it does not abandon them.
To its accomplishments it lays no claim.
It loves and nourishes all things,
but does not lord it over them."

Both scientists sit for a while in silent communion. Finally, Karl says thoughtfully, "I think of the Tao as the ever-present, unmanifest source before the Big Bang."

"Like the cosmic fog, that moment of unpredictable subatomic interactions with light?"

"Yes, only this source must be ever present in the continuum of nature. We should be able to access it and move in harmony with the Tao at all times. As Lao Tzu says, the Tao does not abandon us. We in the West call it God."

This brings another question to Yu's mind: "You're of German descent, are you not?"

"Yes."

"In a philosphy course, I studied Nietzsche, who declared that God is dead. Your God cannot be the same as the Tao, for if the Tao died we could not depend on it." Yu laughs at the irony of the Tao being dead when it is life itself.

Karl takes up the thought in a serious vein: "Nietzsche was nihilist, a precursor of the Antichrist. His main archetypal character was Zarathustra, who offered redemption to those bound by the past through a change in orientation from 'It happened' to 'I will it'. The individual became a creator. Past and future were seen as opposites in a one-way direction of time and destiny."

Yu is puzzled: "It seems that the Western way is to polarize. I still cannot fully understand the Western mind. In old China, the Tai Chi of yin and yang is bound by the circular unity of the absolute emptiness of the Tao. Unity precedes and supports polarity more as a complement than as an opposite. The direction of the past and future is always in the present. Only the present moment is alive. This is 'mutual arising'."

Karl is engrossed: "Yes, even Nietzsche may have been caught by time. The old linear arrow of time as a direction toward the future is false, for the future never arrives. It exists only in our minds, just as the past does. In the West, God must die because of what he represents—an authoritarian God who can save. People have abdicated their power to create. God must die within one's memory to live within one's creative will. Maybe that is what Nietzsche meant by 'God is dead'."

"I think what is lost is not so much the will to create," responds Yu smiling, "but the cosmic power of being immersed in the waves of spinning yin and yang, or what you call the continuum of a spacetime curvature. Lao Tzu used the term *hun* to describe the state before heaven and Earth arose. *Hun* means obscure, turbulent, chaotic. Isn't spacetime continuously being created from chaos?"

Karl laughs, "Yes, I see now. That's why I went into chaos theory in the seventies."

"The Western mind seems uncomfortable with both chaos and death," muses Yu. "I believe the denial of death plus an obsession with progress is leading to a shattering of order and a breakdown of civilization."

"I am still trying to find the usefulness of chaos," says Karl.

Yu continues, "Chaos contains the secret of the renewal of the Tao within people's lives. Maybe the Western mind is only now opening to the mutually arising unity of the ancient Tao. Do you see, Karl, how the Tao is like chaos?"

Karl's blue eyes radiate primal wisdom: "If you mean the turbulence, the flow, wherein all patterns mirror all other patterns, yes. It is the linear sense of history that inevitably leads to the rise and fall of civilizations. The Tao and chaos flow on, in all directions. Our terms are different, but our meaning is the same."

For a moment Karl is silently immersed in the formlessness that precedes all form, but he soon grows restless and asserts, "Chaos must be a form of exchange like birth and death, the creation and destruction of pattern or identity. The Western way *does* want to add order, control, and progress, but I know that nature doesn't work in a progressive linear way. Your father and the ancient Taoists are right. Particles borrow energy needed for their creation, which they pay back when they disappear into light. Forces arise through particle exchange just as they did in the primal fireball. We receive life and pay back in consciousness. Everything is interconnected in exchanges. Chaos is phase transitions of exchanges of energy. Death is as important as birth.

"In the whole of spacetime, a human life is less than a gnat!" continues Karl, waving his hand. "But energy exchange is circulating forever. Perhaps, if we just keep participating, making exchanges in which we give back energy in a more refined way, we can immerse ourselves in the Tao. I feel we must take some risks. How else can we find our direction?"

"The direction of the Tao is ever creative," comments Yu. "It is ever curving back within itself to renew itself. I now know what my father meant when he said, 'You may seem to depart from the Tao, but the Tao will never leave you.'"

They are silent for a while on their return to the hotel. But Karl's thoughts are racing and soon he begins again: "I see molecules as oscillating, vibrating energy complexes. Life molecules consist of electromagnetic and other forces—all vibrating in an interactive web that science is only beginning to investigate. To analyze the atomic arrangement of molecular structure does not go far enough. We need to explore the inner energetic vibrations and the harmonics of those vibrations."

"The direction must either be toward the unity of the Tao or in conflict with it," responds Yu. "When we are one with it, we feel intrinsic harmony in our innermost being. All energy is charged vibration in the ocean of the Tao's great emptiness."

"In science, we call that great emptiness the vacuum and assume it to be nothing, but it is the plenum. It is full of the potential of everything."

Yu continues Karl's thought: "Since everything is a mass of patterns of energy, how does order arise in your view?"

"By vibrational resonances."

"That is what my father calls harmonics," affirms Yu. "The human endocrine system is, I believe, the intermediary between the body and the cosmic vibrations of light, heat, sound, and all the other frequencies of the electromagnetic spectrum. But the endocrine system also responds to more subtle fields."

"What do you mean?"

"The energetic patterns of hormonal molecules represent the vibrational harmonics of the more subtle cosmic fields, polarized according to yin and yang functions. The endocrine system links the subtle energy and the nervous system through different plexuses of the body."

"You are truly a find! I have wanted to meet someone who knows about the effects of cosmic energy on life and consciousness. I'm just beginning to explore this relationship. I'd like to invite you to our home in Karlsruhe. What are your plans after this conference?"

"I am considering going to China to visit my family, but there is no hurry. I accept your invitation."

While passing by the main conference room, Karl and Yu hear a prominent physicist concluding his lecture with a poem. Struck by its fortuity, they stop and listen with complete attention:

Death Dance's Song of the River

I am the primal energy in every atom.
I spark the polarity of electricity and magnetism.
I am the pulse and limitation of matter by antimatter.
You can find me in the density of accumulated light waves.
I am the mass that creates boundaries.

I am death's door where emptiness knocks.
Look for me in the clash of metals and lattices in stones.
I live in the parabolic trajectory of gravity.
I am the inertia that makes resistance possible.
You can find me in every blank wall.
I live in the patient and the humble.
I am the teacher of demandless commands.
I am the marrow of bones and the renewal of blood.
You can find me in every material and sentient being.
I create the arrow of time that is otherwise a cycle.

Are you infinite or infinitesimal?
I am the eye of God inside every atom.

THE LIFE MOTHER

With chaos oozing between her fingers, the Creatrix matches the harmonics of matter with those of the divine plan. Spun from the etheric substance of the Primal Waters, the diaphanous bodies of the Primal Pair fall into matter and become life upon the Earth. Male and female souls feel the etheric vibrations of pleasure and pain as they anticipate taking on physical form.

However, the Trickster claims the Creator's work as his own and struts into matter with the shadows of the soul. He veils the reality of the spirit, distorts the Shaman's imaginal mirror, and once again steals the sacred fire, now from Death Dance's whirling atomic light. Born of collusion between the Antagonist soul and Trickster mind, the human psyche suspends like fog over River waters that bubble and sparkle with molecules of emerging life.

The splitting polarities of body and soul, body and mind, mind and soul, twirl in the River without full consciousness. Distressed at the illusion of matter's predominance over spirit, the Creatrix enters the Third World of nature to maintain the wholeness of the emerging life web. Seeing the River clouded with diverging chains of possibility, she charges the Life Mother with the nurture of all forms upon the planet.

As each fetus is born from water into air, the Creatrix inspires the recreation of life through a fusion of spirit and matter. The burning waters of her blood unite fire and water, but the other elements contend in the struggle of matter. The organs give substance to the Trickster's abstract thoughts. United with the feelings of the soul and the impulses of the body, the mind creates images out of desires. Humans struggle to forge a solid identity, but they do not yet see who they really are: immortal spirits encased in flesh. Desiring the full revelation of her children, the Life Mother infuses the divine plan with genetic codes that weave protoplasm into patterns of life. Growth becomes the process that fulfills her intention until a limit is reached and she realizes that decay is equally necessary. Using the great cycles of the Heavenly Powers, the Life Mother weaves birth and death, growth and decay in her tapestry of life.

Species upon species swim upstream in perfect correspondence between image and matter. Spiders spin from the intelligence of the greater web of life. Earthworms undulate in rhythm with waves of devic light. Fish and snakes—cold-blooded ones with little mind or voice—live beneath the chorus of warm-blooded birds and mammals who sing and growl to express their souls.

The Creatrix imbues the meridians of living viscera with the harmonies of colored light. As the great dragons coil and curl, the Life Mother moves among liquescent clouds as nature's vital force, drawing streams of love through fin, wing, and bone.

Enveloped by furtive elements, the oceanic powers of the soul, body, and mind enter through light waves into crystals, chlorophyll, and hemoglobin. Spiritual light, drawn from the farthest reaches of the cosmos, meets the counter force of Earth, creating vast reservoirs of energy swirling in the River—chakras that burst through the plexus of mortals and spin outward to reveal the balance of every living thing.

The human psyche, maintaining the rhythmic connection between inner and outer, now rides as a winged goddess on the breath of the Creatrix. Using the gift of reflective self-awareness, humans begin to decipher the script of the River. They understand that the body, replicating both Earth and cosmos, conducts the Shaman's imaginal reality into electromagnetic forces, where the play of yin and yang unfolds from desire.

And so the Creatrix and the Life Mother orchestrate the paradox of free will and self-determination. Their wisdom brings the Immortals, the Antagonists, and the Primal Pair to work within nature herself. From amoeba and snail to salmon and bear, consciousness expands as matter evolves. The divine plan, fixed only in the mind of the fearful Priest-Seer, flows with the stream of creation.

THE MIGRATIONS
AND THE WATER JAR

Planet
Gold of white within red

The invisible
and visible streams
entwine
throughout the planet.

Tectonic plates carrying the history of the Earth shift and separate while the planet quakes deep within its molten core. Stressed continents rumble from the fracturing of spirit from soul, soul from body, and body from mind. But even the Trickster is not aware of the divisions in his consciousness that cause such tumult. Only the drifting lands once formed into the single continent of Pangaea hold the akashic memory in their crystals. The lands recorded the cataclysmic collision that pulled the Moon out of the Pacific and spun it into space. Seeking to heal the ocean's primal wound, land masses divided from a balmy Antarctica as the smaller plate of India moved north and the immense continent in the south divided into Africa and South America. The widening cleft in the womb of the Earth gave birth to the southern Atlantic as the Eurasian land mass rotated and began to close the eastern end of the Tethys Sea. Madagascar was carved away from Africa while the northern Atlantic moved eastward to a formative Greenland.

In time the Eurasian plate collided with the floating Indian continent, the clash of their ridges forcing the upward thrust of the great Himalayas.

Wickvaya and Lomo

The Life Mother knows that the perennial wisdom is like a spore that travels across oceans to continents where it can grow. Wickvaya carries this wisdom in his heart. The old Hopi shaman knows that the rocks hold the prophecies and speak the ancient tongue. But will his own children carry the wisdom? Will they understand the place of the planet within the universal plan of creation?

Wickvaya rests in the shade with his youngest son, Lomo, who has just returned home from school in Phoenix. Like his brother Starlie, Lomo struggles with the cultural conflict between the city and the reservation.

Wickvaya sits silently for a long time before he speaks: "Tuwanasavi is the center of the universe right here, my son. We live in the center of the four arms of the cross where, long ago, the magnetic messages were sent by the Twin Gods of the poles. The arms of the cross make the four arms of the swastika where the clans made their migrations. You do not need to wander off to a school to find truth."

"But I'm not sure those legends have any real meaning, Father."

"Lomo, listen. Masaw said that every clan—the bear, the fire, the snake, and all the other clans—would have to make migrations in the four directions before they could arrive at their real homes. So the clans went out from the center of this Hopi country. As they turned at the seashores that we call *Pasos*, they formed a giant swastika, clockwise or counterclockwise, according to the movement of the Sun. The chief clans went to the right and the lesser clans went to the left before they turned back toward the center. When they migrated back toward Tuwanasavi, the patterns of their movement formed spirals that grew smaller and smaller."

Wickvaya points to a series of spirals carved in rock and lights his pipe, "You can see the carvings as a sign of completion—not just here at

Oraibi, but at Chaco Canyon, Gila Bend, and Mesa Verde. Isn't that proof enough that the migrations were fulfilled?"

Lomo listens intently, trying to understand. His father continues: "Masaw gave the clans sacred tablets. To the Fire Clan he gave a small tablet with one corner broken off. He said to them, 'After you migrate to your real home, you will be dominated by a strange people. You must live as they dictate or you will be punished. Do not resist, for Pahana, your lost white brother, will return with the missing corner of the tablet. He will release you from the persecutors and will work out a way to achieve brotherhood with them. But if your leader accepts any religion other than the Hopi truth, he must agree to have his head cut off. This act would save his people.'

"This is what Masaw said. You know that I did not resist when I was imprisoned for refusing to fight the white man's war. You were angry because I was so far away. That was a test for me—to see if I could abide by the Creator's will even though my family was suffering. Now *you* are being tested, I believe."

"This drought is a test for us all, Father. I don't see how the migrations of our ancestors can help us now, when we are threatened with famine."

"Listen, when the clans completed their migrations, they returned to the middle of this great continent. Who do you think helped them? The kachinas! They brought blessings from the stars and from the depths of the Earth. In answer to our prayers, the spirits helped us bring abundance to this high barren plateau. We did not depend on streams to water our tobacco, corn, squash, and beans. No, we kept in balance with the Earth, and the water we needed came, direct from the source of all life."

Lomo is silent for a while: "I'm trying to remember the story of the water jar."

"Yes, my son. Masaw gave each clan a small water jar before it set off on its migrations. In times of drought, they were to plant the jar in the ground and water would flow from that place."

"How is that possible, Father? And if that really happened, why don't we do it now?"

"The jar was to be carried by a holy person who would pray and go without salt for four days before he could move on. Then he had to fast, pray, and go without sleep for four more days before planting the jar again. Not until the water started flowing could he resume his normal life."

Lomo questions with his dark eyes. "Aren't there holy people who can do this now?" he asks. "Aren't you holy enough to do it, Father? Our people are facing starvation. Many are leaving for the white man's cities, but there they just get sick."

Wickvaya puffs on his pipe, the smoke curling up around his wizened face. "Things happen as they are meant to, according to the greater plan," he begins. "Many of our people suffer from their ancestor's refusal to finish the migrations and perform the sacred rites. To know the future, you must know the past. Some clans did not complete the four migrations before settling here on Hopi land. Some even settled in tropical places where life was easier. These people lost their spiritual power. They could no longer remember the prophecies. But those who persisted and completed the migrations kept the door on the top of their heads open. This helped to overcome the evil left from the Third World. They found their home on this desert between the Colorado and Rio Grande rivers. Those were our ancestors. We know our title to this land is that the Creator sends us only scanty water. We keep our traditions, center our faith in the Creator, and accept what we have. Remember, Pahana, a special white brother, is to return from the east."

Lomo stands up. "But he still has not come," he protests. "Aren't we waiting for an illusion? I believe in science. It has tests and proofs. We have no way to know if our legends are true if we can't see results. I believe our existence is jeopardized because we have been waiting for a foolish fulfillment of a legend."

"Why do you speak in such big words, Lomo? Jeopardize? You don't need fancy words to understand the future. If we remember and awaken, the Fifth World *will* emerge."

"But how?"

"Maybe talking to the rocks is the way."

"I have been learning about the layers of the Earth from studying geology. But I want to find a language that links science with the way of our people—if that's even possible. I don't know." Lomo shakes his head and sits down again, staring at the ground.

"That is a good wish, but how can you do that? Your science doesn't include spirits at all, and without spirits we are helpless. The Hopi Road of Life has always shown that we must pray to the spirits first. Otherwise we have nothing. People who rely on outward things do not rely on prayer. That is why we were chosen to live on this arid plateau—because we know the source of all things. From our prayers and fasting, water will come."

His father's ignorance of technology and science frustrate Lomo: "Listen, Father, I hear what you say, but I must tell you something. Maybe the spirits are what are called electrostatic fields between the ground and the ionosphere. Such fields exist in the layers of the Earth, too. Science shows that insects and birds respond to geomagnetic fields that are in turn affected by the Sun and Moon. These 'fields', these invisible forces, may be the same as our 'spirits', Father. You know how the stars and planets affect us. You've spoken of it many times."

"Yes, that is so," replies Wickvaya with a nod.

"Some scientists explain these influences by saying that electrical frequencies and planetary pulses affect our brain waves."

Though the language is strange to him, Wickvaya smokes his pipe in silence and considers what his son has said. He then comments, "Yes, it is possible that you can help Pahana return to us through the white man's way. Can you find the roots of this Earth language? Learn how the terms of the white man's science relate to our kachinas and legends. But remember that we need to be conscious and understand *how*, not only *what* anything is. The connection between mind and Earth is not simply an object or thing. How you see and how you live will open you to the mysteries of our planet. The rocks you collected and talked to as a child are sacred. You understood more then than now. You know about the different layers of rock. You know they are formed from fire and earth, earth and water, pressing upon each other. But what are they really? How do they touch your heart?"

His father's words remind Lomo of when he first learned about tectonic plates that shifted and moved over vast periods of time. He knows well the scientific story of the planet's evolution. He knows that the molten core of nickel and iron is the remains of the primal fiery Earth, and that the Earth's mantle is mainly silicates. Momentarily flooded with childhood memories, Lomo recalls when he collected the slates, mica-shists, gneiss, lavas, and basalts all thrust up from volcanoes.

Wickvaya smiles as he blows a last puff of smoke and puts his pipe in his pocket: "Do you remember the song you and Kuksu sang in the school pageant?"

"Yes. I'll never forget that."

"Through your voice, you opened yourself to the spirits of the Earth. The vibrations of your voice carried everyone there on a journey to the center of the Earth. If you leave your voice, your eyes, and your heart out of your search, my son, your science will become dead and mechanical. You can know nothing that way. You can hear the heartbeat of the Earth through your own. Our planet was sung into existence long before the formation of any rock that science can measure. Find your way about the Four Worlds through song and art and ritual, and you won't need so much technology. We have a severe drought now, but if we pray and perform the sacred rites together, we shall have enough water to irrigate our crops. I know that one is coming who will perform the rite of the water jar. I say to you, find the sacred well in yourself and you'll find it on the Earth."

"I believe you, Father. But how do I speak to the white man about it unless I learn his science?"

Wickvaya stands up. He looks first to the sky and then down at the ground: "Heaven and Earth are made of light and sound. Our own Hopi language carries some of the old root words of the Earth. From what you have told me, I see that the white man may be looking for the spirits, too. But his methods appear to miss the very thing he seeks. If you can remember all the way back to the First World, you will find your way into the Fifth World and the prophecies will be fulfilled. Don't forget the power within you, my son—the power that creates and destroys. There you shall find the water holes, the rain, and the sacred wells."

Kuksu

Kuksu was always able to hear the heartbeat of the Earth. Unlike Starlie, she never went to college, though she was as brilliant as her brother in another way. Her awareness pierced the veils of the ordinary world. She learned from the rivers and trees, and talked with the stones, snakes, and badgers, who had become her childhood friends. She felt the exhalations of the desert, the northern forests, and the plateaus in diverse aromas, colors, and sounds. She intuited the resonance of each place with a specific group of stars. And when she danced on the ground, her bare feet sensed beings deep in the Earth. She knew they had halos and spiritual names.

Roaming the land with her younger brother Lomo, she played with scorpions and snakes, and watched prairie falcons and hummingbirds. The arid plateau was an Eden of the eternal present, for her soul flowed directly into the wild places where the life force flowed. She remained instinctual, as though her whole life founted from some invisible primordial stream. At first she felt its magnatism in her back, guiding her to places where she could commune with the creatures. Later she felt it in her hands. The antenna of her body could anticipate changes in weather and divine water.

She never forgot when Wickvaya took her to the caves that breathe. Something other than air passed through the wind cave of Wupatki, something finer and more subtle, something of the invisible world that brings form and life to the senses.

Now, during the time of drought, Kuksu wants to bring water to her village, as told in the old Hopi legends. The story of the water jar had always seemed very real. She knows that, when the human conduit is open, the water hidden in the sky can pour down upon the Earth. She knows intuitively that the water jar acts as a magnet for the stream of hydrogen and oxygen ions condensing out of the air.

She prepares for her quest by praying. Carrying only a small jug of water and cornmeal for an offering, she wanders for three days without eating or drinking. Finally, at dusk on the third day, she sees a small patch of wild grass on the edge of the mesa. She climbs down the mesa and, upon reaching the valley floor, stomps firmly on the ground.

Suddenly, she is swallowed by the opening Earth and tumbles into a tunnel suffused with an eerie light. She proceeds hesitantly until she reaches a cave that has no outlet. There, deep in the bowels of the Earth, a white man appears naked before her.

He gives her a mushroom to eat. She is afraid of both the man and the mushroom, but she is so hungry that she eats it immediately. In a few moments the spirits of the underworld appear, singing and dancing in flickering lights. They beckon her to follow them, leading her to a giant horned Goddess with serpents coiled around her arms and ankles. Strange beasts cling to all sides of her immense body.

"Why have you come here?" the Goddess asks Kuksu.

Kuksu places the water jar and cornmeal before her. "I seek water for my people who suffer from famine," she says. "I pray for rain or a spring that will bring life to our crops."

"First you must learn the language of the Earth and her plant and animal children," responds the Goddess.

"How can I do that?"

"The spirits will teach you. Follow them into the darkness. Eat or drink nothing until you can speak their language."

Kuksu follows the singing and dancing spirits back out through the winding tunnels. Without thought, she begins to imitate them. *These are not kachinas,* she says to herself, *but spirits of the plants and animals.* They teach her breathing techniques that will enable her to become one with a particular plant or animal. The spirits vibrate with color and sound, their many inflections revealing the manifold qualities of the Earth.

Suddenly Kuksu finds herself back at the cave where she originally encountered the naked man. He sits, watching her movements. She finds him attractive in a strange, magical way, but she does not touch him.

Eventually the man speaks: "Each animal quality must be preserved so that it can resonate with the stars from which it came. Otherwise the Earth will cease to circulate energy."

"Is this why famine blights the Earth?" asks Kuksu.

"All of life may perish from blinding ignorance," he replies. "Man is a predator whose enlarged brain leads, not to greater harmony with Masaw, as was planned, but to universal annihilation. Famine results from insensitivity to the language of the Earth. Her ores are gouged like bones from her flesh. Her vegetation is destroyed, causing the labyrinthine waterways to sink deeper into the ground The organisms in her soils are poisoned. But it is the animals who cry the loudest."

All is silent, except for the nostalgic notes of the Earth song that she and Lomo sang as children. Dancing animals appear before her. She sings the song, riding it like a subterranean wave, following the animals along a golden vein and then across an amethyst chasm. Covered in paint, beads, and feathers, imbibing the passion of the animals, she moves toward the center of the Earth.

One by one, the animals turn into men and women dancing like herself. She beholds the lineages of the creatures in their scales, flesh, and feathers. Their halos resonate with the auric light of the stars from which they come. All are vibrating in the colors of assorted skins and feathered headdresses. The jeweled wings of the dragonfly, the lone howl of the wolf, the curved horns of the sheep all mingle in the body images. Adorned with symbols of the deep script of the River, people of every race dance arm in arm—except some of the whites who have not dressed themselves in the nobility of their aura. Most become one with the animal kingdom, dancing upon thousands of emeralds and crushing them into a liquid green essence that swirls up and out toward the surface of the Earth. But in those places where the soil is spent, the animals needlessly slaughtered, and the flora smothered by ribbons of concrete, the emerald waters do not rise.

Kuksu feels the vitality of the dance. She knows that the crushing of the emeralds into a river is a promise yet to be lived. Having touched the very secret of life, she rejoices in ecstatic arousal as her genitals pour forth an emerald sheen that flows into her burning heart and out the top of her head.

She loses all consciousness of her body as her spirit flies up to the ceiling of the cavern. No longer hungry or in want, she feels the flow of the Emerald River. She hears the mountains singing and observes the intimate movements of the elements mingling in the creation of life.

For hours Kuksu reverberates in a timeless happiness until she is awakened by a large, horned sheep licking her face. The sheep breathes into her nostrils and brings her back to normal awareness. She scintillates with energy, yet desires nothing except to slip into a reverie of her experience. Pure in being, she hears the guidance of the Emerald River running deep in the core of the Earth: *Return to your people. For eleven months, you must live a simple life.*

Just prior to Kuksu's return home, a small spring of water founts out from the mesa and runs down into the field beside the village. The Hopi people are joyously amazed and full of praise for the Creator, but they do not know how it happens. "Perhaps it is a sign of Pahana's return," Wickvaya says to the tribe.

Three months later, Kuksu realizes she is pregnant. Her mother pleads to know more about the circumstances of the pregnancy. "If you are carrying a child, you must have a mate!" Nesaru says. "Please acknowledge the father. You have my word that we will accept him— even if he is white."

"But, Mother," Kuksu replies, "I had sex with no man."

A BATTLE WITH THE ELEMENTS OF CHANGE

Elements
Black of white within red

The Sun
within the stone
brings forth
clouds and rivers.

The Creatrix spins and chants, lifting the human spirit and dispelling the shadows of the soul. She utters different names into the elements, enabling the anonymous loom of life to weave human bodies of varied shape and color, each with distinct traits of voice and bone and limb. The River turns and churns the races into being—red, black, white, yellow, and brown—each carrying a different destiny within the great human mandala.

The races emerge through gene pools and are shaped into tribes and clans by the constrictions of fire, ice, desert, and mountain. Each one seeks to return to the whirlpool in the River. Yet it cannot. Sheathed in flesh, the single human spirit wanders in multitudes through steaming jungles, wind-swept deserts, and rock-studded mountains.

Their northern Eurasian homeland ravaged by the Pleistocene Ice Age, the Caucasians descend into Europe, the Iranian plateau, and India. Only when past the Suez gate do they face the Congoids and

289

Capoids of Africa. Yet they remain apart. During the glacial and inter-glacial periods, the Mongoloids meet the black Australoids in Indonesia and southern China. Yet they remain apart. The Congoid Negroes and Pygmies and Capoid Bushmen cross water and desert and meet in the jungles of Africa. Yet they remain apart.

The major barrier to racial mixing is human consciousness, emerg-ing in the many dialects of the script of the River. Diverse tongues and cultures draw the races forward into time and apart from each other. Differences in spiritual rites, dietary taboos, and artistic expression emerge far stronger than the forces of geography.

Long before the races can mingle, it is necessary for the earth, air, fire, and water within the evolving human body to slowly blend in the formation of culture. The people turn within to probe the mysteries of the gods and goddesses working through their respective ways. The growth of wisdom requires the development of language, art, and tools over millennia, culminating in the journey of the Shaman. Through vision and voice, the people meet the Great Spirit of the Creator and the Creatrix, and they reinvoke their presence through ritual.

Always, elites emerge. The Parsis of Iran, the Brahmans of India, the prophets of the Jews, the blacksmith-shamans of the Negroes—all transmit the perennial culture of the First World into their human world. Yet the weaknesses of the elders are inherited and passed on as a reminder that free will is born out of necessity.

Channon

One of the elite, Channon carries a thread of the perennial wisdom in his brain and heart. Yet he now ambles forlorn through the great stone house in Malta where his teaching and art once inspired many. His suffering has intensified with time, for he insists on waging a battle with change itself. His grand project, the immortality chamber, has failed. Desiring to consort with gods and goddesses, he finds himself only in the company of an occasional drifting seeker. His fire for the ancient ways is now obscured with delusions.

He longs for Fariba. She calls from time to time, but on her last visit made it clear she would not return to him. During their most recent phone conversation, she said, "Find your kin."

"What do you mean, my kin?"

"Your totem, your roots. You are always longing for something beyond, something transcendent. It is not there that you will find yourself, or real friends."

He had reacted strongly: "Totemism is animistic, bestial! The Egyptian gods are superior to all that. You should know better, after all I have taught you."

"Look at the heads of the Egyptian gods. Your gods *are* totems. You reject nature as inferior and deny the elements that made you. How can you achieve immortality by denying the nature that brought forth your mortality?"

Channon had been unable to respond to her words. He was surprised, though disgusted, by her insight. Now he stands on the edge of his destiny, stalled between creation and destruction. Obsessed with immortality, he begins to have delusions of grandeur to compensate for his failure. The very thought of totemism stirs his hatred of being incarnated at all.

He stares at the golden statues of Thoth, Osiris, and Isis on his desk, remembering when he and Horst, as the priest Manesis, sought to control the programs of the world. He would like to be doing that now. He thinks to himself, *To be in a carbon-based body that is part of the food chain is repulsive. I must find escape. Immortality is the way out. I know it.*

At night he is restless. The fear of death has him subconsciously in its grip. Age has begun to affect his memory. His body, which he has come to hate, is changing. He questions his very identity. When he finally does sleep, he dreams of the jackal, the hawk, and the lion-headed Egyptian gods—the animal qualities that repel him. He awakes with hatred for the organs inside him where these powers are embodied.

One night he becomes feverish, dreaming in his delirium that he is in a cave before a monster covered with coiled serpents. It sits on an infernal throne, breathing clouds and speaking fire.

"I will devour you!" claims the creature.

"Who are you?"

"I am the originator of the elements. You have refused my place in your consciousness, so I live in the cave of your soul and in the cavities of your body."

"What is your name?"

"Some call me Typhon, others Set, or Satan."

"Can you overcome death?"

"Death lies within the elements I control. The chemistry of mortality changes every moment. Death is always within you, transforming what was into what will be. I live in all elements, and they in me."

Typhon's organs transform into crystals and metals of the Earth, then into billowing clouds circulating through his lungs. His blood and lymphatic fluids gush into a teeming river. He bursts into flame, his thoughts shooting out like fiery stars. The sparks descend upon a strange land where painted aborigines dance around a serpentine form that undulates between circles and spirals made of bird down. In his dream state, Channon is captivated by the chanting and the compulsive rhythms of clacking sticks and drone pipes. Several dancers in fantastic totemic headresses transform into animals that, in turn, enter into a man lying on the ground. Suddenly aware that the dreaming man on the ground is himself, Channon jolts awake.

Drenched in sweat, he sits up and shakes himself as if expelling demons from his psyche and body. The dream remains vivid. He becomes fascinated with the idea of some secret life-force embedded in Typhon's sexuality and his own. He is aroused and frightened at once.

Over the next few days, the fever abates. He continues to ponder the dream, knowing that what happened was somehow *real*. He has changed, becoming perpetually hungry for food and sex, appetites that have never before driven him in such an extreme way. He feels he must go to Australia and find the aborigines in order to understand what has happened.

His immediate concern becomes financing such a long sojourn. When he receives a fortuitous phone call from an old student, Marlena Strom, he is convinced that the gods still smile upon him. Knowing of his powers in working with Egyptian magic, Marlena appeals to him for a kind of exorcism. Since she is desperate and talks as though money is no issue, he invites her to the house in Malta.

Marlena arrives one week later, complaining of an overly dependent friend who angrily turns upon her when she doesn't get enough attention, but whom she is reluctant to totally abandon. Channon, wielding his pendulum, informs Marlena that she is suffering from a psychic and physical parasitism that drains her vital energy. He tells her she is sexually repressed, unconsciously spending time with this friend to protect herself from a real sexual experience.

Schooled in how to psychically draw in the emotions of others, Channon charmingly seduces Marlena with the enticements of tantra and its esoteric, erotic magic. He convinces her that she has been sexually violated in the past and offers to "heal" her in five sublime sessions at two thousand dollars each. Having long idolized Channon, Marlena agrees to those terms.

Reclining back amid the first-class luxury of the Qantas jet, Channon recalls his encounters with Marlena. When the five sessions were completed, he departed, cash in hand, leaving her broken-hearted. He feels disgusted with himself, not because he so coldly exploited a needy human being, but because of his obsesssion with organic desires to which he had previously felt superior. He abhors the endless web of nature's tooth and claw, mouth and genitals. He sees kissing and sex as just a kind of eating. The elements have seized hold of him and continuously give rise to new states of becoming and dying. He realizes that his ancient plot to control others has rebounded back to him within his own body. The thought of Marlena repels him.

He sips from a glass of red wine, growing more irritable as he reflects on kissing and killing. He hates the amoeboid consciousness of being absorbed by the organism of the universe itself. *This is Typhon, Set, the archenemy! Mouth-to-mouth contact is as fatal in a kiss as it is for the prey of the carnivore!* He begins to mumble aloud, waking the man snoring in the next seat.

His fear of the loss of his identity haunts him throughout the flight. He prays to the gods he knows: *Oh, Osiris, guide me to beloved Fariba. I have lost what could have given me immortality! I didn't realize. Without her I shall fall into the jaws of Typhon, the devouring mouth of nature herself. Isis, help me!*

The drone of jet engines lures him into a semiconscious state. Struggling to understand what has happened to him, he remembers when Fariba used mouth-to-mouth resuscitation to save him from drowning. Ever since then he has lived in fear of death. He tries to recount the series of changes that has brought him to this suffering, this decadence. Recalling when Horst recognized him as a priest in ancient Egypt, he thinks, *We tried to separate the time machine of the stars from the body of flesh, but it was too early. Now it may be too late. I must find out what the aborigines know. The elemental connection in nature feeds the time machine. I must rediscover the key that turns the wheel of birth and death.*

Suddenly a great wheel looms before him. From far away he hears an ancient chant he learned while studying magic:

> Fire flame and fire burn,
> Make the mill of magic turn,
> Work the will for which we pray,
> Io dio, ha he yay,
> Air breathe and air blow,
> Make the mill of magic go.
> Work the will for which we pray,
> Io dio, ha he yay.
> Water heat and water boil,
> Make the mill of magic boil,
> Work the will for which we pray,
> Io dio, ha he yay.
> Earth without and earth within,
> Make the mill of magic spin,
> Work the will for which we pray,
> Io dio, ha he yay.

In a visionary state induced by his sleepless searching and the heady wine, Channon sees the elements pulsating, sparking, and grinding—the very chemistry of nature bursting through the Earth's body as clay, water, stone, and fire. Passing before him are nymphs, sylphs, and gnomes who mix the elements for the unfoldment of life. They are under a spell brought about long ago by the incantations of himself and Horst.

As the galaxy rotates, the Sun spins, and the Earth turns, the hypnotized spirits weave the elements through structuring, centering, and dissipating energies. They pass through the cardinal, fixed, and mutable signs of the zodiac, transmitting the elements in an endless round, creating the circle of reincarnation for all sentient beings. *Nature's devouring food chain is the beholding, being, and becoming of fire, air, water, and earth. I am caught in a web I myself created! In the Dreamtime I shall find the way out.* Channon is still light-headed and dizzy when the plane lands in the city of Darwin in northern Australia.

Although tired from the long flight, he spends the next two days wandering in the Outback. While in Malta, he had researched the emblems and body painting of various tribes, discovering that the patterns worn by the people in his dream were identical to those worn during totemic rites by members of the Gunwinggu tribe. Through esoteric channels, he had managed to obtain some secret passwords, a bone amulet, and a map of the area where the Gunwinggu rainmaker and shaman, Jingo, might be found.

After whispering the password to a half-aborigine, half-white interpreter, Channon is finally led to Jingo. An anthropologist who had years earlier befriended the Gunwinggu introduces Channon as a rare elder among the white people. But Jingo has already seen the nature of Channon's soul from his Dreamtime journeys. In a quest to understand why the elements have been out of balance and why the rain has ceased to fall, Jingo has discovered various black magicians scattered about the Earth. Having seen that Channon's magic was part black and part white, Jingo has entered Channon's dream, intending to either transform him or destroy him.

Jingo takes the bone amulet from Channon, then speaks through the interpreter: "We have been expecting you. The purpose of this bone was to guide you here. But it can kill. Be careful. If anyone among us dies from your handling it, we will know you are a sorcerer."

"But it was not my intention . . ."

"Do you really know your intention?"

"My intention is to become immortal. Was it you who danced around me that night in my dream?"

"You can remember the Dreamtime?"

"I wish to enter Dreamtime at will."

"What will you do then?"

"I'm not sure. Do you know the wheel of life?"

Jingo grunts.

"I will take the central pin out of the wheel," Channon declares arrogantly, thinking he will impress the shaman.

Jingo becomes intensely serious: "You are a lame and blind old man. You do not even know why you are here. How can you presume to stop the vortex of heaven?"

Channon is disgruntled. No one has ever talked to him like this. His tone changes to diffidence: "Perhaps you can tell me why I am here."

"To find your totem and to become a man. You are still attached to your mother."

Repulsed and startled, Channon sits in silence, his eyes growing wide behind the thick lenses of his glasses. He ponders his longing for Fariba in the light of Jingo's penetrating insight, and he eventually realizes that, yes, his ongoing desire for her return *has been* a longing for his mother's protection, for her exaggerated sense of his own importance.

Jingo is unrelenting: "You still resent your son's abandonment of your teaching."

"But I have no son."

"Your son still lives within your psyche. He blinds you and cripples you with a fear of death. Long ago he left you and the temple in which you wanted him to carry out your plots. He refused to assume your role. How could you not see him as he is?"

"As he is?"

"He lives now as a woman. It may be possible to see her, but only if you are willing to submit to the *Pukamuni* ceremony."

"What is that?"

"A rite of death."

"Whose death?"

"Your own."

Channon is afraid, but he knows he must not turn away.

"I long for immortality."

"First you must die."

THE CRY OF THE FORESTS

Growth
Red of white within red

The groan
of the Earth
quickens to
an inexhaustible force.

Long ago, when the Creatrix sat between the converging streams of the River and chanted in two voices, her burning waters modulated the life currents to embrace infinity through patterns of light. Four billion years of teeming life swelled in the River as one organism. Her chant echoed over the mountains, through the forests, and under the tides of the sea. Sylphs and salamanders, gnomes and nymphs, danced and slithered through the body's life-web. Unconsciously, paramecia responded to light, took in nutrients, and changed direction. Cuckoos called in happiness. Bears mated, while helical forms of limpets and gastropods spiraled out of whirlpools. Jellyfish and anemone fed, contorted, and defecated as single flowing axons. Sea creatures moved in global swells, at one with the song of the Creatrix. Protozoa lived but for one crystalline moment in the elemental water, while whales embodied three thousand qualities of the emerald sea.

Now, however, the contention of the elements in the human soul brings drought, famine, and devastation to the Earth. Amid summer's inferno and winter's ice, the Life Mother wails for her children. Fractured by the Trickster mind, the fragments of the Primal Pair shriek in the winds of change. One species devours another. Tigers lick the blood of starving rabbits from their paws. Snakes gulp the meager flesh of mice while antelope search for parched grasses and leaves. Grizzlies attack the invaders of their habitat. The eyes of owls stare down at highways. Salmon struggle and die in silt-filled waters.

The Life Mother sighs at the loss of her emerald sheen. Witness to her own emerging corpse, she recalls the scripture of the Earth. She remembers weaving designs of Precambrian species upon the fiery floor of the ancient sea, and she remembers the hissing hot springs and bubbling mud pots that poured carbon dioxide into the primal atmosphere. She remembers the primitive algae that first released oxygen into the air.

The Life Mother watches the motion of light turning to dark, recalling the winter of three million years. After the melting of that glacial night, her body flourished with plants and animals. But even those children would eventually perish, except the ones who dwelled deep in the caves or the seas. That was 250 million years ago. She shifted her continents then, causing massive seaweeds to blanket her shores with new tides of life. Rains poured down to spawn tropical forests that became home to the giant dinosaurs. Another 30 million years passed before the next disaster, when red cinders blighted the sky. She cannot even recall what began the scourge. An asteroid falling from heaven, perhaps, or fire erupting from the depths of her belly.

The Life Mother is tired, but sleepless. She wonders why she must die once more, the shadows of a fragmented humanity clinging to her soul: *Though I am dying, new life is ever evolving. I remember when the maple, ash, oak, and alder first sprouted from my crust. Is this life cycle finished? Even the scavenging fungi cannot live in poisoned soils.*

She struggles, trying to weave the souls who care into the tattered fabric of her rainbow robe.

Erhardt, Johann, and Rudolf

Erhardt's hands carry the love of the Earth, through which he tries to temper his anger. But his nights are spent tossing with the fury of being born son to a tyrant. Only by going secretly to Austria has he eluded Horst's agendas for the family business. Now, walking with two friends around three hundred acres of farm and forest land, he once again feels joy. The grass seems to shimmer especially for him. The pine needles shoot hope into his heart. He feels his irradiated body revitalized with the qualities of emeralds.

"Together we can begin to alleviate the suffering of this land," he comments. "We can grow organic produce for ourselves and others and try to regain our health."

"But both winters and summers are more severe than ever," replies Johann. He is tall and spirited, but also cautious. "Snow has been reported in the Persian Gulf. Sea birds have died due to ice over the waters of the French Riviera. I've read that extreme winds and cold have assaulted the American Midwest. If an ice age is actually coming upon us, it will strike here, too."

Rudolf, the eldest of the three, kicks at the soil. Although a wealthy business man from Munich, he has maintained a lifelong interest in agronomy: "You can see that the blight of *Waldsterben* is spreading. The white fir is gone entirely. If we buy this land we must know what we are up against. The trees are dying throughout Germany and Austria. In Poland and Czechoslovakia it is even worse."

Rudolf gazes at the contrast between the trees on the north end of the property and the ones to the south, which stand like spindled telephone poles: "As far back as the nineteenth century, Julius Hensel proposed using rock dust to refertilize the soil. He often repeated the Hindu saying, 'God sleeps in stone, breathes in plants, dreams in animals, and wakens in man.' But we haven't awakened yet. Germany did not listen to Hensel. Fifty percent of the West German forests were gone by 1987. It may be too late. But I'm willing to buy this land and put it into a trust if you two will farm it."

"I'll put my heart and soul into it. Muscle, too!" responds Erhardt, who wants to learn the hidden secrets of the Earth. "Rudolf, you know about rock dust. With your knowledge and our labor, we can re-mineralize the soil."

Despite his strong skepticism, Johann also wants to do something: "We *must* attempt to regenerate the Earth, regardless of the odds. The last glacial period began when the carbon dioxide in the atmosphere reached 290 parts per million. We are past that already. Hurricanes, earthquakes, and forest fires are increasing. And the radiation from the war penetrates us slowly. It's all interconnected. The wasteland is upon us, but I want to try."

From deep within the forest, Erhardt hears the appeal of the Life Mother:

> My creatures are dying. No longer do the deer nibble at my foliage, nor do the boars tear through my grasses. Humanity is the blight— yet I appeal to you. My robe was once emerald, dotted with the plumage of birds and the petals of wildflowers. You have disrupted the fluid splendor of my organic patterns. You have raped me, torn my spirit from my body, and turned my ancient compost into cash. Try to understand me. Over 300 million years ago, when giant insects flew among carboniferous forests, what you call fossil fuels were laid down within my depths. Your oil barons fight over my refuse, but these dark secrets are to remain within me. I have untold powers, but I cannot regenerate without you who have laid me waste. You waiver between caution and conviction, but you have no choice. The emerald deep within your heart touches mine. The River still runs.

Erhardt feels the power of her words. He envisions revitalized forests, fertile farmlands, and the return of living waters that run deep within her veins. He stretches out his arms toward the north: "Anything is possible! We can awaken from the nightmare of this wasteland! We must!"

Rudolf looks out toward the trees standing like gravestones in the south. He is moved by Erhardt's enthusiasm: "Perhaps we can get para-gneiss rock dust from an aquaintance of mine near Melk, not far from the Danube. If not, then the basaltic diabase in the quarry between Innsbruck and Kitzbuhel may be our answer. Mixed with dried cow manure, it can revitalize the soil, but only with very hard work."

Johann gazes up toward the mountains: "Glacial grinding is nature's way of bringing rock dust to the fields and forests. As much as I abhor a coming ice age, I know our lives are mere specks in the stream of time. We all grow tall and then return to dust. The Earth is in all parts of us.

We try to ward off destruction, but decay and death are part of growth."

The men stand silently for a while, each musing privately about the mysterious cycles of life. Finally Erhardt speaks: "Even so, we must think of future generations. I want to fight for the life of these forests. I want to work hard. The trees are hungry."

"And thirsty," adds Rudolf. "If we're going to do this, we need water as well as rock dust. Without the cooling effect of thick forest and diverse vegetation, the rain water cannot penetrate deep into the Earth. It either evaporates or runs off, which causes erosion. The water doesn't penetrate deeply enough to draw up the mineral nutrients, which then lie trapped in the Earth. We need the roots of trees to draw the underground water up. To break this vicious cycle, you two will need help."

"We need labor," says Erhardt, his green eyes shining. "Not paid labor, but hands and hearts that can live off the land."

"A community?" questions Johann, who seems startled at such a prospect.

"Can you manage this all at once?" asks Rudolf. His wrinkled face reveals the concern behind his smile.

"How else is it possible?" replies Erhardt, eager to experiment with some new form of community after so much frustration with family and business. "People committed to enlivening the water and restoring the land must be drawn together."

"What do you mean, enlivening the water?" asks Johann. Approaching the western end of the land, they stop and gaze at the river rushing in the hot Sun. A stray warbler perches on a dead cedar and directs its glittering eyes at them.

"I've read about Victor Schauberger's research," Erhardt responds. "He claims that even the water can die. For water to live, it must move in vortices and spirals, generating the centripetal energy that is the basis for all life. Above all, it must complete its cycle."

"You mean the cycle between the atmosphere and the soil?"

"Yes. As Rudolf said, trees and vegetation are the link between heaven and Earth. Without their cooling effect, water evaporates from the warm surface or runs off. The cycle between heaven and Earth is incomplete and the water dies."

"How can we enliven the water when the trees are dying?"

"Fortunately, we have a river. Near the running water, willows and alders will take hold easily. We must start planting here to provide shade to keep the water cool. In the areas where it is needed for cultivation, we can begin installing wooden pipes in zig-zag patterns and surround them with sand. This directs the water into a serpentine flow that will enliven its molecular structure. Then we'll invite the local community to learn about what we are doing and see who turns up. Since the land will be in trust, people with common interests may be willing to offer us the help we need.

"I'm confident that one day we shall walk through emerald forests with our bountiful harvest and deliver the secrets of nature to our children."

Speaking With Spirits

Consciousness
White of white within red

The voice
of nature
vibrates
with prophecy.

Kau Chiang

Kau Chiang sits lost in a trance on Dragon Hill, swept into an ecstasy that burns away the pain of his severed soul. The Red Bird of the south has flown through the heavenly vortex and opened him to the heart of his original vow: to remember the Creator and regenerate all life. The bird's fiery plumage fills the night and illumines the holy lake from which he drinks.

Through the tongues of flame, Kau Chiang sees drought moving like a phantom over the face of the Earth. He shudders and sighs: "O Red Bird, I am clothed in your light. I feel the red depth of change, the fugitive fire in your feathers. I am grateful. But your scourge has dried up the blood of the multitudes. The floods that once battered us have gone, and now, in your summer, the rivers run dry and the clouds cease to rise. What will appease you—that the waters not be consumed by your heat, but reflect the warmth of your heart?"

The glassy waters reflect the evening stars as the Red Bird speaks through Kau Chiang's consciousness: "When humans are angry, when they refuse to hear the 1,694,443th harmonic in my voice, the world becomes my provocation."

Kau Chiang phases in and out of a subtle awareness: "You mean the healing harmonic of compassion?" He hears in his reveries the incisive iridescence of a distant Zarian light.

"Anger in the human soul is the source of the hot dry sands," responds the Red Bird with a piercing cry. "Spite bakes the Earth when forests are cleared without thought of the life within them. Fear not the dirge, the mass, but live the ancient wound and tears of compassion will spill from your eyes."

"How can I touch the angry hearts and the idle dead? How can I heal the hurt and anger in my own soul when I cannot see them?"

"Run barefoot in the burning sand with love running fluid in your heart. Already your soul aligns with your spirit and music vibrates through your voice. Speak to the humble, the worthy, the ones whose anger is turning—and the bleached sky will be filled with rain." With that the Red Bird spins and dives into a scarlet river that spreads into millions of capillaried branches absorbed by the stars in the heavens.

Kau Chiang falls asleep as the rivers stream into the eyes of ones suffering from drought. He dreams of the dark wound of his own white bones, severed and scraped by oyster shells when he was murdered as Hypatia. Recoiling into an anonymous darkness that swells out into black waters, he beholds the soul of Zapana separating from himself. The "other" within him at once draws and repels him. He recognizes Zapana as a power filled with exalted fire, a lens turning spirit into light, a knower of the logos, the Sun God. Yet the inner recesses of his soul turn and reel like infinite fractal patterns caught by the strange attractor of Zapana's Western stream. He feels the tempest of Zapana's fire colliding with the watery depth of his own being.

Kau Chiang awakens and declares to himself, *I cannot provoke the world! My whole being is filled with waves, but I have not lived the fire! I cannot speak!*

Anger surfaces from his memory of Hypatia's wound. His consciousness parallels the universal stream where the script of the River sprays the air with dynamic patterns of energy. The Taoist Immortals watch silently, anticipating his rising courage as the renovating water rushes toward forgiveness in his soul. Fountain and fire fuse, washing and burning, sloughing off the evil elements into a physics of purification.

Kau Chiang reads the meta-language in the matter of the River: *Now fire and water join in my being. I will run barefoot on the burning sand with love running fluid in my heart! May I speak with others as in times past! May humanity befriend the dragons and spirits, and may the Earth turn emerald once again!*

He curls up like an embryo and dreams in ancient fragrances, energized by diamond-white glitter in his bones. Soon he merges with Zapana's spirit in the West, where raindrops filter through a pristine stellar paradise reflected in the holy lake. Yet he dreams awake, lucidly conscious, floating through former days as Zapana and as himself. He sees the tides of history in counterpoints of power and humility, logos and eros, ambition and acceptance—all rushing through a thousand faces.

His consciousness embraces the River that has no beginning or end. Acknowledging the wrongs of East and West, he feels the assault upon the dragons and spirits subside. He remembers the emerald calligraphy of the trees, the scripture of the Life Mother undulating through wind and water with patient care for all her creatures. Longing to see the Earth green again, he prays for the union of East and West in the depths of his being.

The healing harmonics of the burning waters charge Dragon Hill. The White Tiger emerges out of the west, striding to the tones of bells and flutes. Its glassy yellow eyes speak: "The Green Dragon, the Red Bird, and I bind the energies of the Earth together against the stress of human confusion. We can hold it no longer. A new era is about to dawn, but first you must find the ancient jewel that charges all waters with compassion. The demons stole it when the sacred fire was taken from heaven and the River became trapped in limited consciousness. The Trickster mind ruptured the web of life."

"How do I find the jewel?"

"There is a formula. Twenty spurts of clear water with six of metal and four of wind create wood out of the Sun, but even mortar and stone cannot fix twisted minds and broken hearts. Reactivity obstructs the flow of the River where the jewel is hidden."

"You speak in riddles, but I *feel* the meaning of your words. Is the River the Tao?"

Kau Chiang hears the notes of the pentatonic scale as his chakras swirl in an alchemy of subtle elements reflected in the White Tiger's eyes. He beholds the broken fabric of life in the cities of the world as the chakras shake off dissonant notes. He sees both the future travail of the addicted cultures and the poetic vivacity of those who reveal the reality of love. He beholds the multidimensional facets of the jewel shining in a matrix of unspeakable language.

"The jewel is within you," says the White Tiger, who then turns and strides back toward the west.

The words enthrall Kau Chiang. He feels Zapana vibrating through his spirit. He can envision any city, any landscape, any person through the focus of his thoughts alone. Transforming the shape-shifting Trickster in his mind, he begins to open into a flower of pure consciousness. But he feels resistance in his throat, where the chakra trembles with the tug of demons.

"Will I ever be able to speak of this incomprehensible truth?"

The demons writhe and shriek, momentarily feeding on his doubt.

"Who are you?" he asks, seeing the jewel in their hands.

"Temp–or–ary temp–er–a–ture choral, char–coal, temporal all! We speak through the satellite, the computer, the vibrating air you will never catch. We are time stolen from eternity, a spark of gold. We ride on the energy of air and ear. Hear! Here is fear. Ha! Ha! Still you fear!"

But Kau Chiang, heartened by the words of the White Tiger, responds with mockery and laughter. The tonal polarities in his thyroid struggle to balance as the demons disintegrate and release the jewel to the holy lake.

Hearing a low drone in the far north, he turns to behold a swelling black ocean. Clouds cover the sky with the swirling secrets of the River. He clutches the stone, the gift from his mother, Shu Lao, and struggles not to lose himself in the specters of his visions, for the spell of the dark Moon lies within him. An island rises from the waters and moves slowly toward him, its domed back marked with strange symbols. Its head spews an emerald-green substance into his mouth.

The Black Tortoise emerges from the water and speaks: "Persevere and remain constant. You can carry all of humanity on your back. Mongols and Tartars ride swiftly, but humble humus supports green with its black moistness. Be silent in the darkness. Humanity is in its winter."

Suddenly the dark clouds curdle and implode, bursting forth with fingers of lightning that reveal the jewels inside Kau Chiang's chakras.

The Tortoise continues: "Find the one who tells of the Tao and whose eyes speak the language of the trees. She sleeps in your inner space, but longs to awake. The petrified one, the one who has kept you from speaking when the demons are in your throat, is yet unknown to her."

"Who is the petrified one?"

"Peter, the unrestricted wanderer, the wandering restriction, the fixed stone that betrays the shadow that it loves."

Once again Kau Chiang enters a cosmic consciousness, beholding any person, any place to which he extends his thought. He sees a woman—afraid, desperate, and searching—pacing the streets of Beijing.

"Is it she who was Peter, the petrified one? Can I help her?"

"You have already forgiven her," responds the Black Tortoise. "Now you can let the River heal her through your voice."

Kau Chiang feels fear and compassion at once: "May I be united in mind, soul, spirit, and body! Keep me from shattering!"

Cosmic consciousness explodes inside the dark cave of his skull as the Black Tortoise disappears into the black waters. Akashic reflections of biochemical incarnations flood his veins with the scourge of the burning waters. Zapana's spirit speaks within him: *Find my beloved. I am you and you are me. She and I are one.*

Mystified, yet inwardly knowing, Kau Chiang stands on the summit of Dragon Hill, open to the four directions. He beholds the Green Dragon curling in the milky clouds of the east. In the south he sees the Red Bird spinning rings of color that gather like laughter resounding above the drought. To the west, amidst the sonance of jewels and metal, the White Tiger roars for the reign of joy and the circulation of ch'i everywhere. From the northern darkness emanates the still presence of the Black Tortoise. Kau Chiang cradles his stone firmly in his hand, feeling the constant love of Shu Lao and Heng-O. As the heavens open, he turns to leave, graced with the song of the rain upon the Earth:

Life Mother's Song of the River

I am the planetary gift of life.
You can find me in the levity of laughter and the gravity of despair.
Look for me in the expansion and contraction of all things.
You can find me in the chemistry of sexuality.
I am the weaving of matter into tissue.
I am fire, air, water, and earth swimming throughout akashic space.
You can find me in the folds of water curving around stones.
I am born from the spiral arms of galaxies and ferns.
I am the fields of grass, forest, and desert.
Look for me in the leap of squirrels and the flight of doves.
You can find me in the consciousness of rock, bee, and flower.
I am the will of God beholding itself.
I am the purpose of elemental life.
I am the fulfillment of evolution's path.
Hear me in the voice of nature within your body.

Do you have form or are you formless?
Form is my mother before I was born, but I come from the formless and return to it.

THE FOURTH WORLD

Free will surges through human consciousness, bursting forth not only in arrowheads, clubs, and thatched huts but in computers and robots. Not only in love, but in war; not only in invention, but in money. Not only in crime, but in law. Sounding through the electronic latticework that covers the Earth are the last desperate words of the Life Mother: The River still runs.

Where does the River run? The River runs in the music of creation, in the vitality of the body, in dolphins, delphiniums, and the hidden hearts of the dispossessed. The River flows through all living things.

Since the Antagonists divided the human soul and the Trickster stole the sacred fire, all worlds have suffered. The Primal Pair twist in alternating pleasure and pain while the Immortals withdraw into transcendental escapism. The Fourth World of culture remains embroiled in the ongoing struggle between eros and logos, the widening schism between chaos and cosmos. Burning waters swirl in the luminous darkness—unseen, unfelt, unknown.

The old priests attempted to control the River by separating law from sentient life. The new priests, seeing the cosmos as a machine, cast their script in megaliths of concrete and steel. The Fourth World stands encased in patriarchal domination—logos, order, and the regular cycles of the Heavenly Powers. Humankind bolts down the lightning it fears, harnessing it to drive technology. Repressed eros erupts in the rape of women, the slaughter of animals, the devastation of the land, and the scattering of tribal peoples until the clamor for hierarchy and order sounds again. The revolutions of chaos and cosmos turn over and over while archetypes of the natural world moan in desperation.

Ultraviolet rays rip the ozone shroud of the Heavenly Powers, stinging the human membranes with the blight of cancer. Their cycles disrupted, planets stray from their orbits. Time, taken from the eternal return, now stretches out toward the apocalypse. Did no one listen to the oracles of old who warned against the misconception of time?

An Oracle emerges and proclaims, "The wasteland is upon you! Be not hardened by thoughts of blame! Embrace the ancient values of alignment with the Earth, for the trees are the living pathways of the dragons. Forego judgment and seek justice within yourself."

The Oracle's form fades into the mists of time, which congeal into the precisely chiseled features of the Judge. He once sought discernment and accordance with cosmic law, but law turned into rules and arbitrary power. Each time he pronounces judgment, the traditions petrify, forests die, and true divination is rendered more obscure.

The Shaman, remembering the archaic rapids tumbling down toward tribal villages, tries to read the script of the River in the cracked mud of the Earth. Circling the medicine wheel, his feathers blow in the wind as he smokes tobacco, inducing visions. The script unfolds into hallucinogenic visions, unknown to a populace hypnotized by the obsessions of the senses. The primal language is lost in the drone of the freeway, the dissonance of the city. Yet still the Shaman desires to heal. Embodying the imaginal in the brightening transmutation of his being, he turns into the Alchemist.

Swiftly moving vehicles made of metals gouged from the bones of the Earth trample on uncomprehending creatures. Such is the Dance of Death, who enters into the cyclotrons of physicists and spins out subatomic particles and pulls the desires of humans toward the fires of radiation. Within the Dance of Death is the Hero, who longs to rectify the abuse of the once-sacred fire now fallen into matter. From the conflict of right and might, the Hero/Demon is born.

The Life Mother feels helpless before such rampant exploitation and cries out, "Let my children not die a permanent death! I shall become the Virgin who brings living light to every creature. My child will be the enlightenment of life." She metamorphoses into the Virgin/Child, a holographic image that promises a new world born from the unconscious maelstrom of the old.

The end of the age is an unfolding of all explosive forms back toward their origin. Pressing together like cells of an amoeba, the Primal Waters flow on through the technological kingdom as the struggles of order and chaos, logos and eros, reverberate through a dying history. All turns toward its opposite. Evangelism and system cybernetics combine into a new totalitarian ideal. Corporations repackage New Age products to numb the pain of civilizational collapse.

The Creatrix, foreseeing the Fourth World in danger of becoming more violent than free, places herself between the Third and Second Worlds. Balancing free will and fate in her dance, she aspires to heal the schism of spirit from soul, soul from body, and body from mind. She releases the burning waters into the places between vision and love, between shadows and the human image, and between intensity and imagination. The wind of her breath stirs the Primal Waters, drawing eros down into the Fourth World. She seeks a new justice as a foundation, a justice that lives in the supple body of nature, fluid and sensitive to the wholeness of each being.

THE JUDGE/ORACLE

To choose justice is to divine the relation of being to beholding, of beholding to becoming, and of becoming to beknowing. Fluid and pliable, the beholder then flows in the Emerald River, open to knowing how each person, creature, and plant is related in the Tree of Life. This art of knowing is not belief, but divination, as the Oracle well knows. Infused with the eros and logos of the First World, she teaches birds and men to speak from the depths of the Primal Waters and the heights of the Word of the Kingdom.

Though the poetics of the elements become lucid through her speech, to most the Oracle remains invisible. By chipping away the hardened accumulation of blame, she seeks to reveal the cosmic law hidden within a massive mound of plastic. As her divination chisels through the debris of the ages, she weeps at the voidness of vision, finding only the mechanical automatons of the twentieth century. Newspapers telling of tanks crushing students in Tiananmen Square lie crumpled beside video discs showing the glass coffin of Ruhollah Khomeini in Teheran.

Searching the folds of history, the Oracle pulls back the values of time and finds Moses, Manu, and Hammurabi, the lawgivers of ancient times. She finds, not cosmic law, but the guilt created when blame is believed and one's life vow forgotten. Now hypnotized by the priests of politics and industry, humans lose their own knowing and fall into self-conflict.

Seeing how criminal voices torture humanity from the depths of the denied unconscious, the Oracle withdraws unseen into the Immortals. The blameless Immortals turn like angelic architecture toward the Heavenly Powers, where time was born. Turned into the twisted patterns of the Trickster's fear of nature, time explodes into a hypnotic power. Most people believe in time and live by it, and from their faith in time's authority, trials emerge. Time and trials control production and consumption, money and manna. Time and trials terrorize the body, the feminine, the natural world, the unruly feelings that flood against the wall of monotheistic judgment.

Time and trials are not inherently evil—only to blame, is evil. Born of time, linear rational thought runs through left-brain circuits toward judgment, separating the right from the wrong, the true from the false, the proven from the ambiguous, the innocent from the guilty.

The Judge/Oracle stands as a statue at the crossroads of addiction and creativity, possession and self-empowerment. Once an interpreter of motives and events, the Judge is now the critic grown rigid with condemnation. Obsession with perfection and control are held in his solar plexus as failure rears its head through his furrowed brow. The Oracle dwells within him, visible only to those who carry no blame. Furtive bifurcations of Judas and Jesus, the betrayer and betrayed, divide his right and left. The double helix woven from the conflict of good and evil stands in his backbone. The compensating polarity between right and wrong struggles in his unconscious and conscious minds; struggles also in the creative act, in the brutal predation of nature, and in the seething dance of matter. Only in the human does this polarity stand forth as judgment.

The Judge casts his shadow over the ambiguous, paradoxical language of the River. He evaluates precisely with hard-edged perfection. Reductionist proof and objectified science replace the tyrannical authority of medieval priests. Conformity and passivity weaken the human spirit.

What has frozen the River into the Judge? Those addicted to the status quo become the guilty and the penitent, falling in line with the circle of hell drawn by the condemnation of those who rule. But even the Judge changes into his opposite, for violence emerges when piety prevails. Through codependent illusion, the self-righteous and the criminal sustain one another. From within the Judge the Oracle watches, for she knows such false attribution must eventually give rise to conscience.

THE FORCES THAT SHAPE US

Cosmic Law
Gold of gold within white

The laws
of divination
ever elude
the rational mind.

In ancient times, some looked to cosmic law to resolve internal and external conflict. Justice spoke through the tablet, the burning bush, and blazing star. Those who saw the flames of justice communed with the Creator and sent the lightning of the First World directly to the Fourth World.

The new priests became counselors of chieftains and kings. But they swelled with the Trickster's titanic pride and in fiery oration declared themselves to be God and law.

Through the ages, some sought to find the balance of divinity, humanity, and nature. As divine power fell from the sky and life rose from the dust, they beheld heaven and Earth entwined within themselves. Consciousness discerned what was right and what was wrong. Some said cosmic law lived only in the inner light. Others said it dwelled in the axis of heaven. Consciousness became values and values became law.

Christa, Karl, and Yu

Opening more each day to the mysteries of the burning waters, Christa feels the rush of past-life memories and the River washing them clean. Baptized by water in the Rhine, she discovers the vibratory immersion and the fairy world of nature. Baptized by blood in her home, she loses herself in the colored sunlight of ancient shapes. She searches for the source of these streams of incarnations in her paintings, where the distant metaphors of her soul journey are woven into vibratory patterns. To focus the energies she feels in her body and the incessant visions, she attends weekly Zen meditations in Munich.

Christa wants complete enlightenment or nothing. Even death is preferable to unillumined existence. She has grown impatient with the discussions of Karl and Yu that stretch well into the night. No longer is Karl beside her when her sight opens to the pain of past incarnations. Though the visions temporarily blind her to everyday reality, she glimpses the paths of divination.

Tonight, stirred by recent visions and unable to sleep, Christa decides to get up and paint. In the adjoining room, Karl and Yu are conversing about elementary particles, energy levels, and vacuum states.

Karl has seen in his experiments with nonlinear iterations how the random, chaotic motions of molecules in solution give rise to forms in time and space. He sees cosmic law as the emergence of order out of chaos. But he is amazed that the spiraling forms in Christa's art are replicated in the patterns in his chemical dish. He is coming to realize that order gives birth to chaos, just as chaos gives birth to order.

"How, Yu, do you really view chaos?" he asks his young Chinese friend, whose visit has extended into several weeks.

"Dissonance in a given system," Yu responds in a matter-of-fact tone. "What is chaos to one system may be order to another. The rhythmic flow of blood pumps the heart. The pulsations expand from a point in a circulating wave across the surface of the heart. But if the wave is broken anywhere, spiraling patterns self-replicate and disturb the heart's rhythms. What you call fractal forms and period doubling then lead to heart failure."

"It's interesting that you put it that way," says Karl, "because I have been asking myself what is causing civilization to collapse. Is civilization having heart failure? According to the second law of thermodynamics, every irreversible process is accompanied by an increase of entropy. The universe has been running down ever since the Big Bang. Entropy is order tending toward chaos."

"Yes, we spoke of this in Munich," replies Yu. "In the Taoist view, chaos is as necessary as order. When chaos and order are in rhythmic interplay, the Tai Chi of yin and yang revolves in harmony. Male and female, order and chaos, reciprocate each other. Entropy is yang, a centrifugal dispersing energy. But yang must come from an extremely focused and orderly source or it could not radiate and expand into wholeness, health, and civilization. Yin is within yang and yang is within yin, just as the feminine is within every man and the masculine is within every woman. If the universe were only running down, the order of life and consciousness could not have arisen. We would not be able to have this discussion. I believe, on a deep level, that there is creativity in the chaos. Even now the seeds for a new culture are gathering in the yin centripetal center."

Karl glances over at Christa's paintings—the crosses, circles, and pentagons forming patterns of interlocking, multidimensional realities. "I agree that life, culture, and art are all regenerative," he responds, "but our modern civilization seems irresistibly driven by the expansive, consuming, running-down force. It's as if the Big Bang opened time, and time opened history, and history is rushing toward its end in apocalypse. Now we are running out of fuel. Modern technology is all yang—explosive, dispersing, entropic. The order of technology creates chaos by dissipating energy rather than regenerating it. What can reverse this trend?"

"In China we view history as an honoring of our ancestors," responds Yu. "We do not feel this rush toward the end. Is it this fatal view of the future that is causing the heart failure of Western civilization? It is truthful intent that turns chaos into creativity, and eros into art. China became violent and corrupt when it moved from an aesthetic perspective to a purely pragmatic one. Something from the West has plagued the whole world. I wonder, too, what is at the root of it."

Overhearing the men's dialogue, Christa can remain silent no longer and moves to the doorway of the next room. "It is monotheism that cut through the regenerating oscillation of what Yu calls yin and yang," she exclaims. "It is monotheism that created a *beginning* to time, creation, and history and that brought the longing for an *end*. How well I remember from my days as a nun and abbess! Monotheism killed the old gods and goddesses of nature, and the spirits of the rivers and mountains. Its tyranny is absolute."

"Monotheism could be seen as a domination over the circulation of the yin and yang," continues Yu with intellectual dispassion. "To try to impose yin over yang or yang over yin is to court destruction. Yin is the source and fuel for the yang expansion. Current technology uses fire as the fuel for all its power, but we need to use water as well."

"We have polluted the crystal waters of the Rhine," interjects Christa. "The Black Forest is dying. I've read that professional planners won't allow fish ponds there—only settlements, reservoirs, autobahns, and high tension wires. When the forests die, we die—for the forests circulate the waters. The drought is our own doing, and monotheistic beliefs are the source of it all."

Though he believes what she says to be true, Karl feels Christa's reaction is exaggerated. Christa, aware of his judgment, moves back to the easel and sits down to work, furiously brushing white over the patterns she had just painted, her heart pounding and her face flushed with release. *That is part of the story I am to tell*, she thinks, astonished at her own revelation.

Karl says to Yu, "We can invent new technology, based on centripetal yin energy, perhaps using water as you suggest. Also, nuclear fusion does not have the dissipating effect of nuclear fission. From all the forces available to us—nuclear, electric, magnetic, and gravitational—we should be able to tap free energy."

"Yes, but the free energy I look for is more subtle," says Yu. "The other night I had an incredible experience. I was seeking to understand nature's unknown energetic processes. For a moment all became totally still, as though beyond time. I heard the song of a nightingale deep within me, yet it was also all around me. There was no outside at all. In that state I asked, *How can I discover the harmonic patterns of waves that must be the unknown source of free energy?* I experienced my own chakras as undulating, rotating flowers of subtly changing colors. I then saw that ch'i patterns the five elements, moving as energy through the meridians. I awoke as if from a trance, realizing that ch'i is within and without—that inner and outer have no absolute meaning."

"I've never experienced anything like that," says Karl, puzzled. "Can you define ch'i?"

"Ch'i is the subtle energy that enables the whole universe of life and consciousness to unfold." Yu's mild yet direct manner adds lucidity to his words.

"Where does ch'i come from?"

"It is generated in the world through the harmony of the yin and yang, the centripetal and centrifugal forces. But ultimately it comes from nothingness, non-being, the void. Taoists call it the *wu ch'i*."

Karl glances up at some of Christa's canvases on the wall and reflects upon how her painting has changed. He wonders if ch'i is the energy animating her art. The circling, spiraling, and branching forms of her earlier paintings have been replaced by a vibrating tapestry in which forms metamorphose into each other. Boundaries dissolve into scintillating colors. *I wonder if ch'i is in the form or the formlessness of her work?* he asks himself. He notices that, in Christa's current piece, even the vibrating tapestry fades into subtle spaces—misty, impressionistic points that evoke the nuances of rippling water and shimmering sky. Without hard edges, her strokes are more spontaneous, like a dance originating out of a void.

After a long silence, Karl turns again to Yu: "You say that ch'i comes from the void—what science calls the vacuum state, I believe."

"Yes, it comes from the void of the *wu ch'i* that endlessly founts forth into the tai ch'i of yin and yang. This is what those who seek to divide and dominate have forgotten. It is what enables the cycles of growth and decay to constantly evolve into new forms of order. Humanity has simply lost touch with these laws."

Karl is still wrestling with cyclical as opposed to linear time: "But the past can never be symmetrical with the future. Reversal of time is impossible. Everything has been dissipating since the Big Bang. It has never been proven that the universe will eventually collapse again. I cannot reconcile the idea of irreversible entropic time with the function of novelty and creativity."

"You mean we must submit to fate, to the collapse of civilization?" retorts Yu with a knowing smile. "Have you succumbed to the Western view of irreversible time? That is a kind of monotheism, as Christa calls it. Don't you see?"

"You misunderstand me. I find the cosmic law in the formative forces that shape all things. In my experiments, patterns arise out of chaos. Novelty and creativity do arise through the relentless march of time. But how? What is it that turns decay and death into new life?" Karl stares out the window in wonder, reflecting on the infinite unfoldment of evolution and culture.

"The rotation of the Earth, and the orbiting of the planets, winter and summer, day and night—these reflect the cycles of yin and yang," answers Yu. "Novelty comes from within the universe itself, and it expresses itself in cycles that govern all of life."

Karl laughs: "Cycles are just tiny, local events in the expanding universe. There is nothing absolute about cycles. No real law lies here."

Tired of hearing the endless talk, Christa cleans her brushes and walks out into the night. She is feeling extremely sensitive and open, and she continues past the city on into the woods. She longs for an answer to the question the old man and woman asked her to write about many years ago. Coming to the edge of the river, she realizes that water, like time, moves only downhill. *Is gravity, or what Karl calls entropy, the only law of life?* she wonders. Pensive, she watches the moonlight flicker on the Rhine, pleased that the pollution is less visible at night.

Images float like dreams through her mind as the sound of the river fills her ears. *Water is the source of life*, she thinks. *Life flows in cycles, not linear pathways. Yu is right. All that regenerates flows in cycles. The river runs uphill through evaporation and clouds. I hear my soul speaking, as though calling me to some great void. The song of the planets runs in my cells. Something from many lives is summoning me now.*

She hears the Primal Waters calling from the First World: "We are the mystery, denied and defiled throughout history. Within our rolling waves float the patterns of imagination. Within our depths is the story of creation, told by the Moon and stars and mirrored as a reverie in your soul. Marry the Moon, flood your soul with compassion, and the waters of the Earth will be purified. Then humanity may move at ease within our mystery."

Christa feels subtle fire and water fuse inside the fluids of her own spine. She sits down on the riverbank and watches the moonlight play on the water, recalling images from the dream she had the night before she left Horst: Her father Manesis is damming up the river and plucking flowers and fruits from a large tree. Then the tree splits into two and bursts into flames, as a wail rises from the other trees on Earth.

Christa hears the trees crying now, accompanied by the familiar hoot of an owl. She is determined to judge herself, to find the truth. *Manesis has changed the course of the River. The old priest still haunts me— still seeks to control nature and humanity within me. Who is he? Is he really Horst, or is he an authority within me? How can I reach the root of this evil?*

She looks mournfully into the darkness of the river: *Help me be free from all domination—from all tendencies to dominate.*

The waters seem to weep with her as a soft rain begins falling. *Are Karl and Yu any different from Horst or the old priests?* she momentarily wonders. *All seek to explain, to control by knowledge.* But she knows in her heart that Karl and Yu are trying to live another way. They are trying to release domination, though Karl still does not trust the dark mystery of chaos. Christa thinks: *Compassion lies within life, which is ever involving and evolving. Priests can't control life, but they can destroy it! Mechanical technology is killing the Earth! How can nature regenerate? Where can I go to find serenity and wholeness?*

At that instant, her blood and spinal fluid tingle with the burning waters of the Creatrix. She feels ecstasy, then pain, as thoughtforms from past lives flood her awareness in a final surge of resistance. *Is it possible for the incorporeal to join with flesh?* she wonders. The burning waters of Zapana's etheric blood hover in heaven and fall with the rain, merging with her tears as she releases her last defense. His energy joins with hers. Ancient Peruvian symbols flash in her mind. No longer afraid of death, she gazes into the river and is lifted into mystic rapture. Time and space dissolve with the flash of lightning as she and Zapana again become one.

BIG BUCKS

Self Conflict
Black of gold within white

Right motives
using wrong means
writhe
in conflict.

Toda, Starlie, Tamio, and Tei

Toda slides into the niche of nanosecond technologies like noise that destabilizes the world and flips to another attractor, the attractor of a New Age. He knows the grim reality: that people have been feeding on each other for millennia. Now his interest is to make the New Age mainstream—to turn visualization, meditation, and astral projection into big business. He gathers the best minds he can find and assigns them a singular goal: to incorporate the glitter of New Age metaphysics—pyramid power, crystal consciousness, and mantra magic—into a portable computerized technology. Filtering the deluded human psyche with his cyberpunk, he desires to manipulate consumers through their emotional imprints. His brain helmets and chakra churners are created to ensnare questing souls.

Toda knows that the information system of the global mind extends beyond continents. In competition with American venture capitalists, he colludes with psychic demons who carry thoughtforms through the electronic network. Not evil in themselves, the demons are anonymous messengers who relay thought without motivation or purpose.

Humorlessness—the disease of failed psychospiritual connections— spreads through cities connected by the silicon chip. The psychic tension in the world has become implosive. That is obvious from the behavior of the populace. But Toda knows, too, that millions have not yet succumbed to the collective amnesia concerning their purpose. It is these, the ones who still resist his Big Brother ideal, whom he wishes to attract by stimulating an energetic drive in people that will culminate in them feeling as if they are expressing their creative power. Then they will be in his grasp, and they will behold the demons of the integrated circuit as angels.

Starlie knows that all the technology of civilization is perishable— but not the tribal prophecies. Awareness of the Fifth World both attracts and mystifies him. Close to losing his tribal identity, he tries to look backward and forward at once. His traditional culture is dying, his people drugged by alcohol, narcotics, and television. The world is becoming an electronic war field, dominated by the Japanese and Americans.

He still believes in the possibility of regeneration for all people, even though his studies of psychology and modern culture—both in the university and in the streets—have given him no definitive answer. What can check the power of the multinational corporations except a massive return to tribal ways that teach a way to live in symbiosis with nature? The only other check on this power would be the very collapse of nature herself.

Three years out of Berkeley, Starlie now works for a high-tech corporation in California's Silicon Valley. His keen perception and imagination have produced a video game he calls "Crystal" in which the various facets of a crystal light up on the monitor as one's series of choices bring one closer to one's true destiny. The goal is to find one's star by lighting all the facets.

Although he hasn't had enough time to develop the game fully, he knows it is his best effort and sends an outline of the concepts to game manufacturers. One, Hashigawa Games, actually responds by sending him a roundtrip ticket to Tokyo in order to personally discuss his proposal.

Starlie regards most people as puppets on a stage. He wants to use his skills to catalyze unconscious behavior into true creativity. He has read in Hashigawa's prospectus that part of its corporate philosophy is to distribute games that tap the nerves of creativity and open new doors in the psyche. He feels enthused because this view seems so aligned with his own.

Now, riding in a taxi through the streets of Tokyo, Starlie tries to focus on his game and what he will say at the meeting. He closes his eyes, reflecting on his father's perception that reduces everything to zero dimensions. This still puzzles him. To be a single point, the point of emergence into the Fifth World, seems like no perception at all. But he follows his star. He knows when it is glowing and when it is growing dim.

He struggles to lift his thoughts out of a time-space deadlock. *The world is wired together, but what will we send through the wires?* he wonders as the cab lurches around a corner, nearly hitting two old women. He thinks how "Crystal" can help a person open the doors of creativity: *The obscured truth of one's soul can grow bright by playing "Crystal." But is this what people want? Will they buy it? Will they prefer horror movies and games filled with sex and death? The ego is a video of the demons and kachina spirits contending within us.*

The cacophony of the crowded streets pulls him back to the world before him. He opens his eyes and stares out the window, momentarily overwhelmed by the density and clamor of traffic, people, and buildings jammed into something called existence. His mind spins in a whirl of separate motives: to serve humanity and to make big bucks.

Once inside the corporate headquarters of Hashigawa Games, Starlie rides an elevator up fifty-one stories to the executive offices. When he enters the visitor's lobby, he immediately encounters a young man with a shaved head.

"My name is Tei Shikan," the man says affably, extending his hand. "Are you also here for an interview?"

"Yes, I'm Starlie Talashoma."

"Where are you from?"

"California. This company has paid my way here. I have a game that interests them. Have you met with them before?"

"Yes. They are smart. You have to be careful."

"Well, I *am* nervous."

"Your name sounds Tibetan or Asian."

"I am a Hopi Indian."

"Oh! I thought the whites still ran everything in America. Do natives have full rights of citizenship?"

"Yes and no. It's difficult for my people to enter into the business world, but I have done so. I don't think of myself as different from others. Most of the older people in our families want us to remain apart, to keep the traditions, but we can't easily survive that way."

"I understand. I myself am Buddhist, but Buddhism doesn't interfere with what we do in the world."

They are interrupted by a man asking for Mr. Talashoma. Starlie nods, his dark face full of questions.

"I am Tamio Musashi, senior vice president. Please come with me."

He ushers Starlie into his luxurious office and motions him to sit down. After a polite inquiry about Starlie's satisfaction with his hotel accommodations, Tamio gets right to the point.

"Ever since we received your proposal, we have been eager to discuss it in more detail."

Starlie pulls the flow charts and plans of "Crystal" from his briefcase: "The basic intention of my game is to encourage people to live by their star."

Tamio's eyebrows rise: "What is their star?"

"Their inner force, their spirit."

"How will you do this in the game?"

"The facets of the crystal light up as a star when the player gets closer to reality."

"And what is reality?"

"It's not the same for everyone, but that is the point. Each individual expresses the facets of the crystal of reality in a different order. That's why it's called "Crystal.""

"I see. With your permission, I will show your game to our CEO and also to several of our programmers to get an estimate of the costs. Please come back at ten o'clock tomorrow morning." Tamio stands and bows. Starlie does the same, imitating his host.

As he enters the corporate headquarters again the next morning, Starlie is apprehensive. He senses that a day of reckoning lies ahead. *If I can succeed this day, I will bring abundance and happiness to my people*, he thinks. His heart is as wide as the sky, but once he approaches the elevator his temples throb and anxiety fills his belly.

Tamio meets Starlie in the visitor's lobby and escorts him into the office of Toda Hashigawa, the corporate CEO. Toda sits pensively behind an expansive desk, making notes. When he sees Tamio and Starlie enter, he stands up and bows. "Welcome to Tokyo, Mr. Talashoma," he says with a broad smile.

After they sit down, Tamio gets right to the point: "We think your game could have mass appeal. That would mean substantial profits—for you and for us. But there is one problem."

"What is that?"

"We would like to alter the game to sharpen the conflicts between the different types of perception—the different facets, as you say."

"Sharpen the conflicts? Why?"

"To make the game more exciting. Also, it may enable people to get through their conflicts sooner."

"I see. Well, OK," Starlie replies uneasily.

"First of all, you must realize that the more people play your game, the more it will mirror reality and the more money it will make for us all."

Starlie's star begins to grown dimmer, but the thought of doing meaningful work and getting rich also keeps its hold.

Tamio is quick to continue: "Try to imagine here and now how each of the game's four facets would work. You call them spirit, soul, body, and mind, but we want more imaginative words. It might help to think of a more negative connotation of each. There is the term *airy fairy*, I believe."

Toda and Tamio look at one another with knowing smiles. Starlie realizes that he is not the first to walk this road of investigation. He sees immediately that his two hosts are experts in mass psychology and are well schooled in American hip vernacular.

"Can you think of such an expression relating to the spirit?" asks Tamio.

"You mean like space cadet?"

"Yes, space cadet. What about the soul?"

"Juice, jam, bloods . . ."

"Yes, bloods," repeats Tamio, making notations. "That will do for now. What about body?"

"How about bigs?"

"Good! And the mind?"

"Wires."

"Fine. Now, can you tell us how as space cadet behaves?"

Starlie feels pressed to translate his view of the human constitution into new terms and sharper contrasts. He answers with as much confidence as he can muster, but he feels faint shadows entering his soul.

"Well, the space cadets tend to be inattentive to what is happening. You could even say that some cop out altogether."

"Yes, and the bloods?"

"The bloods tend to be very reactive, quick to anger. In the extreme, they become criminals or go insane."

"How would you motivate players to commit crime or go insane?"

"I wouldn't. I mean, if they are prone to violence it would be easy enough to push their buttons. But why would you want to do that?"

"Don't worry about that for now," interrupts Toda. "How could you devise the game to, as you say, push people's buttons?"

Starlie feels in the grip of Toda's power and answers mechanically, as if hypnotized: "Their answers to the initial questions would indicate what they are hiding or defending. It would be easy to expose them."

"More specifically, what?"

Starlie tries to think fast: "A miserly women would have all her wealth stolen, or her house burned down. A big, a man who is uncertain of his sexuality and feelings, would maneuver to become empowered in these areas, but the result would be powerlessness. Or, the pet theory of a wire would collapse like a house of playing cards."

Toda smiles: "You are doing well. Now tell us about conflicts between the four different types. And how could you create them through scenarios in your game?"

Starlie is both excited and disturbed, but his mind is bustling with ideas: "Well, someone who has both space cadet and blood facets might create myths and theologies but also cling rigidly to belief."

"None of this college stuff, please. Get to the core of it. We want to reach masses of people and must condense the game to crucial moves. Give us a concrete example of a conflict between the space cadets and bloods."

Starlie wrestles with his shadow, with his values, and with foreign ways all at once. But he clings to the idea of making it big.

"American New Agers at war with fundamentalists. I don't know if that is prevalent here. Buddhist and Shinto seem to be less . . ."

"Too intellectual, Starlie. What in the game . . ."

"A married man falls in love with another woman. His wife is cold and distant, but his faith prohibits divorce."

"That sounds more like it."

"In the game, he must choose between the woman and his faith. If he chooses the woman, he loses his faith. So he goes into despair and winds up losing her anyway. If he chooses his faith, his love dries up, for his wife is unresponsive and he has no fulfillment."

"Good—a double bind in which one can't win either way!" exclaims Toda. "You see, creating such situations brings people into self-conflict. The conflicts induce people to want more games."

"I don't get it."

Toda's thin veil momentarily drops altogether: "Differences energize the ego, which loves adversarial positions. In these times, people are splitting apart and tuning into the psychograms of everyone else."

"What do you mean—psychograms?"

"That's what you have devised with your game. When people are frustrated, they experience emotional tension from the conflict of energy. This conflicting energy is at the core of your game, don't you see? People get excited to the point of feeling explosive. That's what lights up their star! But there is another thing that needs to be changed."

"What is that?"

"The title of your game. Change it to something more dramatic. Are you a space cadet?"

"No, sir. I'm very grounded."

"'Crystal' is too static and dull. What about something like 'Blockbuster' or 'Sabotage'?"

Starlie looks into Toda's eyes and is repulsed by his own reflection: "If you want to change everything in my game, what is the use of our talking?"

"We do not want to change everything," intervenes Tamio, smiling. Your game contains a multiplicity of perceptions, a way of seeing the world that can encompass many types of people. We want a game that will appeal to a broad spectrum. Changing the name is not changing the game. For now, let us call it 'Blockbuster'."

"What is the point? What are you really getting at?"

"People will have the feeling of breaking the power of the *other*. Now, describe a conflict between the bloods and the bigs."

Starlie feels about to burst from frustration. *Bloodshed between the Hopi and Navahos couldn't be worse than this*, he thinks. Stumbling upon his own thoughts, he is swept away by the swift currents of the two businessmen.

"Environmental preservation versus corporate profit," Starlie spurts out.

"Not so intellectual. Be concrete, specific."

"A politician wants to be elected, so he espouses policies that will bring him votes. He advocates a few token tax incentives that he claims will encourage businesses to employ sound environmental policy. He promises economic growth *and* environmental protection. After he is elected, the air quality worsens, the deforestation continues. . . . What is the point of all this? Why conflicts?" Starlie leans forward and puts his head in his hands.

However, Tamio is relentless: "The excitement of the game is in the *conflict*. Don't you agree that people are tired of authority and want to assert themselves?

"Yes, but . . ."

"Games are a way for them to release energy without harming anyone."

"Without harming anyone?" Starlie looks up and stares into Tamio's thick glasses.

"Now, describe a conflict between the space cadets and the bigs."

"Tribal versus technological," Starlie answers mechanically.

"Too abstract, Starlie."

"A man is born into a native culture that embraces the Earth and the ancestral traditions," says Starlie, his rage slowly rising. "He wants to be accepted by his ancestors, but the world has turned into a mega-machine. He can enter the machine by working with computers or he can return to his people, but he can't do both. His people won't accept his technology, and the larger world won't accept his people." Starlie falls suddenly silent as he realizes he is describing himself.

"How would you put it into the game?"

"By creating isolated groups. The player can choose. It's all either/ or . . ."

Starlie has reached his limit. He stands up and shouts at Toda: "I won't do it! You want to encourage people to fall into their own traps. You want me to go against the whole purpose of the game! I see the conflicts of the world, but I won't contribute to them."

Starlie storms out of the office, his whole body shaking. To his surprise, Tei is standing in the visitor's lobby. Seeing Starlie's obvious agitation, Tei puts his arm around his shoulder. "I know," he says. "I met with them, too. Let's get something to eat and talk about this."

Starlie's confusion and anger continue to build as they descend fifty-one stories on the elevator. "How did I get myself into this?" he wonders aloud.

"You wanted to make big bucks," Tei responds.

THE DILEMMA OF BEING

Trials
Red of gold within white

The holiness
of innocence and guilt
stretch
each other.

All that is known is change and impermanence. Society oscillates between establishing the logos of the Kingdom and embracing the romanticism that searches for the lost language. The tides of history propagate kingdoms, republics, and oligarchies as a way to rule the people. But as long as cosmos is separate from chaos, and as long as order is imposed upon the rampaging hope of the people, there are trials.

The rage against the rich is equalled by the oppression of the poor. Villages grow into towns, towns grow into cities, and cities grow into sprawling miles of dehumanized tenements. Yet there are fierce souls who break free of the urban bondage and roam the Earth.

Petruska

Something from long ago calls Petruska to China—something haunting from within that she needs to uncover. Still struggling with depression, still hoping to free herself from lifetimes of painful illusion, she leaves the astronomy academy with enough savings to wander, gypsylike, through Asia.

She rides the Trans-Siberian Railroad to Irkutsk near Lake Baikal, then south into the Mongolian capital of Ulan Bator and on to the Great Wall, where she reminisces of ancient times. Continuing west to Paotow, she gazes upon the Yellow River Valley where China was born. She knows there are places in this country where she once knew happiness.

Finally, her train makes its way eastward to Shandong province and the holy mountain of Taishan. Petruska feels eager to climb to the temple at the top, but upon leaving the train and seeing the thousands of granite steps crowded with pilgrims and tourists, she decides to put off her ascent until evening.

At dusk, Petruska silently sets off carrying only her drum, a small bag, and some food. Ever since her experience with Bear-Looks-Twice, she drums to keep herself both grounded and entranced. Upon reaching the ridge below Taishan's summit, she sits down and begins beating the deerskin. Young boys in the distance, lured by the intensity of her rhythm, match her cadences by tapping sticks. Oblivious to them and to everything but her own hypnotic rhythm, she enters a visionary state. She sees herself sailing on the black Nile, so close to the banks that she can pick ripe olives and figs from overhanging branches. She disembarks and climbs a stairway to a temple, at once beginning to tremble at the sight of the hierophant Manesis inside. Her blood pulses through her veins and spirit fills her heart, for she has prepared long and dutifully for the five-day initiation in the coffer. Eager to proceed, yet filled with trepidation, she enters the dark chamber breathing heavily.

Suddenly the drumming stops. Petruska's face is like an open grave, paling in remembrance. Her failure in that initiation hurled her into an unceasing feeling of abandonment and into lifetimes of futility, depression, and rage. Unable to face the shadows that dominated her ever since, she projected them onto others and spit out spiteful darts of hatred.

But what can I do about it? she involuntarily declares to the dawning sky. Seeing the faint streams of violet and magenta in the east, she picks up her drum and begins the climb to the peak, hiding in a shroud of hurt from the ancient mysteries still within her. Her body survived the

Egyptian ordeal, but her soul was almost destroyed. She continues tenaciously up the steps toward the high temple, thinking how long she has hated Manesis—and now Channon and that terrible man Horst! *This hatred is within myself!* she realizes. Dismal thoughts and quickening hope dwell together in her skull. Her heart is dark, afraid to open, but something in the Chinese landscape echoes memories of ancient peace. She weeps with a mixture of joy and sorrow, thinking, *I want to see old China and feel something of the happiness I knew before my encounter with Manesis.*

Finally the gates of the Taishan temple loom before her, but a priest appears and holds up his hands to ward her off.

"Do you speak Russian?" she asks.

The priest only stares, his eyes grim and cold.

"English? I have journeyed from Russia," she tries to explain. "I visited here long ago and now wish to enter."

But the priest stands rigidly and shakes his head.

"Anyone should be permitted to enter!" she cries, then turns and rushes furiously down the 6293 granite steps, flooded with memories of past failures.

She spends the afternoon wandering like a vagabond, but as the hours wear on, she is able to embrace the pain in a more accepting way. Curled up later that night in a youth hostel, she dreams of torture, humiliation, and burning at the stake as a witch. Her soul opens to become a releasing ground for the filth that she has so long denied, and the rage within her begins to subside. She realizes that her hatred for her sister began in Egypt when her sister passed the initiation and abandoned her to her fate. Then, in Alexandria Petruska was born a man, became a monk, and became enraged when her sister was the star in the Neoplatonic school. It was then that she killed her sister. Petruska later incarnated as a Christian monk to oppose her once again. In her dream, she passes through another abyss and floats to the surface with her own essence intact. Toward morning, her soul opens to the vast unknown and drifts amidst the etheric clouds. She longs for the stars and sees them reflected in water.

Upon awakening, she remembers little—only that her dreams were full of trials and that she killed her sister. Filled with new hope and a passion for deeper self-discovery, she offers herself to the day with firm determination. Picking up her drum and bag and heading into the street, she realizes that she must find someone to talk to.

She enters the station and boards a train to Beijing. As the train stretches into the countryside along the Yellow River, she looks out at the laboring peasants and farmers as a transformation works within her soul. The experience of her shamanic rebirth glows with the lights of heaven. Ancient memories and possible futures converge in the bubbling currents of the River that at once courses through her veins and flows freely before her.

Ariel

Ariel crosses the continents seeking to know both himself and the world about him. Emotions strong, he travels alone, saturating himself with the hungry eyes of a child, a baby suckling its mother's breast, and an old man's embrace of death. His sorrow at the pollution in the world knows no respite. He walks the crime-filled streets where the terror behind love rends the hearts of humanity. He feels it all, and he fills his journals with poetry and reflection, for his innermost thoughts connect him to the eternity that gave him birth.

His soul remembers. The moment of birth is now. The eternal breath of the Creator moves through his body. Rainbows shine in his mind and heart. Having quit school at seventeen, he has been wandering for two years, a sensitive youth repulsed by mindless American materialism. A rebel in his San Diego high school, he walked into fire whenever he stood his ground, refusing to perform repetitive math problems he had already mastered. He did not believe in wasting time on superfluous assignments when he could be exploring in the Outback, painting landscapes, or feeling the rush of the wind. Nature became his altar, and the Earth herself his beloved, despite the signs of the wasteland upon her face.

Now Ariel stands in the rising water near the banks of the Yellow River. Love, laughter, and rushing currents carry his memories forward into the swirling mirage. He wonders what is real and what is not real as he moves toward the cry of a child in the willows. The bloated body of a fish sweeps by him and spirals downstream. Grabbing the child's hand, he feels it as his own. He pulls her to shore and into the sweeping arms of her terrified mother. Ariel believes his memories are like children— they need hands of love to reveal their poetry. Fugitive as the rain or wind, they vanish whenever he grasps for them.

Days later Ariel walks the crowded streets of Beijing, feeling unusually lonely amid the vendors, the traffic, and the thousands of bicycles moving like mechanized ants. Recalling the landscape paintings at the museum in Hong Kong, he decides to go to the country. Something in those paintings refreshes and nurtures him. Perhaps the landscape itself will also do so.

Getting a train ticket, however, seems impossible. Seats are available, but not the cooperation of the ticket agents who bear the ingrained Chinese resentment of foreigners. Always there is a problem, and always another line. So Ariel waits, his attention drawn to a gaunt Iranian in tattered clothes. The man moves as if in ecstasy, singing songs with the ardor of divine love. If someone shoves him, this fool thanks him! If someone smiles at him, he kisses their cheek. Ariel is fascinated. Is this person a lunatic or a saint? Curious and delighted, he decides to approach him.

"Do you speak English?"

"I speak the word of Mother Mary!" the man replies. "The holy mother lives in my poverty, in my joy. I am renewed in each moment."

"Who are you?"

"A child, a servant of Allah."

Ariel returns to the ticket line and watches the stranger for the next few hours. That night he decides to sleep on a bench near him. Whenever he wakes up, he sees the man kneeling in prayer. Losing all concern about the train, he begins to regard this strange fool as his teacher.

Fariba and Abhar

To ease the painful loss of love in her marriage, Fariba decides to accept an offer to teach at the International University in Beijing. Channon's work is well known among Egyptologists, and now, through him, her own expertise is also being recognized. She and a visiting professor from Cairo are to jointly teach a class in Egyptian healing. Beijing has become a place of great change, open to the study of diverse philosophies.

Fariba is relieved to depart from an India she now associates with dirty flock bedding and the matted hair of double-faced gurus. She arrives in China and, several days later, feeling well rested, she is pleased to be attending a reception for the teaching faculty and some foreign dignitaries. Attractive and well-styled, she stands out easily, impressing everyone.

As the evening wears on, Fariba is approached by an obviously wealthy Egyptian who introduces himself as Mr. Abhar. After offering a few compliments, he announces, "I have two tickets and a letter of passage to the sacred mountains of Shaanxi. Please come with me! It is a rare opportunity."

Fariba sees the man's apparent loneliness and confusion. She doesn't trust him. "Good man," she replies, "reap your life in the moment. Thank you, anyway." Having tried to be polite, she excuses herself and moves across the room, only to be followed.

"Come with me," Abhar implores. "You are my Isis, and I shall buy you anything you wish. You will never regret it."

"If I am Isis, how shall you divide your own members? Osiris died for you—now you must rise and live for him within yourself. Gather your own members."

She walks away again, but he calls after her: "You say I must rise and live, but I say to you: Rise and live with me and whatever diamonds or gold you desire you shall have."

Fariba's patience is gone and she speaks sharply: "Nothing in the world can buy my love. I give it freely! You must find yourself, for you are a reprobate. Give your tickets to the first fool you meet and you will be absolved."

Stunned, Abhar turns away and leaves the party. He meanders about in the streets for several hours and eventually winds up at the train station. Seeing a wide-eyed fool singing praises to Mary, he flings the two tickets in his face. "It is you who are to have these," he shouts despondently, then promptly turns and disappears into the night.

Seeing this, Ariel gets up off the bench. He picks up the tickets and hands them to the fool.

"Passage to Taiyuan," he laughs, waving the tickets in the wind. "Who wants these?"

Petruska, standing nearby, reaches out her hands: "I do!"

Ariel, the Fool, and Petruska

"Why don't *you* want to go to the mountains?" Ariel asks the fool.

"I am nourished by Mary, who is everywhere," he responds. "I pick the fruits of love from these trees." He points to bare boughs trying to survive the assault of drought and carbon monoxide.

Ariel cannot comprehend how someone can be so content living nearly naked in seemingly miserable circumstances. "Where will you go?" he asks.

"I go where Allah wills. Allah is the Buddha. Allah is the Tao. Don't you see?" laughs the Fool. "It's all the same!"

Petruska, too, is fascinated by this man. "Do you never rest?" she asks.

"Rest. I *am* rest. The joy of *being* is rest."

Ariel feels the man is a light shining in his sky: "I can learn from you. Why don't you go with me to the mountains?"

"Hah! I would be a marvelous companion, but this dear woman wants to go," the man answers, handing Petruska a ticket. "Behold me in her and you will find the hills of the Immortals."

Ariel feels horrified. Petruska's face is wrinkled and pocked and her eyes are dark and blood-shot. Her nose is too large for her face, and her head too large for her small frame. Ariel senses her depression, yet he is able to feel compassion for her. He looks at the fool, thinking, *Yes, to travel with her might be difficult, but perhaps that is what is to be.*

"All right, but I wish you could come, too."

"I am but a bag of bones," replies the fool, who weighs only ninety pounds. "I spread myself everywhere. Think of me and I will be with you."

Ariel, having never met such a man, speaks his heart: "Please come!"

"I live as a flame in the eye of my Lady. I will be wherever you want me to be."

A whistle signals the train's imminent departure. Petruska starts toward the passenger cars, but Ariel, still amazed by what has just occurred, stands motionless. The fool goes over and urinates by a tree, then comes back to where Ariel is standing and hands him the other ticket.

"I will never forget you," says Ariel, embracing him.

"Nor I you," replies the fool.

Ariel runs and boards the train and begins looking for Petruska. He knows she represents some kind of trial in his own rite of passage. After walking through three cars, he sees her thin frame on the seat behind a tea wagon and sits down beside her. He takes some time to settle himself and then asks, "Where do you want to go?"

"To my destiny. I seek to return to myself."

Ariel wonders if this woman is the fool in disguise. "Is China your past?" he asks.

"And perhaps my future. I am a star, but no one recognizes me."

The gleam in her eyes reveals a longing. Looking at Ariel with a bulbous stare, she continues: "I am powerless, but in the sky I will find my power. I dwelled here long ago, but now I am a stranger to Earth— ever since the trials in the initiation chamber."

"What trials? What chamber?"

"I failed—in Egypt. But in China, long before that, I was happy. What passed is what is real. I am as old as the stars. Now I return. I seek to empty myself of the jealousy that led me to kill my sister. I thought she abandoned me. But I see now that she is innocent, and I seek her forgiveness. I was reborn in Siberia, but I am still searching for the thread of ancient happiness. Last night I dreamt that I, as a monk, lunged at her with a knife and killed her. In that horrible moment my soul was almost lost in oblivion. But something called me back. My sister was in China, too. Perhaps I shall find her in the old village—if I can locate it."

Ariel finds Petruska hard to understand. Her English is fragmentary and spoken through a thick Russian accent, but he is fascinated by the honesty of her confession.

"I can detect evil anywhere," she continues. "But your snakes are asleep. Your innocence helps me. I curse the day I was born! Yet bodies stream from the womb to remember."

"Remember what?"

Petruska feels she has found the person who will listen, and she pours out the truths stored in her cells. The contradictions clash like cymbals, her tongue issuing flame one moment and rot the next. All day they travel, the train stopping and starting, as Ariel is initiated into the journey of her soul.

Finally the train pulls into Taiyuan. Greeting them there is the radiant face of the fool.

ABORIGINAL JUSTICE

Conscience
White of gold within white

The courage
of self honesty
absolves
the pain of denial.

Gus

Gus lies slumped in the corner of his prison cell filled with utter desolation. He wishes he could die, for death has never frightened him. Only pain frightens him; now the pain is so great that even his fear is gone. It is the pain of humiliation, the loss of his sense of being. Where is his soul in the madness of a loveless life? All he has left is his love for Anita. He respects Pahulu for having the courage to face him and to bring Tawhiri, but he doesn't love her. Occasionally Tawhiri sends him a drawing—the fleeting blue brushstrokes of the sea, the colored petals of a hibiscus flower. How distant Hawaii is from this dismal grey cell!

Beyond the tumult of existence, bereft of purpose, he desires only one thing—Anita's forgiveness. Time and space seem to have disappeared. Locked away in his cells are memories from before birth, unknown until they burst forth from denied experience like sparks, flashing and expanding into other dimensions beyond the monotony of everyday reality.

Gus bolts upright when one such spark explodes in his brain: *I am a killer.Why?* But he lapses quickly into desire as sexual fantasies again assert themselves against painful recollection. *I would make love to a woman, any woman, if she were here.* He stays lost in that reverie until startled by the clanging of the opening cell door.

As he has hundreds of times before, Gus follows the guard down the bleak corridor to the mess hall. Not quite a living corpse, he moves like an automaton, whether he is walking, working, or spooning his oatmeal.

Since it is Sunday, he decides that after breakfast he will go to Mass, one of the religious services offered by the prison. Basically, he just wants a change from the dreary solitude of his cell. He was raised Catholic and reacted strongly to the constant cant of sin and hell and suffering. At twenty-two he pronounced himself an atheist. Now, concerned only with the immediacy of his own being, he doesn't know what he is.

During the Mass, Father Flaherty reads from Ephesians 6:11: "Put on the whole armor of God that ye may be able to stand against the wiles of the devil. For we wrestle, not against flesh and blood, but against principalities, against powers, against the rulers of the darkness of this world, against spiritual wickedness in high places."

When the Mass is concluded, the priest urges the inmates to go to confession. But Gus has become riled and suddenly speaks out: "The scriptures say the devil works wickedness in high places, not within our flesh and blood. If the devil, as you say, brought me here, why should I confess?"

Father Flaherty, appalled by the outburst, says nothing. But Gus, feeling trapped by the concept of evil as an astrally imposed fate, continues: "If devils exist, they are within me! I feel the war within my body. Jesus cannot save me from what I have inflicted upon myself!"

Gus's aura is so perforated from past transgressions, and his soul so fragmented, that spectral parasites periodically take possession of him, dwelling in the hollows of his confused existence. But he is able to renounce the false authority of the priest, just as he had renounced the false authority of his alcoholic father.

"I worship the phallus!" he shouts back at the priest as the guard shoves him out the door of the prison chapel. "Only two things are real—orgasm and death!"

Once back in his cell, Gus feels relieved for having asserted himself. But sex is really his despair, the introverted conflict that causes him to masturbate night and day. Struggling against the body and fate, he fills the emptiness of his days with the power of his memories—of exploitation, shame, and his own river of semen mixing with the menstrual blood of his mother. He remembers once again how his mother, drunk and seductive, urged him to enter the cave of her womb—the place from which he emerged fourteen years before.

Since that first ungodly orgasm, he has detested women and anything associated with the corporeal—even animals. Ancestors swim in his mind like screams in the throats of the frogs, monkeys, and dogs he tortured in his experiments. He dreams of creatures leaping from the astral onto Earth, roaming the wild as invertebrates, then apes, then men.

I am less than an ape! he mumbles aloud, curling up like an embryo, his head between his knees, wrapped in his long arms. Torn between the impulses of the body and the longings of the soul, he knows he wants only one thing—Anita. *Do I love her?* As feelings for Anita arise again, his spirit ignites his vision, and he realizes that his ultimate fear is to live without love.

Wracked by the disparity between what he wants and the truth of his being, he reassesses his life, overcome by the sense of a sacrifice that seems impossible. *Must I give up the one thing I value most? Anita!*

Fifty years in prison would be less excruciating than this love, which finally illuminates the horror of every wicked thing he has done. Knowing he has made a terrible assault upon life itself, he struggles to separate his inner remorse from the imposed sin of the church. *Is my lust for women pathological, or is it the natural pulsing of eros? Is lust linked with my cruelty to animals? How does it differ from what I feel for Anita?* For a moment, his stark honesty faces what seems like an inferno. He feels grateful to be locked up, confined. Initially outraged when the judge announced his sentence, he now thinks his term should be longer: *Three years are nothing for lifetimes of violence.*

Suddenly, the visage of a wise woman appears.

"Who . . . who are you?"

"I am your Oracle. Dispel your fear and face your demons, and I shall be with you. You must realize that you can find freedom even in this cell."

"How can this be?" Gus mumbles, awed by a new sense of justice.

Through the Oracle, he realizes that destructive tendencies can only be changed from within, not by law or decree. Of this he becomes certain. Only *he* can know the cause of his violence and madness. The killer in him will not die by his being locked up or by his issuing false confessions. *I am not a sinner,* he whispers inside. The stalemate struggles within him like comfortless love, an unspent passion, while the Oracle watches and waits.

She speaks with a different kind of authority: "Your conflict embodies both the contest of the weaponry of *Homo sapiens* and the ceremony of nature's libidinous sympathy with all senescence. Your body's erotic impulses lie side-by-side with the cannibalism of nature and the calculated war of humankind."

"I am not a sinner!" he cries aloud as his frustrated desires and unfulfilled self-awareness clash in the Oracle's underground temple. She speaks from within him: "Your wound is self-inflicted, but nonetheless malefic. Find aboriginal justice, and you will know how to heal the wound of your ancestors—of all ancestors whose domination and victimization have plagued you." As Gus begins to fall into doubt, the Oracle continues more forcefully: "You are a scientist who knows about genetic heredity, but what about the qualities of the soul? Are they not passed on from generation to generation?" With that she disappears.

Are rape and murder a collective or individual responsibility? muses Gus. *Where does it all begin and end?* Tormented with questions, he takes stock of the dirty, barren cell with its leaky toilet that keeps the floor damp and reeking of stench. He hates it, yet he begins to realize that it is somehow just, that it suits his selfish soul.

All night long, Gus meditates on the meaning of his life. He stares into the dark room and sees nothing—neither the stars nor the hills in the shaft of moonlight. Yet he sees what lies within his psyche and suddenly realizes, *What I do on the outside depends on what happens here. I want to face my God and pay for my abominable acts.*

His mind and soul spin with probing: *How could a good God create evil, or even allow it? Is evil real? An unconscious agreement? Will I be judged? By whom? I don't want to be numb any more. I want to awaken. Who is the real killer, the alien within me? This body was inherited from the brutes of the jungle. Why do I torture them and torture myself?*

He knows he is not unique: *I belong to a race that has created concentration camps, nuclear bombs, and toxic waste. What hope can there be in a world addicted to war? Yet my life is my responsibility. What mask do I wear? That of a martyr? Rapist? Killer? Do the demons of fate await my death to tear me limb from limb? What of my soul? Even now I am possessed. Will my love for Anita survive my death?*

His mind reels with questions until, exhausted, he falls asleep on the threadbare mattress. He dreams he is in a fiery caldron of unbearable intensity. Through the acrid black smoke billowing out from the turbulent golden flames, he can see Anita. She is passionate and beautiful. He reaches out to caress her and to ask for her help, but she changes before his eyes into a hideous hag. The excruciating heat of transformation turns his liquid lust into a dry burning and fury. Deep is his resistance to change. Still reaching for her, he returns to a primal light that glows with an animalistic erotic fervor. His lust is driven within himself. Receding still further into the Primal Waters, he bathes momentarily in the mystery of their uncertainty until he cries out at Anita's horrible image reappearing through the flames.

To live through another is itself the source of agony. Each inner life is its own secret. Half conscious, Gus's soul asks, *Are we each a differentiated individual? Isn't all of nature a chain of one species interpenetrating with another? How can we emerge from the collective eros of our animal ancestors?* He knows intimately that sexuality is itself a language of signs, body images, and chemistry. Back in a dream state, staring at Anita's repulsive features, he declares, *This is a test. May my illusions and rage die in my blood!*

Out of the cry of his heart in the comfortless night, conscience is born. Anita transforms yet again—this time into a snake that devours the swarming astral parasites that have plagued his entire life, the demons that have entwined with the congenital dysfunction in his cells. He understands that his aberrations are those of the entire human race. The primal beginnings were erotic, but the march of civilization brought a mirage of progress, and of technological domination over nature. He has participated in that domination. The demons, exorcised by the fire of his awakening conscience, scream and flee, trying to alight and feed on the compulsive habits being consumed. Along with the demons, the projected ideal of Anita is absorbed by the labyrinthine passageways of his brain. The mirage is gone.

Gus awakes. Animal muteness struggles to speak, but he finds his own voice, *Where is my beloved? Does the universe care about me? No! Only Anita cares, and I abused her.* He opens to a new identity shorn of the pathology of the past, but he knows nothing of himself. He wonders how to see where his self parts from his loveless ego like a light that goes on beyond the extinguished torch of his dismal existence.

Gus is jolted by the opening of the cell door. It is the guard, informing him of a visitor. Gus gets up, not yet fully conscious of all that has taken place, and follows the guard to the visitor's window. Through the glass he sees Anita waiting patiently. She appears now as a stranger, yet one that vibrates with life. She stands before him in simplicity. His veils have burned away.

"You have come?"

In the seconds before she speaks, he hears a song rumble from the depths of his being:

The Judge/Oracle's Song of the River

I am the earthquake and seismic waves of judgment.
Look for me in self-evaluation.
I can be found in the voice of prophets and the courts of justice.
I am the hologram of the cosmic law in the social world.
I am the self-conflict and dialogue of the blaming mind.
Look for me in the prisons and the ways of rehabilitation.
You can find me in the skull and crossbones when you feel doubt,
    and in the rose of truth when you feel confident.
I am authoritative conditioning and the disentanglement from the past.

You can find me in your conscience and the hope of radical dreams.
I am the honesty of my ancestors and the release from negative values.
I live in self-acceptance and discernment of right and wrong.

How can you know who you are?
Do you ask a mirror what it reflects? Look at yourself.

THE ALCHEMIST

Nothing is fixed. The endless vortex rolls with waves obscuring and revealing the essence of the gift of the River itself. Eros animates every Sun, flower, and organ of nature. Logos vibrates through all concepts and forms seeking expression in culture.

"There is only one universe, but who can fathom it?" asks the Alchemist.

Wellsprings of infinite light, perennial culture, and powers of sacrifice issue from the spiritual world into the Alchemist's home in the Fourth World. He receives them as exalted mystical experiences. Streaming outlets of visions, shadows, intensity, and thought pour down from the human world. He receives them as limpid perceptions and shapes them into ritual processes. The nature world spills over in stars, forms, directions of energy, and diverse levels of consciousness. He receives them as substances of transformation—as erotic, wondrous realities.

The streams issuing from the Three Worlds teem into the Alchemist's body, making it fluid like molten metal, for he has emerged from the imaginal realm filled with the Shaman's hallucinogenic power. Mindful of only one goal—the healing of the incarnate soul through the perfect substance of gold—he pours the streams into a golden caldron created from the soul's own contents. Through the human genius, he seeks to fuse the Three Worlds.

Knowing of the Alchemist's desire, an angel appears and tells him, "To heal humanity and culture is to prepare the jewel. To draw the jewel from the vagaries of life, you must pass through all phases of transmutation."

"What are they?" he asks.

"You have known the essential gold of mystical experience, but you have forgotten it. This is natural. It must lie obscure in the darkness of human nature, for black is the hieroglyph for lead, the primeval pattern of the human in which the seeds of Noahs are spread."

"Of this I am aware, but how can the darkness be dispelled?"

"Through incarnation into sentience, in which dawn breaks the darkness with the reddening power of nature. Red is the volatile and fusible process, the primal vitality of change."

"What happens then? The human alone in nature is helpless, for even the elements suffer when the human soul is torn in two."

The angel is luminous, her voice shaped by the waterfall of her being: "The purification of mind and feeling can bring a purification of civilization. White is the color of diamond clarity and purity. Free the sentient body from endless change through commitment to flawless truth."

Through the gold, black, red, and white of transmutation, the angel instructs the Alchemist in the history of the universe and the migration of souls. The colors fuse in his caldron as the burning waters are released from the body of the Creatrix.

Over the aeons, nature enters the Alchemist's metabolism, art assumes supremacy over his rhythmic heart and lungs, and religion takes over his head and nervous system. He seeks to become the free man, Adam Cadman, the whole human embodying the universe.

However, as time goes on, the mysticism of the First World turns into organized religion. The perceptions and rituals of the Second World congeal into art, psychology, medicine, and logic. The primitive, wondrous realities of the Third World of nature become analyzed, categorized, and mechanized.

A few courageous souls seek to find the golden origin within the caldron of the Alchemist's being. But the gap between subject and object widens as history unfolds, culminating in the identity crises of the twentieth century. At the time, the three branches of the River emerge in the language of the priest, the artist, and the scientist. Fearing one another, these three take refuge inside the Alchemist, who embodies their collective shadows: the fearful rigidity of the self-righteous evangelist, the self-indulgent narcissism of the struggling artist, and the frustrated idealism of the space engineer.

The Creatrix knows a great healing is needed—both within the human being and within the entire cultural world. The Tree of Life inside her moves in the nervous systems and bloodstreams of mortals. Living within the gossamer world of essences, she suffers, watching religious leaders tyrannize humanity through judgment and fear. Even mysticism has become authoritative, losing its source in the First World and deteriorating into cults that worship the supersensory chimeras in the human mind. She mourns at the decline of art into expressionist op and pop outrage, severed from the oneness of inner knowing and the beauty of natural forms. She sighs at a science that sees the stars and stones as lifeless and the genesis of life as statistical and random.

Unseen, unknown, the compassion of the Creatrix dwells within all things, waiting to be experienced as inherent joy. Refusing again to interfere with free will, but desiring to ward off the potential destruction of creation, she finally charges the Alchemist: "You must bring awareness to humanity."

Secretly, silently, in the basements and caves of civilization, the Alchemist performs the great experiment on himself: to become whole and integrated and to harmonize the contending streams of the worlds. But how will he bring humanity an awareness of the three worlds as one? Only the Shaman, the Alchemist, and the artist who remain true to a vision behold the Creatrix within nature and within themselves.

Knowing that spiritual metaphysics cannot be mixed with scientific objectivity, and that scientific empiricism can never reveal the deepest secrets of life, the Alchemist sorts human emotion, body, and mind into inspirational symbols and sounds. He struggles with esoteric and chemical texts in order to heal the psychic schism. Violence, tyranny, and dogma must all be melted down within the human unconscious, and within the sacred fire of the Priest-Seer before he can draw forth the elixir. The elemental powers still contend for the human will that is not yet free, and that will become so only through surrender to the creative influx of the Creatrix within.

From within the human body, the Creatrix awakens the Alchemist to the reptilian hindbrain, the midbrain, and the cerebrum. As the animism of the Primal Waters, the dynamism of the Antagonist, and the healing of the Shaman mix together, the inexorable momentum of the River splashes down upon the Fourth World with the hope of integration.

But humanity, seeking to avoid the pain of clashing paradigms, has forgotten the Alchemist within, who struggles to comprehend the disparate languages of religion, art, and science. Once liquid life, and molten metal, the script of the River, flowing in multidimensional reality, now collapses into three dimensions as the Alchemist's cast body crystallizes. The image of the Alchemist hardens into metallic sculpture as space and time compress toward a singularity impossible to reach by division.

THE MEMORY OF BLOOD

Healing
Gold of black within white

The deep stream
of the fertile Earth
responds
to loving care.

Fa and Buba

Her beautiful black body burns from within. The dark shapes of racial injustice writhe unconsciously through the Earth and into her groin. But Fa's gift of empathy encompasses all people, for she is infused with spirit. Her New York world bustles with gaunt Europeans, vivacious Latinos, and cautious Asians. But of all her university friends, she is closest to Buba, a student from Mali. Americans call him Bob, but that is not his name. A teller of tales, Buba describes the strange contrasts of Africa. He speaks of the vast jungles still bursting with life, but also of the blood of starving millions seeping into the Earth. His Africa is at once a natural paradise and a modern hellhole where corrupt governments widen the rift between the rich and poor.

Fa listens to Buba with only one thought—to go to Africa herself. "I cannot *not* go!" she declares to him at the end of the spring semester. In an academic environment that stresses the mind, she moves by instinct: "I can taste the longing of the Earth to heal in my people."

"You feel the Africans are *your* people?" responds Buba in surprise.

"They may not recognize me as one of them, but my body knows we are kin. I feel a burning within me to change my blindness to sight. Here in the city, I feel cut off from the primal and tribal ways."

"But Fa, Africans are struggling to live by small cash-crop farming, illegal brewing, and private transport—not by the old tribal ways. My Aunt Kasa may tell the old myths, but until we put food in our bellies, we are bound together only by misery."

Fa is determined: "We could be inundated by the Earth's bounty if we work together. I know it. You have studied history, and you know that the real story of the African people has not yet been written. A seed planted in the Earth will bear fruit if tilled and tended with care. Our desire for harvest propels us to split the seed. I will go to Africa even if I die in the process. A seed sacrifices itself to become a tree. Let me go to Mali with you. Otherwise I will go alone. I want to understand. I want to help if I can."

Buba's soft eyes glisten: "You cannot go to Africa alone! God knows what would happen if you did!"

He stands silently for a moment, then reaches forward to embrace her: "All right, Fa. Come and stay with my family."

Fa feels as though she is standing in the molten core of the Earth, her face flushed and her heart full of gold. She dances and shouts with joy: "The fire within me transforms hope to gratitude. May I remember my people through the winding river of time!"

In the weeks prior to her departure, Fa spends as much time in reflection as anticipation. Thousands of years ago, her ancestors traveled south and west as part of a movement away from the Sahara, where the desert encroached upon the surge of life. Two hundred years ago, the curse of slavery brought her grandfathers and grandmothers to America. Of those times she has no conscious memory. Only her blood knows.

She remembers the lush fields of Alabama, where she roamed happily as a little girl. She was only six when Zoa took the family to New York, away from the circle of green that shaped her childhood. But it was there, exposed to the extremes of wealth and poverty and a diversity of cultures that she found her heart. She sought the truth of the Earth even in the urban environment, finding in her study of science a revelation of the worlds of nature. Often lost in a pool of memory, she tries to fathom a future in the distant land of her ancestors.

As the plane descends to land in Timbuktu, Fa looks down upon a mixture of ancient ruins and ramshackle huts. She feels herself entering a world that is strange, yet somehow familiar. She knows that in centuries past this city was the cultural capital of the Songhai empire, a resplendent center of learning and commerce.

Once inside the airport, Buba embraces his wife, Halima, and introduces her to Fa. Fa follows the couple to an old jalopy that carries them bouncing through the city streets and beyond to a small village southwest of the city. Several of Buba's closest family members have assembled to greet him and his American friend, who has brought gifts of beads, colored braids, and cloth. Later they fill the evening with music in a welcoming celebration.

Fa spends her first morning walking along the Bani, a river that flows through the gentle savanna near the small mud huts of the village. There, many people are busy tilling the soil, herding cattle, or weaving cloth. The village lies six miles from the edge of a small waterfall, where the jungles begin. She knows that, although the country is beautiful, it harbors deadly vectors of disease—tsetse flies that spread sleeping sickness and mosquitoes that carry malaria and yellow fever. In both city and country, thousands have contracted AIDS. The prevalence of suffering everywhere distresses her.

Fa wakes each morning pierced to her heart by the problems of soil erosion, disease, and starvation. Yet the souls of the people remain loving and poignantly real. Their eyes shine like dark pools. Her compassion grows, even as the wasteland continues to spread across the Earth. She mourns for the animals driven from their habitat, for the elephants slaughtered for ivory, and for the barren Earth stripped of the gold in its veins. She senses that jewels and precious metals are the blood and nerve-centers of this vital, massive continent.

Frequently Fa walks alone and prays:

Oh, beam of light! Come into my people with your strengthening power. Help me to see how they can heal themselves. I walk with the grace of your rays in my body. My voice speaks from the energy of your divinity. Open my eyes that I may see how to remove this sorrow. Oh, Mother Earth, instill me with the living heart of your being. Help me to understand, but not to interfere. Help us all to move to your living pulse and stay true to your purpose.

As days flow into weeks and months, Fa begins to learn the local dialect and way of life. Halima shows her how to work the Earth. Halima's elderly aunt, Kasa, graciously teaches her how to weave. But Hardo, Buba's brother, scorns such labor, preferring to sell imported secondhand clothes along the road.

On the morning of the new year, Fa announces to Kasa, "I feel I am one of you."

Kasa laughs, her old face wrinkling like dried autumn leaves: "You *are* one of us! During these months, there's not been a shadow between you and anyone. You've blended in like rain in a river."

After a tribal dinner gathering later that evening, Kasa offers to tell a creation story customarily told at that time by an elder.

"We've heard it so many times!" protests Hardo. "It means nothing. We live in a different world now, Kasa. You'd do better to salvage packing cases and sell them for furniture."

However, the children—Ala, Marwe, Yero, and Batogi—encourage Kasa to tell the story. So does Buba, who knows Fa would appreciate it. Hardo grunts in protest and leaves.

Kasa winks at the children and begins: "Here in the western Sudan, at the bend of the River Niger, our people, the Dogon people, dwell. Some myths and legends say the Dogon people came from the star Sirius. But it was a blind old man, Ogotemneli, who gave the secrets of the tribe to the wider world—so that humanity might awaken to its destiny."

Kasa tells of the creation from the one God, Amma, and the emergence of the twin Nummo spirits in the life-force of the great River that contains all other rivers. It is a River of light, radiating constantly through the shimmering movements of the Nummo spirits.

Kasa smiles at the young ones, her aged voice conveying the sense of tradition: "The Nummo spirits looked down and saw the Earth naked. So they clothed her with fibers from the heavenly plants. The water in these plants was the River itself, where language was discovered."

Fa's eyes grow wide like the children's while Kasa continues her story: "But a jackal became jealous of the Earth Mother's language, and it seized the earthy fiber skirts. The Earth resisted, but to no avail. The jackal gained the power of speech and revealed the plans of Amma to diviners, who use this power to this day."

"Does divination really work, Kasa?" interrupts Fa impulsively. "If it did, wouldn't we be able to overcome our problems?"

The old woman is quick to answer: "You get divine messages all the time, but do you follow their advice? In the old times, humans had more integrity with spirit and nature and followed the oracles. The spirit of divination is still with us, but people don't listen. When we do listen, we often don't act. Let me continue the story and maybe you'll see for yourself.

"Now, Amma decided to create live beings without Earth, but the Nummo spirits grew afraid that they might no longer have twin births. So on the ground they drew a male form and a female form, each one with twin souls."

Kasa looks at Fa with seriousness and then breaks into laughter, slapping her hands on her lap: "You see? Our ancestors came from the twins! The oldest male ancestor went into an ant hill and has never been seen since. But Ogotemneli tells us that the male Nummo spirit led this ancestor into the depths of the Earth, where he shrank into seed. Six ancestors were changed in this way before going up to heaven, where the first pair of Nummo spirits dwell still."

"Do they really?" asks Marwe. "Can I see them when I go to heaven?"

"First you have to *get* to heaven," says Kasa with a loud laugh. "Now listen. The language of the River was revealed to the seventh ancestor in the art of weaving. He was also shown how to build mud huts. All this we learned first from the ant-people!"

Kasa points at the ground where ants trail across the mud floor: "In heaven, the eight ancestors were changed into the same essence as the Nummo pair, but they fought among themselves, so the Nummo spirits separated them to keep the peace."

"Were they spirit people or real people?" asks little Batogi.

"They had bodies and forms."

"What did they eat?"

"Each of the eight ancestors ate a different grain," replies Kasa.

Fa listens intently, sensing that this story might reveal some secret of the soil, some secret of healing her people and the Earth. Kasa picks up a clay pot with four handles and continues: "Now, the first ancestor used a basket and some clay to mold a model of the world system with a circle at the base and a square on top. A ten-step stairway ascended each of the four sides. The stairs were both male and female, and together they represented the children of the ancestors, the animals, the insects, and the stars. The model was called the Granary of the Master of Pure Earth, and in each compartment was a different grain, one for each of the eight ancestors. These ancestors also held the powers of the organs in the human body."

"Were the people and the Earth in balance then, Kasa?" asks Fa.

"Listen and you'll see. After the first ancestor stole fire from the Nummo blacksmith, the Nummo hurled lightning, causing the first ancestor to open the Granary. The lightning came down as a thundering rainbow that struck the Earth. People, plants, and animals were all scattered. The first ancestor went down the steps of the Granary and marked out fields for the descendants, teaching them how to tend the soil. He taught arts and crafts as well."

Fa can't resist another question: "What did the Nummo spirits teach about the Earth?"

"Grow just a few crops in a small patch of land, then move on so each patch has time to refertilize itself. Now, at that time, the people were growing in number and needed to be organized. There were eight families, descended from the eight ancestors. But death had not yet come into the world, and there were too many people living on Earth. After great purification, the eighth ancestor finally remembered the original Word of God. He realized that the script of the River spoke of death as a way to balance growth. The oldest descendant of the eighth ancestor was called Lebe, and it was Lebe who died first."

"How did he die?" asks Marwe.

"He was swallowed by a snake who was the seventh ancestor in disguise. After it ate Lebe, the snake vomited up stones that resembled the outline of the human soul. The stones held the life-force that each of the eight ancestors sent to the eight families."

"Where are the stones now?" asks Yero.

"They are kept by the priests."

"Do the stones still have power?" wonders Ala.

"Lebe lives in all the descendants through the Word in the stones. I'll tell you a secret if you can keep it to yourselves. Can you keep a secret?" All the children nod, along with Buba and the others.

"The secret is that Lebe is not really dead. He only appeared to die so that humanity could have the life-force. Lebe is restored to life through the food we grow in the Earth. Lebe is restored when we heal ourselves."

Fa feels a shaft of hope come into her heart, although she is still concerned: "But if the soil is depleted, won't Lebe really die?"

"If Lebe really dies, we will all die—our vitality will be completely spent." Kasa's wizened face grows serious.

"The exhaustion of the soil is the first sign of real danger, isn't it?" says Fa, looking intently at Kasa. But the wise one sits silently, knowing Fa has the answer within herself.

Kasa stands up and leads Fa and the children to a structure where two stones mark east and west. Its roof is shaped like the heaven of the Granary of the Master of Pure Earth. Kasa speaks of the mysteries of soul and body, explaining, "The rooms of the house are both male and female. The four posts supporting the end room are the arms of man and woman embracing in copulation. Their union brings fertility to the Earth and health to our people."

Lying on her cot later that night, Fa cannot stop her thoughts: *There can be no rest. We live on the edge of starvation. When the soil is tired, we are tired. I know the purpose of Lebe. The plants of the Earth are to nourish our bodies as the ancient myths nourish our souls. We must act now, or our children will die and there will be no tomorrow.*

When she relates these thoughts to Buba the next day, she is encouraged by his response. "You are a messenger of hope," he says.

"Maybe this is the split seed you spoke of in New York. You must speak your mind, Fa."

A group of elders gather at Buba's request on the following evening. Fa stands when it is her turn to speak. Her words have been forged in the fire of her own heart through long nights and days: "You all want to see the jungles return, filled with animals and wild birds. You want most of all to restore life to the soil. Lebe may really die if we let the soil die."

Some whisper among themselves. "She knows Lebe. How does she know our secrets?"

Fa goes on: "Do you want Lebe to live? Do *you* want to live?"

"What are you saying, Fa?" asks Dogo, a gaunt, middle-aged man.

"We must embrace the land. From it we can find the powers that make the stars shine. Your own stories hold the secrets of soil, a healthy life. The old gods and goddesses of the Earth are more powerful than the overlords who have destroyed your ways over five hundred years. The Earth and your own bodies are crying for your attention."

"Just what do we *do*, Fa?"

Buba intervenes, knowing the group will be more receptive to his words than those of an American female: "We must make some changes. If we are to survive, there need to be rules for the management of common land. I suggest that each family work a limited pasture for a certain period. Those with herds can let them graze on separate land at different times."

Some of the men are shaking their heads. "Are you one of us or one of them?" challenges Hardo. "You've lived in the city too long, Buba. You can't come back and just expect us to change our ways."

"I've learned what will build up the soil. If the soil dies, Lebe dies. If Lebe dies, we die. For a whole people to die is not good."

"How do we build up the soil, Buba?" asks one of the elders. "We've been using fertilizers, but the soil is dead."

"Fertilizers that are simply mineral salts eventually deplete the soil, whereas dung and other organic refuse add to its structure and mineral content. The secret is in getting the humus, the life-force of Lebe, back into the soil."

"How can we get the life-force of Lebe back?" asks Dogo.

"There are only two ways—by growing it, or by human labor. If we had rotary tillers, we could grow it using cover cropping. But we don't have tillers, so we must do the work. We can use manure from our animals. It's a good source of nitrogen. And potash and rock powders are needed to maintain phosphate levels. We can use wood ashes, cocoa shells, and other plant refuse."

A few of the men and women nod their heads. Some are silent, still suspicious. Most begin to respond to the love conveyed by Fa and Buba.

Buba, sensing that he is being heard, continues: "We also need earthworms. Earthworms work the soil and keep it loose so that it can quickly absorb the rainfall."

"What do the worms eat?" asks Dogo.

Fa smiles: "Truth is in the belly. Earthworms know that just as you do. They eat organic matter and mineral rock powder. But the chemical fertilizers kill them."

Buba reinforces what Fa has said: "Western technology has developed chemicals that force the growth of plants for a few years, then deplete the soil for decades. Ammonium sulfate is the worst. Pesticides that contain lead, arsenic, copper, lime sulphurs, and tar oil are also very destructive to earthworms and helpful bacteria."

Realizing that he is getting too specific for this initial discussion, Buba smiles and continues, "If birds are poisoned by eating insects full of pesticides, the insects become a plague. Look at our crops! They are infested with insects! We must fertilize with manure instead. We should drive our cattle and goats onto the stubble after each harvest.

"Listen to the voices of our ancestors. We can rebuild the soil. We can resurrect Lebe and be healthy."

TWO CHERRY BLOSSOMS

Awareness
Black of black within white

The vanity
of ambition
obscures
the treasures of life.

Toda and Ono

Toda is methodically engaged in his weekly tour of the production lines of Hashigawa Games, where thousands of women assemble electronic parts on minute printed circuits. All of them wear magnifying lenses over their eyes, giving them the appearance of robotlike drones. The bell has just rung for their hourly break, signaling the women to stand up and bow all together. For the next five minutes they perform *do* breathing exercises, instructed by tones sounding through an intercom. They inhale with the high tones and exhale with the low tones, after which they again all bow together and chant in unison, "May our business be successful!" Then everyone sits down and silently resumes work.

Toda feels proud as he walks through the factory, pleased that all is in order. He continues to the units where programmers hunch over work stations designing the latest games, but his moments of satisfaction are interrupted by a voice over the intercom: "Mr. Hashigawa, please come to the main office."

Toda goes immediately to the elevator, anticipating that the overseas phone call he has been waiting for has finally come through. But he returns to his office to find Tamio waiting, tense and grim. They bow to each other.

"Why have you interrupted my rounds?" Toda asks. "This had better be something important."

"Please sit down, my friend. I have some bad news."

"What is it?"

"There was an auto accident this morning. Rai and Ozaki were killed. Apparently, they had been drinking."

Toda gasps in a state of shock and disbelief. He says nothing at first, then grabs Tamio by the shoulders and shakes him: "My sons dead? This can't be true!" He sinks into a chair, feeling stunned and dazed. For the first time in years, he cries.

Tamio goes to the phone and calls Toda's chauffeur to take him home.

An hour later the limousine drops Toda in front of the high-rise building where he lives. He is barely able to function—barely able to find the button that will send him up to his penthouse on the forty-fourth floor.

When he enters, Ono is there. She sees the sorrow in her husband's face immediately. "What is it?" she asks, knowing he never comes home at this time of day.

Toda stammers, then finally forces out the words: "Rai and Ozaki have been killed in an automobile accident."

"Ai!"

Ono stares out the window in silence for a long time, but says nothing more. Raindrops fall lightly against the glass. Toda is amazed that she does not weep.

"How can you be so calm, Ono?" Toda stares at his wife in disbelief.

"I have a source of strength that I haven't told you about."

"You have held secrets from me?"

"Secrets of loneliness, sorrow, and meaninglessness. It has been hard for me, Toda, being the wife of a busy, high-ranking executive. I had to do *something*. Now perhaps I can tell you."

"*What* did you do?"

"Two years ago, I went to the temple. From that time on, I have been meditating regularly. I know you think this is trivial compared to business, but it helps me accept things as they are."

"Why have you never told me?"

"I *couldn't* tell you. You would have ridiculed me. Now, perhaps you will listen. I go to the temple as often as I can. The roshi there is very kind. On the weekends that you are away, I usually go to the Zen service."

"Zen?"

Toda's eyes begin tearing again: "But Rai and Ozaki are dead! If meditation makes you so unfeeling, you must stop . . ."

Ono still feels afraid. She focuses totally on her breath, trying to bring all her attention to the present moment. "My heart cries as much as yours does," she replies.

Ono gazes into Toda's moist eyes: "Don't you see? Our sons were calling us! Their tongues wagged to imitate you. They took on *your* thoughts and *your* ambition. How could they be themselves? We robbed them of their memory of simple things. They had been drinking for years. You thought they thrived in the churning waters of business, but they drowned in alcohol. I tried to be obedient. I *was* obedient, but we no longer enjoyed the simple procession of the seasons, the sound of crickets, the miracle of the lake beneath the moonlight."

Toda knows the truth of what Ono says, but he is too forlorn to acknowledge it. Now his anger flares up: "How can you be romantic at a time like this?"

Ono realizes that he is in no place to understand her now, and she shifts her attention to his immediate needs. She smiles through a sorrow that presses from her heart toward the tears in her eyes. "You are tired and disturbed," she says. "Take a shower and then put on your kimono. I will serve you some tea."

When she returns, she places two cherry blossoms beside the finely glazed cups. In silence, she fills Toda's cup, then her own.

"If you like, I will serve you in our traditional way and refrain from drinking tea myself."

"No, please stay with me," replies Toda. He is confused. His awareness dims and then flickers toward insight: *Why did they drink so much?*

Why did I not see it? Did I really dominate them so much that they had no lives of their own? How could I be so unaware?

Ono puts her hand on his shoulder and says softly, "Born when the leaves fall and the gourds are gathered, they die when the cherry blossoms bloom." She cries inside. Like molten lava embedded in the Earth, her tears hide from the surface of her eyes. Struggling to let her intemperance fade, she begins breathing and concentration exercises.

Toda carries his tea over to the window and gazes down upon the city of Tokyo spreading out below. His pain is excruciating. His ambition, his wealth, his power seem like nothing. He has lost his successors and with them all meaning. "I trained them for twelve years," he says to Ono. "They were to inherit everything. Not one in a million would have as much! Now they are gone." *Where, where have they gone?*

"Please sit and just drink your tea, Toda. Your thoughts will change."

Toda glances at her and then at the two cherry blossoms in the slender crystal vase. *My two sons! How fragile is life!*

Shapes of good and evil gnaw at his thoughts. He feels desperate. "Who will succeed me?" he mumbles half aloud as his tea cup slips from his fingers and crashes upon the floor. Ono stoops and carefully picks up the scattered pieces.

Staring at the rain that now pounds against the window, Toda remembers the joys of his sons' childhoods. "Saki. Bring me saki!" he cries, as the root of his despair scalds his heart. *I did not even* know *my sons! I was too busy to listen. They simply obeyed me. I made them into automatons like the women who work in the plant.* "Now I'll never know them!" he shouts as Ono returns with the saki.

He sips the saki and continues to cry. But he is unwilling to absorb what he has just acknowledged and grows irritable: "Call Tamio for me!"

Ono dials Tamio's number, pauses, and then puts down the receiver: "He is gone for the day."

Toda holds his head in his hands: "Too many things at once! You attend to our son's bodies. Call Nigisa. I'm going out!"

"Drive anywhere, Nigisa, just drive!" Toda orders his chauffeur as he climbs into the limousine waiting near the front entrance of the building. Nigisa drives toward Kamakura, but the passing scenery does little to distract Toda from his pain. He groans from time to time as the rain splatters the windshield. In the distance he can see the statue of the Great Buddha, dedicated to Amida. "Stop here, Nigisa," he says. "I want to get out."

He feels momentarily comforted in the presence of the immense Buddha. He hasn't been in a temple since he was twenty. He recalls that Buddhists believe that all beings will be reborn in one of the six realms of existence. *Will Rai and Ozaki be reborn as humans?* he wonders. *As gods or demons? Or even beasts or hungry ghosts? What becomes of people who lose their souls? Surely they won't be born in hell! What will become of* me *when I die?*

Fear grips his soul as he fastens his raincoat and stands in the pouring rain gazing at the statue. "Isn't there a Zen temple near here?" he asks Nigisa as he gets back into the car.

"There are several, sir."

"Take me to one."

Nigisa drives to the parking area adjacent to the Kenchoji temple complex. Toda gets out of the car and instructs Nigisa to wait.

For a while, Toda stands under the roofed gate and listens to the rain. When it finally stops he proceeds on to the Buddha hall. The gardens are beautiful in their order and simplicity. He sighs spontaneously as he sees the cherry blossoms, some fresh, some faded, along a pathway being swept by a monk. Thoughts again overtake him. *My sons are gone! Who will succeed me!* He bows to the monk, holding back his tears. "I am Toda Hashigawa, president of Hashigawa Games in Tokyo. I wish to see the roshi."

The monk ushers Toda to the portico and tells him to wait there. Then he disappears inside the hall.

For fifteen minutes Toda waits, feeling at first impatient, then insulted and dishonored. His impulse is to leave, but he does not. He somehow senses that he may find peace here, if only he can see the roshi. He waits another fifteen minutes, his mind running nonstop: *Can I trust Tamio to succeed me? Why have my sons been taken from me?*

Restless and irritable now, he watches several monks pass by, one with a wheelbarrow, another with a rake: *What a life! Have they no ambition? This seems like a kind of slavery.* Then he becomes aware that the methodical routines of the monks are not different from the routines of the workers in his company. *What keeps monks in this kind of life? What could Ono have found here that enables her to accept the death of our sons? Is she cold and indifferent or truly serene and accepting? What is the difference? I would give anything to be relieved of this torment!*

He feels the breeze and watches it carry more cherry blossoms to the ground. Through the doorway of the portico he can see a trail of blossoms left by the monks along the pathway.

After another hour passes, Toda slumps on a bench and falls asleep, exhausted from his sorrow. He dreams of holding a baby Buddha and having no place to put it, but he is jolted awake by a monk ringing a bell. The monk bows. Toda gathers himself, stands up and bows, then follows the monk into the great Buddha hall where the roshi is sitting serenely in a full-lotus position. He motions Toda to sit on the cushion opposite him. To Toda's complete astonishment, he recognizes the roshi as the monk who was sweeping the steps when he arrived.

"You?"

"You?" repeats the roshi, laughing loudly. "Sit, please."

They sit face to face in silence, the roshi's compassionate gaze embracing all of Toda's sorrow, pain, and confusion. Toda's eyes fill with tears. He doesn't know why. The rain patters hard on the roof.

Toda finally attempts to speak, "I have come . . . to . . . seek your help."

"Help yourself!" snaps the roshi.

"I don't know how. My sons . . . they are dead."

"How do you know?"

"How do I . . ."

"Who died?"

"My sons."

"Who, who?"

Toda stares at the roshi, aware that he is asking about something beyond appearances.

"I will give you a fortune if you bring them back."

The roshi whacks his stick on the arm of Toda's chair, shattering all his thoughts with one incisive gesture.

"You torture yourself."

"I? Myself?"

"Who?

Suddenly Toda feels something sweep through him. He feels somehow empty, yet more lucid than before. The roshi laughs, stands up, bows, and leaves the hall.

A monk conducts Toda out through the portico. There, bowing to him, is Ono, standing on the path where the cherry blossoms fall.

THE MYSTERY IN THE
MOUNTAINS OF SHAANXI

Will

Red of black within white

The dialogue
of destiny
opens
to the will of God.

Pravin, Krishna, Luqman, and Ariel

"Brother! What are you doing here?" exclaims Pravin, startled at seeing Luqman in the Beijing train station. Luqman embraces his old friend warmly. "Oh, it's wonderful to see you !"

"This is my son, Krishna," says Pravin. "I have just finished conducting a tour through Xi'an and met him here. We are anticipating a leisurely journey to Shaanxi. Why don't you come with us? It will do you good to be in the mountains."

"The bloom of youth," says Luqman. He looks at Krishna's own bright countenance and thinks about his decision not to accompany the admiring Ariel. "Yes, I will go with you."

"How are you?" asks Pravin.

"You know that long ago I fell face down on the Earth. Even though I have been trampled, all of heaven has opened to me. But now I am tired and troubled."

Pravin looks at Luqman's eyes blazing with light out of his thin body. "I go with the changes of each day," continues Luqman, "but I still long for eternity. I cry when moments of ecstasy fade. I don't know what's wrong. I've never been so tired, except during the war."

Pravin looks concerned: "We can rest in the Shaanxi mountains. You can tell me about your trials on the way. I have an extra ticket. My wife had hoped to go, but she is at home with our younger children."

The express train carrying Pravin, Krishna, and Luqman arrives in Taiyuan a half-hour before the slower train carrying Ariel and Petruska. Having heard all about Petruska's mottled soul journey, Ariel is eager to refresh himself in the hills and possibly climb one of the higher peaks. No sooner has he kissed Petruska goodbye than he rounds the corner and encounters the fool.

"You? Here?" Ariel exclaims, astonished.

Krishna and Pravin stand on each side of Luqman. Ariel looks from one to the other, not believing his eyes: "Pravin, Krishna, is that you?"

Pravin is uncomprehending. Ariel has grown up in the fourteen years since they were last together.

"I am Ariel! Don't you remember?"

"Ariel!" Pravin cries, and he opens his arms to hug him.

Krishna, realizing that he is looking at his childhood companion, joins in the embrace. Filled with memories, the two young friends open to each other in the evening light, sharing their joys, sorrows, and dreams of what is possible.

The four explorers spend the evening reminiscing at an inn and set off with rucksacks in the early morning. The day is bright, and the sky arcs above them with soft stratus clouds hovering like Taoist immortals around the pinnacles of the mountains.

Luqman is gaunt, his long arms and legs seeming to will their way up the steep mountain path. He is pensive and moves slowly. "I will come along in my own time," he says to Pravin, who has fallen behind to accompany him. Luqman senses that it is here, in this high range, that he may even pass on to the western horizon. *May I drift like smoke from the incense offered to the holy mother,* he prays. The mountains sing, but he cannot hear, for his own song has become buried within himself.

"I have nowhere to go," says Pravin. "Already we are here. The mountains continue on like an endless procession of sapphires. The boys can run like wildfire on ahead. I have peace here with you."

Luqman usually delights in Pravin's companionship, but not now. "Please, go on ahead," he urges. "I will find you when you return. My blood is thin. All I need is the ambrosia of the holy mother. Her food is like milk from the stars."

Luqman's words bring Pravin an image of the Milky Way reaching down to Earth and forming the rivers he knows so well—the Ganges, the Yangtse, the Nile, the Tigris, the Euphrates. Reluctantly he leaves Luqman and runs to catch up with Ariel and Krishna. Perspiration forms like crystal dew on his brow. Soon out of breath, he stumbles and laughs at himself, recalling his long search for Savitri. He feels her presence near, yet a battle still rages within him. His war with the Turanians over many incarnations divided him from himself and from his beloved. He sees a series of lives that open and close like doors leading him farther from his goal. *I grow old as Luqman does,* he reflects, *but time shall not overcome me. If I could be just once in her presence, I could leave mortality and suffering behind.*

While Pravin hurries to join them, Ariel and Krishna burn through the mists of time. Krishna is animated, his body vibrant: "My teacher is a direct student of Ali Akbar Khan. I play sarod and am learning tabla, too. Our tradition teaches us that sound is God—*Nada Brahma.* Playing the sarod and singing certain *ragas* according to the time of day and year bring me into harmony with God and the universe."

"I am envious," responds Ariel. "I wander the world looking for direction, a teacher perhaps. I thought maybe the fool—Luqman is his name?—could teach me. He is so delightfully present every moment."

"Luqman?" laughs Krishna. "He is mad! He has no direction, no will, no sense of purpose."

"But that's exactly how I feel," declares Ariel. "I do well in everything I try, yet I have no purpose. Playing in a jazz band energized me, but only for a while. I have done carpentry, painted pictures, won prizes in poetry. But I am still discontented. Now I circle the world like a hawk circles the sky. I long for something more—I don't know what. There is an emptiness in me. When that woman Petruska was telling me about her life, I felt that her emptiness was my own. She was like the shadow I cannot see. I came here to find peace in these majestic mountains. They inspire me to paint, but painting is not my purpose. Luqman's surrender of will inspires me more than anything."

"You can't be like that," replies Krishna adamantly. "It will get you nowhere. Maybe you should just express your feelings. That's what led me to music. Eventually, music took me beyond feelings to spirit, and behind spirit to being one with every change of the Sun. Then the eternal shines through."

"I express my feelings in poetry, but who can make a living writing poetry?"

"I would like to hear some."

Ariel hesitates for a few moments, then takes his journal out of his rucksack and reads:

> *The unshapeable shock of a cheerless child*
> *scatters the gifts of the heart.*
> *Deeply, surely the world is wrong*
> *where marbled currents of the wild,*
> *unseen, split the zodiac apart,*
> *and sound their truth through an unheard song.*
>
> *I am the sky, the stars singing,*
> *a brain burning in the world I roam.*
> *I am flesh yearning. I am ears ringing.*
> *I am insatiable, but I have no home.*

"It's very beautiful, but very sad," says Krishna, obviously moved. "Could I set that poem to music sometime?"

"I would be honored."

The two companions feel like soaring, their hearts are so full. Out across the mountains, past and future seem to dissolve into a writhing dragon of the present. Krishna sees the panting figure of Pravin approaching and yells out, "Father, come look! The river in the valley winds like a beautiful blue dragon!"

Pravin arrives and, standing between the youths, places his large loving hands on their shoulders: "The flow of nature is one with the gods. I remember long ago roaming the Asian plateau with the gods Indra, Agni, and Vayu. Here, they may appear as dragons. When we are one with them, we release ourselves to our true destiny. Only when we surrender with our own volition do we find happiness."

"I don't know what my destiny is," complains Ariel. "In my travels I see mostly evil and suffering. Here I feel like a god, but I know that as soon as I enter a city, any city, I will wind up praying for the end of difficult days. I want to *do* something about the problems of the world, but I feel helpless."

"Ariel, take a walk with me," offers Pravin. "We'll use this majestic vista to find inner strength and still our frustrations and fears."

Krishna remains behind, smiling at the thought of Ariel and his father in communion. He pulls his flute from his rucksack and begins to play, his breath merging with the hollow reed, his ecstasy becoming a stream of sound that reverberates through the hills like sinuous trails of blue smoke. The glorification of Krishna's music soars with the birds overhead.

Ariel and Pravin walk ahead into the eastern light. "You know, Ariel," says Pravin, "many years ago in Rome your father, Raphael, helped me see that love is within me. Maria, your mother, had come there to hear me lecture, but I believe the real reason she was there was to meet your father again."

"But she has not seen him since! He abandoned me!" Ariel's anger flares up uncontrollably, like a cobra.

"I knew your father when we were both students at the University of London," says Pravin, embracing Ariel with his words. "At that time his pride made me angry, but my real disturbance was due to the clarity of his revelations. His brilliance made everyone uncomfortable. When I saw him in Rome, he was more humble. He had changed. He knew it, and he said it was due to a friend named Zapana. At least then I could listen to him. I remember his exact words—'I feel you still hold the secret of existence within you, Pravin.' But I didn't know what he meant. I kept wandering the Earth like you, searching for something. I thought it was Brahma.

Pravin feels the stillness between breaths, the truth that stands on the tongue but cannot be spoken. Recalling when he first met Ariel as a child, he breaks the spell: "Remember when you fell in the Tungabhadra River? Luqman was there then, too."

"He was?"

"Yes, don't you remember? He was suffering from the wounds the war made in his soul."

"That was Luqman? But now he is so full of light. What brought about the change?"

"He surrendered to Allah," says Pravin. "Again, it was your father who made me realize that Luqman is enlightened. I had seen him as a fool—a lost, neurotic person. But as I observed him more, Luqman showed me that it's possible to burn through the pain of lifetimes of denial and anger and actually dance on flame."

"I love Luqman," responds Ariel, "but how, in a world becoming more violent and chaotic every day, can the whole of humanity regenerate? Very few go through what Luqman did. I feel insignificant next to the task of human transformation."

"Why be concerned with the collective shadows of humanity at your age? Sow your own field and harvest what you can from life. Enjoy these mountains and rivers."

Ariel hears the tranquil sound of Krishna's flute, but he feels a storm within. "What inspires you, Pravin?" he asks. "How do you remain so positive?"

Pravin reflects for a while before responding: "Centuries ago, India gave up worldly ambition and turned to inner truth. I have followed the Aryan stream through all my incarnations. I learned that worldly success does not fulfill my desires. I have a passion for one thing: Savitri, my beloved."

"Do you think she really lives?"

"Raphael dispelled my quest for abstractions of God—for the mere *image* of Savitri. He shattered my projected ideals of a perfect woman, or even a perfect God. He turned me to finding Savitri in the flesh and blood."

"Have you found her?"

"No," Pravin shakes his head. "I am here to dispel my past karma, to burn off any hatred that still lingers in my heart. My will is still too strong. I am not easily cracked open to the light of the spirit. Being in

Luqman's presence helps me to surrender, but his path can never be mine. We share a love for the holy mother, but whereas I seek her in reality, he finds her in some realm I can only imagine."

"What is behind your longing for Savitri?" asks Ariel, feeling more calm.

"My imagination brings me new metaphors for an old love, the love of one who is one with the River I spoke of long ago. That is Savitri. It's true that all finite loves come from the infinite love for a mother. A Vedic hymn tells of the maternal waters that make sacrifice by giving their milk to us."

From the top of a knoll they can see the sky embracing the blue mountains. The subtly shifting tones of Krishna's song merge with the morning light on the river. Ariel's voice breaks as he looks into Pravin's black eyes, "I love my mother, but I am angry. My blood is determined to find peace, but I only see contradiction and paradox."

"What do you mean?"

"Something in me longs to die, to experience a primordial funeral. And something longs to rise like the Sun at dawn. I don't know what it is."

Pravin feels the intensity of Ariel's longing. "Your self-will and your love-will are in conflict," he says gently.

Ariel grinds his teeth in silence. Just as Krishna rejoins them, he blurts out, "*I* feel guilty because my father has never returned! He attends to a thousand children and ignores me. How many nights I have cried out for him. My mother pines away for him, even now."

Pravin lays his hand on his shoulder: "No guilt, my boy. Something in you agreed with one mind and heart to be born of Maria and Raphael, to separate from them, to forget your vow to life, and then to remake yourself."

"Why?"

"To find your way back to God. Whether it is through your parents, or through religion or art, it will be done. The gods and goddesses dance within our bones until we dance with them."

"I don't know how to remake myself," Ariel replies. "My experience with my father has taught me one thing: though I was abandoned, I must never abandon myself. I see you, Pravin, growing old, still searching for your beloved. I see you, Krishna, bright and happy in the world of music. But whatever I try, I feel limitation. Nothing holds me. I've had glimpses of eternity through art and nature and in moments of love, but I long for something more. I must find a purpose that fills the emptiness my father has left. How can I remake myself from a void?"

Pravin is silent a long time before he speaks: "Perhaps the emptiness is a blessing. Your father once told me, 'Return to the source of the River of life. You must cross the abyss between intangible memory and tangible life.' I'll never forget that. When you feel a great emptiness, there is a promise of great fullness. What do you really want, Ariel? What is your highest will?"

"I want to be like a god, an immortal, to go beyond the human condition. Existence is suffering. Sometimes, when I become too distracted or proud, I forget my vow as you say. Then I cling to what I think I know. I congratulate myself, then fall into fear of loss."

Pravin looks directly into Ariel's blue eyes: "There can be no loss. Your father's destiny calls him as yours calls you. The question is what karmically hinders you from being an immortal? A lifetime is but a ripple on the surface of water. To become immortal you must first be *in* the world. You must find yourself."

Ariel stares into the sky. "My highest will is to be free from conditions—clinging, suffering, pain, death—and I want that for all of humanity."

"You sound like a Buddhist, a Bodhisattva."

"Is Buddhism any different from the will of the heart?"

Pravin answers, "Krishna's song may be the will of the heart. Buddhism sees the heart and soul as ephemeral as clouds in the wind."

"I want to live my life without a self," says Ariel, striving to find the source of his longing. "I often feel bound by my own will. Beauty attracts me, but I want to base my life on truth. I sometimes think I wander because I have no father to guide me. My mother clings to me even though, for her, I am but a living shadow of him. When I was a child, I often felt that Raphael was the light, I was the shadow, and she was the eye that bound us together. Her way of seeing could never be realized. I'm struggling to free myself from her expectations. It's not easy."

Ariel gazes down at the series of switchbacks on the trail behind them. "Luqman. Where is Luqman?" he blurts out suddenly. "I thought he was behind us. I don't see him anywhere . . ."

"Luqman!" he yells.

"Don't worry, he urged us to go on," says Pravin, trying to calm him. "He'll meet us on the way back."

At that very moment, they hear Luqman shouting their names.

"He's over that way!" shouts Ariel, pointing to the south. "How did he get there?"

The swans follow the Sun's path to the south. After Pravin leaves him, Luqman falls farther and farther behind and then wanders off through the bushes, finally coming to a small hut beside a lake. There he encounters an old hermit with three missing teeth, whose first words are, "I've been waiting for you."

Even Luqman is astounded.

"Come in and rest yourself," offers the old man, handing him a steaming brew of green tea.

Luqman takes the tea graciously and sips it: "I have never tasted anything so fine!"

"The condensation of the universal spirit falls from heaven to Earth here," says the hermit, his eyes ablaze. "This tea is celestial dew. What is it that you seek?"

"I have ceased seeking. The holy mother is here with us now. My will is hers. But something disturbs me . . ."

The old hermit smiles, "I know. Let me tell you a story. There once was a poor man who desired to get rich. Walking through a busy street, the poor man saw a man carrying gold. He rushed up, stole some of the gold, and ran. He was caught, of course. When the magistrate asked the poor man how he expected to get away with the gold while so many people were around, he answered, 'I didn't see the people, only the gold'."

Luqman laughs heartily. The old man continues, "You cannot get away with the gold of your own enlightenment and the holy mother if you do not give of yourself to ordinary people. You have emptied yourself and become detached. Though full of ardent devotion to Allah and holy Mary, you don't see people as they really are."

Luqman sighs in recognition.

"You will burn out in ecstasy with too much gold. You need to distribute it to others."

"How can I do that?"

"By seeing humans as mortals, not only seeing the divinity within them. Whenever you see a person, only the slightest touch, or a glance from you will bring vitality to the person, and your own balance with humanity will be restored. I have a mixture here, a solution that, if you take three drops every day, will help you with this."

Gratitude fills Luqman's heart as he sprinkles three drops into his mouth. Feeling the fire in his body fuse with the fluids, a deep peace enters him.

It is then that Luqman hears Ariel calling his name.

"Ariel, Pravin, Krishna! I am here!" he calls out of the hermitage door.

Following the sound of Luqman's voice, Krishna and Ariel come crashing through the brush. Pravin follows immediately behind, the clouds of heaven around him like a shroud. The air becomes silken, the mountains translucent, shining from an inner light that touches them all. Jeweled rocks line the shore of the lake that shimmers like a mirror of eternity.

As the three approach the hermitage, they hear and feel the music of water running through their bodies. They enter to see shelves lined with vials of various shapes and colors. Magical talismans in fine calligraphy hang from the ceiling.

Luqman looks years younger than when Pravin left him not two hours ago. "You seem renewed, Luqman," he says, embracing him. "What has happened to you?"

"I have found true peace."

Pravin addresses the hermit, who is busy fixing more tea for his new guests: "Luqman looks so much younger than when I left him. He is so happy and peaceful now. What magic did you perform?"

The old man's eyes slant, smiling. "The transient body is combustible," he says, offering Pravin a cup of tea. "To achieve immortality is to animate mercury. Animated mercury rises from the conflict of heaven and Earth."

"You speak in riddles."

"You need only surrender your will, and you will feel the solvent coagulating like minerals in your blood. Savitri is within you."

Pravin is stupefied that this man could know of his longing for Savitri. Before he can respond, the hermit commands, "Surrender your quest and you will find yourself."

Suddenly, Luqman laughs wildly, for he sees Pravin as a human being in need.

The hermit goes on: "You need ch'i—prana you call it—the vital spark of life. The body has seven letters in which the burning waters are created. Through these you receive the twelve rays. Your friend has just found the true way of nondoing. His wheels turn while his mind is as still as the lake."

Pravin looks out at the lake and wonders, *How can one take action in the world by being still?* Then he looks at Luqman, whose loving glance pacifies him.

The hermit, aware of Pravin's thought, speaks softly but clearly: "The body alone cannot act. Read the letters of your body and you will feel the *spirit* acting through you. Choose one of the nine elixirs to be prepared. The body must be digested and absorbed, and the nutrients separated from the excrement in the darkness."

Pravin wonders, *By darkness, does he mean what we cannot know—the unconscious?*

The hermit responds to Pravin's thoughts: "The primordial mother can only be touched in the absence of solar light. Fecundation and generation take place in obscurity among the creatures. Seeds, too, germinate in the sunless realms. Healing unfolds in the shadows of sleep. Light destroys fragile substances and enhances those that build structure. Then the mirror of mercury condenses, for every mirror is backed by darkness. After mercury is raised from the conflict of heaven and Earth, it must become fixed with incombustible salt."

Complete stillness fills the old shack. Ariel and Krishna sit enthralled by the understanding they feel in their hearts. The hermit's words have pierced the barriers between intent and speech, between speech and silence.

Yet Ariel feels compelled to ask, "What do you mean—incombustible?"

"Pure with virtue," answers the hermit mirthfully. "You have inner fire, my boy, which is far superior to herbs. Cinnabar produces mercury. You need to find water to match your fire."

"Who are you?" asks Ariel bluntly. "How did you come here?"

"Like you, I sought teachers of wisdom in my youth. Then I did not know that to find the teacher is to taste the elixir, and to taste the elixir is to emerge from black mire and float upon the waters. I did not know how to lock the sperm in my belly and focus my eyes on the axis of the universe. I did not know how to use my will to still my breath, nor that, by stilling my breath, I could draw the Sun, Moon, and stars to my forehead. I did not know how to tend the fire to keep the crucible from boiling over."

"Are you an Immortal?" asks Krishna.

The hermit laughs: "When buried deep, hidden snow and ice last through the summer."

Suddenly, a whirring high frequency sound envelopes them all. In an instant, the hermit and all of his apparatus vanish, including the hut. The others stand, incredulous, looking out at the lake and the sapphire mountains.

Was this all an illusion? Pravin wonders in amazement. Luqman simply sings.

THE SHAPES OF DESTINY

Integration
White of black within white

The solitude
of the soul
participates
in all things.

Christa and Karl

One with Zapana, Christa swims in the darkness. Lifetimes converge in a bubbling froth of emotion as the Rhine's swirling waters unveil her transgressions against God, others, and nature. Floating suspended between life and death, her soul flying upstream while her body drifts downstream, she remembers how the ancient elixir of the Creatrix once enabled her to read the script of the River. It is the same elixir that now drops from her brain and permeates her body, revealing the dynamic shapes of the hidden language. Entranced by the mysteries of the Primal Waters and the Kingdom, she dreams, adrift, she knows not where.

Late that night, when Karl and Yu finally exhaust their conversation, Karl goes into Christa's studio and reflects for a moment on the eerie, mistlike quality and subtle haunting beauty of her painting. All at once he senses her absence.

"Where is she?" he asks, looking over at Yu.

"I saw her leave quite a while ago. She's probably out walking."

380

Karl grabs his fur coat and rushes to the door: "I must find her. I realize now how art follows its own laws. Christa is searching for something that I, too, want to understand."

Already the purple hues of dawn glow in the clouds and reflect upon the meadows and hills. Seeing Christa's footsteps in the dampened Earth, Karl follows her tracks like a mystery within himself until he comes to the Rhine. He looks down into the waves. *Could she have?* He runs along the bank looking for a sign, any sign. The realism of death renders thought useless. He grows pale, realizing he has dreamed this nightmare before. His love, the part of himself that seeks integration, is severed from him. *How could I have not seen her?*

He closes his eyes and then looks downstream. *She is a good swimmer. Surely she would not drown.* His essence reaches for hers. *Where are the gods and goddesses now? Why did I talk so long? My mind has blurred my awareness of her. Her moodiness has bothered me lately.*

"Christa!" he calls aloud.

Now the Sun is soft and pink in the east, casting its hues through the lingering mist in the trees.

Christa feels as though she has been swallowed by a dragon. The wave of deep memories she sought to capture now devours her as she relives the moment in Alexandria when she and Zapana, as one being, split from the dark oriental spirit of Kau Chiang. Is she in purgatory? What realm cradles this confusion? She feels the intensity of the burning waters, as if something were trying to consume itself within her. Macabre visages of the medieval abbot who opposed her move to the nunnery transform into images of Peter, the wild-eyed monk, lunging at her. "Heretic!" Peter shouts. "You shall die!" He drags her through the Alexandrian tumult to the Caesarean Church where she is beaten to death. All at once, she realizes that the abbot and Peter are the same.

She reenters the pain with white fire. There is destruction, invisible power, and unspeakable glory. It is another life, another time. Kisses of death and rebirth—kisses of the burning water—move up and down her spine. As she emerges from the depths of the vision, her mortal sight is blinded, but she has seen. *Love is light,* she realizes. *My name was Hypatia. Now I can release that life as a voluntary sacrifice. Nothing can ever be truly taken from me. Though forms change, the soul is eternal. Yet the Eastern and Western paths have parted. Where is my Eastern soul?"*

The bright word is stuck in her throat. She cannot speak. She was killed for speaking. Kau Chiang was killed for speaking. Hypatia was killed for speaking. Time clashes against the roar of the word, the pain of separation. The body of the dragon undulates through the twisted pathways of the ethers. Peering out of its eyes, she sees Kau Chiang speaking to the Red Bird on Dragon Hill.

Then she hears Kau Chiang speak within her: *Now I join fire and water in my root, heart, and brain. I will run barefoot on the burning sand with love running fluid in my heart. May I come forth to speak with others as in the days of old! May humanity befriend the dragons and spirits and may the Earth turn emerald once again.*

The jewel that charges all waters with compassion looms suspended before her. She looks at its facets through the eyes of the dragon— through the eyes of Kau Chiang. The facets interweave in a multi-dimensional matrix of unspeakable language.

"The jewel is within you," declares the White Tiger, who has appeared from the west. The jewel's luminous colors permeate her chakras as she drifts into the consciousness of the Black Tortoise, who whispers, "Find the one who tells the story of the Tao and whose eyes speak the language of the trees."

When Christa awakes, cold and damp on the riverbank, she realizes that it is *she* who seeks to tell the story of the Tao. She gathers the pieces of her shattered soul into the curves of her heart and lets the burning waters purify her being. She spins in an ocean of cosmic energy, becoming one with Kau Chiang's spirit. She knows there is something beyond memory that cannot be spoken. A beauty born of nothingness, it lies beyond sound, form, and thought. The Green Dragon winds through the milky clouds of the east, dancing with the Sun that kisses her face.

She looks up into Karl's bright blue eyes streaming with grateful tears.

Christa spends the next several days resting in relative silence. When she has fully recovered, she approaches Karl one evening after dinner.

"I am feeling the call of Zen very strongly. There is an alchemy turning within me."

"Yes, go on," responds Karl, knowing Christa is leading up to something.

"My friend Tessho at the Zen center says his father is a roshi at a temple in Japan. I would be welcome there. I thought we might accompany Yu part way on his return to China."

Karl is astonished: "You've already had a monastic life in a medieval nunnery. What can you find in Oriental traditions that is not alive here?"

"You know I've studied the shapes of tradition in symbols. I've painted the tree as symbolized in the Minoan cross, the Mayan cross, and the Toltec and Christian crosses. I'm finished with the cross. I'm called to the circle of Zen."

"What about the circling cross of the swastika? I still haven't healed from its abuse by the Nazis."

"Perhaps that is why you should come," continues Christa. "The swastika is a symbol of the Sun, the triumph of the logos moving across the Earth. Something deep within the swastika itself can heal the past abuse of its power. It is a symbol that calls to the wandering mystic in us both."

"What is it that you *really* want to explore?" asks Karl, somewhat irritated.

"I long for something as ungraspable as the Tao that Yu speaks of. There is something toward which I tend, something unfathomed. I glimpsed it when I was immersed the river, when I didn't know whether I was alive or dead."

"How do you expect to find the unfathomable mystery in a traditional religion like Buddhism?"

Christa hears a voice within: *You have been baptized in the waters of the Rhine and the blood of your love. Zen is the baptism by fire.*

She tries to make Karl understand: "The essence of Zen is not traditional. Buddhism is a *practice*, not a religion."

The voice continues: *Zen is a way of emancipation from suffering. Not only your suffering, but that buried in the history of the Earth. It is suffering born of the human defiance of spirit and nature—born of a refusal to be human.*

"I need the discipline that I cannot give myself," appeals Christa, now very animated. "I suffer still. Through Zen, the Tao shines through."

At that moment, they hear Yu returning from his evening walk. Karl calls him into the room.

"We were just discussing your return to China. Christa wants to go to the Land of the Rising Sun."

"What will she do there?"

"Study Zen."

Yu's face lights up: "Zen is a Buddhist stream of the Tao. Come to China with me and I will show you the root of Zen."

At Yu's words, Christa hears a song beckoning her to the East:

Alchemist's Song of the River

I am the forger of inner transformation.
I am the vulcanism beneath the sea.
I am the the source of all culture in the core of the Earth.
You can find me where birth and death are known as one.
I am the inner force of the person that cannot be revealed.
You can find me in the molten state of metals and the metamorphosis
*   of rocks.*
I am the heat and pressure that forges human integration.
I create magical tools and staffs to guide you on a sleepwalk.
I am the formative power of your awareness.
You can find me in all true healing.
I am the conscious seeing through the light of the spirit.
You can find me wherever will overcomes time.
I am the mythic imagination at the time of the world deluge.

Are you creative fire?
I am the dragon of the deeps.

THE HERO/DEMON

Beholding the inner tensions and outer explosions of the three tongues of the River, the Hero emerges through generation. He remembers the vow he made when the world was formless and empty—when he was whole and innocent. Now the vow shines like a star of immortality, leading him on a journey from youth to manhood and from manhood to becoming the god he knows he is. His call to adventure is a call to rectify the world.

Nevertheless, the warring spirit, soul, body, and mind turn dark within him and within the social order. The divisions of self and other, male and female, and culture and nature manifest as the violence of the emerging heroic ego struggling to overcome the projected enemy of its collective shadow. The old fear of the priests emerges once again—as a fear of the wild, the feminine, and the animal, the sympathy between cell and soul. Seen as Demon, eros swells within a genital cry and twists into the indecipherable rambling of the human psyche. Nations appropriate aboriginal homeland and spread lattices of uniformity throughout the global marketplace. The land itself, pulsating with the life-force of plants and animals, abounds in erotic splendor.

The Hero is wracked by a moral duplicity as he crosses the threshold of his unconscious mind. Should he love the Goddess or kill her? For she appears as a devouring demon when fear enters his soul. Long ago, the torrents of the Heros ran from the Nile to the Yellow rivers as the River divided into currents of those who value the Earth and those who abuse it—currents of those who want reciprocity and those who want domination. Inside the magma of hardening Earth, limestone skeletons were pulverized between humanity's swords and twisted thoughts. The blood of Heros who longed for apotheosis still waters the ground where they once fell.

Horrified at religious warfare's desecration of art and nature, the Hero seeks to defend the innocents and what naturalness remains. But, in time, fearing the mystery of the Goddess, he himself is lured into the black magic of war. The battle changes from railing against the devil to the active slaying of the feminine shadow: Leviathan, Dragon, Hydra, Medusa. Embodied in the chieftain, the warrior, the technocrat, and the politician, the Hero forgets the root of his desire—to love himself and fearlessly surrender to the belly of the Goddess that he may drink the elixir that brings him wholeness. Devoured by fear, not by the Goddess, he appears as the nomadic warlord, creating revolution. Agamemnon, Menelaus, Kubla Khan, and Huascar ride the barren plains of nature, turning the barbed wheels of chariots against the pain of unconquerable love.

Throughout the millennia, Stone Age Heros emerge as imperial conquistadors: Huizilopochtli of the Aztecs, Ares of Greece, and Thor of the Norse. Turanians fought Iranians, Huns invaded the Chinese, the Hyksos stormed the Egyptians, and the Vikings marauded the Celts. Helmeted warriors, plumed with pride, marked the bloody hour of genocide.

In modern times, the Hero's longing for the Goddess manifests in pornography and rape. The underlying cause of mass murder, the death squad, and the torture chamber is lost. Desire and mutilation move together as a weeping soul. The march of progress anesthetizes the wounds of loveless life.

Unconsciously seeking to unite with the Goddess, the Hero becomes the Demon he seeks to slay. From Alexander to Machiavelli, from Napoleon to Hitler, the warring phallus shoots rockets of fire. The thundering Paleolithic hammer escalates through technology until it explodes inside the atom. The bomb of frustrated desire falls into matter, wounds the Earth, and incinerates civilization.

Divided within himself, the Hero still struggles to awake within the mystery of his inseparable Demon. One with humanity and with nature, the Demon falls unconscious in the belly of the Goddess. She becomes a distorted metaphor for the mystical states in which the perennial wisdom infolds into the erotic intensity of the body. One with the proliferation of armaments, the protection of prison, and the strategy of the think tank, the Hero feels he is in conscious control. The division between his ego and his Demon widens.

Finally, the unceasing accumulation of social debris turns the Hero into a statue, his outer shell a mixture of drug-trade plaster and anti-Christ cement and his inner chambers lined with computerized access codes.

His Demon, hacked into pieces and wailing in the wasteland, struggles to reconnect her bloodied tissue and remember the play of the divine plan.

As she watches production and consumption trample the Earth, overcoming the fluid exchange of nature's deeper rhythms, she longs for regeneration in a new culture.

The script of the River eludes those who identify with the symbols of civilization. At first solidified into monumental structures, the symbols now run like fluid in electronic currents, relaying the past and future into holographic virtual realities that brainwash the multitudes.

Banished from the old Kingdom, the Hero and Demon each seek to find the lucid language of the River. They know that, inside the ocean within the Pacific rim, the Land of Zar vibrates with renewed hope. But logos will seize what eros denies, just as eros will seize what logos denies. The bodies of the victimized and the repressed become embedded in the Heroic figure that dominates the plaza of the profane while, silent and anonymous in the biosphere, the mystical body of the Creatrix awaits recognition.

The Quest for a Totem and the Fluid of Life

Generation
Gold of red within white

The life force
of the rainbow snake
renews itself
in ego-death.

Jingo and Channon

By submitting to the aboriginal rites of subincision and circumcision, so rare for a white man, Channon hopes to find the secrets of sex and generation—the secrets of the vital force—and thus regain power himself. *In this fluid essence lies the secret of immortality,* he thinks. Unwittingly, he has put himself in a position to be stripped down to the truth. The experience promises to change him. He has come to recognize the wisdom of Jingo, who continues to confront him. Through Jingo, Channon learns that, although he was once a great shaman, he has thrown away his power.

Now the time for the *pukamuni* ceremony, or funeral rite, has come. Accompanied by his interpreter, Jingo leads Channon into the Outback. They stop at the foot of a witchetty tree that is covered with slithering grubs.

"Here you shall enter the Dreamtime and find what you need."

"Will I find immortality?"

Jingo only grunts.

Channon stands naked, his entire body painted with black charcoal. Magical emblems drawn in white cover his chest. He looks at the grubs on the witchetty tree but says nothing.

Jingo speaks and the interpreter translates: "Lie down and remain here until you reach the lips of the devourer—Typhon, you call him. You must look straight into his jaws until you find your totem. Only then will you be a man. Only a man can find immortality."

Channon lies down on the desert sand. The two men leave quickly. Over the next few hours, the grubs drop from the witchetty tree and swarm over his body. He groans, caught between the terror of being eaten and the compulsion to follow through on his quest. The larvae absorb the perspiration on his chest and limbs, then begin boring into his flesh. Sensation turns into pain and pain into delirium.

For the next several days and nights, Channon endures the stinging grubs and the searing Sun until, out of a bloody vision, he beholds a great golden eye. It seems to say, *I see you, Father, but in all this time you have not seen me.*

Channon feels a sense of familiarity and recognizes the eye as that of an ancient unitive consciousness. His vision is obstructed by the abandonment of his son in Egypt. The air crackles with his remorse as he cries out, "I see you now, my son! Do not leave! I need a successor!"

He beholds the reincarnation of the son that he and Horst, as one soul, seeded through a priestess of the Temple of Amun. Channon's tears mingle with the blood and sweat of his trembling body. Naked, open, rife with fever and pain, he enters death. Within the eye, he seeks to remember something deeper about the time when he was a demigod and was about to impregnate a goddess in a divine ritual to seed a new king. He feels no love for her. Instead, he is repelled—afraid of being enveloped, swallowed. She is like the night, an immense but intangible power over all of nature. He is afraid, and with his fear, his direct contact with nature is lost. He goes into convulsions, part of him repulsed by the flesh and part of him compelled, even as pain now sears his flesh.

As Channon's consciousness shifts, his spirit moves like mist across the Australian Outback. He drifts across the burning desert, taking on the lithe and powerful body of a young aborigine who carries only a dilly bag and spear. He comes to a lake and drinks, but finds the waters bitter. Turning around to leave, he is confronted by a coiled snake staring at him with amethyst eyes, its scales glistening in changing colors. The snake circles around him and then speaks: "I am Ngalijod. Follow me if you would be born a man."

"But I am a man!"

"You are a ghost of a man. The unborn and the dead have lived within you ever since you tried to sever eternity from time and sought to control the world. *Ghosts cannot pretend in my world.*"

Channon's dark flesh becomes translucent. He feels borne aloft on a venture he cannot reverse: "Deliver me to my fate then."

The snake slithers into the acrid water.

As Channon obediently enters the lake, the grubs on his body change into insects that fly off into the vast sky. They transform again into geese, sparrows, quail, eagles, owls, swallows, ravens, and finches—all calling out together, *We are the wings of the life-force. Free us from the madness of humanity. Help us mediate heaven and Earth.* Channon sees their lines of flight reflected as interference patterns on the rippling surface of the lake.

The swirling patterns of the life-force glow in the translucent skin of his spectral body. He is a living *tjurunga*, the aborigine's sacred emblem where the totemic ancestor lives. His essence runs like a silk thread through every particle in the universe. The waters ripple with his slightest thought. The Dreamtime appears to him as a living River in which his boundaries are nullified. He is repulsed by his entanglement in this vibrating tapestry—this symphony of waves where all beings mingle with all other beings, living and dead. He turns away, only to face the gaping jaws of an alligator.

But I am a ghost! Channon thinks to himself, clutching the last threads of reason. *Nothing can harm the dead.*

Waves heave from the alligator's undulating body and thrashing tail: "I am your soul. I wander the Earth in search of a way to escape the wheel of birth and death."

"You? My soul?"

"I am necessity, the inevitable jaws that devour all to which you cling."

Images of his beloved library, his immortality chamber, even his imagined light body, lie impaled on the sharp crystalline mountains of the alligator's teeth. The reptile grinds and chews Channon's memories of Fariba, his mother, and the son of long ago, until only one final treasure remains—his longing for immortal identity.

The alligator speaks: "This desire is so strong that it has hardened into your own coffin, but I can digest anything." Channon writhes in pain, watching his values dissolve and disappear into the alligator's throat. Noxious odors assault him while he beholds his cruel and atrocious deeds from lives past. The longing for eternity dies only as he himself vanishes into the bottomless black gullet and the swirling Primal Waters.

The robes and headdress of the priest, and the crook and flail of the pharaoh float to the surface to be seized by vultures, who fly in red flames toward the consuming light of the Sun. Ngalijod, the Rainbow Snake, reappears and slithers down Channon's throat, spreading its rainbow colors through his entire digestive tract.

Channon falls totally unconscious. The snake clears ancient memories of black magic and reactive karmic imprints from his astral body, where intense, etheric poisons have concentrated from lifetimes of trying to sever the pulse of life from the eternal creative source.

The old priest has died. The remnants of Channon's karma are ground to dust that blows across the plains. Over a period of fifty-six centuries, Channon had sought to withhold the power of self-mastery and free will. Now his own will is lost. For ten days he lies unconscious, incorporating the experiences of millennia. He is shorn of all insignia, stripped to aboriginal truth. His multiple lives rise and set in his sleep, which is his oblivion, his unconscious baptism.

When he awakens, he stretches his boney frame under parched, taut skin. The grubs are gone. The stench of his wounds rises to the sky to be purified while his blood, no longer churning with passion for survival, seeps into the Earth. He is spent, with no before or after, no past or future.

He beholds his son as a real person instead of the shadow of his desires. Across continents and oceans, Erhardt sees Channon in a dream and calls out to him: *For generations I have longed to find you. I have wanted your understanding for having followed my own light. My love for you is eternal, Father.* When Erhardt awakens, he recalls the dream in vivid detail, but has no idea of its meaning. Yet he feels changed.

Jingo arrives on the thirteenth day. He knows Channon has entered the Dreamtime of no past, present, or future, where all spaces are carved like the *tjurunga*, the house of one's totem. Jingo has seen the alligator, the ancient digestive tract of the food chain that so repelled Channon. It is the jaws of the abyss, the vertebrate emerging from the slime of the Primal Waters to stalk the land for sacrificial victims.

Channon opens his eyes to find Jingo standing over him and the hollowed carcass and open jaws of an alligator lying next to his head. He recognizes Jingo as his ancient mentor-shaman from Paleolithic times. He sighs deeply, aware that immortality has lost all meaning and that he lives in the eternal now.

Jingo speaks: "The work is done. The river of generations can flow. Your successor is free of the spell you once cast on him. The circling digits in the sky run in every organic body. Eternity and time live in each other. No more will you cling to the womb of your mother where you can imagine anything you want. No more will you long for an unattainable future. Your body is now a living *tjurunga*."

Channon is emaciated and too weak to respond, but he feels the elixir of the Rainbow Snake moving throughout his body. He is one with the vital force of the All Mother and All Father.

Jingo puts the alligator carcass over Channon and signals two men to carry him back to the village where the flesh of kangaroo and wallaby will revive him.

HEART MEDITATION

Uniformity
Black of red within white

The habits
of the automaton
change
through the heart.

Petruska and Fariba

Despite all her seeking and wandering, Petruska begins to doubt that she will ever be healed. In Beijing, as in all cities afflicted with the erosion of their former culture, daily life is monotonous. A society once rich with dance, theater, and storytelling is now filled with television and newspaper reports of the world's conflicts. It is not the ubiquitous technology itself that troubles her, but the uniformity it seems to impose.

She feels anonymous among the city's millions—not only the Chinese, but the Indians, Africans, and North Koreans who move robotically through the streets like ghosts cased in flesh. She is one among many, and many are the fragments of her original soul. Her outer and inner worlds clash in alienation as once again she feels on the verge of oblivion.

Petruska searches for the scattered fragments of her being in memory. However, she finds that the village near the Shaanxi mountains, where she and her sister long ago knew happiness, is completely changed. Once again, she realizes that the past can never be the present, except in the mind.

She reflects upon how Bear-Looks-Twice brought her original soul back to her awareness. How can she hold it steady? Like ships meeting in the night—one weighed down with the dead and the other with the unborn—she feels her past and future pressing together in the storm of her present.

Still, her search continues, and her interest is piqued by a course in Egyptian healing techniques at Beijing University. It is taught in English and covers reincarnation and karma. Despite her dwindling finances, she decides to attend the class.

The course Fariba teaches focuses on the cosmogony of the *Coffin Texts* and the *Papyrus of Ani*, but her real intent is to distill the ancient Egyptian teachings into a practical way of healing the soul.

On the evening of the first class, Fariba presents an overview to an ethnically diverse and eager group of students: "This course will be taught with the intent that you apply its methods to your own life," she begins. "There is little point in gaining abstract information about Egyptian gods that you cannot practically apply to yourself. Since the attendance is small, there is time for each of you to introduce yourselves and ask any questions you might have."

Each of the students takes some time to describe the reasons he or she is drawn to this particular course. One woman speaks proudly of her enlightening experiences. "Be patient," responds Fariba. "You will find greater peace when you surrender your attachment to sanctity." The others, obviously startled, turn and look at one another.

Another woman asks, "Is it necessary, as you say, to experience hell before being reborn?"

"All opposites arise together," answers Fariba, her gentle strength already becoming apparent. "If you love solitude, you will become an exhibitionist. If you desire beauty, you must first discover the ugly. Too great a desire for gentleness will erupt in violence. Through such contrast the soul learns."

A lithe, gaunt, black man hesitates before speaking: "I want to know the meaning of my dreams, and to be able to dream what I want."

"Your dreams reflect your appetites. In that sense, you do dream what you want. What is it that you want?"

The man looks around furtively: "Someone who loves me."

Everyone sits silently in recognition.

"Thank you for being so honest."

Fariba is pleased with the sincerity of the questions, her bright face lit from within: "In this first class I will present a theoretic overview of the human constitution according to ancient Egyptian theology. It is ourselves we have to work with. We can work with the gods and goddesses later. We have all suffered and undergone untold pain, but also untold bliss. The majority of the Earth's population is both unconscious and unrepentant of the ills it has committed, the suffering it has caused. But there is a living fire that burns inside our hearts and sings aloud to the heavens. It will not go out. This warrior of light within us is our *ab*, our spiritual heart, linking the physical and spiritual aspects of our being. According to Egyptian theology, we are not limited to either our *khat*, our physical shell, or our spiritual being. We are a complex web of interconnected dynamics."

Fariba writes *khat* on the board and draws a human form beside it. Then she draws the hieroglyphic picture of the *sekhem*, a lotus scepter.

"*Sekhem* is the heavenly power that enables us to incarnate. But incarnation itself is not enough to be fully human, let alone to be born into the light. The wisdom of the *ab*, the spiritual heart, must be awakened if you are to be more than an automaton wandering the Earth."

"How can we awaken this spiritual heart?" Petruska asks with obvious sincerity.

Fariba fixes her eyes on Petruska for some time and feels her scarred, fractured heart: "When you join your breath with your intent, the fire in the heart begins to ignite from the center of yourself. Later we will do an exercise to help you with this." Petruska relaxes, feeling Fariba's heart touch her own.

"Is this spiritual heart one with the physical heart?" asks one of the young Chinese men sitting in the back row.

Fariba smiles as she responds: "Veiled in the flesh, it lies between the physical heart and the solar plexus, yet it is the source of impersonal love and intuitive knowledge. Daily *ab* meditation on this center, regardless of the trials you are facing, will open it to an inspired message from heaven—to the radiance of divine intelligence. This heart opening can then heal and guide you out of uniformity and toward wholeness."

Petruska remembers the opening of her heart and the brilliance of her star when Bear-Looks-Twice descended to hell to rescue her soul. But she is unable to keep her heart open. She wonders how shamanism relates to the ancient Egyptian techniques of trance induction.

Clairvoyant, Fariba answers her silent question: "After the fifth week, I will schedule a day-long intensive during which we will practice trance techniques and the meditation methods of the ancient priests and priestesses. We will begin the *ab* meditation at the end of this lecture."

Recalling the failure of her initiation with Manesis, Petruska relishes Fariba's broader patience and acceptance. She senses that she made the right choice in taking the course and feels deeply relieved.

Fariba continues, trying to impart the relevance of Egyptian teachings to current lives: "We incarnate. We swallow the world and are supported and nourished. Then we in turn are swallowed by the world. But the world of becoming is only a part of ourselves, the Osirian part. Osiris is the god who changes, and who gives birth out of death. He was killed by his brother Set, and his members were scattered. But Isis gathered his members together again. Isis represents the power to re-create yourself through your personal witness."

"But what does it really mean to re-create oneself?" asks Petruska. "I feel trampled by fate, unable to make anything of myself. Where is Isis in me?"

"Isis is your spiritual heart, which can begin the process of resurrecting your scattered, disassociated parts. Osiris is an immanent god who suffers with mortals. Though he is dead, he brings revival and fertility, for he is paradoxically the source of all life. Above all, Osiris is identified with the black Nile, the River itself, the watery inundation that brings life to the land. He is the immanent power of change that is also one with the eternal source."

The passion rises in Fariba's voice: "Hear me now. It is imperative that immanence and transcendence never be completely separated. Set, who represents the separation from the Creator, manifests as the automaton."

"What do you mean by automaton?" asks an English woman. "Is it that part of ourselves enslaved by the humdrum aspects of life? I have trouble because I'm always getting distracted. I can feel divinity within me, but I become bound by repetitious thought patterns and habitual routines. Is Set the evil that makes us slaves of habit?"

Fariba considers the question before replying: "Set is the mortal automaton who is ignorant of the true meaning and value of his brother, Osiris. He follows his instincts, mates with Nepthys, and lives by the impulses coded in his genes. Your automaton can perform daily tasks. It believes it can evaluate and make decisions, but it cannot. The modern world is increasingly dominated by the unconscious automaton, which, seduced by technology and brainwashed by rampant materialism, has lost contact with the inner power of the heart. Consequently, the life and death cycles of Isis and Osiris are muted, and the automatic nature of a fragmented life is multiplied. Set, who controls the autonomic functions, is jealous of Osiris because he doesn't understand him. He understands only Osiris's power, not how that power was acquired. So he plots his death. When Set seals his brother in the coffer and floats it down the Nile, he unconsciously cuts himself off from his own creative source. Can't you all recall automatic reactions that have killed the cycle of truth—that have aborted the emergence of self-discovery and creative power?"

"Yes," blurts out Petruska, "but I feel helpless to change! Has Set taken possession of my soul?"

"Had he taken possession, you would not be here. Have patience with yourself, my dear."

Fariba stares out at the faces trying to grasp her point, then continues with her lecture: "According to Egyptian theology, you have two souls—the *ba* and the *ka*. They are both psychic and cosmic forces. Each of you has your own *ka*, which is expressed as outreaching, embracing arms. The *ka* is a creative and preserving power of life. Your *ka* is your double, and when you die it lives on. The *ba*, on the other hand, is the universal soul that is one with the gods. It appears as a bird." Fariba draws the hieroglyphs for *ka* and *ba* on the blackboard.

Petruska reflects that it must have been her *ka* that saved her when she walked through so many incarnations of darkness. Some power within her invoked a presence that could deny the nightmares of guilt and fear.

"What is the point of learning these functions of the human being?" Fariba's question brings Petruska back to the present.

"To know ourselves—even if we don't like it," responds an older Chinese woman whose steady voice breaks into light laughter.

"Yes. We have little experience of the high vibrational power of our divine *kas*. For the most part, we are automatons, controlled by our organic functions and emotional reactions to external events. We are conditioned, both by evolution and culture, so that the higher functions of consciousness cannot fly to the spirit. Why do you think that is?" Fariba looks out intently at the diverse faces.

"I am caught by distractions in the world!" replies a Turk.

"I get bored and tend to give up," admits a Korean girl.

"I don't know what flying to the spirit means, except when I first met my husband," offers a young African woman. "How can I reach that state again?"

Fariba nods: "To do so, we must first become a witness to the automatic nature of our lives. Then we need to eliminate the personal point of view that was so necessary to the first awakening of consciousness. The personal witness desires personal experience, but it gradually learns not to identify with it. Then the heart can open, and you can begin to experience an energy flow that you all felt as children. With that, your intuitive mind can receive the ecstatic energy that clears all ills. The aim of this course is to make it clear that we can heal deeply only by uniting with our divine *ka*—by getting in touch with our personal witness and opening our heart."

The students try to comprehend what Fariba is saying. One of the Americans asks, "When our heart unites with the divine *ka*, do we lose all individuality?"

"No, but your individuality is no longer tied to a personal point of view. Individuality is expressed through the center of your *ab*, your spiritual heart that mediates between your automaton and your *ka*. Through your spiritual heart you tap the root of the *ka*, the true source of individuality. But it needs the animating spirit of the *ba*, which is impersonal."

"I don't understand the difference between the *ka* and the *ba*," admits a young Chinese man.

"The *ka* is what distinguishes individual souls. It is the link with the Creator. You cannot comprehend the higher *ba*, for it is a free spirit that links with the human only through consciousness. Both the *ba* and *ka* operate in the soul as well as in the world. The *ba* and *ka* interact, but the cosmic soul of the *ba* is in everything. It is the breath that creates life and can never be extinguished. The cosmic power of the *ka* bears the vital force from your regenerative system and manifests in the world of form and substance."

"I sense that the *ba* takes care of itself," concludes the Chinese man, who decides to let part of his question go unanswered.

"Everything takes care of itself if you open your heart, feel deeply, watch what is happening, and allow yourself to expand to higher frequency energies."

The classroom fills with a silence that is finally broken by Petruska's question: "What happens if our heart never unites with our divine *ka*?"

Fariba speaks from an inner voice: "In some sense, you become a wandering ghost at death. In your next incarnation, it will be yet harder to link with your divine *ka*. You identify with the automaton and have no notion of your true identity or your destiny. Moment by moment, cycle by cycle, life after life we must follow the inner sense of our *ka* through the intelligence in our *ab*, our spiritual heart. To put it simply, what I intend in this course is to give guidance on discerning the difference between the automaton, your personal witness, your heart, and your divine *ka*, so that the delusions brought about by your past conditioning can be rectified. Unless the automaton becomes conscious of the *ka*, you are little more than an animal following its instincts."

"Are you saying that the personal witness is the consciousness of *both* the automatic nature of the body *and* the divine *ka*?" asks the English woman.

"In simple terms, yes. To unite the consciousness of both, we must link with Osiris, the personal witness that records our continuity as individuals. Those who lose the Osiris witness shatter into many automatons. It is the destiny of Horus, the divine son of Osiris, to redeem us from karmic chains. Yet, from his lofty vantage point as the hawk or falcon, Horus is pure spirit and cannot easily be grasped. Your divine *ka* resides in heaven, but you must be *conscious* of it or you remain an automaton. Then the *ka* will never nourish the emergence of your true individuality. When the blissful energy of the spirit spreads from your heart to your entire body, you can feel the wings of Isis embracing you. Your heart energy gathers your fragments together and brings them to life. Thought, bone, and blood burst into a flight of ecstatic union, whereupon Horus is conceived as a great eye, a vision of wholeness."

Fariba gazes into the eyes of all her students and, with feeling, continues: "Otherwise, as automatons, we have a massive unconscious population explosion and untold problems upon the Earth. If we cannot give up pills, alcohol, or cigarettes, how can we stop war, famine, and pollution? Civilization reflects the degree to which humanity truly individualizes or remains an automaton. The spreading of a uniform electronic technology through computers and television is not evil. Set has a place—to wire the world together even through the fragmentation process. However, to redeem the world is to open our hearts. Then our vision opens and we can see how things are. We can begin to change the world by changing ourselves."

"Do the scattered members of Osiris represent the fragmentation of the world?" asks a stout man from Brussels.

"Yes. In the Osirian liturgy, the places where the members of Osiris were scattered became shrines. But for the sacred to emerge in the midst of a uniform modern world, the center of yourself must not only ignite but burn constantly and consume the reaction of the mechanical person. You must live from your center. Otherwise, repetitive habits may lead to annihilation of the soul."

"You mean a soul can be annihilated?" asks Petruska, suddenly gripped by fear.

"Not as long as there is some consciousness of both the automaton and the divine *ka*. But the personal witness and heart simultaneously must collaborate with the *ka*. Then cosmic consciousness, symbolized by the Eye of Horus, is continuously present."

"How can we know if this collaboration is happening?" asks the English woman.

"If you give your power to another, *especially if you feel you love them,* you forfeit your own soul. This is addiction, a sign of losing touch with your witness. But if you try to dominate others in order to prove yourself, you will lose contact with the *ka*. The personal witness can also be termed *mindfulness* or *awareness*. Such mindfulness is under voluntary control, but the opening of the heart is involuntary. The heart energy drawn up in rapture allows you to surrender to the divine *ka*. You are not only made whole, but you are vitalized and ecstatic."

"When I give my power away," interjects Petruska, gesticulating with her hands, "I get angry and often do something destructive to myself or someone else. Then I feel guilt, which leads to my giving my power away again. I'm so tired of this!"

She pauses, then continues in a calmer manner: "I know I am a star in heaven, but on Earth I feel trapped in this vicious cycle. I am out of touch with my heart most of the time. I cannot control my thoughts. My mind wanders day and night. Often I feel alienated. What can I do?"

"Don't feel bad," responds Fariba compassionately. "You are a witness to vicious cycles, which have caught us all at one time or another. But you have also lived with truth and love in your heart or you would not know the difference. You have had moments of re-creating yourself when you witnessed your powerlessness, cried for direction, and took action. You came here. Forgive yourself and breathe, for breath is the link between your automaton and consciousness. Become more aware of your breath and allow your heart to expand."

Realizing that this is an opportune time to introduce the *ab* meditation, Fariba asks everyone to form a circle. As they position their chairs, a common sense of unity and purpose becomes tangible. After a while the fidgeting stops, and everyone becomes silent and still. Fariba speaks from her place in the circle: "Sit with your spine straight. Observe your breath passing in and out of your nose. You are a sentinel to the door of your house. Watch your thoughts as they come and go, without judging or blaming—either yourself or others. This is social conditioning that has contributed to the automatic process, and we have all suffered from it. Let it be. Just breathe. Watch your breath, your thoughts, and your feelings as they arise and disappear."

Each person centers and breathes. One by one, hearts ignite and pulse with power. Thoughts pass through. Recollections murmur. Fears arise. Wills seek to hold hearts steady. Minds run off, but hearts watch through them from the centers of being. Forgetfulness spreads until the witnesses renew themselves. All persons watch in their own time, in their own way. Slowly, steadily, the hearts awaken the delusions of the wandering minds, as the ecstatic wings of Isis fan throughout the circle, nourishing each soul with awareness of the eternal now.

THE DIALECTICS OF CULTURAL PARADIGMS

Revolution
Red of red within white

The trail
of history
flails
in search of purpose.

Henshaw

About two hundred people have assembled in a New York hotel for Professor John Henshaw's lecture and workshop on his new book, *The Dialectics of Cultural Paradigms*. The work has been lauded as an imaginative analysis of periodic cultural crises and transitions.

Henshaw, now sixty-six-years old, paces back and forth while those attending settle into their seats. When the hubbub has diminished, the moderator informs the audience that questions are encouraged if they are pertinent to the discourse. Henshaw looks out at the expectant men and women, his steel-blue eyes gleaming through his glasses. He centers himself until everyone is quiet, then begins:

"Has the hubris of Western civilization—based on science, technology, national sovereignty, and a world economic market—destroyed the freedom it so highly values? After two catastrophic world wars and innumerable others, humanity remains undeniably divided. I want to differentiate civilization from culture here. Any social collective that creates and uses tools, language, art, and ritual comprises a culture. I reserve the term *civilization* for more complex collectives in which institutions, technology, and art are informed from diverse cultures.

"I have based my interpretations on archaeology and scripture, two primary sources. You will find specific references in my book. Here I shall only highlight the general trends.

"What are the cultural patterns that have worked in the past? Why are some revolutions liberating and others debilitating? Is it possible for a civilization to endure through vast periods of time, or do all eventually disintegrate? How did humanity fall into such addiction and confusion? How can we regenerate ourselves from the destructive habits that envelope us? These are questions I'd like to address today.

"My work addresses the relevant questions about cultural processes. I believe the fourfold dialectic described in my book can help with this. It is necessary to review history, and even prehistory, in order to transcend our current mindsets.

"Let me review how the fourfold dialectic works for those who are unfamiliar with it. In this dialectic, the *thesis* and *antithesis* give way to a process of *synthesis*. But the fourth phase of *paradox*, or what I also call *metathesis*, is crucial if the dialectic is to be regenerative. In cultural evolution, the thesis is a source, a sacred gift, whereas the antithesis is a societal response to the source. The antithesis is always a polarity, a crucial separation or choice point. It involves human will. Sometimes it manifests as antagonism. The synthesis is a reconciliation of the thesis and antithesis, often becoming a cultural tradition, for culture seeks to preserve and remember what it values. The paradox is a contradiction, for it destroys and yet brings renewal to all the previous phases. In the deepest spiritual sense, paradox manifests as a relinquishment of the self toward a revelation of the divine. It is through the divine in the human, and the human swept up into the fires of the divine, that the cultural paradox presents itself. It reveals the purpose and fulfillment of the original gift, the thesis.

"The teleological nature of the dialectic is unmistakable to those who observe and reflect. To look out and then look within is to complete the cycle as a way of being in creative relationship with God, nature, and one another. In other words, I believe there is a purpose built into cultural evolution. Let me use the blueprint of a house as an example. Its purpose is not only to manifest in a structure but to manifest in a place where the design itself enhances the richness of the life ongoing within it. It results in something new—something unexpected and creative.

"In a study of cultural evolution, I believe we must include the primordial patterns of the creation of the universe, for light affects life as life affects consciousness, and it is consciousness that responds to crises and recognizes new cultural paradigms.

"The origin, or thesis, must embrace the awareness that the light waves of which all of creation is composed are a sacred gift. The thesis is always a gift. Ultimately, a gift is given, a priori, from the silence and darkness of the Creator. The gift is sacred. The eloquence of divinity shines in all light waves that beam across the expanse of nothingness.

"If we forget to appreciate this source, we experience only conflict in the antithesis, and we foul the result with our tampering. But in reality, we live in a fountain of light that is a mystery. What is light? What is a photon? Its place is nowhere and its mass equals zero. It can be seen as a divine thought speeding across the void."

The audience seems intrigued by Henshaw's cosmic perspective. He goes on: "When an electron or proton emits a charge, it makes a choice. The antithesis is always a polarity, a choice. Our modern awareness is only on the edge of seeing that every particle in the universe has consciousness, but this is the vantage I am taking. It is an old animistic viewpoint. How can choice or differentiation be possible if it is not inherent in subatomic particles themselves? The possibilities of freedom of choice open to these first divine agents. Through positive or negative charge, up or down spin, centripetal or centrifugal motion, they polarize and then combine to create the harmonic chemistry of the universe.

"The synthesis here is the circulation of energy. In the case of light waves, particles are messengers that have memory and that circulate the harmonic information of the cosmos.

"Every event, then, is conditioned by memory: memory of resonance and dissonance and a perception of the world. And the result is the creation myths of the archaic peoples. These myths emerged in the face of the awesome mystery of light and the information that light transmits about the forms of creation. The paradox lies in the fact that, through creation myths, one can glimpse the gift of light and reveal its direction through life and consciousness. When they are enacted ritually, creation myths fulfill the renewing purpose of perpetual gratitude for the gift and understanding of the process."

A young woman raises her hand and asks, "Are you saying myths *still* have a renewing purpose?"

"Yes. Through myth we re-create the world in the human image. The archaic language of myth is lush in imagery and metaphor that reveal hidden meanings under the efflorescence of story. The mythic process flows from the River of the spirit into the chaos of the unconscious and rises with collective creativity. Myth holds the memory of a way, the polarity of tendencies, and the renewing purpose of the gift. This way of looking at the unfoldment of culture can be observed in the dialectic of the paradigm shift. Paradigms are the myths of the modern world."

Henshaw looks out at the audience, then continues: "A true paradigm shift always occurs between the fourth phase of metathesis and a new thesis. Otherwise, the changes are either antagonistic or revolutionary. The fourth position of paradox both contains the original gift and simultaneously brings forth creativity. When a paradigm becomes too self-conscious and rigid, it shatters and a shift takes place. A culture then breaks down and stands on the edge of a dark abyss, unknowing of the new paradigm that will be born.

"We are in such a period now, but to understand, we must forgo an easy answer and expand our view. The archaic peoples were more in touch with what we term the unconscious than we are. In fact, it was probably not unconscious to them at all. We live amid one large sound—one stream of light—but don't know it. We are a chorus seeking to understand how the orchestration of creation—the crucial gifts, the ways of continuity and discontinuity, the paradigm shifts—can be seen in perspective over thousands of years. We might then break through to the unconscious and pull forth creative possibilities. We might find a greater resonance with the trend of the cosmos as a whole and harmonize with the oscillating rhythms of the divine plan.

"To obtain this perspective, let us touch upon the paradigm shifts experienced by our ancestors during the cultural transitions from hunting to agriculture to the city-state and to our modern civilizations."

Henshaw takes a drink of water, gazes out at his audience and breathes deeply before he begins again: "The emergence of hominoids took millions of years, but culture accelerated once tools were used and symbolic signs were engraved on rocks. It is as if the cosmos were enfolded in the human mind to accelerate the transformation of nature into culture through art and tools.

"Let us imagine what the essential patterns of the dialectic might have been in Paleolithic times. We know from cave paintings that the hunting culture developed art, magic, and tools and lasted for thousands of years. The cave of the underworld, the unknown to our Paleolithic ancestors, must have been a mysterious womb from which a sacred gift could be born. The first gift beyond that of light itself was *vision*, the inner life of the imagination. Under the pitch-black sky perforated with stars, our ancestors awakened to speak to the Suns that illumined both eye and mind.

"It is the rich inner world of *Homo sapiens* that distinguishes us. Most of the creative anatomical potential of organic life had been exhausted two million years before the Paleolithic era. All manners of form, color, and chemistry had evolved before humans walked the Earth. Animals excel in size, power, and speed. What sets us apart is our ability to imagine, remember, and anticipate."

Henshaw gestures from heaven to Earth in a large, quick, sweeping motion. "Where lightning struck was a gift. To take the fire and use it for light, warmth, and cooking was to choose. The fire of the Sun gods came to Earth in lightning, but the control of fire was born of the firestick.

"The use of fire by the Paleolithic hunters was more significant than any subsequent discovery. Control of fire was the antithesis to the gift of vision in the dark unconscious of humans emerging out of the prehistoric Ice Age. The axis of the human spine and nervous system was ignited through the control of fire. The antithesis receives and becomes an agent of choice. Will added to imagination creates action. In some sense, fire outwardly mirrors the inner life, the imagination drawn down as a gift from heaven."

Henshaw imaginatively enters the world of the hunter: "Fire has light, heat, and power: light to overcome the fear of nocturnal predators, heat for cooking and bodily warmth, and power to change the face of nature.

"When the inner life was awakened and fire was controlled, language and ritual emerged as a synthesis, a sacred way of life. To our hunting ancestors, the inner and outer realities rolled together like waves teeming with magic and animism. Sticks, stones, and stars had life. This animistic universe is largely denied to modern awareness and is therefore unconscious. Language and ritual moved from unconsciousness to imagination, and from the perilous, celestial excess of the inarticulate body of the cosmos toward meaning. Language and ritual were blood listening, body harkening, and bone drumming in response to the gifts of light, fire, and imagination in the dark unconsciousness. Gestures, sounds, and actions became a way to express and regulate the wild, creative, welling-up from within. The synthesis of ritual and language was a reconciliation of the inner and outer worlds through memory, which then became tradition.

"Tradition and culture served to ward off the unpredictable and frightening aspects of life. The hurling of creation through chaotic whirlpools, waves, thunder, and volcanoes awakened awe and wonder, but also fear. Culture emerged with pattern recognition—something familiar recalled. To remember was to find pattern. The half-divine human stared out of the primeval jungle of unconscious energies and recorded the dance and word in the brain. With memory, the continuum of nature's glissando stream fell neatly into harmonic patterns that began to articulate the cosmos through human song, dance, and symbol.

"Culture emerges as a ritualization of significant patterns that reconciles the inner life with the environment. Human beings are born and pass away, but language and ritual remain as ways of honoring the sacred gift of life. The synthesis of language and ritual then becomes a myth, a cosmic story that offers some order and predictability to the troubled heart."

"What is the paradox in the Paleolithic hunting culture?" queries an elderly gentleman at the side of the room.

"For the Paleolithic people, the thesis of the inner life revealed its purpose through the paradox, or metathesis, of totemic magic. The animals particularly were revered, and their powers were taken on through totemic rituals and art. The cave paintings are full of such magic. To exercise this magic was to surrender one's will to the spirit of the animal. The animal then changed from a feared enemy to a spiritual power. The totems became a form of identity and creative power that was one with the forces of nature. The unconscious was recognized, absorbed, and transformed.

"In our modern culture, the killing of an animal without connection to its spirit is a profane act that our hunting ancestors could never have imagined possible. Before hunting, they thanked the animal spirits. The sacred and profane were completely united in this action, for empathy with the 'other' is the basis of the sacred.

"Now let me move on to the second major revolution in culture that, though inherent in the first, turned from the magical identification with animal powers to the control of fertility of the fields. During the Neolithic agricultural revolution, sometime around 9000 B.C., a dramatic shift took place. When paradox evolves into a new thesis, the polarity in the paradox shifts to a new focus. Totemic power was largely a male process. But the women who gathered berries and grains had a deep understanding of the cycle of birth, death, and rebirth in the spirit world. They experienced the continuity of sexuality, death, and afterlife in their own lives, in the seasons, and in the ways of the plants and animals.

"The male-dominated hunting period shifted more toward the feminine through the domestication of plants and animals. Sex became ritualized as a method of control. The love and war of the sexes has a convoluted history, but here I want to stress that life became eroticized through awareness of fertility cycles within the body and the Earth."

"Do you mean that the people were more aware of sexuality in Neolithic times?" asks a woman. "Or did the roles of male and female simply shift?"

Henshaw paces back and forth a few times and then gazes into the woman's eyes as if looking for an answer there: "During Paleolithic times, the ithyphallic birdman of Lascaux represented the climactic, discontinuous male principle. He was juxtaposed with the enduring continuity of the feminine associated with the bison. In the Neolithic era, the male became the sacrificed god and later the phallic pump that died into the spacious watery womb of the Goddess. The female shifted from being a *symbol* of fertility to being a conscious *active agent* in bringing fertility to the land. The myths shifted from the animal totem ancestors of male societies to those of the sacrificed god of the Great Goddess.

"In Neolithic times, the ritualization of work through the seasons mirrored the human cycles of birth, growth, death, and rebirth. The mother who gave birth also brought death. The reconciliation or synthesis of the agricultural revolution was the enactment of the eternal return within nature and within the body of the Goddess, who held the sacred and profane together.

"The Neolithic people saw the land as a fertile gift, a bounty to be drawn out and controlled. The environment became more responsive to humans. The pig, duck, ox, sheep, and goat were domesticated along with the hunter's dog. The horse became a draft animal. Edible beans, aromatic seeds, juicy flesh, and colorful flowers emerged as alchemy within the vessels of staked fields. The male became a husbandman as domestication of animals helped balance the sexes. Cooking, fermenting, dyeing, and brewing took place in womblike pots, baskets, and vats. The emphasis was on protection, storage, and continuity as opposed to risk and danger in the unpredictable wild.

"The Neolithic metathesis evolved as capital emerging in the storage bins of grain grown by the women. The irony lies in the fact that although the village was rooted in the protective womb of the Goddess, it produced capital that could be stolen, bartered, or sold by men. The split between the sacred and profane began here, when God as man sought control of the wealth. This split mirrored the division of the interior life from the exterior life, which in earlier times were a unified experience. Consequently, no true paradox was attained.

"The division between the sacred and profane severed intrinsic values from money and goods. Humans became blinded to the Epiphany of nature herself. The spirits in the plants and animals were valued less than the foods of their flesh.

"And so, in the third millennium B.C., the golden grain, ripened in the Sun, gathered, and stored, became the consummate gift of yet another revolution—that of the city-states. The sacred became profane insofar as the *source* of food, fertility, and abundance was forgotten. Consequently, what might have been cooperation between nature and humans developed into the exertion of humans *over* nature. Nature became a resource to exploit rather than a gift to cultivate through the gardens of the heart.

"The numinous mystery of nature and the Goddess began to be denied and became unconscious. But it became more threatening in the underworld of the human psyche than if it had been consciously integrated. Throughout history, what humans refuse to face becomes increasingly unconscious and eventually erupts in irrational seizures, orgies, and violence.

"In the great river valleys where the Neolithic villages accumulated wealth, fire and earth were fused into metals. Swords, plows, spears, and wheels emerged as a male effort to control wealth through both domestic and military powers.

"Strangely, during the emergence of the city-states, it was in the domain of the sacred—in the temples—that priestly power dominated the populace. Priests controlled the sacred knowledge—the symbols that became scripture—just as merchants controlled the capital spilling over from the agricultural revolution. But authentic priests and priestesses kept the sacred way through prayer and ritual, their own divinely directed consciousness providing a link between the gods and goddesses and the Earth.

"The synthesis of the city-states was reflected in a theocratic, hierarchical caste system and an inflexible bureaucracy. Bureaucracy is an ancient code of mechanical operation of a megamachine model that has been transmitted from civilization to civilization to this day. Once established, there was no limit to the number of people the bureaucracy could control. The methods were geometric rather than organic in form—accurate in measurements, colossal and regimented in the organization of the working force. Standards of weights, measures, language, and laws overcame the isolationism of the Neolithic village, but they imposed hierarchical orderly knowledge from above. At this time, the regularity of the gods of the sky dominated the Goddess of the Earth. There emerged a trust in the lofty, distant, regular, and predictable orbits of the planets, Sun, and Moon, guided by priests and ruled by the king or pharaoh. Insofar as the city-states were truly theocratic and the priests sought to divine heaven's will, benevolence prevailed. But corruption eventually emerged in most high places.

"In the city-states, the social pyramid consisted of only two classes: the dominant minority, who were privileged with wealth and leisure, and the majority who were condemned to a life of hard labor. Submission and obedience divided not only male and female but the rulers and the ruled. Everyone had a place, but they could not change places."

While Henshaw pauses to sip some water, a man in the audience offers a question. "But the greatest monuments of civilization were created by this authoritarian system: the pyramids and temples of Egypt, the Yucatan, China, Sumeria, and Babylonia. How do you explain exploitation and grandeur as simultaneous phenomena?"

"Civilization stands on the bodies of slaves and summons many from a hierarchy of gods. But the dead cannot speak. The monuments reflect an intelligence accelerating the civilization process and a connection to the divine source. The priests used the telluric and heavenly forces in conjunction for the timing of rituals and the placement of temples. They were aware of an energy field that pervades the entire universe, and they used this energy to enhance the kingdom.

"The paradox of the city-states lay in the emergence of the power to understand and control yet more energy of the Earth and Sun, even though the cost in human lives was great. For a paradox to be fully regenerative, however, the offering of life, labor, and capital must be *voluntary*. Then it becomes sacred. When it is forced, the paradox reverts back to the antagonism of the antithesis, and a reconciliation or synthesis is not fully achieved. A wholly profane paradox or metathesis is impossible."

The same man continues his thought: "I'm astounded at the greatness and endurance of the ancient civilizations. Extreme intelligence was represented in what they did, whether they forced the populace or not."

"Yes, civilization accelerated at an unprecedented rate during the time of the city-states. Written records, measurements, astrology, geometry, anatomy, medicine, and mathematics all came under kingship. You are right, sir. The achievements were impressive, and the origin of kingship was divine, but when secular powers seized control, the interior life of the common people became repressed. The sacred link with the Goddess and the mysteries of nature were driven underground. The repressed side was forced into a collective unconsciousness that later, in the Middle Ages, erupted in magic and occultism."

At this point, Henshaw stops and removes his lapel microphone: "With these issues in mind, please break into discussion groups of not more than twenty. I will resume the lecture in one hour."

While some take an intermission, most assemble into circles. Henshaw wanders among the groups until, to his surprise, he sees Fariba. She stands up and they go aside.

"My, my!" he exclaims, opening his arms. "I didn't expect to see you here. What a pleasant surprise!"

"How could I miss your lecture, my friend?" she responds after they embrace. "You are, as usual, covering the breadth of life that rises amidst the forms of culture. You always give perspective to my more specialized studies."

"I thought you were in China."

"I've just returned. My courses are over for a while. May I ask a question?"

"Of course."

"Do you think that the progression of civilization and the growth of unconsciousness are inevitably in tandem, or is it possible to integrate cultural order with nature's more chaotic rhythms?"

"As you know, nature only seems chaotic when we live in fear of the unknown. Integration is possible when we realize how unconscious we are and begin to embrace what we fear. Tribal peoples who have never severed the sacred and profane live in a culture integrated with nature."

"But we cannot revert back to archaic ways of life," protests Fariba, looking slightly disturbed.

"No, the new culture will take a form unknown to us now. The key is the unity of the sacred and profane."

Fariba grows more calm as she clarifies her thoughts: "The Egyptian priests had great wisdom. They knew the sacred techniques that could awaken the unconscious automaton to the cosmic and transcendent. But this was possible only through witnessing honestly while feeling deeply. I agree that the turbulence of nature must be felt and embraced before fear transforms to exaltation. But then, with expanded heart and clear mind, the unconscious automaton can awaken to the service of the cosmic purpose."

Henshaw shakes his head: "I believe what you say is true, but will a significant portion of the population ever see this, let alone dare to undergo such transformation? The collective shadow looms large. I hope for such realization, Fariba. I work for it. But something yet unknown to us needs to intervene. We must actualize a synthesis and metathesis on a global level. Then I believe something new will grace humanity, bringing transformation on an unprecedented scale, in spite of ourselves."

He glances at his watch: "My dear, let's continue this after the lecture. Tomorrow I have the whole day free."

"Can we spend tomorrow together? It's so good to see you."

"I'll meet you in the hotel lobby at nine in the morning."

Henshaw takes a few minutes to gather himself before resuming the lecture. He watches the audience reassemble, feeling heartened that Fariba is there. He breathes deeply, glances around at the attentive faces, and begins:

"During the break, I heard some of you questioning whether the dialectic reflects natural stages in the completion of a purpose or whether it is merely imposed thought. This is a good question. I regard the dialectic as a useful intellectual tool for modeling how nature and culture evolve or devolve.

"The more unconscious humanity is, the wider the split between the sacred and profane and the greater the degeneration of both civilization and nature. This fracturing tendency is an incomplete dialectic, remaining stuck in the antithesis wherein a dominant tier of society represses the rest. Revolutions overturn rulers, but they often lead to other forms of oppression.

"Let us continue our survey of human culture through the Axial Age of Prophets, the Middle Ages, and on into urban capitalism. In the era that Karl Jaspers and Lewis Mumford call the Axial Age of Prophets, the ordinary person revolted inwardly against the autocracy and social rigidity of the city-states. This led to a spiritual revolution. In a relatively short period, from 900 to 500 B.C., the inner life emerged so virulently and powerfully that it threatened kings, who were astonished at the large followings created by some invisible power.

"The prophets initiated a new thesis of enlightenment. It was to be achieved through spiritual practices that required facing one's greatest fears, and it often meant undergoing social exile and persecution. It came through the deep unconscious and therefore frightened rulers who were in denial. The prophets, who emerged as illuminators of the poor and downtrodden, were themselves from the laboring class. Amos was a shepherd, Hesiod a farmer, Socrates a stonecutter, Jesus a carpenter, Paul a tent-maker. Confucius was chronically unemployed and not welcome at court. Buddha was born a prince, but renounced it in his quest in the wilderness.

"The possible enlightenment of the common person recapitulated the gift of vision and the inner life known to the Paleolithic hunter. A new choice was available: to base one's work on devotion to God and service to one's fellow humans.

"The difference was motivation. The accessibility of spiritual experience to the common person made voluntary worldly work possible, and the work that emerged was the astonishing antithesis of this new revolution. All classes could participate in the axial religions. It was as if the stream of creation were working toward a new synthesis in which the daily rhythms of life enabled greater participation in creation through prayer, farming, and craftsmanship. To become a whole human being was to reject the curse of forced labor and to bring joy back into work as a part of a community.

"Monasteries emerged out of the Axial Age of Prophets as a social synthesis, built from the commitment of *free* people. A new class of masons, monks, and nuns brought discipline, offering spiritual service to the community and enabling production of the arts, wine, and cheese. The monastic integration of work with moral aesthetic expression created an unprecedented social security.

"The early monasteries drew upon the harmonics of the mystery of the universe to find the patterns that could both liberate the soul and sustain the body. The unconscious reservoir, tapped through spiritual discipline, became a wellspring of creativity. Glorious cathedrals, illuminated manuscripts, stained glass, sculpture, and music brought spiritual fire and light into material form. Guilds were formed. Art and spiritual practices became in themselves a memory bank, a tradition that guided multitudes and gave them hope. This social security became a way of life, based on the awareness that what humanity shared in the cosmic matrix of nature and spirit superseded the power of any particular group or king.

"Any organization, to be sustainable, must cooperate with nature and give thanks to God. This is worship, from which comes all harmonic growth and fulfillment, resulting in a peace that makes war unthinkable. The creative tension of flourishing arts is revelatory, enabling one to be more fully oneself and bonding a community.

"The creative metathesis that emerged from the monasteries was the mystery play, the pilgrimage of the soul—the spirit journeying in body and mind to rediscover its source. In Asia, the story of Buddha's life and the places of his pilgrimage served the same purpose. The wealth of the monasteries was in the meaning and beauty of the art as well as the lands and temples."

Henshaw takes a question from a gentleman in the audience who says, "I believe the monasteries were an attempt to bring the sacred back into an increasingly profane way of life. But, by setting themselves apart, didn't the monks emulate the discipline and structure of the city-states? Also, what do you think about fear of the opposite sex, which was institutionalized in monasteries?"

"Yes, there were aspects of both wholeness and denial in the monasteries. Sexual energy became redirected toward devotion to God. The threat and distraction of the opposite sex was abolished, but so was the possibility of full cooperation.

"The monastic way of life reached a fully regenerative paradox only among visionary heretics who kept alive the illuminative way of embracing opposites. It seems impossible for society as a whole to sustain the phase of paradox. Perhaps the Cathars lived in this dangerous interior terrain where one's lifestyle was more important than one's conformity to outward rituals. Certain Sufi and Zen orders at particular periods also attained this state. But most monastic orders were orthodox syntheses and were eventually more characterized by conformity than revelation.

"The irony of monasticism was that the thrift and discipline of devoted monks led to worldly success. Gradually, as the guilds expanded, a mercantile world emerged, split off from spiritual and aesthetic values. The gap between wealthier and poorer guilds grew, especially when machines were incorporated to increase the production of those who could afford them.

"Again, with a splitting of the sacred and profane, the creative energy in the mystery plays, arts, and crafts was converted back into the antithesis, in which the spiritual and material values were in conflict. The arts and temples in themselves were not in conflict with the spiritual intent, but they became so when they were used primarily for profit.

"With the rise of the machine, the aesthetic quality of the entire human experience was reduced. No longer were the heart and hand synchronized to reveal the patterns that would open people to the grander cosmos. The machine took over weaving, printing, the making of bowls, and even locomotion. This furthered the relinquishment of the sacred to the secular, and a new thesis of progress emerged.

"The pain of repression produced by the strictly secular life created a longing for transcendence, which became part of the progress thesis. Again, this new thesis did not spring out of a true metathesis, embodying creative paradox, but instead reverted back to the antithesis of worldly work. The sanctity of work that predominated during the early monastic period almost disappeared.

"When one works only for money, and the sacred aspect of the human being is not engaged, the wholeness of the will is lost. One is then motivated only by external rewards that can be manipulated by others.

"Historically, the desire for a more prosperous life lured people to work harder. But, separated from the sacred source and the intrinsic rewards in work itself, humans became more vulnerable to addiction. This became the cultural and economic backdrop for urban capitalism."

Henshaw looks at the audience with an ironic smile: "Industrial societies emerge when the sacred is forgotten. The desire for limitless wealth has little relevance to human welfare, but urban capitalism is based on it. Wherever capitalism prospers there is a calculation of quantities, a regimentation of time, and a focus on the abstract rewards of money, regardless of other human values. Urban capitalism is the fragmented synthesis, containing the same perversions that prevailed in the city-states. Its aim is power and profit, resulting in competition and domination. Armies are trained to defend wealth as much as people. Urban capitalism contains no true paradox or metathesis.

"In a world moving toward mechanization, the sacred and profane divide further as scientific 'advances' are made. Science studies nature, but in such a way that nature's spiritual forces are denied. It analyzes and categorizes the fractured parts that are observable by the senses. The unconscious dimensions of the reductionist scientific method are then driven deeper into the irrational wellsprings of both mind and matter where the Goddess sways her heavy hips amidst the dry bones of a sterile world.

"Early twentieth-century science was the most repressed form of profanity on Earth. The scientific revolution, in extending the thesis of progress, signaled the complete collapse of the paradigm of the Middle Ages. Empiricism completely separated objectivity from subjectivity. Only in modern physics, with the discovery of Heisenberg's uncertainty principle, did this dichotomization begin to be transformed.

"In a profane and increasingly scientific world, the sacred was seen as occult and superstitious. Mechanism was substituted for the failure of occultism. Social cohesion could not be found, for the rhythms of community practice—the basis of the way of synthesis—became split and atrophied. Descarte's famous dichotomization of mind and body was but one refrain of the fragmenting process."

A well-dressed man interjects a question: "Is *all* our progress based on tension and conflict—a division of the sacred and profane, as you call it?"

"It depends on what you mean by progress. When it comes from the drive of the profane to conquer—to overcome the archaic, the natural, the female, the Earth-based, the body—then it is ultimately debilitating. Although the outer person develops more powerful tools, the inner person feels driven to transcend in some way. The drive of progress is inwardly climactic, either striving toward a peak or a pushing toward apocalypse."

"Are you saying one shouldn't want success or high points in life?" asks the same man, who seems angry.

"What is your motivation?" replies Henshaw calmly. "Is it to dominate others or to awaken to their intrinsic gifts and cooperate with them? Perhaps if I continue my discussion of modern times, you will see how important the source of motivation is.

"Colonization emerged from the thesis of progress. Kings and queens sent ships to sail uncharted oceans. But what began as a spirit of discovery grew into a desire to conquer and exploit. Colonization widened the split between the sacred and profane, the inner and outer life, and led to a breakdown of cultural values. The antithesis ramified as a tension between peoples with differences. This polarity was now internalized as self-hatred, projected onto the other—the other races, other religions, and other nations.

"We can only overcome this fear of otherness through a resacralization of the world. Like the hunter who internalizes the feared animal, when you see the 'other' as sacred, you become spiritually empowered. The denial and unconscious reactions of our lives must be faced, whether their objects are racial, religious, sexual, or national. The monsters are not to be slain but *transformed*. When you see the sacred in the 'other,' what you fear becomes an ally."

Henshaw pauses to take a drink of water and then resumes: "Let us explore recent times in more depth. What we had in colonialism was the clashing of two radically different phases in the dialectic of cultural history. Africa, a blind spot to Europe, was the continent most exploited during the rise of European imperialism. The native peoples, like those of the Americas, knew that Mother Earth belonged to all who lived in harmony with her. Tribes lived in different territories according to the affinities of land, vegetation, and wildlife. There were tribal wars, but nothing on the scale of Western militarism born of modern technology. The intrusion of Western civilization into the cradle of Africa—full of mystery, wildness, and naturalness—continues still.

"Let me give you another example. The people of China were similarly exploited in the nineteenth century. In China, there had been a safeguarding of an old culture—a hierarchical one from the city-states model, including a bureaucracy that guarded China's art. But China fell prey to delusion by trading silver for opium. Eventually, gold, silver, jade, and pearl were pillaged from the emperor's palace. As the sacred gave way to the profane, the principles of the Chinese sages became less valued than worldly treasures.

"You see, when the gift of the thesis is no longer acknowledged, and when wonder, awe, and prayer disappear, the profane power struggle takes over. The antithesis, instead of being a polar dialogue or dynamic complementarity, becomes a conflict. Then there can be no real synthesis—only temporary treaties or agreements, because the loser is forced to compromise.

"For nearly one hundred years after the Opium Wars, the Chinese lived under horribly degrading treaties imposed upon them by the English, French, Germans, and Russians. The polarization of East and West—the "barbarians" and the "cultured"—created an increasing schism of inner and outer values. The Chinese looked to opium to compensate for the malnourished soul—to appease the longing for the sacred.

"Here is another an example. The West forced Japan and China to sign treaties surrendering control of their trade and tariffs. Foreigners residing in Japan and China made themselves exempt from local laws. In the late nineteenth century, the United States used the presence of its navy to pressure Japan to open up trade. Hurt by this domination, a weakening shogun encouraged the learning of the technological and political ways of the West. In two decades, the resourceful Japanese laid miles of railroad track, instituted mail service and telegraphs, conscripted a state army, set up factories, and increased their literacy. When Japan won its war with China in the late nineteenth century, the West raised its eyebrows, for its own thesis of progress was being enacted."

"Was it inevitable that, once colonization had run its course, European powers should fight among themselves?" asks a troubled-looking woman.

"Probably. By 1914, the European rivalry over the Middle East,

China, and Africa was at its peak. A European war could not be a localized war, for the whole world had been colonized, most of it falling deeper into unconsciousness, an amnesia of the source and purpose of life."

Henshaw's intensity brings images of the war to the listeners: "The machine gun of the Triple Entente, a seeming advantage, actually prolonged the war. After two years, the British captured 120 square miles at a cost of 400,000 men. The next year they lost 240,000 men to gain 50 square miles! Two more years of agony gained nothing.

"All countries were bleeding, not only on the front, but at home from food rationing and fixed wages. The psychological damage ensuing from death, poverty, and disease was inestimable! Scientists developed synthetics to offset natural materials that were in short supply. They invented more powerful explosives and fertilizers. Everything became forced.

"Do you see how breaking with the cyclic rhythms of spirit and nature drives people to violence? It increasingly bifurcates the culture."

A serious-looking woman raises her hand. "History seems to be a horror story," she remarks. "How can we keep these atrocities from happening again?"

"It *is* a horror story. The fact that civilizations that pride themselves on progress use thirty percent of their national wealth for warfare is insanity. Again, this resulted from the division of the inner and outer life and the repression of what was feared. Unconscious men were trained to kill like robots, never considering their inner life. The human war machine has been the single most efficient organization humanity has effected—but to what end?

"War is the epitome of antithesis without a synthesis. After World War I, Wilson did attempt a democratic synthesis. He advocated world economic cooperation and the right of national self-determination as embodied in the League of Nations. But the smaller nations had no voice. The peace treaties were made by the leading powers and consequently they did not endure.

"The attempted synthesis retrograded back into the antithesis of a conflict of power. Japan still held its wartime gains in China and the Pacific, but the Allies did nothing to support Chinese occupation of her own ports. So China withdrew from the peace conference. Germany resented the 'war guilt' clause in the peace treaty, which forced it to accept responsibility for the war."

"Why couldn't we learn from World War I? How did it lead to the second world war?" asks a young American.

Henshaw's steel-blue eyes move from the youth and penetrate the eyes of those seated in the front rows: "We were still hypnotized by progress after the war. The United States emerged as the leading industrial and financial power. But industry and economy, as we have seen, were means, not ends, and when divorced from any true value of life, they spawned only tension and violence. Even industrial progress was a search for intangible values. But when force was applied, the human cost was horrible. One need only look at the profane push of industrial progress in Russia under Stalin."

"Don't you think there really was progress?" asks a tall British man. "Why did the Depression occur?"

"Herbert Hoover spoke of indefinite progress, comfort, and security. But was it progress? The value of the dollar continued to grow as stocks went up in an unregulated market. More wealth was being produced than ever before, but the workers were receiving less. Industrial production fell in 1929 and declined thereafter while the stock market continued to rise. This seesaw economy was a direct reflection of the conflict of powers, locked into the antithesis with no sense of a resolution.

"The stock market crash exposed the myth of industrial success based on profane values alone. Even the gold standard was abandoned for promises and paper money. There was no realization that money and wealth had anything to do with integrity, kindness, or beauty. Art and charity were the first to be forsaken when money got scarce. They had an extremely minor place in the industrial society.

"Here was a good example of how destruction emerged out of illusory values and unconscious behavior. Real values, the beholding of the sacred in real goods, were not seen or were neglected. Farmers had no money to buy feed for animals, and vegetables rotted in want of a market.

"Roosevelt's New Deal brought social security, farm subsidies, and low-cost mortgages. But the government spent beyond its means. Roosevelt may have been motivated by justice and goodness, but in a civilization habituated to greed, the needed transformation toward a synthesis was not possible. People could have taken initiative and banded together in a spirit of community and reevaluated priorities. Land, food, friends, and tools were the essential things that needed to be shared in a spirit of cooperation.

"Eventually, the scourge of the Depression merged with the greater scourge of World War II. One war was a spin-off of the unbalanced antithesis of the other. Seventy million men fought in the second world war. Thirty million soldiers and civilians died. Japan, after the horrors of Hiroshima and Nagasaki, became dedicated to economic security above all.

"Again, I want to point out that, after World War II, just as after World War I, peace was imposed upon the vanquished. No true synthesis was ever reached. A legacy of this imposed peace is the raging ethnic conflict following the breakup of the Soviet bloc."

At this point, Henshaw realizes that it is time to break for lunch and concludes the morning session.

Two hours later, after everyone has settled into their chairs, he begins again: "After such a brief historical overview, we must ask, 'How can we rediscover the sacred?' Humanity, having lost contact with the source, the true thesis of the gift, suffers from deep repression and depression. The more we deny the unconscious, the more power it has over us. Through the dialectic of key paradigm shifts, there has been increasing robotic behavior and uniformity, punctuated with reactions of violent crime, insanity, and war.

"Now the sacred is buried beneath the skyscrapers, freeways, and nuclear power plants. The danger of the split between the sacred and profane cannot be emphasized enough. Technology is seen as an end rather than a means. The horrors of all the world wars, including the Cold War, occurred because gratitude for the gift of light, vision, life, and consciousness died.

"In the nineteenth century, Nietzsche proclaimed, 'God is dead.' Other philosophers argued over whether the world existed *a priori* or because we sensed it. Prisons and insane asylums escalated. Psychology and psychiatry were born as an answer to the splits among soul, mind, body, and spirit. The feminine nature of this repression erupted first in romanticism and later in revived worship of the Goddess.

"The child's dream, vision world, and bodily spontaneity were transmuted through the Newtonian and Cartesian society into controlled behavior. Consequently, creativity was lost as well as health. When we condition our children to the same unconscious behavior, they become armored. Spontaneity, joy, and creativity are not frills but human necessity. Ecstatic highs are sought through drugs, sex, and occult rituals because we suffer intensely when the deep cosmic rhythms are not lived and shared in community. Even the psychedelic phenomenon of the 1960s was a reaction to the dominant technological paradigm. Unfortunately, while it opened some to the spiritual wealth within, it also destroyed many minds and bodies.

"The widespread use of psychedelics helped addict seekers to the glamour of spiritual sensationalism, one aspect of which is an obsession with ascension. The desire for ascension is generally an attempt to escape the pain of the split between psyche and body. This happens when the *wholeness* of the dialectic is not fulfilled. The ascension paradigm includes a manic-depressive tendency that needs to be released before the natural dialectic can return. Although illusions about ascension characterize parts of the so-called New Age movement, this same movement has also adopted traditions such as Buddhism, Sufism, and Hellenic polytheism that have stood the test of time. Much authentic experience has come from the central nerve of the New Age, which is an honest attempt to find a more wholesome, organic way of life."

Henshaw's energy intensifies: "We are both somatically and spiritually hungry. Alcohol, television, drugs from the street and pharmacy, sex—none can substitute for real ecstasy. Bourgeois alienation and worldwide depression and inflation are all signs of a deep anxiety about the meaning of life—a loss of contact with the sacred gift of the source. The gift cannot be conquered. It can only be surrendered to."

For a few moments, the room is totally silent until Fariba, sitting near the front, speaks up: "How can we heal this three-thousand-year-old split of the sacred and profane in human consciousness?"

Henshaw looks up and speaks slowly and deliberately: "Through a resacralization of the world. The sacred is now referred to as archetypal energy, but it is a repressed and frightening energy to most of us. Humanity will be renewed when it lays down control at the altar of the divine. Consciousness transmits patterns and creates changes that break down and dissolve, but also renew. If this is not done, unconsciousness seizes control and forces us to our knees. We are experiencing the greatest social disintegration in recorded history.

"Healing will not come through government policies or economic prosperity. We must refind the sacred, the thesis wherein a new gnosis can emerge. This gnosis must be brought down into agriculture, industry, and the arts. It must be transmitted through computer technologies to create global links between eco-villages."

Henshaw pauses amid silence until someone shouts from the back of the room, "What *are* the new paradigms?"

"What do *you* think? It is up to all of us to discover. I can only sketch possibilities. Due to the denial of the natural dialectic, we will likely see increasing revolution in all areas. New forms of fascism and fundamentalism will continue to emerge, as well as occult societies. You will see efforts to create a universal religion as an antidote to the splintered sects. But any form of religion imposed by an elite group is but another form of monistic totalitarian rule. Worship of the Goddess, political turmoil, armed conflict, and urban shamanism will continue to gain momentum. These movements, which are expressions of the conflictual tension within the antithesis, seek to bring about a natural synthesis. And so let me ask you: What *is* the new thesis?"

"A cry for holism," calls out one man.

"Realization that God permeates every mundane action," shouts another.

The chorus of responses continues:

"To be able to dream and know it can be a reality."

"The freedom to express diverse viewpoints."

"To see the order inherent in nature."

"To be wild and creative."

"To return to scripture and the truth of God's law."

"Yes, all of that," responds Henshaw with a smile. "The new thesis erupts as a chaotic flow. It involves emancipation of women, the body, and eros. The new physics and spirituality arise together. The New Age and fundamentalist movements may be opposite faces of one being. Turning into your enemy is the order of the day. The destructuring of one movement both destroys and enhances others. We have a decentralized process of fracturing and refusion, with chaos theories heralding the new forms of order.

"We live in an information age rife with the possible emergence of a new paradigm. But artificial intelligence and systems cybernetics cannot replace the inner life, nor can the inner life be fully realized through escape into altered states. We need to come into a holism that respects embodied differences."

"What role will computers play in the new paradigm?" interjects a young man.

"Computers are wonderful tools. They connect the world, and because of this they can enhance communication and thus our understanding of one another. But it is from human beings that values must arise. There is a crying out for holism amidst the vanity of acquiring more and more information without the ethics or vision that can guide its use.

"Blake and Reich saw the values crises coming and addressed the issue. Whenever a new thesis emerges, there is a period of transition when we face the unknown. If we grasp at some idea before it has become one with the real thesis that is a sacred gift, we reel around in short-term revolution and dissipate our precious energy. The new paradigm will emerge from *within us* when we behold the sacred in all beings and embrace differences. We cannot figure it out, project it as an ideal, or even cling to it as a hope.

"We live in Earth-shaking times. The numinous shines from within when we abandon our habits, our concepts, and even our beliefs. There is no question that this emergence, this recognition of the sacred gift is heretical to many religions, but it is not heretical to the perennial wisdom flowing as a living stream through the fourfold dialectic."

"What can we do, then? Just trust?" asks a seemingly distraught woman.

"To face this abyss, we need to be present, feeling and witnessing what each instant brings to us—from the inside out and from the outside in. Ordinary life then becomes a miracle and the quest ceases. We must watch, then do what needs doing. The core of any religious tradition, if practiced, will open you to it."

"How can you encapsulate this core of religious tradition?" asks the same woman.

"As sober ecstasy. The kaleidoscopic arena of human experience can be encapsulated as joy in ordinary life. Ecstasy is a natural condition—one needs not turn to psychedelics. When ecstasy is forced, the spirit, soul, body, and mind split apart. The ultimate paradigm is the mythless myth—one that releases worldviews and cosmologies and disappears altogether. One learns to live in the now. To be whole, we must break through the conformity of religious ritual and into the heart of the practice. This means being practical, sober, and ecstatic at once.

"Christ told us to 'become as little children.' We continue to create new relations as they arise. Everything comes to pass. New monks and troubadours travel the world to inspire the populace. Eco-villages are planned and begun. By remembering the gift of the River of creation—by staying with the Source—we will find new ways to give thanks and praise in daily life. This is to walk in balance.

"Our reflexive awareness is bringing us to our knees, but ultimately to our creativity. May you find yours. What we have destroyed, we can create anew when we acknowledge the sacred gift and work joyfully as inspired humanity to build a new culture."

THE FALL AND HOPE
OF A DEMIGOD

Regeneration
White of red within white

The pain
of terminal illness
deepens
the path of regeneration.

Horst and Erhardt

When Horst learned that Erhardt had disappeared, flinging his entire inheritance to the winds, he crumbled and fell into a deep depression, withdrawing from all activities and remaining on his estate. Now, gripped by illusory nostalgia for the days with Christa and Erhardt, he moves futilely between hope and denial.

All he has left is his wealth, comprised of assets from three main sources—his inheritance from his father, his stock in Hashigawa Games, and his holdings in African gold mining. The mines unconsciously attract him because of his former life in Egypt. At that time, gold and jewels embellished the temples and statues that had been part of the crystalline treasury upon which the star patterns beamed their codes, linking cosmic intelligence to Earth.

However, Horst remembers nothing of this. His attachment to wealth is a defense that substitutes for love. His green eyes have turned an eerie grey that matches his once-blond hair. When he finally falls seriously ill, he cannot fathom what has happened. It's as though he is turning to ashes.

Eventually, he is diagnosed as having lymphatic cancer and admitted to the hospital in Munich. Grasping for some link with life, he decides to telephone Christa despite her steadfast refusal to communicate with him. Thinking that she knows where Erhardt is, he calls Karlsruhe only to be informed by a close friend of hers that Christa and Karl have departed for China. However, the friend does know where Erhardt is living. Aware of Horst's illness and sensing his desperation, she decides to let Erhardt know of his father's condition.

Horst lies in bed, the physical pain drawing up nightmares and memories. He returns again to the time, not long ago, when Petruska cursed him to his face for her failure in the Egyptian initiation. She is one of the unpetitioned shadows that gnaw at him. Others are from lifetimes he can only vaguely remember.

The energetic complexes of these past lives now gyrate through his soul. Thousands of years ago, he and Channon existed as a single demigod. Now he is caught in the net he wove then, a prisoner inside his own body. The reverberations of his conspiracy to separate the vibrations of the star intelligences from the erotic pulses of humanity karmically rebound against him as he writhes in pain.

In his internal struggle, Horst begins to understand what happened over so many lifetimes. He and Channon, as one demigod born of an extraterrestrial father and mortal mother, exalted in the light of the Sun behind the Sun. Originally the power of the Great Goddess, this divine eye opened the third eye of mortals. It could do so only when a person's exalted feelings of love expanded to cosmic dimensions. Then a golden stream of light infused heaven and Earth—the star intelligences and the erotic vegetal root. Earth became a paradise.

In ancient times, a demigod would ritually mate with the Great Goddess in order to conceive a new king. The eye—the daughter of the High God—could only be dilated with the opening of her womb when both she and her mate were in a state of complete love. Then the blazing light of the Sun God Ra would stream within the sky, the underworld, and the single eye of the Goddess and demigod. The music of the spheres would resound in praise of the Creator.

At that time, many thousands of years ago, the Goddess opened her womb to the Horst-Channon demigod in the center of a circle of couples erotically aroused in tantric union. But the demigod felt *nothing*. Neither love nor desire moved within him. In that instant, the all-seeing eye between him and the Goddess shattered into six parts. From that moment on, the demigod could no longer behold the star intelligences nor see into the crystalline emerald core of the Earth.

In this way, the unity of the Horus Eye fell into fractions: 1/2 + 1/4 + 1/8 + 1/16 + 1/32 + 1/64. But a fraction was always missing because the eye shattered infinitely, resulting in the recursive fractal patterns of chaos theory that continue to enthrall and bewilder the scientists of the late twentieth century. The mysterious attractor is a complete fusion of love and sexuality. The wholeness of vision can never be restored as long as they are divided.

As the high priest Manesis, Horst's soul was given one last chance to heal the rift between sex and love, but Manesis wanted only to control the erotic energy that moved within nature and the priestesses. The intelligence of heaven became a cosmic computer, severed from the vitality of the Earth. Cut off from the cosmic source, Manesis became afraid of beholding the light directly, yet he arrogantly tried to assume its power. Together with Channon, he calculated the angles, orbits, and velocities of the stars, but, with the division of the eye, he no longer embodied the zodiacal qualities beamed from the galactic center. No longer could he decode the information within light itself. The two-stranded DNA imprinted in the physical world still held the patterns of the zodiac, but only those with a single eye could see them.

When Manesis died, his soul shattered. It has searched the world for the Goddess ever since.

Now, while Channon pursues his quest in the Australian Outback, the conflict in Horst's soul erupts with the memory of a sixth-century incarnation as a Roman general. The general learns of a certain St. Illtyd who founded a monastic college and seven Celtic churches where twelve monks chant unceasing praise to their God. Fearing that the

Druidic churches and megaliths may still be alive with numinous power, the general commands all singing to cease. The devotion expressed through the perpetual choir terrifies him.

In Horst's delirium, the general is courageously confronted by St. Illtyd and one of his monks. He looks into St. Illtyd's eyes and begins to tremble, for there he recognizes the soul of Christa, the Goddess he seeks. Zapana suffered with her then, as one being and one soul whose single intent was to reconnect the intelligence of the stars with the human heart and vital energy of nature. The images of Christa as a virgin Egyptian priestess awaken Horst's dying flesh, and he clutches the hospital bed as the vision continues.

Suddenly the monk accompanying St. Illtyd begins singing a plainchant once sung in the temples of Egypt. The beauty pouring from the monk's throat in courageous defiance penetrates Horst's heart. In the monk's eyes, he fleetingly beholds Erhardt's soul and is stirred with compassion. But his words betray him. "The Druids must cease all worship. Your songs shall be silent, your churches closed, your stones toppled."

Tossing violently, Horst unconsciously screams at hearing his own command. He awakens to a resurgence of feeling, and with the feeling, remembrance. The mortal in him awakens to the demigod and the demigod awakens to the mortal. This feeling moves from pain through anger to desire, and from desire to moments of love. But he is afraid. To love is to drop his armor—to become defenseless and vulnerable and to surrender to the Goddess within him. Somehow he knows that to be one with the Goddess is to *see* eternity and *be* love. Yet he still wrestles inside the walls of his fortress as death stands nearby and darkens the pallor of his face. Heaven and Earth begin to weep within him, spreading their salty tears down his greying cheeks.

Two days later, standing at his father's bedside, Erhardt is appalled to see how much he has aged in one year and how vulnerable and helpless he is. Ravished by disease, Horst seems a mere skeleton, yet the harsh, square features of his face are the same. *What do I feel now? Is this even my father?* thinks Erhardt, who knows only the stout man filled with anger and given to harsh commands.

All Erhardt's repressed anger, directed at himself for being so submissive, rises into a ball in the pit of his stomach. When Horst reaches out for his hand, the ball rises like a red-hot coal into Erhardt's throat. Saddened by the incomprehensible complexities of a soul unable to love, Erhardt speaks with perturbed assurance: "I'm here, Father."

To return to what he most hates opens the way for possible conciliation. Erhardt's struggle to feel something other than animosity for his father eases only because of the devotion he has given to restoring the land in Austria. Invigorated and at peace from his work there, he is more able to see Horst simply as a man who failed to live his life and who failed to know himself.

The mere presence of Erhardt at his bedside begins to crack Horst's hardened defense and open his third eye. His half-glimpsed reality of having been both mortal and demigod over so many loveless lives softens him. Unwittingly, he senses the arched golden thread connecting him to Channon, who is being equally humbled at the opposite end of the Earth. The core of his inner reality is sucked through drifting shadows and nightmares into the shining instant of a living now. His heart bursts open at the moment Channon beholds a great golden eye while enduring the stinging grubs and searing Sun of the Australian Outback.

Gazing into Erhardt's eyes, Horst is able to say, "I'm sorry, Erhardt, for whatever I've done that takes you away from me. Why? I don't yet understand. It hurts me so."

Erhardt trembles, feeling everything his father ever denied. He is becoming aware that he took on Horst's transgressions himself. To this he agreed long ago, realizing that the Roman general who silenced the songs in St. Illtyd's church could only be in great misery. Erhardt vowed in that life to be reborn as a relative in order to understand and heal Horst—to transform his malevolent will and restore the praises to God.

"It is good, Father, that you feel hurt," he responds after some time. "Perhaps that is why I left—so that you could feel again. We don't always know why we do things."

Horst is puzzled by Erhardt's words but feels his compassion: "Tell me about your life, Erhardt."

Erhardt stares at him, uncomprehending this expression of care. He pauses a long while.

"I live on a farm, Father," he begins, feeling a tenderness rise. "A few friends and I are working to revitalize the land."

Horst smiles faintly and speaks with effort: "Erhardt, I know you have refused to receive the inheritance that is rightfully yours, but you remain the beneficiary of my will. If you don't want my money, I trust you will give it to a good cause."

Tears come to Erhardt's eyes, for he realizes that his father has truly ceased trying to control him: "Thank you, Father. I will receive it gratefully, but you have long to live yet."

"I'm not so sure." Horst stares at the ceiling and closes his eyes.

At the moment that Ngalijod, the Rainbow Snake, slithers down Channon's throat, Horst, like Channon, falls totally unconscious. The magical snake simultaneously clears crusted memories of black magic and loveless dominance from their two astral bodies.

Erhardt remains with his sleeping father all night long, regathering the ancient chants of praise while the compassionate emerald fluids rise up from the center of the Earth into Horst's still-beating heart.

Horst experiences neither rest nor joy nor peace during his dying days—only the depth of insight from suffering. Erhardt, realizing that he chose a father whose guilt would challenge his power of forgiveness, remembers the dream in which he called out to Channon: *For generations I have longed to find you. I have wanted your understanding for having followed my own light. My love for you is eternal, Father.* He realizes that the dream could well apply to the man dying before his eyes, though he does not understand who Channon is.

The seven-day vigil at Horst's bedside brings to Erhardt memories of the chants he sang when Druidic sacred science linked the stars with the megalithic stones. As the last vestiges of evil in Horst's soul crumble to dust, choirs of heaven assemble in expectation of coming to the Earth again and exalting the trees and flowers. The musical intervals burst forth in a resonance that makes whole the fractions of the eye. When Horst breathes his last, Erhardt places the soul of his father in the center of an imaginal stone circle and draws the harmonics down from heaven to Earth. Propelled into mystery and terror, Erhardt's memory gives birth to beauty, until at last he hears the voices of praise to the wholeness of the single eye.

The voices restore Erhardt's faith and hope. He asks no return on what has passed—only that the chorus of star intelligences return to renew the land. Like chlorophyll, whose energy is linked in double symmetry with light through the reflection of green, Erhardt absorbs the extremes of the spectrum of life and reflects them back through the center of his being.

With fierce eyes Erhardt now evades nothing. He knows that civilization will be redeemed only through listening to the Earth. And he knows that this healing intent must be wed with vibrational means. Fire and water will hiss and steam until they fuse in the blood memory of an awakened humanity. Light and soul will shake loose the shadows and be used to create a new testament. As Erhardt walks out of the hospital, he hears a song from out of the sky:

Hero/Demon's Song of the River

I am the blood of the tribes and the succession of chieftains and matri-
    archs.
You can find me in every cultural renewal.
I am the challenge to every act of greed,
    the rectification to every social wrong.
I am the dam that controls the waters of the river.
I am a reservoir of strength for the past and future.
Look for me in the alternation of mother and father rule.
I create revolutions where corruption is rampant.
You can find me in all social bonds.
Look for me in the mythic history of nations.
I am the power of regeneration in the acceptance of difference.
I am the journey and the journeyer to find the treasure.
I am the treasure when I return home.
I am the way-shower to men and women.
Look for me in blood and gold.
I am the succession of past and future generations.

How can you be of the ancestors and of the unborn?
I am the heroic lineage of the present that reflects both ways.

THE VIRGIN AND CHILD

The Fall, incarnation, and redemption at the end of time and history stream forth from the Big Bang and back toward apocalypse. The scarred Earth drowns amid the cacophonous hum of electricity, the violence of warfare, sirens, sonic booms, the screeching of trains, and the grinding of machinery. The unconscious maelstrom of civilization seeks a new birth while the music of the Old Earth drives millions into movement.

Humanity panics when the music stops. Four billion people playing musical chairs are caught without seats. Nomadic, dislocated refugees of the Earth changes, they are the homeless, poor, and unidentified. Migrating families wander and wonder as time and space collapse into the black hole of memory being purged of illusion. The twisted thoughts of humanity spin in the air against the vermilion sunset of a dying age.

The Creatrix watches from the splendors of the biosphere. Her faith in humanity endures, despite humanity's amnesia of its source and purpose. The quickening energies make one thing clear: past thoughtforms—evocators of violence—must dissipate. The singularity that draws near depends on the courageous vision of a New Earth. She knows that the inner sanctity and purity of the Virgin can birth children of radiant vibration. But such children cannot survive in a world of psychic and physical pollution. Of more subtle, fragile frequency, they circle in heaven, beyond time, waiting for the Earth to be purified.

As the great god Pan returns to romp over the wasteland, summoning the divine Virgin out from the clamor and confusion, old collective projections begin to vanish. Pan brings both panic and a panorama of history. The hologram of the profane speeds into reflections that mirror the split beam of eros and logos. The split beam sinks inward until a singular light presses it back into the reality of I and Thou as one. Cataracts of eros flood the collective dream, shaking history out of time and time out of eternity. Long light-waves of logos retrieve the divine plan from crystalline star-shapes, radiating information toward a new destiny. The Primal Waters rumble between the computer chips and the shores of continents, signaling a new reality born of the script of the River.

Those who embody the full spectrum of being awake to the reality of Pan. He is the all-encompassing divine imagination, weaving purpose into paradox and paradox into purpose. While Pan shakes the continents, the Virgin softens the tribulation with lucid laughter and ecstasy. She lives in tender breasts, thirsty mouths, and shuffling feet searching for home. The perennial wisdom long lost within the spores of human souls, she now awakens from within. She stirs the air with wonder, the Earth with love, the oceans with tears. She shakes the fruit from the Tree of Life which falls to Earth as constancy, truth, and creativity when energy flows without obstruction. Kundalini rises up the spines of mortals, purging the demons from their souls.

With lightning, Pan smites the golden gates of heaven, bringing the swift grace of the Creator to shatter the casements of armored hate. Heaven and Earth fall together in the arched embrace of rainbows, summoning sweet tears from those in long pursuit of their divinity. As the courageous and constant ones rise from the labyrinthine ruins of civilization, the facets of the split crystal in the First World shoot forth hope. The infinite power of the Second World streams down and turns again upon the choice of mortals: to be free of mindless conformity and the illusory limitations of the three dimensions—to be free to create new ways of life.

The Virgin springs to life wherever mortals shatter the illusion of inner and outer and create a future from the fluid script of the River. Like minimal music, the circle of patterns shifts, revealing the order hidden in chaos and the harmony hidden in dissonance. The way of the waves rises from thundering tremors of implosion while the veil of the Virgin is thrown back, and the malefic web of thoughtforms is forever purged from the atmosphere.

Angelic voices resound through the iridescent obelisk in the Land of Zar while the River teems with renewed possibilities of service. The bright spheres of the heavens clash together, entwining rarified vibrations and flinging out new orbits that mock the pain of troubled times.

The Council of Nature Spirits, impelled by the sacred trust of those who walk in balance, speaks silently in the midnight hush before preparing the womb in the turbulent Old Earth. As the new children are conceived, orderly fluctuations of chaos spin in the photons of their light bodies, drawing life and consciousness into an unknown future.

Now the children come from heaven, calm and centered in the divine intent of freedom. Rushing down, their fragile bodies shimmering in the light of each compassionate instant, they sing, "We have followed you through the ages. Now light your inner tapers. We come to raise the dead and spew the wild wisdom of eternity to the four quarters of the Earth."

Their forms are invisible to all but the lucid minds that evade nothing. Their songs fall silent except to those who open their ears to the beauteous intimacy of nature—those who behold the Earth as a Virgin and the children as themselves.

THE AGNIHOTRA CEREMONY

Ecstasy
Gold of white within white

The renewal
of life
begins
with rapture.

Krishna, Ariel, and Athene

When the time comes to leave the mountains of Shaanxi, Ariel decides to go to India with his three friends. On the first day of their arrival in Delhi, Krishna receives a letter inviting him to play in a ceremony at the agnihotra center in Shivapur. He is elated and asks the others to accompany him. Though Pravin wants to attend to business obligations and Luqman feels called back to Iran, Krishna continues to encourage Ariel.

"Shivapur is only three hundred miles south of here. We could start hitchhiking in the morning. The ceremony will be the day after to-morrow."

"And agnihotra—what is that?" asks Ariel.

"*Agni* means 'fire'. *Hotra* means 'the act of purification'.'"

Ariel remembers what the Immortal told him: *Find water for your fire*. He senses that the water is the female inside of him.

"I already feel fire raging within me. It's water I'm looking for. What does music have to do with this purifying fire?"

"Are you willing to find out?" challenges Pravin, winking at Ariel like a knowing father. "It is a ceremony for the purification of the waters and the Earth. The vibrations of particular chants amplify the resonant effects of the fire's rays."

The two youths set off the next day, Krishna carrying his sarod, and easily find a series of rides. As they approach Shivapur toward evening, the hills grow noticeably greener and the air fresher. Flowers line the pathways and streets and the sound of *raga* music is everywhere. Ariel feels an ease he has rarely known and is glad that he has come along.

Krishna inquires about lodging, and they are directed to a nearby hostel where a young Hindu greets them warmly. He leads them to a room with dozens of worn mattresses where the two travelers happily fling down their rucksacks. Though weary, they are excited and decide to go out to survey the area. They are barely outside the hostel when they encounter Rahu, Krishna's teacher.

"Krishna! You made it after all!" cries Rahu. "Does your friend play?"

"No, but he can chant."

"The ceremony is at dawn tomorrow. We'll rehearse at seven tonight on Agni Hill."

"Good. See you then."

After practicing well into the night, Krishna is so energized that he cannot sleep. He gets up and goes out to the hills. There, he softly sings into the night sky.

About an hour before dawn, Ariel is awakened by the muffled voices of those walking in casual procession toward the ritual site. The music of the stars fades as magenta paints the eastern horizon. A medley of ages and nationalities moves slowly toward the crest of the hill. Knee deep in grass, the children run and kiss the flowers, darting in and out of the line. Some walk holding the hands of aged grandmothers and grandfathers. People come from all directions, many carrying inverted pyramids filled with a mixture of cow manure, ghee, rice, and a pinch of redolent sandalwood.

Passion builds toward the moment of dawn, when a chime sounds. The thousands assembled assume an enthralled silence and turn to face the east, where a short, heavyset yogi in white robes and with a long white beard offers a Sanskrit prayer. As the first rays of the Sun touch the sky, the yogi ignites the mixture inside his pyramid and others do the same. Amid the glowing fires and the scent of sandalwood, the voices chant in unison.

Ariel is wholly uplifted and transformed by the chant. He feels not only the resonance of the purifying energy, but the vibration of the original Word, the *aum* of the universe. The impulse that drove creation now trembles in the gathering clouds about to release a sacramental rain upon a drought-ridden continent. The gods and angels seem to stir the prana through the rain and into the Earth. Feeling the fire in him returning to the source, Ariel spends the entire morning in silent ecstasy.

At noon, Ariel joins Krishna and others around a large table laden with fruits, vegetables, dal, and curried rice. People of all ages encircle the bounty, an elemental sacrament of nourishment brought forth by the spirits of the skies, hills, and streams.

As Ariel stands waiting in silent gratitude, his eyes fall upon the jet black hair and fair skin of the young woman standing next to him. When, unexpectedly, she raises her eyes to meet his, he feels a rapturous current sweep away the loneliness of his soul as his heart opens to an unknown mystery.

When the blessing is finished, Krishna notices a sphere of light around the two and comes over: "Ariel, I want you to meet an old friend, Athene. We went to school together."

A faint smile spreads over Ariel's lips as Krishna goes on: "Ariel is from the United States, but he has been a vagabond for many years now. Athene, you know about agnihotra. Perhaps you can explain more about it to him."

Athene smiles shyly. Delight without desire runs free in her. Her beauty impels a flustered Ariel to speak.

"Are you Hindu?"

"My father is Hindu," she responds. "My mother was Greek, but I do not remember her. India has been my home, but I teach about agnihotra throughout Asia."

"I feel the ceremony has changed me for life. What happened this morning?"

"The life-force of the Earth is vitalized by agnihotra. The ceremonies are performed at power places around the Earth."

"Do you know how it really works? I mean, is it magic or real?"

"What do *you* feel? You saw how it created rain. This area has become fertile because of these rituals." Athene's forehead is clear. Energy seems to focus around the painted dot at her third eye.

Ariel knows words are inadequate for what he feels, and he struggles to keep his mind centered: "But how does it work? Have scientists studied it?"

Athene spoons some curried rice onto her plate. "Let's take some food and sit in the shade of that tree," she suggests. They walk over and sit down, and she begins responding to Ariel's questions: "I'm studying agnihotra as well as what many people think are other strange phenomena—crop circles and megaliths."

She continues her explanation. Speaking in English with a charming Hindi accent, she tries to shield her attraction to Ariel behind the articulation of her thought: "So far, I have found that in agnihotra there is an informational transfer through atomic and molecular processes that are mediated by the resonance of ultraviolet photons. But the main thing is that it works."

"It worked as a transformer on me," responds Ariel, his face lighting up. "How else does it work?"

Athene now seems to be giving a discourse: "The ash produced in the ceremonies can be used as a disinfectant and anticoagulant. And through its contracting effects, it aids in the healing of living tissue. But I think its most significant potential is in restoring the ozone layer and clearing atmospheric pollution."

"That's incredible! How can it do that?" exclaims Ariel, dumbfounded by her claims for agnihotra.

"It hasn't been proven yet," Athene continues, "but it seems that the smoke from the colloidal molecules of ghee and cow manure grabs pollutants in the air and transmutes the particles by charging them with life-force—prana. It returns life by transforming a substance back to its original nature. When the electrical charge is diminished, the particles coagulate and become dead. A charge from the agnihotra repels the particles from each other and keeps them in colloidal suspension, full of vitality. In this way we can transform pollution back into clear air."

Ariel feels awestruck by this bright, beautiful, spiritual woman: "Are you a scientist, too?"

"Not really, but science interests me insofar as it can help us repair the environment." She takes some rice with her fingers, and Ariel does the same.

"What did you mean when you said that the particles become dead? Aren't they dead anyway?"

Athene laughs: "No, nothing is *really* dead. Prana flows through particles that are charged and in suspension. But the Vedas say that when pollution reaches a certain limit, the cellular structure of plants is changed and they should not be eaten. These plants are toxic to the human system. That is the problem with most of the so-called 'fresh' food in supermarkets everywhere."

Ariel is so energized that he jumps up and braces his body against a tree trunk: "I can learn a lot from you. I've heard of living and dead water, but I had no idea that pollution could be cleared by chanting through the flames of burning cow dung and ghee."

He slides down the tree trunk and looks up at the sky through the leaves. After reflecting for a few moments, he asks, "Why isn't agnihotra more widely known and used?"

"To light a fire and chant at dawn may not be in accord with some people's religions. And others cannot manage to rouse themselves at dawn—no matter what their religion!"

"But, surely, clearing pollution and restoring the ozone should override mere differences of custom and religion!"

The conversation between Ariel and Athene stretches on into a walk and then a swim in a nearby pond. When Athene tells Ariel that she is leaving for Europe in a few days to teach agnihotra and conduct ceremonies, Ariel's heart sinks. He swims alone in circles, feeling forlorn when moments before he was happy. *Is this the water the Immortal spoke of?* he wonders to himself, sensing that Athene may be the catalyst to finding the feminine within himself. *Never have I felt such passion and delight. What will I do when she leaves?*

He draws his dripping pale body from the water and sits down beside her. The Sun is intense," she says tenderly, throwing a shirt over his shoulders. "You had best cover yourself or you'll burn." He feels the care in her gesture.

"Why don't you and Krishna come to Europe with me?"

One week later, the three companions leave Shivapur, their gentle days in India abruptly ended by cross-continent travel. When they arrive at Green Farms in Austria, Erhardt, Rudolf, and Johann are there to greet them.

"We are so happy you have come!" exclaims Erhardt, embracing Athene and kissing her on each cheek. He and Athene then proceed to introduce their respective friends, after which they all walk along the river that flows through the land.

"You are all welcome," says Johann. "We are trying our best to revive the land. I first heard about agnihotra when I was in Poland a few months ago. Some farmers there spoke of amazing results—of actually weakening, and in some cases nullifying, radiation."

"We are a small group," says Athene, "but if we align our intentions properly, agnihotra will work well." She bends down and takes some river water in her hands. "It is polluted still."

"Come downstream," suggests Erhardt. "The water there has passed through the vortices, or what we like to call the dragons."

After a day's rest, Athene calls everyone together, including six volunteers from the local community. "We need more pyramids," she observes. "They are easy to make if you have copper and a soldering torch."

"I have all the supplies," says Johann. "We obtained them as soon as you said you could come."

"Good. The pattern is simple: four triangles! Perhaps you, Johann, can assist two or three others in making pyramids while the rest of us gather dried manure to burn."

Before beginning the work, everyone stands in a circle and invokes the help of the spirits in making the pyramids and gathering the ingredients for the transmutation.

Ariel feels a paradisaical energy flow through him as he works the copper with shears and a soldering iron. He looks over at Athene, who feels sensitive to the fire in his eyes. She is like an opal, changing her watery iridescence with the shifting angle of light, inwardly responding to his every glance.

She goes out to the knoll where the ceremony will be conducted and gathers the prana from within herself and the elements about her, fusing it with her uplifted intention: to clear the pollution in the Green Farms environs. She also prays to be able to anchor in Virgin purity the passion she is feeling for Ariel. She knows how the clouds arise, how the light penetrates the planets, and how the wind shapes the stones. But this strange, blissful force is beyond her control and knowledge, and to it she must surrender.

Well before dawn, while preparations are being completed, Erhardt, Johann, and Rudolf walk silently to the knoll.

"Great God," prays Erhardt softly, "we give thanks for the opportunity of life on Earth and the gift of this land. Help us clear away psychic and physical pollution. Caress these leaves and this grass, so that they may be vital with life. May we live in harmony with the Virgin Earth, and may the prediluvial forest return."

Erhardt's prayer gives way to the distant singing of the six volunteers who are weaving their way up the hill. Ariel, Athene, and Krishna arrive carrying inverted pyramids filled with cow dung, ghee, rice, and sandalwood. The twelve assemble in the still-dark morning like the arteries of a single heart, the soft notes of Krishna's flute focusing their intention. The prana that circles through Athene enflames Ariel. They glance at one another, sharing their ecstasy, as spiraling whirls of energy dance above their heads.

No one speaks while the fires are lit. Feeling the Earth's sorrow, like that of an ancient mother, forgotten and abused, they vow to restore her to her pristine state. As the first rays of dawn pierce the purpling sky, angels descend to join in the sacred song.

THE CONVERGENCE OF WAYS

Creativity
Black of white within white

The shape
of destiny
gyrates
in hidden forms.

Petruska, Kau Chiang, and Christa

Able to relive the Egyptian mysteries through a contemporary priestess, Petruska knows at last why she came to China. After the course at Beijing University ends, Fariba continues to guide her through the entire winter. Petruska's heart discovers love through truth. Able at last to glimpse freedom and the healing of ancient wounds, she feels like a bird freed from its cage.

Now it is spring, and Petruska tries to continue the relationship by working as a secretary for Fariba, the only source of resurrection she knows. But Fariba, foreseeing Petruska's disempowerment if she remains too close, suggests she move on to practice the teachings elsewhere, even though she knows Petruska's disappointment will be as great as her attachment.

Petruska returns to her hotel room and falls on the bed weeping. Trained to watch the timorous snares of her muddled mind and reactive feelings, she beckons her personal witness. Feeling abandoned once again, she breathes deeply and consciously, awakening the power of her heart. *I cannot afford to fall back; I must continue to re-create myself,* she thinks and bolts upright, her soul still storming with Fariba's love and wisdom. Her mind clings to the lucid moments of meditation in Fariba's class.

The following morning, she boards a train for Dengfeng. Soon after her arrival, she comes upon the giant tower built by the astronomer Guo Choujing in the thirteenth century. Despite the strong wind, she climbs the tower at dusk, hoping to abate her sense of loss and release the familiar pain of rejection. To watch the stars is to hold the light and to remember who she truly is. *My star is my divine* ka, she thinks. *If I burn, I burn to heal. If I live in darkness, it is to dispel the shadows. If I feel alone, it is because I have not opened my heart.*

Still struggling with old guilts, she gazes at Saturn and then Jupiter emerging behind the scattering clouds. She wedges herself between two stone walls to retreat from the wind and watches the clouds alternately conceal and reveal the white beams of the stars. With conscious breathing, she comes to feel one with the cycles of the gods. Alone, her soul becomes a rain of tears.

Kau Chiang stands outside his mother's house in Angkang. Amidst the midnight stream of heavenly rays, he clairvoyantly beholds Petruska gazing up at star beams sent forth light-years ago. There at the tower of Dengfeng, he finds the one who carries the guilt of his death in Alexandria sixteen hundred years ago. Kau Chiang knows what is in her soul as he listens to the night wind intoning the hieratic chants of Egypt. In Egypt, as in China, he was her sister. With his heart he calls her to him here and now, in Shu Lao's house.

Unpetitioned, the burning waters flow through all that was sealed off from the flux of Kau Chiang's life. Zapana sails in and out of the eye of the Sun, the eye of Mama Ocllo, and the eyes of Christa and Kau Chiang, beholding their uncharted destiny. Kau Chiang's own freedom guides him to heal the unreachable wound beyond death. The Horus Eye summons him to make whole the vision that includes the rejected.

Unknowing, Petruska follows the wind of wisdom to Angkang. On the train she feels an awesome peace and expectancy. Did she actually hear the passionless voice of her divine *ka*? Did she dream it?

In a spring that melts the ice of taciturn years, Kau Chiang is at the train station to meet her. In his eyes shines the clear emerald light. The person who reeled him into the depthless deeps, splitting East and West in his soul, stands before him. The pain of betrayal still stings as it is transformed through compassion into rippling creative energy. Here is the source of the Emerald River—the eternal mystery of the Tao— where the shapeless deep turns the pain of violence into beauty. Beauty shines through Petruska's homely face as she responds to Kau Chiang's timeless smile.

"Do you need lodging?" he asks.

"Yes," she responds to this apparent stranger, surrendering to the swell of the emerald current that sweeps her to the source of her eternal pain.

"My home is simple, but my wife and I would be pleased with your company."

For the first time in countless incarnations, she feels welcomed. Having beckoned her star, she basks in its rays like a child standing in the soothing ripples of a pond. They walk to Shu Lao's house in intuitive silence, opening to the mystery in one another.

When they arrive, Kau Chiang introduces Petruska to Heng-O and explains that he has invited her to stay a few nights. Old Shu Lao comes in from the back, her face wrinkled like a dried flower. "Come and have soup, my daughter," she says. "You can sleep where Ho Liu does when she comes to visit. She is married now."

Heng-O speaks no Russian and little English, but she feels the felicity between this guest and her husband—like a renewed ancestral childhood of sweet and wild things.

The next morning, Kau Chiang and Petruska amble along a nearby tributary of the Han Kiang. As they walk together, Petruska sees the countryside scattered with light as it was during her happy times in China. She is irresistibly drawn to Kau Chiang's luminous darkness, and her shadows fall away with each step.

For the next three days they walk, moving like dreams through memory, recalling the marrow of both joy and sorrow in the murmuring

River. Petruska cannot yet comprehend the ancient connection, but she delights in moments marbled with wonder, awakening again to the subtle mystery of sunlight, water, and stone.

Kau Chiang shows her the paths of the dragons and the swerving way of the Tao that moves in ungoverned freedom, spilling the wealth of the world from emptiness. They talk of the Earth, the spirit, and the quest for intangible things. Kau Chiang feels that to walk with her is to shed his barriers against trust. He realizes that not only his mind, but the lightning in his ravaged soul, the very aureole of the Tao, has forgiven her.

"Are you at peace?" he asks.

"I am still afraid of death, for I feel guilty," she replies, casting a sidelong glance and stepping into the River.

He thinks to himself, *Come! We can journey beyond the black waters of death by closing our eyes and releasing old imaginings. Let the River break upon the past like a slow tide upon the beach and dissolve the rocks of pain.* Aloud, he says, "The burden of guilt is unreal and can be forgotten. Let it go. It obstructs the power of your heart. The heights of heaven have room for all that is and is not."

Immersed in the fearful sacrament of the River, she realizes that he knows her past. "But I have sinned!" she screams. "I killed the sister I loved!" Her tears are hot, her hands trembling. She cannot measure the span of lives in which self-forgiveness would have been a simple act. The wave of emotion passing through her is like a flagellation preceding the clarity of renewed imagination. The good and evil memories in her soul splinter into light as the voices of the past rise, echo, and fade away.

When they return to the house for dinner, Heng-O greets them at the door with news.

"Yu is coming home at last!" she announces.

"After all these years! When?" asks Kau Chiang, overjoyed.

"Tomorrow. A letter arrived this morning. He is bringing two friends."

"I don't know where we will put them all, but we'll manage."

Yu is delighted and proud to bring Karl and Christa into the majesty and simplicity of China. As they approach the house of Shu Lao, they sense that it stands in etheric light, saturated with a wordless essence from the past, from the living present, and from the breath of the Creatrix.

Yu's natural grace immediately dissolves any initial discomfort among all who have assembled in his grandmother's house. Though surprised to find Petruska there, he casually asserts, "I am happy to sleep outside. The nights are already warming and the poppies are almost in bloom."

When Kau Chiang beholds Christa, her essence permeates the air like sanguine flowers dried in the Sun. Mates of one soul, the innocence of their unity survives the phantoms of division. The diversity of incarnations in Atlantis, China, and Egypt tumbles like weeds in the wind as their beings enmesh through the burning waters in their veins.

"This is a time of gathering!" exclaims Kau Chiang, who feels the sweep of the divine plan pulse within his bones. "I will sleep outside with Yu and his friends."

Jealousy at once wracks Petruska's heart. Growing heavy with fear once again, she remembers to breathe and watch. She withdraws to her room, attempting to distance herself from the source of pain, and tries to remember the trance techniques she learned from Fariba. But her practice weakens in the face of her distress. Her trust is fragile and cannot withstand the strain of such sudden shifts.

She stands and stares until, unable to bear it any longer, she loses her witness. Self-pity and pride press together into vengeful blindness. She storms out of the house, wandering aimlessly over the hills and groping for peace. After many hours, she comes upon Christa walking alone by the river. Her rage uncontrollable, she confronts Christa and spits accusations into her startled face. "You look upon him as if you were a single star! I hate you! You have stolen what little I knew of joy."

Shaken by Petruska's outburst, Christa focuses to settle her trembling auric field. In Petruska's panicked glare, Christa can see both the abbot and Peter, her nemeses in former lifetimes. But she overcomes the turbulent test of retaliation with the greater gift of compassion. Both an impetuous storm and heartfelt love arise within her, and strange words fall from her lips: "Thunder-driven, you are wonderfully wild! Now you can be traitress and true at once, tremendous lover. It is not I you attack, but the hidden part of yourself. Kau Chiang entered the invisible dark-ness. He and I are a conjunction and can never be parted. I am your friend and sister."

Petruska is caught in a creative chaos beyond human and divine thought. In her whirling flurry, she is caught by her star, the divine *ka* embracing both the traitress and killer in the folds of laughter. Petruska feels God following her, running after her, stirring the air into savannahs that smite the burden of her long-treasured shame.

"My sister! You?"

She turns swiftly to gaze upon Christa and beholds the eyes of the one who once stood with her in the flowered fields of China.

THE BIRTH OF PAHANA

Service
Red of white within white

Honoring
each child's birth
honors
all of creation.

Kuksu, Wickvaya, and Nesaru

The kachinas come as spirits, gathering around the rundown shack where Kuksu lives with Nesaru and Wickvaya. Wickvaya's shamanic knowing tells him that it is Pahana, the lost white brother of the Hopi prophecy, who grows in Kuksu's womb. Now, after the trials of time, the long migrations, and the slow emergence from the former Three Worlds, he returns to release the Hopi from their persecutors and to find a way of brotherhood. Wickvaya has forbidden whites to come near his home, the women's lodge, or the kiva, for he is determined to protect the entire mesa for the duration of the pregnancy. There can be no quarreling— only the expression of pure feelings and thoughts.

Kuksu senses Pahana's every feeling, just as she hears the messages pulsing within the Earth. She remembers her ecstasy when, opening herself to the emerald waters in the core of the planet, she conceived Pahana in the wild heat of the dance. It was then that the bright sperm of heaven entered her womb in divine rectification of loveless human sex.

Opening to the immensity within her, Kuksu can perceive the

embryonic development of this divine/human child called from his master's heaven. The formation of his hands, feet, and vestigial tail brings his tree-climbing past and linkage with the creatures. The formation of his eyes and ears brings the panorama of the angels. He longs for the milk of the galactic River just as he longs for the milk of mother's breast. There is no moment in his waking uterine sleep when he ceases to be aware or when he ceases to live in eternity.

When Kuksu reaches her fifth month of pregnancy, Wickvaya prepares a number of men to impersonate the visiting Kachinas in order to link these formerly human spirits with the perfect passage of birth. Remaining celibate until Pahana is born, they dance to weave the spirits of heaven and Earth into the organic life of his developing body.

Kuksu laughs with delight at each stage of Pahana's journey. Eros erupts within her as his genitals form in the night of her womb. Buddhafields and the light of the Christos ripple through their joined breath and blood. His spirit, baptized in the waters of a suffering humanity, now lives in the full rainbow spectrum of light, shimmering beyond the power of vibration. Already attuned to the music of Zar, he is the forerunner of children conceived in love and embracing all of creation.

Through Pahana's third eye, the divine dream begins to awaken. Pahana feels his spirit seeping into the protoplasmic depths of the biosphere where the Creatrix dwells unseen. He deciphers every photon buried within the chemistry of the Earth, learning to weave new patterns of energy in accordance with the Creator's plan.

Pahana's presence sends transformative energy surging throughout Kuksu's body. Guided by the Kachinas, the energy moves along her meridians, explodes within her cells, and reconstructs her chemistry. Full of compassion, these Kachinas have lived as humans in the past according to the pure pattern of creation, and they have already passed into the Fifth, Sixth, or Seventh Worlds where evil does not exist. They return now to the Fourth World to support and honor the birth.

In the ninth month of Kuksu's pregnancy, Wickvaya dances to awaken the crown chakras within all who will be attending the birth ceremony. The dance is a vestige of the First World, when the door at the top of everyone's head was open. As Wickvaya moves, the white conductor of the Holy Spirit ascends through Pahana's third eye up to heaven, leaving a brilliant corona of white fibers around his crown. The dance awakens Pahana to his greater destiny: to vibrate all his rainbow chakras, bringing eternity and compassion together in the brotherhood of all.

Weeks later, Wickvaya sits shaking his head, for he feels both joy and sorrow. The coming of Pahana promises the restoration of the missing corner of the sacred tablet given to the Fire Clan. *The great healing between the white people and the native tribes will be difficult,* he reflects, puffing on his pipe and gazing out at the mesa. *This means a greater intermingling in the world.* He ponders the maze of profane artifacts in the white civilization and the stress that produced them: *How can it ever be made sacred?*

He stands up, puts away his pipe, and goes into the house to see Kuksu, whose belly swells with expectancy in the eleventh month of pregnancy: "You honor our family and our tribe, my daughter."

Kuksu smiles: "The Kachinas guide my every move, Father, though I live my own life as truly as I can. I am often in wonder that I have been chosen."

Wickvaya sits in silence and contemplates the coming of an awesome change. He feels the singularity of zero dimensions within his soul, a soul stressed from living in integrity throughout the tumultuous changes of the worlds.

It is after midnight when Kuksu feels the first contractions and calls out for Nesaru and her helpers, who accompany her into the women's lodge. Wickvaya tells Lomo to awaken the tribe and announce the ceremony for Pahana's arrival.

Only those who hold to the old ways and believe in the prophecy of a Fifth World may attend the ceremony. Others must leave the reservation. Upon entering the dark kiva, the tribesmen go to the raised eastern end while Wickvaya, Lomo, and the priests sit at the lower altar in the west. The kiva represents the Fourth World from which they will emerge. It is named *Hawiovi*, meaning One-Way Trail. Their purpose is to ritually affirm the pure pattern of creation intended by the Creator, that is to be repeated by every newborn child. Wickvaya determines that no one there will come out alive whose intent is not aligned in this way, for their clarity of purpose creates the Virgin field into which Pahana will be born.

In the upperworld, One Horn and Two Horn priests patrol the dark, vacant streets. To anyone who is wandering they call out, *"Haqumi?"* meaning "Who are you?" If the response is, *"Pinuv"*—"I am I"—they know it is a spiritual being traversing the One-Way Trail. If not, they drive the person off the reservation to protect the ceremony from being defiled.

It is past four in the morning, and Kuksu's contractions pulse stronger and more frequently. The men in the kiva wait in the darkness. As Pahana's tiny head arrives at Kuksu's cervix, Wickvaya intuitively knows it is time to remove the plug from the hole in the floor of the altar. This is the *sipapu,* the place of emergence. While the seven Pleiades rise into view through the ladder opening, Wickvaya recounts the Road of Life up through the Four Worlds and the promise of the coming Fifth, Sixth, and Seventh Worlds.

The firelight reveals Wickvaya's radiant brown face as he speaks: "Life in the First World was fiery, but it came to be contaminated. Our ancestors thought that this world was destroyed, but it only became invisible when we passed into the Second World. Here we thought we knew who we were, but through arrogance and the theft of the First World's fire we lost our way. This Second World also became invisible and inaccessible to almost all. Passing into the Third World, we realized that we were family with the stones, plants, and creatures. But at this time many Hopis used their sexual energy without love, and most of our power was taken from us. Without our full capacity, we forgot how to sing praises to the Creator.

"So it was that we eventually passed into this Fourth World, for the Creator is merciful and gives us many chances. Here, as you know, Masaw is the caretaker. He told us to divide into clans and migrate over the Earth. Now we have come to the time when the Fourth World, too, will vanish. Only dust and ashes will remain, like the ones from this fire. The light of the burned wood shall return to the sky."

Wickvaya falls silent as he attunes more deeply to Kuksu's labor in the women's lodge. Just as Pahana is about to be born, Masaw himself appears to those in the Kiva, attended by brightly garbed men with four-pointed white stars painted on their foreheads. Attuning to the rhythm of Kuksu's breath, they emit deep guttural sounds to accompany her labor.

The women attending the labor are also chanting in rhythm with Kuksu's breathing. As she makes one final heave, Pahana, riding on the tides of creation, bursts through blood into the open hands of Nesaru and the dawning sky. Kuksu shrieks as her breathing changes and her entire body rejoices in orgasm.

The child's skin is white, like that of the man Kuksu encountered before the spirit dance in the center of the Earth. Nesaru holds him to her, exalting in his blissful energy, then offers the baby to his mother. Kuksu takes Pahana to her breast, their hearts becoming one with the Earth, the Sun, and the Sun behind the Sun.

At the moment Pahana is born, a being in a white robe appears in the kiva. "I am the beginning and the end," he proclaims, then disappears. The men accompanying Masaw immediately throw a large flat rock on the fire to extinguish the Fourth World, then strip and begin to shriek and dance madly. They dance in the crimson light, frenzied and wild, beaded with sweat as if in labor for their own rebirth. Wickvaya and the others leap up and rush to the place of emergence, climbing up the ladder before the Fourth World is destroyed. At last they emerge into the full dawn of day, a premonition of the Fifth World.

After three days have passed, all who were reborn during the kiva ceremony are permitted to behold the mother and radiant child and to honor the Virgin womb that brought forth Pahana, the promised one.

DIRGE FOR THE DEATH OF THE OLD EARTH

Freedom
White of white within white

Facing
one's shadows
brings
freedom.

While ominous expectancy ripples from pole to pole at the dying of an age, strife-weary dragons hold together a tremulous maze of brooding seas and oppressed continents. Scattered about the planet are those called to the depths where the crushed emerald waters rise in vortices of hope. With the joy of intrinsic knowing running through their channels, they live their vow amid the tumult of the decaying world. The poetic fountain of divine imagination can flow within the heart of anyone, but only these courageous ones feel it and use it.

Lomo travels the land, drumming in the hills where people meet in sacred trust. He knows the loneliness of humankind, except for those whose drums beat to the pulse of the Fifth World. Starlie, who left Tokyo reeling in confusion, at last has surrendered to the inner music that tells him, *The prophecies will be fulfilled.* Now his games reconstruct the world from the prophetic traditions of his people. He meets Lomo in New York, where they pour old Hopi stories into a cup of revelation and drink the new vision.

At a concert a few blocks away, Pete's Holocaust Rock band is blasting through the imprisoning thoughtforms of urban automatism. The uniform, repressive monotony of the first movement, "Entropy," builds into the blaring tones of "Holocaust" in which drums, marimbas, and synthesizers explode in a crescendo of spirit. Thousands, feeling the ancient beat resound through the concrete beneath their feet, begin to dance, touched by a tincture of God. The music falls like shrapnel upon the hip crowd that responds in hallucinogenic abandon.

Allen and Martha cling to their seats, trying to reconcile the heretical visions of a New Age son with their own crumbling fundamentalism. Allen gapes at the dizzying scene, which reminds him of the fertile bramble of junk at the dump back home. But the noise presses him back into life.

The band, in a thundering cry for liberty, turns metal into music and sound-waves into light. The electronic vibrancy is lifted by the white dissonance that shatters the shadows of the Old Earth. Starlie laughs as he and Lomo walk toward the flashing lights of the concert hall. They arrive just in time for the apocalyptic surge of heavy metal. Pete calls out over the microphone, "We shall no longer believe in purity while living in hell! This monstrous system of contradictions calls for the final movement, the 'Cosmic Dirge'. Let's go!"

Within the drumming and strumming rises the voice of the River, crushing the casement of meaningless lives and spinning them back to renewed purpose. Sonics become the "Word" that ripples at one with the River. The babel of human speech merges with the inarticulate muttering of matter and seethes in the quaking Old Earth.

A storm brews all over the world. Visionaries behold Satan rising up toward Christos. Some behold the kachinas dancing with demons, others the conflict between devas and asuras. A phoenix cries. Dragons hiss and roll through the electrified air. Crowds in cities everywhere assemble and dissipate in an uneasy melding of hope and trepidation.

"The eternal return is returning!" shouts Starlie, dancing amid the throngs around the band.

The dirge resounds with the pain inflicted in the past: The lamentations of not living one's life, and of succumbing to hatred and anger; the lamentations of neglected children; the lamentations of crime and warfare; the lamentations of the amnesia of paradise, the golden age, and love. The dirge billows with the death of racism, genocide, complacency, and apathy.

In the music is the eternally pathless path, the face of the unknown. The scourge of history, nations, and races brings the end of messiahship and of clinging to false hope. The demise of the Old Earth brings destruction to the caves of Plato and the Paleolithic tribes. It topples Teotihuacan and the tableland of Anahuac and it pulverizes the Sumerian cuneiforms at Nappur.

Crowds wander down the River, chanting and mourning through the ruins of New York, Paris, Bombay, Beijing, San Salvador, Jerusalem, and Calcutta. Homeless people roam the streets or huddle in taverns and the caverns of condemned buildings. Lomo and Starlie add their drums to the flutes, whistles, sticks, and bells that sound the living dirge. In Berlin, Bangkok, Budapest, and Moscow, thousands join the procession swelling with the pulse of life.

Intensity builds as the clouds condense into tightening spirals. Rain torrents down, creating a sea of mud. Lifetimes of pain are released in the wailing, which rises and spreads like the concentric circles of Atlantis. Okeanos, the god of the ocean, rises into a hurricane that swirls in violence from Earth to heaven.

"Come, mysteries of chaos!" call out the Primal Waters. "Reveal the harmonies in your deep order! The island of New Earth rises from the sea! My waters are in your bones and the salt of your blood."

"Holy Europe, holy Asia, holy Africa," sings a chorus of angels amidst hallelujahs. "Holy Polynesia! Holy Australia! Holy Atlantic Ocean! Whole Earth holy! Holy! Holy we call! Kukuklan! Atum! Zeus!"

"None but the Sun," Pravin calls as he feels Savitri within him.

Languages pulsate with new meaning. Forms reveal their hidden beauty. In the quickening energy of life and love, the fall of rain is felt as a kiss, the darkness as a blessing.

Throngs migrate across the Earth. The Mother of the World, invisible to all, churns the poisons of the planet into a roiling brew, cast into storms over the face of the waters: the Atlantic, the Pacific, the Indian, the Arctic. The Trickster in nature hurls cyclones, mudslides, and volcanic eruptions.

The burning waters rage inside the human spine. The Mother-Creatrix-Sophia is everywhere, offering not even a hell for a refuge! Every pain and experience is transformable in the metamorphic soup of the River of Compassion. The turbulence stirs the memory of millennia, releasing the addictions of the ages, and separating seed from weed, wheat from chaff, and life from sin. The end of the River meets the source, turning and churning pollutants toward purity.

The veil is rent. Some see the turbulence, some the hand of the Mother, and others the vortex—the projection of denied desire flashing in the darkness. Unbelievers believe, and false believers believe no longer. The holographic screens of the universe have shattered.

The geometry of the Earth reveals its unkempt lines beyond the continents of dirt and stone. Old dragons—having long held the Earth together—return rejoicing to the whirling heavens as the energy of the ley lines is restored. Poisonous hatred and blame—long hurled at the dragons by an ignorant humanity—are now stirred by the Mother of the World into an oceanic swell.

Rolling tidal waves level the villages of the Pacific islands in a watery baptism. As palm trees twist beneath the sea, Zoa, Mujaji, and Nummo take refuge in underwater island caves. Convening there is the council of ancient scribes, retainers of the esoteric wisdom, who speak in the silence of the deep: "The blood of the Earth shall soon run pure. Brimstone, ashes, deluge, death! Let us dance all night to honor the return of the snake goddesses." Wild, passionate, and ecstatic, the islanders revive the archaic tribal dance, driving out the madness that poses as sanity, so that the true human dance can begin.

As the storms rage above, the iridescent obelisk of Zar rises from the lapis lazuli door on the floor of the Pacific, invisible to all but those who have held the loving vision for humanity. Some already live in the divine imagination of the Land of Zar, where the dolphins dance, the diatoms delight, and the whales circle clockwise around the base of the obelisk.

At home in Malta, Channon enters the massive stone ruin where he hears the music of Zar sailing above the swells of a perishing world. "I see titans raising an obelisk, like those of Egypt, only more clear and translucent!" he cries out in his visionary state. "I see now! I have been intoxicated by my desires—addicted to having and holding. The titans are our benefactors!" *Yes, he reflects, the titans in humanity rise to fall once again. The titans have been unloosed from the mountain tops where the sacred fire of the Immortals flames within reach. It was the titans who lifted the stones of the megaliths and pyramids to align the energy with dragon veins and ley lines. Now they return to raise the obelisk.*

Many die to the Old Earth on this night of nights. In Madrid, Manila, Bucharest, Baghdad, and Dublin, voices rise in chorus to the sweeping Zarian music. Some dance in orgy. Some dance in mystery. Some dance in love. Angels and demons bear witness to the acceleration and chaos of events on Earth as the multidimensional light casts the divine imagination into the confusion of cultures in total transformation. The courageous ones defy time and the laws of a perishing world, for the colors of the robe of the Creatrix vibrate within their awakened flesh. The archetypal forces weave through the migration of souls and press vibrations of new social forms into their bodies.

East and West meet in the Chinese countryside, where Christa, enfolded in Karl's arms, hears the rhythms and tones of Zar rising from the distant shore and beyond, in the swells of the Pacific. She realizes the story she is to tell is unfinished, for a new humanity is coming. It is a story she knows cannot be told with words. Dancing and whirling in sound and color, it surges forth as she hears a song:

The Virgin/Child's Song of the River

I am the waters springing from wells where hearts are true.
I bring ecstasy whenever you summon deep powers.
I am the rising up of purity when you call for truth.
I am the mother of creativity when my womb is honored.
Well, womb, and wonder are the ever-flowing sources of my service.
I am the reservoir within all sentient beings.
I am yourself when you express from the source.
I serve everyone alike though I am silent and unseen.
I am the freedom of not-knowing.

You can find me in wildlife and pristine forests.
I am the sea that births all beings.
The Sun is my lover who brings bliss to the pure at heart.
You can find me when you bask in the light of the Moon.
I am the limit of dominion and render each being the freedom to be.

How can one know one's being?
All that is, floats; all that is not, sinks.

THE MUSIC OF ZAR

Dauntless, the courageous ones are called to Zar, deep in the Pacific Basin, where the divine imagination pours forth in music. Lured by the iridescent tones to a dimension beyond time and space, they gather from all realms of the planet. Here, the symphony of the stars and the sanguine flesh of the Earth vibrate in jeweled images echoing throughout the universe. Here, hearts burst into song as they recognize the orchestration of their soul's vow. The deeper the suffering of humanity, the more penetrating the music. Here is the liturgy of being, of participation in the pure plan of creation. On and on the liturgical rite purifies each ordinary act.

The past is submerged in the onomatopoeia of a language beyond words, a hydrous space of consonants and vowels singing the River's script. Liquid syllables articulate the ongoing genetic and social transformation: the utilization of free energy, the appreciation of cyclic ecology, and the destruction of all conspiracies against a free life. The sounds change pitch as the River regathers her tributaries into a planetary synthesis, and the many-colored tongues move to a fuller possibility of awareness.

From the clarified rainbow colors, new children emerge. Summoned by contrapuntal Zarian rhythms into the wombs of loving mothers, these genetic mutants possess an expanded cortex and pulmonary filters for protection from the remaining pollution. Their slowly beating hearts bring the possibility of longer life, and their finely synchronized endocrine systems bring attunement to the cosmic harmonies. Although only a few cross the time-shift in the 1990s, thousands will arrive by the early twenty-first century. Their greatest ability is to willfully pass between eternity and time—to lift the veils of the subtle dimensions.

Compassion dissolves the veils of many who are transported to the obelisk, then on through the lapis lazuli door at its base on the Pacific floor. There the River spins in imaginal vortices where visionaries burn to make themselves and the world anew. The dawning answers of the

New Earth lie in Zar, where the Emerald River is channeled up from the Earth's core into limitless loving energy.

However, the horror of God rushing into private lives terrifies those still linking their will to illusion. Confounded, they dim the glimmering River and dare it to penetrate their defenses. The last war rages between the expression and repression of the innermost self. Whenever a soul embodies its intuition, the music soars and the Creatrix sighs in relief, for the divine imagination is made transparent.

The glow radiating from the towering obelisk signals the charge of a coming New Earth. The divine moves through prostrate forms and kindles new life through the flame of the burning waters. Changed from liquid to light, the cells of the children vibrate to the free energy of the Sun. From the Land of Zar, they behold the River in the Earth—and the Earth in the Emerald River.

THE EMERALD RIVER

The broken water of the River churns in underlying melody. Upstream, the ancient tongues speak of the parting of the waters into east and west, north and south, and the birth of nature in all its glory.

The mystery of the River remains. The true ones know in their hearts that behind the waves pounding the distant shore is a source that can rise again and rain down upon the mountains. And behind the waves of civilizations—Aztec, Mayan, Roman, Greek, Babylonian, Chinese, Egyptian—lie the echoing images of the burning waters. The precepts of logos mix and mingle with the tinctures of eros in the blood, and in the tide, sweeping trepidation aside. Whether sinful or saintly, bitter or sweet, those who feel compassion know that the shower of the River's spray refreshes the clinging memory.

And so the reverie continues both beyond and *through* history as the laughter of the divine plan summons souls toward their destiny and the healing emerald waves flow into the genes of a new humanity. Outstretched wings sail effortlessly on the winds of time where precipitous waters form. Turning, turning, the swirls of the River empty and fill the vortex that spins in ecstasy. Rapt, the River steals away, forever on and on. . . .

ABOUT THE AUTHOR

Rowena Pattee Kryder lives in the Mount Shasta wilderness humbly chopping wood in the winter and facilitating week-long intensives in the summer. She is the founder and program director of the Creative Harmonics Institute, where she guides year-round retreats for a couple of people at a time. She was trained in Zen with Shunryu Suzuki Roshi for seven years in the 1960s and has taken many Vipassana courses in the 1970s and 1980s. Though sitting meditation is at the core of her practice, it has extended into direct insight into archetypes that guide creation and that are healing agents for the regeneration of the Earth.

Consciously linking with the archetypes and telling the creation story—in art, poetry, myth, film, and live theater—continues to be her way of spiritual teaching. She has taught I Ching, World Myths and Symbols, Sacred Art, and Shamanic Art and Ritual Healing at the California Institute of Integral Studies as well as other universities. She is a way-shower and a bridgemaker for the New Earth children who are incarnating at this time. She has two wonderful sons, as well as many spiritual children and friends.

She has built two temples, produced five visionary films, and is the originator of the *Gaia Matrix Oracle* (Golden Point, 1990), a divination tool for our times. The visual symbols in the *Emerald River of Compassion* are part of this original divination work. *Sacred Ground to Sacred Space*, a work on visionary ecology, is forthcoming from Bear & Company (1994).

Rowena can be reached through Creative Harmonics Institute, PO Box 940, Mount Shasta, CA 96067.